LP

09-2114

STA   Stamos, Ann

Bitter tide

31.95

BITTER TIDE

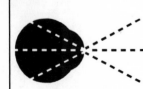

This Large Print Book carries the
Seal of Approval of N.A.V.H.

Bitter Tide

Ann Stamos

THORNDIKE PRESS
A part of Gale, Cengage Learning

GALE
CENGAGE Learning

Detroit • New York • San Francisco • New Haven, Conn • Waterville, Maine • London

GALE
CENGAGE Learning™

Thorndike Press® Large Print Core.
The text of this Large Print edition is unabridged.
Other aspects of the book may vary from the original edition.
Set in 16 pt. Plantin.
Printed on permanent paper.

LIBRARY OF CONGRESS CATALOGING-IN-PUBLICATION DATA

Stamos, Ann.
  Bitter tide : an Ellis Island mystery / by Ann Stamos.
    p. cm. — (Thorndike Press large print core)
  ISBN-13: 978-1-4104-1797-8 (alk. paper)
  ISBN-10: 1-4104-1797-2 (alk. paper)
  1. Ellis Island Immigration Station (N.Y. and N.J.)—Fiction.
2. Immigrants—United States—Fiction. 3. Irish—United States—
Fiction. 4. Fiancés—Crimes against—Fiction. 5. Murder—
Investigation—Fiction. 6. Corruption—Fiction. 7. Large type
books. I. Title.
PS3619.T363B58 2009b
813'.6—dc22   2009013440

Published in 2009 by arrangement with Tekno Books and Ed Gorman.

09-2114
Mhorndike
(Gale)
8/09
$31.95

Printed in the United States of America
1 2 3 4 5 6 7 13 12 11 10 09

To
Jerry and Donna Kerly
with love
and in memory of
Rita E. Berry

What dream came with you that you came
Through bitter tide on foam-wet feet?
Did your companion wander away
From where the birds of Aengus wing?
William Butler Yeats
The Wanderings of Oisin

ACKNOWLEDGMENTS

At the beginning of the twentieth century, the Ellis Island immigration station was a new and complex place — a city unto itself, with several hundred employees who processed hundreds, often thousands of immigrants every day — and yet very little has been written about the guardians at the gate and the administration of the station itself. Without the help of Barry Moreno, Ellis Island Librarian and author of *The Encyclopedia of Ellis Island,* it would have been impossible to bring the station to life. Any errors or license taken are strictly the author's responsibility.

Likewise, thank you to: Diane Trap, Research Librarian at the University of Georgia, whose help and support throughout this project has been invaluable; Thomas McCarthy, General Secretary of the New York Correction History Society for information about police procedures in New York; Doug

Wicklund, Senior Curator of the National Firearms Museum, for his advice and suggestions about contemporaneous firearms; Kevin Kenny, Associate Professor of History at Boston College and author of *The American Irish,* for information about Irish Americans and revolutionary movements; and the members of the H-Ethnic discussion list who, unbeknownst to them, often directed my research and sculpted my ideas about immigration and ethnicity.

In the course of researching this novel, it was my great fortune to find many valuable books on the subjects of immigration, Irish Americans and other ethnic groups, New York at the turn of the twentieth century and the manners, mores and society of the times. While it would be impossible to list all of those sources, I am particularly indebted to the following authors, both living and deceased: Luc Sante for *Low Life;* M. H. Dunlop for *Gilded City;* David C. Hammack for *Power and Society;* Jerry E. Patterson for *The First Four Hundred;* Robert A. M. Stern, Gregory Gilmartin, and John Montague Massengale for *New York 1900;* Gerald W. McFarland for *Inside Greenwich Village;* Eric Homberger for *The Historical Atlas of New York;* Hutchins Hapgood for *The Spirit of the Ghetto;* Moses King for *King's Handbook of New York City* and *King's Notable New Yorkers;* William L. Riordon for *Plunkitt of Tammany Hall;* Terry Golway for *Irish Rebel;* Kerby A. Miller for *Emigrants and Exiles;* Hasia R. Diner for *Erin's Daughters In America;* P. W. Joyce for *English As We Speak It In Ireland;* Peter Morton Coan for *Ellis Island Interviews;* David M. Brownstone, Irene M. Franck, and Douglass Brownstone for *Island of Hope, Island of Tears;* Alan M. Kraut for *The Huddled Masses;* Victor Safford for *Immigration Problems;* Thomas M. Pitkin for *Keepers of the Gate;* Virginia Yans-McLaughlin and Marjorie Lightman for *Ellis Island and the Peopling of America;* Elizabeth Ewan for *Immigrant Women in the Land of Dollars;* Bruce M. Stave and John F. Sutherland with Aldo Salerno for *From the Old Country;* Mario Maffi for *Gateway to the Promised Land;* W. L. Thomas for *Old World Traits Transplanted;* Hamilton Holt for *The Life Stories of Undistinguished Americans as Told by Themselves;* Elsie Clews Parsons for *Fear and Conventionality;* Kathy Peiss for *Cheap Amusements;* and Michael Swan and Bernard Smith for *Learner English.*

In addition, the valuable Web sites which

11

contributed to my research are too numerous to list, but special acknowledgment must go to: the Library of Congress American Memory site; the Museum of the City of New York; the Lower East Side Tenement Museum; the New York Public Library; the Archives of the *New York Times;* the New York Yacht Club; the National Park Service; Cimorelli Immigration Manifests Online; and The Ships List.

Finally, thank you to the friends, family, and fellow writers who provided a network of support, listening, criticizing, and encouraging me in this book in its many incarnations: Harriette Austin, Beverly and Charles Connor, Diane Trap, Larry McDougald, Dac Crossley, Cathy and Tim Conahan, Angie and Andrew Shih, Father Christos, and Mari Mars. And thanks to my agent, Joan Brandt, for her wisdom and eye for detail.

CHAPTER ONE

Maggie Flynn observed her own wake with unaccustomed dispassion. Known throughout County Sligo as "that hard-headed girl of Bernie Flynn," and at home with her sisters and brother as "Mags the Terrible," neither siblings nor neighbors would have described her as passive. But today was different. While the rest of them wept and wailed at their loss, Maggie kept her own counsel, knowing full well that nothing was as it seemed.

"I heard she was seein' that Cormac Doyle," said old Mrs. Feeney. Mary Feeney kept her ear so low to the ground it was a wonder she hadn't grown a potato in it. "And him in all that trouble now. You'll be glad she's gone when they catch up with him. Who knows what your Maggie might do, havin' a mind of her own as she does."

Eileen Flynn hastily changed the subject. "Will ya have some more tea, Mary?"

Voices drifted in on the summer breeze from the dooryard where Bernard Flynn held court with half the male population of Drumcliffe. "Cormac Doyle would scorn a bridge to teeter on a log, I said to her, Father. And I didn't raise ya up eighteen years to have ya come to grief over the likes of him. So she raised her chin, Maggie did, and she said to me . . ."

Maggie silently mimicked her father. "Da, I'll not be courted by the likes of Jimmy Foy with his butterfly ears, and I won't be cuffed around like Michael Loughlin's poor mother. So if ya have some idea thatch'll marry me off to a village boy, ya'd best put it out of your head right now. If I can't have Cormac Doyle, then I'll not marry at all. I'll go to America."

Father Tom Duffy shook his head. "Three American wakes this month, Bernard. Where will it stop?"

Inside, Jerry Flynn took his older sister's hand. "Will ya send me somethin' from America, Mags? Will you write to me?" He laid his head against her skirt. "Will I ever see ya again, Maggie?"

Maggie ruffled his hair and chucked his chin. "I toldja, Jerry, but I'll tell ya again. I'm to work for Mrs. Westcott of New York for two years. It was all in her letter. After two years, she'll pay my passage home for a visit and then I'll go back. And maybe when I do, you'll go with me, Jerry. Wouldja like that?"

Jerry Flynn took one glance around the cottage and nodded his head. But if her plans went right, she'd be back in Drumcliffe long before two years were passed — back a married woman, with her strong, handsome husband by her side.

Tomorrow she'd leave with her father for Derry. She knew how it would be, standing on the dock looking up at the *Cymric.* Da would grow all misty eyed. "Do yer job well, Maggie," he'd say. "That Mrs. Westcott paid good money to bring ya to America. You give her the bestja have."

"I will, Da. You know I will."

Bernard would nod and dab at his eyes. "And don't forget to go to Mass every Sunday. Yer mother will worry about that. Mrs. Westcott seems like a fair woman. I'm sure she'll letcha have yer Sunday mornings fer church."

"I'll go to church, Da. Every Sunday, like always."

They'd be interrupted, then, by the mournful whistle of the boat. An old man with a beard and a cane would bump into them there on the docks. He'd look her

15

father full in the face, raise his hat and make his apologies, because Cormac Doyle could never resist tempting fate.

Maggie would board the ship right behind him, wave a last good-bye to her father and follow the old man to steerage. And there the adventure would begin, because being with Cormac Doyle was always an adventure.

And so it went — exactly as Maggie had dreamed it, and Cormac Doyle had planned it. The crossing was easy and despite the crowding in steerage, Maggie only cared that she was with the man she loved. Together, they passed under the raised torch of the Madonna of freedom and slid into the ferry slip in front of an immense building of red brick and limestone, with towers and spires, arched windows and gables. America.

It was a perfect plan and progressed smoothly, right up to the moment they stepped off the gangplank onto the soil of Ellis Island, when Maggie Flynn drew a gun from her sleeve and shot her beloved Cormac Doyle.

CHAPTER TWO

If Joseph Hannegan had been a man to lay money on a fight, he'd have put a fiver on the bantam lad with the blackened eye. Although his opponent stood eight inches taller and outweighed him by a good forty pounds, the bantam was as quick and lithe on his feet as a dancer — a veritable Italian George M. Cohan. They scrambled on the steerage deck below, shouting epithets and wildly swinging their fists, even as three older men tried to pull them apart. But the bantam slipped out of their hands, leapt onto a hatch and ducked under a web of rigging, taunting his opponent with a come-on wave. The big fellow shook the other men off and gave chase. He lunged after the bantam just as the little man capered backward, grabbed hold of a davit and swung around in an arc, landing two sound kicks to the big man's chest and head, and putting an end to the fight almost

17

before it had begun.

Joseph watched the fight from the second-class deck of *La Gascogne.* He felt as though he had seen it all before. Twenty years it had been, and still he remembered the sudden bursts of laughter and the quick flares of temper on landing morning. Nerves were raw. Stomachs heaved with doubt. Lovingly cultivated and carefully polished dreams were brought out for final inspection and, in the light of reality, revealed to be illusory. America could not be that wonderful. But there was no going back, and suddenly, the burden of the decision weighed heavily.

At ten, he'd been only an observer trying to shield Moira from the turmoil. Now he was a part of the great machine these newcomers feared. He was the one who, with a stroke of his pen, could change the future of every person on that deck. Yet it was so easy to slip back twenty years, gazing toward the harbor, waiting for the brand-new life they'd all been promised. He hoped he'd never forget it, for to forget their yearning was to neglect half of the people he served. He was there to safeguard their interests and the interests of his adopted country — two duties that all too often were in conflict.

He looked out over the steerage deck now

18

and grieved for them. Too many of their hopes would be dashed before they'd gotten used to the feeling of land under their feet again. He was glad he wasn't clairvoyant; it was easier not to know which of them would be returned or held. Which families would be separated, calling for impossible sacrifices. Which of them would say their final good-byes under the watchful eye of his great machine.

But some of them were tough — too tough not to make it in America. They were the ones who found a way, always found a way, to get around the laws, avoid deportation, and rise in a world where everything worked against them. And that was why Joseph really would have put a fiver on the bantam. One way or another, he was going to make it in America. He was standing with his foot resting ever so lightly on the neck of his opponent and a grin so wide it took in everyone on deck and Joseph too. Joseph touched two fingers to his cap, and the Italian bantam took a bow.

Joseph turned away from the rail, almost colliding with a small, dark man in a white jacket. The man, whose brass nametag said Sapelli, held his hand out.

"It is for you, yes?" he said.

Joseph looked down at the outstretched

hand. The man arched his thumb back, revealing a folded stack of fives and tens. Joseph scrambled for something to say — the right thing to say.

"How much? *Quanto?*"

"Thirty, no? You have them?"

Joseph maintained an impassive expression. "Which ones do you want?"

"See-tee-zen," the steward pronounced carefully.

"Ah," Joseph said, extracting the money from the steward's hand. "Yes, citizen papers. Let's see, that would be . . ." He unfolded the bills and began to count. Sapelli glanced around nervously.

"Two men, four women."

"Right. I have them." Joseph patted his pockets. "Not on me. I'll get them. You wait here."

The steward smiled and nodded, turning away toward the rail. Below, a woman bent over the triumphant bantam lad. She wore a scarf around her shoulders, crossed over her breast and tucked into the waist of her apron, but pulled it out to wipe blood off his eye, loudly berating him in Italian. Joseph mounted the stairs to the next deck and hurried to the telegraph room. He scrawled out a quick message and thrust it at the telegraph operator. "Not a word to anyone or you go with him."

The operator blushed, nodded and turned toward the key. Joseph narrowed his gaze. "If I hear that anyone was warned off, I'll know who to come to. Do you know what collusion is?"

"*Collusione, si.* I will say nothing," the operator assured him.

In the second-class lounge, four boarding inspectors moved among the passengers, checking passports, examining the papers of well-dressed women and neatly groomed men who nevertheless lacked the final polish found in first class. In the corner, under one of the mahogany paneled arches, four women and two men crowded around one of the inspectors. Hanrahan, Joseph thought his name was, and that would explain Sapelli's confusion. He was Joseph's approximate height and weight, with the same black hair but a more florid complexion and a rounder face.

Hanrahan shrugged at the passengers. The men's faces were dark with anger. They consulted together before one of them took a step toward Hanrahan and dropped something at his feet. Hanrahan retrieved it and slid it into the pocket of his blue uniform coat. He propped his foot on a low settee, opened a book on his knee, uncapped his pen and scrawled something across the page. The men stood next to him, blocking Joseph's view, but it didn't matter. Joseph knew what Hanrahan was doing. The folded money in his pocket told the story. Joseph casually moved in Hanrahan's direction in time to see the inspector turn, glance his way, and quickly turn back. There followed the sound of paper tearing, and a quick shuffle among the men. By the time Joseph reached them, the passengers were smiling and Hanrahan was a model of composure.

"Everything all right here?" Joseph asked.

Hanrahan smiled. "Fine, Superintendent. Just fine." He handed several documents and three passports to one of the men. "You can prepare to land, sir," he said. "Welcome home."

The dark man nodded and shepherded two women to seats near the saloon door. Hanrahan turned his attention to the second man and the women with him. Joseph studied the passengers openly. Two women, both quite young — eighteen, at best — carefully dressed in modest suits and plain shirtwaists. One wore pale blue and a straw boater, the other ashes of roses with a large, flowered picture hat. One had the orange hair of a henna rinse, the other a deep and suspicious black.

The man, who looked to be about thirty years old, was shorter than either woman, and square, with a stocky build. He was sweating heavily in a tightly fitted suit with a dizzy pattern of black and white checks. Joseph took the papers from Hanrahan's grip and unfolded them, studying them with interest.

"Mister . . . DeLuca, is it?"

"*Si*, DeLuca. Alfredo DeLuca."

"Of Cleveland, Ohio. You're still a long way from home, Mr. DeLuca."

"*Si, si*," DeLuca said sadly. "Next, train. One day, two day." He grinned and held up two fingers.

"And when did you and your daughters become citizens of the United States, Mr. DeLuca?"

DeLuca seemed to struggle with the question. At length he replied, "Long time. One year, two year." He shrugged, as if he couldn't quite recall.

"It says here that you've been an American for six years — since February, 1895. Time certainly passes quickly." Joseph turned to the young women.

"And these are your lovely daughters, I suppose. Which one of you is Sophia?"

They faltered briefly before the redhead tapped her chest. "Sophia," she said. "Sophia DeLuca."

"And that would make you . . ." Joseph said, turning to the other woman. The girl glanced at her companions wildly.

"Anna." Hanrahan took the papers out of Joseph's hands, folded them and offered them, with passports, to the man. "Glad to have you back, Mr. DeLuca. When we come into port, one of the gatemen will direct you to the ferry for the New Jersey Central depot. You can catch your train there."

"Si, grazie," DeLuca said. He shoved the papers and passports into the breast pocket of his jacket and ushered the women out of the saloon onto the second-class deck.

"Sorry, Superintendent," Hanrahan said when they'd gone. "We still have quite a few passengers to get through before docking." He turned toward the next couple, waiting close by. Joseph walked companionably beside him.

"How long have you been working for the Boarding Division, Hanrahan?"

"Three years, sir. I was a watchman at Castle Garden. Joined Boarding when the first station was built on the island."

"Yes," Joseph said. "I thought I remembered you. I was in Registry at the time. Well," he said, glancing around the saloon, "I think I've seen all I need to here. Carry on, Hanrahan."

Back in steerage, the fight was over.
Although the big man was nursing a grudge,
he was doing it at a prudent distance from
the bantam, and no one was paying him
much attention. Instead, they talked excit-
edly among themselves, pointing upriver
where Manhattan, and its promise, lay waiting for them.

Joseph would not travel the final lap with
them, but he could see it in his mind's eye
as clearly as if he were there. The long wait
in port, while the first and second cabin passengers cleared Customs and were sent on
their way. And then steerage removal to ferries and barges by gatemen issuing perfunctory orders that would grow more gruff as
the day wore on. "Move along; get in line.
Get that trunk outta here!"

They would be crammed onto the boats
like cattle in a stockyard, sweat drenching
their best clothes until they were sodden
and limp. Numbered and rounded up by
groupers who did not care if they had a
name as long as they were tagged. Held on
the boats to steam under the summer sun
while the hundreds who had arrived before
them moved from line to line, breathing air
thickened with anxiety, hope, disease, and
despair. Once they were separated, some

would be cut from the herd like inferior animals, others shepherded to more boats and trains and on to destinations foreign and mysterious. Until finally it would be their turn to taste the freedom they had come for. But by then, the taste would have soured. There were four ships in port today — *La Gascogne,* the *Cymric,* the *Lombardia* and the *Furnessia.* Some of the immigrants were going to have a very long wait. Joseph silently wished them all well, and turned away to finish his job.

Four United States marshals and two black marias were waiting on the dock. He held back the disembarking passengers until Ernesto Sapelli, Hanrahan, DeLuca, and his companions had been identified, handcuffed, and removed from the ship. Joseph watched them escorted to the jailer's wagons with a surge of deep satisfaction. McNabb was going to be livid.

Assistant Commissioner Edward McNabb almost tripped over Dr. George Rockwell in the corridor outside his office. He had the unpleasant feeling that the Medical Chief had been lying in wait for him. Ambush was Rockwell's favorite tactic. He cut him off before Rockwell had a chance to speak.

"In a hurry this morning, Dr. Rockwell.

Got to go down to Boarding," he said, walking a little faster.

"I'll walk with you then, and you can step outside with me for a minute. I want to show you something."

"You showed me the hospital yesterday, and the day before that. In fact, we've had this conversation every morning this week and three times last week. Despite what you apparently think, I do not have lapses in memory, Rockwell, and I really do not think there is anything left to say on the subject."

"But you wouldn't want anyone to think you're not supervising the job as closely as you should, I'm sure. Am I wrong that, as Assistant Commissioner, it is directly your responsibility?" Rockwell held the door open for him.

McNabb stopped on the threshold. "You know perfectly well that it is. But so are many other matters of more immediate importance."

Rockwell waited unfazed. He wasn't going to go away. The harangues would continue. Every day he tried a different appeal. Yesterday, it was the lack of emergency surgical facilities. The day before that, their inability to isolate the insane from the other aliens. McNabb didn't give a damn about the insane, but he was getting tired of Rockwell's sob stories. "All right. I'm giving you two minutes."

Dr. Rockwell ushered him out the door with a slight bow. "If they don't get the building finished soon, we'll have to start putting them on barges. The city hospitals are starting to complain about all the cases we're sending them. I'm on my way over to Long Island College Hospital right now to beg for more beds.

"We can't keep crowding them in together here. God knows it's bad enough to arrive with cataracts or rheumatism or a simple head cold without contracting measles while they're here. Right now, the contractor has less than half his normal crew working. Come along. I'll show you." Rockwell started down the walkway around the ferry slip to the construction site on the other side, as McNabb lagged several paces behind.

The second island of the immigration station was composed of landfill and connected to the first by a shallow strip of land bordering a canal just wide enough for two ferries to navigate. The Great Hall lay on the southwestern side of the island, while the hospital, which was not much more than a skeleton of steel girders and a skin of bricks at present, would eventually take up the northeastern side. Rockwell had lobbied hard for the arrangement, which would put sick immigrants in proximity to their loved ones, while still allowing immigration authorities control over both.

"They shouldn't have come with rheumatism in the first place," McNabb snapped. "They can't work when they're all crippled up."

Rockwell waved him away irritably. "All right, maybe not. But there's nothing we can do about that. They come sick and they're going to continue to come here sick and it's up to us to make them well or send them back. But it's not up to us to send them back sicker than when they arrived. Now I'm telling you that we've got to do something. We've got to have that hospital, and soon. We spend half our time here shuffling them around the dormitories, trying to keep them from exposing each other to something worse than what they've already got. The risk is much greater than you think. If we get one incipient smallpox case in here, and we could, we may just end up with an epidemic on our hands." He stuck an unlit pipe in his mouth and clamped down on it.

"Well, be that as it may, they're building as fast as they can over there," McNabb said, gesturing vaguely at the hospital site.

Rockwell had his finger in the air, counting the workmen. McNabb ignored him and continued.

"I would remind you that we are not running a resort for the downtrodden here. If those people across the drink can't weed out the chaff before they get here, then it's the steamship company's problem if their aliens come down with measles on the way back to wherever they came from. Besides, the Commissioner won't be back for a week and Hannegan's just stirred up a new problem for us," he added. "And now, if you'll excuse me, I have to find the Boarding Chief." He turned to go, but Rockwell would not be put off.

"Thirty-six. What sort of a crew is that? At that rate, they might get it built by 1920."

"I'll speak to the contractor as soon as possible."

"That's what you said yesterday. The longer you ignore the problem, the worse it's going to get. Our budget for 1901 is almost spent, with almost four months left in the year. I'll have to write to Powderly to appropriate special funds to get us through."

This gave McNabb pause as no other appeal had. The last thing he wanted was to give anyone, least of all Powderly, a reason to scrutinize accounting any closer than he already did.

"No need to go bothering the Commissioner General, Dr. Rockwell. Let's strike a bargain, shall we? Let me review the budget and see where I can eke out a little extra funding for your department. Give me a few days. In the meantime, you will stop hounding me every time I walk out the door of my office."

Rockwell rocked back on his heels, a satisfied little smirk hovering around his mouth. "Agreed. Just one other thing, McNabb. When the first epidemic comes, and I promise you it will, unless we get this hospital built, who do you think will be blamed?"

But McNabb was not going to be intimidated twice. "Why, you of course, George," he said. "They'll blame you."

CHAPTER THREE

"Just start moving slowly to your right, Miss Bonner. I'm coming behind you. As soon as I'm in place, you run for the doctor while I try to subdue her."

"No."

Rachel Bonner waved away the watchman, but kept her gaze fixed on the young woman who slowly backed into a corner of the day room. She held a shoe in her upraised hand — grasped it at the toe so that the hobnails in the heel would inflict maximum harm. A man's shoe. Rachel stole a peek at the girl's feet — one bare, one swimming in a well-worn mate. Too big, very shabby. Her husband's shoes. Rachel's gaze traveled back to the girl's face, to dark eyes unnaturally bright with fear, and on to the women who shrank together behind her. The girl took another step backward, her glance quickly shifting left and right — looking for a friend, watching for an enemy.

"She's frightened, Mr. Archer. Don't come in, and don't go for the doctor just yet." She turned her full attention back to the young woman. "Teresa . . ."

The girl darted backward and brought the shoe up higher in a clear threat. Rachel gasped a little, in spite of herself.

"Teresa," she said. "Your husband is waiting for you. *Il vostro marito è qui.* Come, I'll take you to him."

The girl blinked uncertainly. "Paolo?"

"Paolo Bastitelli is your husband, isn't he?" Rachel said, repeating the question in Italian.

"*Sì.*" At length, Teresa's hand dropped to her side, but she tightened her grip on the shoe. She looked about at the other women. One of them pulled her shawl close around her shoulders and dared a step forward. "*Andate!*"

"Come along then," Rachel said, turning away. She batted her hand at Archer, a warning to move back so as not to frighten the girl further. Behind her, Teresa collected a basket and a carpetbag. Rachel stopped at the door, holding her hand out to the girl to relieve her of some of the load. She pointed at Teresa's still bare foot.

Some of the other women laughed. Teresa's color rose and she cut her eyes around before she, too, broke into a smile, dropped the shoe and slid her foot into it. Rachel led her across the gallery and down the northwest staircase, with a watchful Archer close on their heels.

It wasn't as if this kind of thing never happened. It happened all too often, and sometimes it ended in disaster. Esther Berman had been stabbed with a kitchen fork. It left a nasty scar on her neck and a worse one on her disposition until the Head Matron finally discharged her for bullying the women. Rachel had never experienced violence herself, but she had always known it was a possibility.

Paolo Bastitelli waited for them in the family waiting room. Despite the heat, he wore a too-large suit of heavy wool and clutched a new gray fedora in his hands. A thin sheen of perspiration glossed his slightly yellow complexion, and a single drop trickled into his unevenly trimmed mustache. Rachel paused, turning away as Teresa fell into his arms with cries of joy.

"I have been sick," Paolo explained to his wife. "In the hospital. They — the doctors — they would not let me come for you until today. No one would bring you a message."

Teresa Bastitelli, an ignorant seventeen-year-old girl, had been living in the detained women's dormitory on Ellis Island and waiting for her husband for over a week. In the nine days she had been there, she had watched the other women come and go, some to husbands or brothers or uncles, others to the ships that would take them back home. She had been repeatedly questioned by the inspectors. Where was her husband? Why had he not come for her? Did she really have a husband at all? Why had she come to America? Teresa had no answers for them. It was no wonder, Rachel thought, that she had been wary and frightened.

Few immigrants arrived on Ellis Island uninformed of the laws governing immigration. They all knew that a woman alone would not be released on her own, and they all knew that they must lie about prospective employment, contract labor laws being what they were. Teresa could not claim to be coming to America to a job, nor had she a male relative to take her into his care. Had Paolo not arrived when he did, she might well have been sent back to Italy — deported as likely to become a public charge, or worse, for immigrating for immoral purposes. Once back in Italy, it would not be easy for this girl to raise another passage.

"Yesterday Regina Curcio was deported

by Special Inquiry," Rachel said to the watchman, as they crossed the baggage room together. "Teresa thought the same thing was going to happen to her. She knew Paolo was supposed to come for her, and she was afraid of what might have happened to him, and what was going to happen to her. Imagine what it must be like, for them, Mr. Archer. Separated, traveling to a strange place."

The watchman shrugged and started to answer, but his words were lost in an explosion of noise. The commotion began at the doors to the pier, swelled and traveled in a chaotic wave across the baggage room — screaming and pushing — men, women, and children clambering to get past one another. Rachel and Archer pushed back.

"What is it?" Rachel shouted. The watchman pointed to the doors, where other guards had converged, fighting their way through the mass of people rushing into the Great Hall.

"Something out on the dock," he shouted, and began shouldering his way through the crowd.

Rachel tried to follow him, but was borne back by the crowd. Archer had been swallowed up by the sea of people still advancing on her. She stood on her tiptoes, but all she could see of him was his boxy blue hat receding into the crowd.

"Rupert, *wo bist du?*" A voice sharp with rising panic repeated the cry again.

Rachel spied a child crouched behind a battered trunk, gnawing on his hand as he watched legs and feet scurry past him. He might have been four years old.

"Rupert?"

He blinked. She grabbed his hand, pulled him out and delivered him to his frantic mother. "Keep a good hold on him now," she said, and to him, "Stay with *Mutter.*"

"*Danke,*" the woman said, scooping him up in her arms.

The groupers inside the Great Hall were beginning to restore order. "It's all right," they cried out in German. "Go back to your lines, please."

Rachel elbowed her way through the remaining crowd, emerging into the sunlight to find that the order inside did not extend to the pier. Straight ahead of her, a doctor, his hands covered with blood, bent over the crumpled body of a man. Next to him a valise lay open, its contents tumbling out onto the cement. A grouper ran past the doctor to assist a pair of watchmen who were holding other passengers back on the ferry. Rachel edged closer until she could see the victim clearly.

He lay on his side, his hands pressed against his stomach. Blood oozed through his shirt and coursed over his fingers. He was breathing hard and fast, his eyes squeezed shut, his face scarlet.

"Is there anything I can —"

"Stay back," the doctor snapped.

Rachel stepped back a pace, stumbling over the open valise. She dropped to her knees and began shoving a book and some clothes into the case, aware all the while of the man's labored breathing. He was a young man, she thought. Twenty-six or -seven, perhaps.

"I help, Mees Bonner."

Rachel glanced up into the heavy features of a darkly complected man. She recognized him as a laborer from the Janitorial Division and cast about for his name — Fotis. Fotis Apostolou.

He squatted next to her and, removing the book she had tossed into the valise, rearranged the clothes beneath it. He took a shirt from her hands and carefully folded it before laying it in the case. Rachel leaned back on her heels and let him take over the task of packing.

"Do you know what happened here, Mr. Apostolou?"

Fotis nodded grimly. "A gun. The girl have a gun and she . . ." Defeated by the effort of explaining, he merely pointed at her and pretended to pull a trigger.

"A girl? Where —"

"Pulled out a gun and shot him right there, she did."

Rachel glanced up at the sound of an agitated woman's voice. "Never seen the likes of it, her shooting him there before God and man and me own eyes."

Several passengers from the *Cymric* clustered around a man in a charcoal suit. Edward McNabb listened attentively to the witnesses, all of whom talked at once. ". . . a queer sort of a pair. Stayed to themselves on the ship."

"I think it must have been some kind of a mistake — an accident."

"An accident? Whatcha mean? I saw it with me own eyes, I tell ya. She just pulled it right out, big as you please . . ."

Behind the ferry, a police cutter was tying up at the dock. The doctor glanced up at the boat, rose and addressed himself to the administrator. "I've got to get him to a hospital. They'll take him," he said to McNabb, with a quick gesture toward the cutter. "I'll see to it."

McNabb agreed. "Take the witnesses'

statements," he said to a pair of groupers. He broke away from the passengers and hurried toward Rachel, still on her knees.

"Matron, come with me," he said, and pointed at Fotis. "And you, if you saw anything, be sure you tell the watchmen."

Rachel hastily rose to follow McNabb, glancing back over her shoulder. A stretcher was laid out next to the bleeding man and two police officers crouched over the body.

Fotis had closed the valise and carried it off to the side of the walk, out of the way of traffic, returning to Watchman Archer to give his statement. Rachel saw the doctor motion to him to help lift the man onto the stretcher.

Rachel picked her way past other immigrants who stared at the scene in shock. A man jostled her elbow, shoving past her to take his wife by the arm.

"Come along then, Rosaleen. We'll not be getting involved in the likes of this."

Rosaleen pulled out of her husband's grasp. "I'll be along, Michael, as soon as I see —"

He reached back, this time grabbing her arm more firmly. "Now."

The police cutter steamed away from the dock as Rachel joined McNabb at the edge of a tight circle of watchmen. "I asked you your name," McNabb said. "It won't do any good to withhold it, you know. I'll get it off the ship's manifest, or one of your fellow passengers will tell me."

A fair-haired wraith of a girl turned her green-eyed gaze on McNabb. She was neatly dressed in a navy blue serge skirt and a shirtwaist of fine, ivory linen. A pert straw hat primly shaded her delicate features. She raised her chin slightly and crossed her arms over her chest.

"Maggie . . . that is, Margaret. My name is Margaret Mary Flynn, and that's all I have to say to ya."

CHAPTER FOUR

"I'll call the mainland right away, sir. The police cutter's just pulled out, but they'll send us another. Sir? Shall I call them, sir?"

Edward McNabb looked blankly at the watchman and then returned his gaze to the young woman in front of him. His mind was reeling as the enormity of what had just occurred pressed in on him. Over the girl's shoulder, he caught a look at Albert Lederman, Chief of Registry, and tried to gauge the expression on his face. A warning, he thought. Why?

Because whatever had happened here was going to focus attention on Ellis Island again and that, above all, was something that he wanted to avoid. The island was overrun with critical press as it was, always sniffing for a scandal, watching for a misstep. The foreign language presses were the worst, skulking in the background, hoping to expose how poor immigrants were mistreated, abused, bilked. And now there would be this blasted investigation of the Boarding Division. McNabb tried to think about how this newest eruption might affect his position on the island.

It was hardly their fault, after all. Officials at Ellis Island had done nothing to incite her, had not provided the weapon. Officials at Ellis Island were innocent bystanders. McNabb glanced up at the watchman, opened his mouth, and abruptly closed it again.

Innocent bystanders they might be, but the press would still love another episode of Ellis Island drama. They might not be able to blame immigration officials, but they would certainly be scrutinizing every move he made from this time forward. For the first time in his career in the immigration service, McNabb wished that Fitchie were there to make the decisions. The responsibility should have been falling on the New York Commissioner, not on his assistant. He licked his lips and damned the summer sun that was beating down on all of them. A trickle of sweat ran down his scalp and onto the back of his neck.

If he turned the girl over to the police now, it would be out of his hands for good — a prospect that appealed greatly. On the other hand, if it was out of his hands, it was also out of his control. What if there was something he didn't know about this shooting? What if a boarding inspector were somehow involved? What if he, himself, were involved in some way? He couldn't possibly predict the ramifications of all the arrangements he had around Ellis Island, after all. The imbecile Sapelli was proof of that. Once the police had the girl, once she'd started talking, there would be nothing he could do to stop her.

But he didn't have to turn her over to the police right away. He had every right — perhaps even an obligation — to restrain her right here on Ellis Island until he had conducted at least a preliminary investigation of the incident. And there were probably some legal issues to sort out. McNabb knew from experience that digging out the law could take quite a lot of time. By the time all the legal issues were put in order, he would have had plenty of time to figure out just how all this was going to affect his job and the hearings that might result from the Boarding Division investigation. Meanwhile, he could play it up to the foreign press — how he was just protecting a naive girl and keeping her out of a mainland jail. Maybe they'd come out on his side for a change.

But then there was Hannegan. Somehow or another Hannegan would involve himself in this, just like he did everything else. God, how he hated Joseph Hannegan. Every problem he'd had at the station in the last year could be traced right back to the Superintendent. McNabb wondered if Hannegan knew that he was keeping score.

"The gun, sir?"

"What?"

"What shall we do with the gun, sir?" McNabb focused on the small revolver lying in the watchman's palm. He grabbed it and jammed it into his pocket. "I'll lock it up for now," he said, and turned his attention back to Maggie Flynn.

Didn't he have enough to worry about without this? You'd think she'd have the decency to look frightened. He turned to the watchmen surrounding her and cleared his throat.

"We'll have to detain her on the island pending investigation. I'll consult with our legal staff immediately. In the meantime you two," he pointed to Archer and another watchman, "move the women from the temporary detention day room into the dormitory." He turned to Rachel.

"Matron, you will be closed into the day

45

room with a watchman and Miss Flynn. I want her searched for other weapons. We'll question her later." He lowered his voice. "See what kind of information you can get out of her, and report it to me immediately."

When the temporarily detained women were safely closed into their dormitory, Watchmen Donald Archer and Friederich Bosch escorted Maggie Flynn through a side entrance and upstairs to the day room. Rachel followed close behind. She was shivering, she realized, still shaken by the sight of the man lying on the dock, blood pouring out of his body. She shoved her hands into the pockets of her skirt and balled her fists in an effort to contain her trembling. The last thing she wanted was for Archer to see it. The matrons got little enough respect from the men without jeopardizing it further.

Even as she followed the men and their prisoner through the corridors and up the back stairs, her mind raced ahead of them. The arrangement could only last for the short term, as the women could not be held in the dormitory indefinitely. There were blankets to be aired and general disinfecting of the beds and furnishings, a process that must be performed every morning without fail, lest one immigrant infect all the others with a contagious disease. In a country already gripped by xenophobia, the Immigration Service had to take care not to fuel the hysterical fear that aliens flowing through the Golden Door were undermining the health and well-being of American citizens on the other side of it. Incidents like this — one immigrant shooting another on the docks — would not better the situation.

"Right in there, miss." Archer urged Maggie through the open door and stepped back for Rachel to follow her. "She's to be searched, Miss Bonner."

Rachel directed Maggie to raise her arms over her head. She patted the girl down carefully — breasts, waist, arms — wishing it could have been done outside of Archer's watchful eye. The girl stared over Rachel's shoulder, pointedly concentrating on a spot on the wall, her face flushed with embarrassment.

"Turn your back, Mr. Archer."

"But if she's carrying a weapon —"

"I'll call out to you. Please turn your back." He hesitated, but finally complied.

"Raise your skirt, please." The girl pulled her skirt up around her waist, allowing Rachel to pat down her bloomers.

"Now take off your boots, please."

Maggie did as she was told, handing them to Rachel to examine. She turned each one upside down and handed them back. "That's finished."

Maggie pulled on the boots, stooping to lace them with her tiny, childlike fingers. Rachel turned to Archer, as if he might have the answer to what to do next, but he merely shrugged. Maggie wandered to the window and peered down on the walk that led to the power plant. Archer pulled a chair in front of the door and took his seat, while Rachel joined the girl at the window. On the sidewalk below, a laborer carrying a toolbox walked toward the power plant. He stopped to examine something on the ground, kicked it with the side of his foot and moved on.

"When will they come back, do ya think?" Maggie asked.

"They? When will who come back?"

"The constables, of course."

"I couldn't say, really. Maybe not at all."

At that, Maggie turned to Rachel, her freckles in sharp relief against a complexion gone white. Her voice rose, her tone growing sharp.

"Not at all, didja say? What will become of me, then? I can't stay here." Abruptly she turned back to the window, stared out at the cloudless sky over the harbor, and chewed her lip. "Will they send me back to Ireland, do ya think?"

She didn't seem to understand the gravity of what she had done. In the aftermath of such a terrible act, there didn't seem to be a trace of violence left in her, not even a hint of bad temper. Rachel felt inclined to crack the girl's composure and see what was underneath.

"I don't know, Miss Flynn. If he lives, if you're not charged with assault or worse, if you're lucky and a judge or jury is moved to clemency, you might be sent back to Ireland." She took the girl's elbow and gently pulled her away from the window.

"Come, sit down here," Rachel said, gesturing to a library table and chair.

Maggie's gaze shifted to Archer at the door, straight and watchful, intimidating in his dark blue uniform. Rachel excused herself to speak to him.

"I'm afraid I can't do that, Miss Bonner. You heard Mr. McNabb."

"Yes, and so did you," Rachel whispered in response. "He asked me to talk to her, to try to get information from her. Now you know that she's not carrying a weapon, and I assure you I'm perfectly capable of defending myself. Besides, you'll be right outside the door, if I need you."

"But —"

"Mr. Archer," Rachel said in a firmer voice, "there are things which women simply cannot discuss in front of men. If something improper occurred aboard ship . . ."

Archer colored and averted his gaze. "You'll agree to leave the door ajar?"

Rachel pulled open the door. "Ajar, it is."

Archer picked up his chair and passed her without further comment. Rachel pulled another chair over to the table, took a piece of paper and a pen from a shelf of writing supplies and seated herself across from Maggie. "All right," she said. "Why don't you tell me a little about yourself?"

"You're overreacting." Albert Lederman calmly eyed his superior over the desk. "The secret is to find a way to turn it to your advantage."

McNabb stared at him incredulously. "Thanks to Hannegan, I have the Commissioner General in Washington and the press both breathing down my neck about conditions here at the station, and now a shooting. And I'm supposed to turn that to my advantage. Just how, may I ask, am I to do that?"

Lederman snatched the telegram from Washington off McNabb's desk and gave it a quick reading.

"Expect thorough investigation of Sapelli incident at once. Stop. Place Hannegan in charge. Stop. Keep Washington posted of all findings."

It was signed Terrence V. Powderly, Commissioner General of Immigration.

Lederman tossed the telegram back on the desk and leaned forward. "All right, so there's to be an investigation. So? As long as you contain the investigation to Boarding, you can handle it. Contact Fitchie, wherever he is, and let him know that you've already begun putting together an investigating committee of your own — with his permission, of course."

McNabb snorted. "Of course. And who will be on this supposed committee? Powderly specifically named Hannegan."

Lederman waved a warning hand. "No, we've got to keep Hannegan in the background. Get in touch with a few reporters — sympathetic conservatives, no bleeding hearts or reformers — and announce the pending investigation. While following up on the Sapelli arrest, it has come to your attention that abuses in the Boarding Division, etc. etc. Once the story appears in the paper, Powderly will have to let it stand."

McNabb grabbed a pencil and took a few notes on a memo pad. "All right, but who shall I appoint to the investigating committee?"

"Yourself, of course. And me. And one more person from the ranks — Crater would be a good choice. Fitchie will probably have to be in on it too."

"Crater," he wrote. "But what about this shooting? You know what *Stats Zeitung* is going to do with that. There'll be more accusations about not protecting our 'huddled masses' and all that nonsense. There'll be no keeping this quiet. They're going to do everything they can to make me the scapegoat. If they can't get me one way, they'll try another."

"If they're looking for a scapegoat, give them Hannegan."

"Hannegan? Why on earth should we bring him into it?"

"To handle the girl's case."

"And have him making wild accusations and bringing more press down on the station? That's all I need."

Albert Lederman smiled. "Exactly. That is exactly what you need. If they're worrying about the girl, and how he's treating her, they won't be paying attention to the Sapelli investigation, now will they?"

"And Powderly? He expects Hannegan to conduct the investigation. You read the telegram."

"Yes, and so did you. But not until after you'd already assigned Hannegan to the shooting. The telegram arrived at two fifty-four, approximately five minutes before the shooting. The shooting, naturally, took precedence over anything else, the girl having to be subdued and all. You called Hannegan in and placed him in charge of the investigation of this Flynn girl. And you didn't get a chance to read the telegram until . . ." Lederman pulled out his pocket watch and looked at it. "Until about thirty minutes from now."

McNabb stared down at the telegram lying on his blotter for a moment, then picked it up and dropped it into his top desk drawer. "Right," he said. "Send for Hannegan."

CHAPTER FIVE

Edward McNabb removed the cap from his pen and scribbled in circles on his blotter. "So I've discussed this with Commissioner Fitchie, and we'd like you to take charge of this young woman's case, Hannegan."

"Case? What case would that be, Mr. McNabb? She shot her companion. She'll be taken into custody and the marshals will handle it from there. I seriously doubt that we'll see her again, unless it's to deport her. If anyone from Treasury should be handling it, it should be the Special Inspector."

"No!" McNabb's hand curled tightly around his fountain pen. "There's no need to bring Washington into this. The Commissioner General has enough to do. We can handle it under our own roof."

"All right, then give it to Special Inquiry. Besides, I expect to serve on the Boarding Investigation."

Joseph watched as McNabb scratched a

signature on the bottom of a form without reading it. McNabb's signature was a tight, spiky scrawl, narrow and illegible. Joseph had always thought that men with unreadable signatures were hiding something. McNabb had plenty to hide.

The administrator signed the last form, tossed it aside, and capped his pen. "You can't. You're our only witness to the incident. If you serve on the committee, it might appear to be collusion. And you, of all people, wouldn't want that." He leaned back in his chair and met Joseph's gaze, a twinkle of amusement in his eyes.

Joseph leaned over the desk, his face only inches from McNabb's. "Don't delude yourself. I am not the only witness. I feel sure that after a day or two in Ludlow Street jail, Sapelli will have plenty to say. You and I both know this has been going on for a long time in Boarding. Now that we have proof, I intend to do something about it. Once Sapelli and Hanrahan open up, you'll have a hard time keeping the rest of them quiet."

McNabb's gaze hardened. "You're Irish, Hannegan. I'd have thought you'd be more pragmatic. Out to make a name for yourself, are you? Joseph Hannegan, the only honest Irishman in New York."

Joseph stepped back, stuffing his fists into

his pockets, lest he land one squarely on the administrator's nose. "That sounds like an admission of guilt to me."

McNabb tilted his chair back and eyed Hannegan. "Merely an observation on your opinion of yourself, lad. Hubris never serves a man well, Hannegan. There's always someone waiting to knock that pedestal out from under you. If I were you, I'd watch myself." He landed his chair with a thump.

"Besides, it's not my decision. Commissioner Fitchie assigned you to the girl's case. I'm merely conveying his orders. Now, we've never dealt with a crime of this nature before. Consult with the Legal Division before you call in the police —"

"The U.S. Marshals. We're on federal land, remember?"

"Fine. Before you call in the marshals or anyone else. And you'll need to get statements from all the witnesses. In fact, the Legal Division should probably get their depositions."

"McNabb, that is not our job. We have an immigration station to run —"

"There is no room for error on this. We're going to be under scrutiny, Hannegan. Our conduct of the investigation must be thorough and above reproach. That's why Fitchie wants you to handle it personally.

And I think that in the interests of satisfying . . . uh, everyone, we should try to procure an attorney for this young woman. She's being held in the temporarily detained day room. Go talk to her. See what you make of her. Oh, and one other thing . . ." McNabb dug in his pocket and brought out a small gun, passing it over the desk to Joseph.

"This is her weapon. Lock it up somewhere, will you?"

Under scrutiny. In the interests of satisfying everyone. Now he understood. This potato was red hot, so McNabb was handing it off to him. Meanwhile, he'd keep Joseph out of the Boarding Investigation and square in the eye of the press. Even with Powderly's support, he'd be walking a tightrope handling the girl's case. One misstep and he'd find himself condemned in the evening papers. And one more thing he knew very well — once the story got in the wind, there'd be Irish immigrant societies swarming the island and, like as not, a crew of long-of-wind, short-of-principle politicians from Tammany, as well. All the more reason to bring in the authorities as soon as possible.

Joseph wondered how much Powderly knew about what had occurred at the station this morning. He knew about the Boarding scandal. Joseph, himself, had seen to that. It was, after all, the reason he was there and in the position of Superintendent.

Under other circumstances, the assignment of informant would have been abhorrent to Joseph Hannegan. But these were not those circumstances. Thomas Fitchie and Edward McNabb were in positions of deep public trust — a trust they abused with abandon. Terence Powderly knew it but, so far, had been unable to prove it. Meanwhile, graft and corruption went unchecked at Ellis Island. In one way or another, everyone had a hand in the immigrants' pockets.

While still Chief of Registry, Joseph had been called to Washington for an interview. The summons was private — by mail, coming to him at home. Joseph had gone, of course, with no idea of what awaited him. It had come as a shock. Powderly had been explicit in conferring the position on him.

"Your purpose, Hannegan," Powderly had said to him, "is to get it cleaned up, and gather as much evidence against those two thieves as you possibly can in the process. I will expect weekly reports from you. I should warn you, though. This job will not make you more popular with your co-workers."

Joseph Hannegan had never sought popularity, although he liked to think that he had the respect of most of the men who had worked under him in Registry. What Joseph Hannegan wanted was to be able to look himself in the eye every morning when he shaved in front of his mirror. He wanted to be able to unburden his soul in confession, knowing that his sins were largely personal, involving himself and God, and perhaps the people he loved. He wanted to believe that, somehow, he had made coming to America easier for some of the thousands of immigrants who, every day, defied the unknown to make new lives for themselves.

"If I might ask, sir," he'd said to Powderly, "why did you choose me?"

Powderly had smiled. "I presented a list to McNabb. You were the one person he strenuously opposed for the position. That was all the recommendation I needed."

Finally he might have a chance to make a serious difference at the station. McNabb sat up there in his citadel, where Fitchie was a mere figurehead, while legions of minions built walls around him, protecting him from exposure. Now, at last, there was a fissure in the wall. It was, admittedly, only a hairline crack. But if Joseph could only chip away at it long enough, he believed he could topple the fortress. He would not allow McNabb to deflect him from that purpose. He'd dispose of the girl's case before McNabb could convene the first meeting of the investigating committee and be on hand for every piece of testimony. Somewhere, there would be inconsistencies — impossible denials, lies, and cover-ups. Joseph Hannegan would be there to find them.

He stopped at his office long enough to lock the little Derringer in his desk drawer, then skirted the perimeter of the Registry Room and entered the north wing, which held the day rooms for excluded immigrants and was always the most carefully guarded. He stopped outside the small witness interrogation room between the Special Inquiry rooms, where a janitor was coursing the hall with a dust mop. It was not a perfect arrangement. Witnesses would have to be interviewed elsewhere, but it was the best he could do. He left the janitor with instructions to set up a cot in the room and went on to the day room where the young prisoner was being held.

"I thought she was going to confide in me, Superintendent," Rachel whispered, glancing across the room at Maggie. "But then she sat down and crossed her arms, and refused to tell me anything but her name and where she's from." Rachel consulted the paper in her hand. "Drumcliffe, County Sligo, Ireland."

Joseph turned to the young woman sitting perfectly erect in a chair in front of the window — a wisp of a girl, of little more substance than her long shadow cast on the floor by the waning light. "What's her name?"

"Flynn. Margaret Mary Flynn. She came in on the *Cymric,* out of — "

"Derry," Joseph supplied. "I know."

At the mention of Derry, Joseph thought he saw a slight quickening in the still body, as though the girl had been secretly listening. He strode across the room and stood in front of her, blocking her view of the window, planted his feet apart and clasped his hands behind his back.

"Miss Flynn, I'm the Superintendent here at the station. I'd like to talk to you."

She gazed up into his face serenely. She couldn't be more than eighteen years old. Despite his outward composure, Joseph found himself shaken. There had to be a mistake. This girl couldn't be a killer. Yet there had been witnesses — according to McNabb, there were plenty of them. The girl said nothing, but inclined her head a fraction, a bit like royalty. He cleared his throat.

"We don't have many shootings at the station, Miss Flynn, so you'll pardon me for proceeding cautiously. I'll need the name of your companion, that is, the victim." She calmly shook her head and shifted slightly in her chair.

Joseph stepped back a pace and glanced up at Rachel, who raised her eyebrows but said nothing. He frowned at Maggie. "You understand that I will be able to get it from the ship's manifest. It's only a matter of time."

"Do what you must, Superintendent —"

"Hannegan."

A spark flared in the girl's eyes. "From Donegal?"

Joseph shook his head. "My father is from County Mayo."

"But I'm from Sligo. We're almost neighbors . . ." Her voice trailed away. She dropped her eyes, stuck out her foot and examined her shoe. Joseph followed her gaze, but found nothing remarkable in the small, slightly scuffed brown boot.

"Neighbors, exactly," he said, seizing on what he hoped might be a friendly overture. He dragged over a chair, took a seat in front of her and elbowed his knees, leaning forward as though ready to accept her confidences.

"Now, Maggie from Drumcliffe, I should very much like you to tell me what happened out there," he said. "Did he do something to you? Is that why you shot him?"

"No. Oh no, Cor—" She stopped, breathed deeply and blew out a long sigh. "He did nothing to hurt me."

"But you shot him just the same, Maggie. Why? Why did you shoot — what did you say his name was?"

Maggie let out a tinkling little laugh that reminded Joseph of Moira's crystal dinner bell. "You're a sly one, Mr. Hannegan. I didn't say his name. You'll have to find that out for yourself."

Joseph pushed his chair back impatiently. "And so I will. This will go easier for you if you cooperate, Miss Flynn."

Maggie shrugged. "Easy or hard, it's all the same to me."

Outside in the corridor a group of detainees was being moved toward the dining room for the evening meal. Muffled voices instructed them to "Come this way" in a half dozen languages. Joseph stood and returned his chair to its place. He opened the door to the corridor and called in the guard.

"Mr. Archer, please escort Miss Flynn to room 205. She will be spending the night there. One of the night matrons will be around to check on her periodically."

He watched as the guard and the girl moved away down the corridor, before turning back to Rachel. "I would like you to be her day companion for as long as she is here. Which I hope will not be for too long," he added.

"I know you're technically off duty, but before you leave the island I must ask you to do two things for me. She'll need a blanket and a few personal items. There will be no one with her at night to escort her to use the —" He glanced away uncomfortably.

"Yes, I'll take care of that," she said.

"Thank you. And then, as you're leaving, go to the baggage room and have her bags sent up to my office."

The two split up in the corridor, Rachel to go upstairs to the dormitories while Joseph turned back toward the Registry Room. The *Cymric's* passengers should have all been processed by now. He collected all the necessary forms for the ship and retreated to his office. There, he snatched up the telephone, instructing the operator to connect him to Long Island College Hospital. At length, a voice informed him that he had reached same.

"I'm calling to check on a patient from Ellis Island — a gunshot wound, brought in this morning. No, I'm afraid I don't have a name. Not yet."

The dormitories were still empty, row upon row of metal hammocks, suspended in tiers from chains in the ceiling, waited for detained women and children. Rather, Rachel thought, like so many wire baskets awaiting fruit and vegetables at a greengrocer. She fetched a blanket from the storage closet and locked the women's dormitory door.

Outside was the visitors' gallery, where politicians and dignitaries, foreign emissaries, notables and socialites were conducted when they wanted to observe the exotic masses assaulting the gates of democracy. Social voyeurs, Rachel had privately dubbed them, titillated by the dark unknowns of poverty and desperation.

A persistent drone ascended from the floor below, the sound of the immigration machine at work. Questions asked in a dozen languages — "Is someone meeting you here? Have you a trade? Where will you live? How much money are you carrying?"

The thunk of baggage being moved up the line, the slam of a metal gate. The call of an inspector — "Next?" "This way." "Messenger!" Brothers teasing sisters; men snoring; women sighing, rustling, questioning their men in worried whispers. And, now and then, laughter that seemed to ring out above it all.

Rachel stepped to the gallery rail and gazed down into the Registry Room. Although the day shift was nearing its end, the room below was still buzzing with activity, as though someone had stirred a great ant bed with a stick. Lines at the money exchange and the telegraph offices snaked all the way back to the registry desks. The detention pens on both side walls were full. In one, dozens of men stood behind chain link fences, their forlorn faces broken up like shards in a stained glass window. On the other side, women wept softly into their kerchiefs, consoled bewildered and fractious children, and stared across the room, perhaps to get a glimpse of a husband or father. Directly below, the last of the medical inspections were winding down for the night. Their pens were equally full, each occupant marked with a chalked letter indicating their disability. They clung to their meager possessions — a bundle tied up in

rags or a rickety basket leaning lopsidedly
— their faces struggling to maintain hope
where there was little cause for it. Because
she worked with the detained women, it
sometimes seemed to Rachel that no one
was ever admitted, at least not without a
fight. But the truth, she knew, was that the
vast majority of aliens were landed without
any problem and remained on Ellis Island
for only a few hours before going on to their
destinations.

Twelve of the fifteen registry inspection
lines were still open, their length varying
from as few as twenty to as many as sixty or
seventy immigrants who sat on iron benches
and leaned against the metal separating
rails, waiting to move another foot or two
toward their goal. From her vantage point
above, Rachel could scarcely make out faces
— only spots of color that, as she stared,
resolved themselves into native costumes,
kerchiefs, and hats. Poles, Italians, Magyars,
Greeks, Germans, Armenians, Russians,
Swedes; Jews, Catholics, Protestants, Mus-
lims; old, young, dispirited, and undaunted.
It was easy to look upon them that way,
harder to remember that they were someone's child or sister or brother; someone's
father, who had left his family in the old
country; someone's mother who had not

seen her son in half a lifetime. Some of them had been waiting for hours and yet, when finally they reached the inspector, invariably they stepped up to the desk with renewed vitality and, when they were passed to land, even the oldest grandmother strode smartly off for the docks. It said something about the human spirit.

Rachel never tired of watching the drama below, and pushed herself away from the rail reluctantly. But they would be there tomorrow or, rather, there would be a new wave of fresh faces, for they lapped at the American shore as inexorably as the breakers of the Atlantic. She sometimes wondered if there was anyone left in Europe.

The inspectors had several hours ahead to clear out the remaining crowd, and she, meanwhile, had her own duties to perform. She went downstairs to the medical office for a chamber pot and washbowl before returning to the witness interrogation room to deposit them with Watchman Archer. From there, she took the stairs to the first floor and the desk in the baggage room.

"You're sure that this is all?"

The chief baggage clerk set down a single, small wicker basket trunk at Rachel's feet. "That's all there is for this number, Miss Bonner. I'm positive. It belongs to that girl

— the one that shot the man out there. One of the groupers brought it in here, said put it aside by itself so it don't get lost."

"All right. You might as well let me have the victim's suitcase, too."

The handler rocked back on his heels and jingled the change in his pocket. "Far as I know, he didn't have no suitcase. Nobody brought it here or I woulda seen it."

"Are you sure? He did have a suitcase, I know that for a fact."

"You got his number?"

"No, I'm afraid we don't even know his name yet, but the Superintendent will find it."

"Well, when you got his name and number, you come back and I'll try to find it for you." He glanced down at the wicker case. "Let me carry that up to Mr. Hannegan's office for you."

"No, no," Rachel said, hoisting the trunk. "It's not heavy. I can handle it. You should be on your way home by now. Have a good evening."

Despite what she had told the baggage handler, by the time Rachel reached the second floor she was struggling with the little trunk. She stopped in the deserted corridor to catch her breath. The Superintendent's office door was open and his angry shouting reverberated in the hall.

"Your own people were there, on the spot, when it happened, and there was a score of witnesses, and you're telling me there was no shooting? What kind of slipshod outfit are you people running over there? This is United States Treasury Department business and we expect some cooperation."

Rachel stopped at the door, but Joseph waved her on into the office even as he paced behind the desk. "Well, that's fine then. You check on the whereabouts of your patrol cutter this morning and get back to me please. And I'll need the names of those officers. They're witnesses in a shooting."

He slammed the receiver back into its cradle, ran his fingers through his hair and glared at Rachel. She set the trunk down next to his desk before he could take it from her. "Is there a problem, sir?"

"Yes, Miss . . ."

"Bonner. Rachel Bonner."

"There is, indeed, a problem, Miss Bonner." Joseph dropped wearily into his seat and gazed up at the matron.

"No one seems to know where the victim is."

CHAPTER SIX

It was still there. Joseph groaned as he eyed the sign in the window — ROOM TO LET, Apply Between 3:00 and 4:00 Daily. And now there was a crack in the glass as well. The third this summer. Probably another stickball game.

So the fourth room still wasn't filled. Moira was just too finicky. When a potential boarder presented himself at the door, she'd size him up in a glance and, if she didn't like what she saw, snatch the sign from the window with quick apologies for having forgotten she'd rented the room just an hour ago. If, on the other hand, the hapless candidate satisfied all her criteria, she would turn him over to her father for Dennis to interrogate and intimidate. No wonder they had so much trouble finding boarders.

Joseph mounted the steps of the house in Greenwich Village and let himself into the front hall.

"Shosav?"

"It's me, Dad."

"So you're home, then. We didn't wait dinner on ya, though."

Joseph dropped his hat on the hall tree and hooked his coat beside it. He followed the sound of his father's voice past the parlor to the door of the dining room behind it. Dinner conversation had resumed, and a new voice was participating in it. It was one Joseph knew well.

The partial remains of the evening meal were still spread over the table. Dennis Hannegan sat in a wheelchair at its head, flanked on one side by a slender reed of a woman, and on the other by a dumpy matron thirty years her senior. And in Joseph's own place sat a man who rose to greet him with a confident handshake. Despite the years they had known one another, Joseph was always startled when confronted anew by his friend's handsome looks — gleaming, dark eyes and a square jaw which was softened only by the deep dimples he flashed now.

"Liam?"

"I've a beer growing warm on the bar for ya, Joe m'lad. I find myself wondrin' when you're comin' to claim it."

Joseph took his friend's extended hand. "The station's been keeping me pretty busy,

Liam. But I'll get there. One of these days, when you're looking the other way, I'll show up in want of a whiskey."

He dropped two evening newspapers at his father's place and pulled out the remaining vacant chair. "Good evening, Miss Dove," he said, nodding at the knobby spinster who sat, hands primly folded, in front of a half-eaten bowl of rice pudding.

Though Joseph guessed that she might only be in her thirties, Grace Dove was an ageless woman. She might have been thirty, she might have been sixty. One could scarcely tell at first glance, and Joseph suspected that men rarely went back for a second. Hair of sepia and clothed to match, she was an unprepossessing package. Joseph always tried to give her a little extra attention.

"And Mrs. Shapiro, how were your undergarments today?" Selma Shapiro giggled, her cheeks turning almost as rosy as her hair.

"Very busy, Mr. Hannegan. We're introducing a new line of . . . well, you know. We're showing a lot of silk this year. I have just the prettiest garment in the store right now — something that would be perfect for Miss Moira —"

"I'm afraid silk wouldn't hold up very well

73

to the kind of cooking and cleaning I do around here, Mrs. Shapiro." Moira Hannegan set a plate of shepherd's pie in front of her brother. "I heard you come in. What kept you this time?"

Joseph glanced at the attentive faces of the others. "An incident at the station. And where's Mr. Kessler this evening?" he asked, smoothly changing the subject.

"At one of his night classes. This time he's learning about photography. I've never seen anyone so bent on self-improvement," Mrs. Shapiro said. "When he finishes his class, I think he should make a portrait of Moira."

Moira laughed out loud, pushed a lock of hair back with her forearm and pointed to her sleeves, rolled up to the elbow. "And what will he call it? Perhaps 'A Bridget in New York'?"

"You're not a bridget, Moira Hannegan," Miss Dove said. "You are an educated young woman, and don't you forget it. Isaiah Kessler would be fortunate to have a subject such as yourself."

Miss Dove's uncharacteristic burst of fervor elicited a surprised silence from her dinner companions. Liam glanced at the others and back at Miss Dove, who stared self-consciously into her rice pudding.

"Don't you worry, Grace. May I use your

Christian name?" She answered with a blush and a nod.

"Well, then, Grace, you're quite right. She's no bridget. Moira Hannegan is a lady born, and you may be sure, Mrs. Shapiro, that there are, indeed, portraits and silks in her future."

Moira merely rolled her eyes, but her father beamed at Liam before returning his attention to his open newspaper. He sat forward abruptly, pushed his rice pudding out of the way and smoothed the paper out on the table.

"Well, well, Redmond is coming to the United States to speak in November, Shosav." Across the table, Liam met Joseph's gaze with lips compressed to hide his amusement.

"Who is Redmond, Mr. Hannegan?" Mrs. Shapiro said.

"John Redmond. Member of Parliament for Ireland and planning to sell us out to the Lion with Home Rule if he has his way."

"Home Rule?"

"An Irish Parliament, but still subject to the queen. A compromise at the very time when we should be striking a blow for independence while the Brits are still fighting the Boer guerrillas. Devoy will set him straight."

Joseph ground his teeth, crossed himself, grabbed his fork and speared a chunk of carrot. Dennis Hannegan's unholy litany, as unchanged as the ancient rites of the Church. John Devoy, *Lord have mercy on us.* The Boer Wars, *Christ have mercy on us.* Home Rule, *Deliver us, O Lord.* Mother of God, he was sick to death of it.

"And this Mr. Redmond is in favor of Home Rule?"

"That he is, Miss Dove."

"But it seems to me that it would be better than the way things are right now, Mr. Hannegan," Mrs. Shapiro said. "Of course, I wasn't old enough to remember it, but my Nat came here when he was fifteen, and he never forgot how bad things were in Russia. The pogroms . . ." She shook her head.

Liam leaned across the table. "But you see, Mrs. Shapiro, if the Irish accept Home Rule, nothing in Ireland will ever really change. The only possible way is complete freedom from English oppression, and that means an Irish Republic and nothing less."

Dennis slammed his palm on the table. "Exactly! You see, Shosav? Liam understands."

"I see, Dad."

An Irish Republic, always the final entreaty. *World without end, Amen.* Once it was out — his father's dearest wish and solemn prayer — Joseph could relax. The others could talk on about it, but for Joseph it was like the dismissal at Mass. *Thanks be to God.*

His thoughts drifted back to what he had learned that afternoon. None of the hospitals he contacted had received a gunshot wound from Ellis Island. Or at least, none of them had any record of it. Why? And which doctor at the station had escorted the victim in the first place?

"I didn't know him," Matron Bonner had said, "but I don't have much contact with the medical division."

Dr. Rockwell would be able to identify the doctor tomorrow and then it would be a quick matter to dispose of what had happened to Michael Finnegan, for at least now Joseph knew his name. After calling all the hospitals, he had compared all the male passengers on the alphabetical passenger list of the *Cymric* with the various forms recording the disposition of immigrants, matching each number on the list to one of the forms until every passenger was accounted for except one. Michael Finnegan had failed to appear for medical or registry inspection, ergo Michael Finnegan must have been Maggie Flynn's companion.

Tomorrow he would check all the hospitals

again, asking about the patient by name. When he knew what had happened to Finnegan, he would call the marshals and let them take over the case of Maggie Flynn from there.

"I'll be going then, Joe."

Joseph glanced up, surprised to find only Dennis still at the table and Liam standing over him, his pocket watch in hand.

"I've a meetin' with some of my voters tonight. They're badly in need of jobs. I'm doin' my best for them."

"Oh, I'm sure you and your cronies down at the Hall will find a way to put them on the city payroll, Liam."

"Shosav!" Dennis glared at his son.

Liam winced in mock hurt. "I'm out of Tammany, doncha know? And in a few more months, I'm out of politics altogether."

"Are ya, now?" Dennis turned to his son. "Didja hear that, Shosav? He's left Tammany. Saw the light, didja lad?"

Liam tucked his watch back in his pocket. "Oh, the boys at the Hall are all right, I guess. And some of them are my best customers. But I don't much care for politics, ya see. I've a head for business, I've found, and the Ballyglass is doin' right by me. But as long as I'm alderman, I've still got a job to do."

He conferred his thanks for dinner, went to the kitchen in search of Moira and left by the back door. The moment he was out of the room, Dennis turned on Joseph in a strained whisper. "What is the matter with you, Shosav? You might think of your sister before you speak!"

"She's got to know the truth, Dad. And when did you become a Tammany man?"

Dennis wheeled his chair around the edge of the table. "Never, and never will. Butcha heard him yourself. He's out of Tammany."

Joseph followed his father into the front hall. "I'll believe it when I see it."

Dennis waved him away. "I'll be goin' myself, then, before ya go climbin' on your high horse."

He heaved himself out of the chair before his son could assist him, grabbed a crutch that leaned against the hall tree and thrust it under his arm. Joseph moved the chair aside as his father turned to face him. He was wearing the expression Joseph knew too well — the one he reserved for meeting nights. Dennis started to say something, but a knock on the door silenced him prematurely.

"This'll be Seamus," he said, opening the door.

Seamus O'Neill stepped inside, whisking

a tweed cap off his head as he entered. He was a small man, all the more dwarfed by Dennis Hannegan's considerable size, but lively and crackling with nervous energy, like one of the dynamos at the station. He had a long, curved nose and dark hair that had receded halfway back over his scalp — a puckish figure whose seed had produced, through some miracle of nature, three exceptionally handsome children.

Seamus stuck out his hand to Joseph. "Good to see ya, Joe lad. It's been a while. I saw Liam on his way out. The lad wonders why ya never come round to the pub. But you're coming with us tonight, eh?"

"I'm afraid not, Seamus. I've had a hard day at the station, and tomorrow will be even worse."

"Save your breath, Seamus. We'll be goin' on. Tell your sister I expect to be late tonight." Dennis adjusted the crutch more firmly under his arm, shoved Seamus through the door and let it slam behind them.

Joseph found his sister poised at the big cast iron sink in the kitchen rinsing the last of the supper dishes. The back door stood open and the faintest breeze fluttered the muslin curtains on the window, but it wasn't enough to stir the damp locks plastered to the back of Moira's neck. She wiped her arm across her forehead.

Joseph wondered why it was that although Moira was closer to thirty than twenty, he never thought of his sister as old-maidish. It might have been her ready laugh and occasionally astringent tongue. But it was also the sharp contrast of her fine white skin with glossy black hair and eyes as glittering blue as a pair of aquamarines, for no man, even a brother, could imagine that a woman so beautiful would be allowed to languish into spinsterhood. There was nothing dull about Moira, and if it were not for being cooped up here with her father day in and day out, she would have married long ago. The boarding house was not conducive to meeting suitable young men. Nevertheless Moira was not short of suitors — Liam O'Neill, for one — and other young men from church and the neighborhood who would have happily come to call, had she encouraged them at all. "I'm particular, Joseph," she'd say. "I'll not marry a lesser man than either my brother or father, and that's a fact."

Privately, Joseph didn't think Moira would have to look very hard to find better men. But he wasn't sure she was quite sincere in her claim, either, for she had been in love with Liam O'Neill for as long as he could remember. He also suspected that Moira was loath to encourage a beau who might take her from the boarding house knowing, as she did, how much he and Dennis depended upon her to keep it running smoothly. Liam O'Neill might be the one man who understood her plight, but his understanding came at a very high price.

If only their mother had lived, it might have been different for Moira. She had started nursing school, and might now be working in one of the city hospitals. But Fiona Hannegan had died trying to give birth to a change of life baby, himself a stillborn. Both Joseph and his father had been working steadily then — Joseph in the immigration service at Castle Garden, and Dennis in his twenty-second year as a longshoreman on the docks. Not long after Fiona died, a two-hundred-pound crate fell on Dennis Hannegan, crushing his right leg and resulting in amputation. In reparation for the accident, Dennis Hannegan's employer had given him a wooden leg, a few thousand dollars and his walking papers.

The money had gone to buy the house — a step up and out of the tenements for the family but, more importantly, additional income. It had given them some stability, but it had also trapped Moira in a life that was far less than what her father and brother had hoped for her. Just as soon as they found a steady fourth boarder, they would hire a daily to help Moira with the housework and send her back to nursing school.

Joseph took a seat at the kitchen table and spread out the newspapers he'd taken from his father's place in the dining room. *The New York Times* had it on the front page. "Big Immigration Frauds" the headline declared, and beneath it, "Wholesale Smuggling of Undesirable Immigrants Going On For Years — Full Investigations Ordered." The article was as factual as it could be, considering that the information had been filtered through Edward McNabb.

A "startling story" had come to light, it said, "when it was learned that one of the employees of the French line steamship *La Gascogne* had been arrested and would be arraigned in the United States Circuit Court on a charge of having tried to bribe a United States Government officer." McNabb had not given out the officer's name. No doubt he wanted to keep the reporters as far away from Joseph as possible. It would come out, of course, when Joseph was required to testify in the case, but by then McNabb would have devised cover stories and smoke screens to keep reporters guessing. Assigning Joseph to Maggie Flynn's case was just one distraction.

Joseph turned to the inside page of the paper, and then to page four, but found no mention of the shooting on Ellis Island. Either it had occurred too late to reach the press, or the *Times* reporters had not considered it especially important. After all, the victim was only one of thousands of faceless strangers who passed through the doors of the station daily. One immigrant was scarcely worth a column inch unless, of course, he could lead reporters to bigger scandals.

"So, are you going to tell me what's troubling you, then?" Moira asked over her shoulder.

Joseph rose and went to the range where a pot of tea steeped fragrantly, took two mugs from the shelf above and filled them. "What makes you think something's troubling me?"

Moira raised an eyebrow in mock contempt. "As if you can hide anything from me. Is it Dad, again?"

"He didn't ask me to go tonight. I suppose I should feel relieved." Joseph carried the mugs to the table, took a jug of milk from the icebox and poured a stream into each one. Moira wiped her hands on a tea towel, tossed it over her shoulder, opened the oven door to let it cool and took a seat across the table. She picked up the mug and blew across the surface of her tea, silently inviting him to continue.

He tapped the open paper. "Look at this," he said, pointing to an article carefully outlined in red pencil. "Capt. Arthur Vine Here. Ex-Military Attaché Denies that He Refused to Meet Bourke Cockran — Says Boer War Is Over," the headline stated.

"And here." Joseph pointed to another article, this one about Irish M. P. John Redmond's proposed trip to the United States. "Home Rule is at hand," he read in a tone salted with sarcasm.

"And this one: 'Boer Spies In England.' "

He closed the paper and crumpled it under his hand. Moira rescued it, smoothing it out before removing it to the sideboard. "He'll want to save these," she said.

Joseph didn't need reminding. Dennis Hannegan followed his program with ritual devotion, perusing all the city papers nightly, carefully outlining his articles and neatly excising them with his penknife. These he compiled in a file until the weekly Clan na Gael meeting, whereupon he presented them to the brotherhood and later added them to his latest scrapbook volume.

"An idle waste of time," Joseph said, reaching past her for the whiskey bottle on the dresser.

Moira turned on him angrily. "What is a waste of time to a man in a wheelchair, Joseph? Is it keeping him from working? Perhaps you think he should be back on the docks, his half leg and crutch be damned."

Joseph poured a slug of whiskey into his mug, but sat back without drinking it. "Of course not," he snapped.

He pinched his brows between his thumb and forefinger, waiting for Moira's anger to abate. She was right and he knew it. But so was he right. Dennis's devotion to his holy crusade far exceeded reason, and his expectation that Joseph should fight for the cause beside him was not only unreasonable but also irresponsible. Joseph Hannegan was an officer of the United States Treasury Department, and any involvement with Clan na Gael could, and would, compromise his position. Despite her anger, Moira understood his predicament.

"I'm surprised he lets you put carrots in the pie, their being orange and all," he said. His sister laughed, easing the tension between them.

"Twenty-three years he's been here, Moira. Almost as long as he lived in Ireland.

They're all like that, you know. But to hear them talk, they've only stopped in to America for a natter on their way from Galway to Tyrone. Why? What did Ireland ever do for any of them but bring them to grief and put them in jail?

"Look at John Devoy. A literate, intelligent man who lives in the worst kind of poverty because he won't get a decent job and get on with his life. Every spare minute he's got is in the service of a country that he hasn't even seen for almost thirty years! What is the point of it all?"

Moira shrugged. "You know how the Irish are, Joseph — full of dreams that will never come to pass."

"Well, the Irish had better get their heads out of the clouds and put their shoulders to the wheel. Look at the Russian Jews. Dad talks about how unwelcome the Irish were when we came here, but no one has it harder than the Jews from Russia and still most of them succeed. And do you know why?" He went on without waiting for an answer from her. "Because they look forward, not back. It's not the Jews, but the Irish who end up on the public dole. Just look at Seamus."

Joseph sat back, suddenly weary. Moira left her mug on the table, went to the stove and stuck her hand in the oven. "The pie cooked over," she said, taking an iron cake turner from a rack over the sink. She got down on her knees beside the oven door, leaned into it, and began scraping. Her voice was muffled by the confines of the oven.

"They're not all on the dole, you know. Liam has done all right for himself."

"On Tammany money. I know you don't want to hear it, but it's true."

Her head came out of the oven. "You don't know that, Joseph. He works hard in that pub of his. And he's left Tammany, you know."

"So he says. But how did he come to own the pub, do you think? You don't think Seamus has been saving up money from his odd jobs over the years? The man never worked more than two days a week in his life, and not that if Devoy needed him."

Moira went back in the oven and brought out the turner piled with charred scrapings from the shepherd's pie. "But Liam is not his father. He's going to make something of himself," she said.

Joseph watched his sister and felt a heavy sadness press down on him. Perhaps it was kinder to leave her to her illusions.

CHAPTER SEVEN

Matthew Bonner liked to say that his family fortune came from peddling trinkets and gimcracks to Knickerbockers and Brahmins. If this understatement minimized his ancestors' importance, it did nothing to diminish the significance of his wealth. The Bonner assets were as robust as the Astors' and Vanderbilts'. They were simply less conspicuous.

The first Bonner on American soil, John, had arrived in 1730 and quickly decided that farming was not the life for him. Instead, he took to the sea, building a small trading business that, by the third generation, had grown into a modest fortune. John Bonner III, a hard-working, astute businessman, turned the family's moderate wealth into a fortune that would endow his family for generations to come. But John Bonner III would have no idlers in the family, and established a trust with one provision: no

Bonner was ever to live on his wealth without becoming a useful member of society in his own right. All Bonners thereafter were educated and contributing members of the world at large. Matthew had gravitated to the law — not to corporate law, or even to the wills and trusts so popular among lawyers of leisure — but to criminal law, a field in which he had made a considerable name for himself without ever attaching it to either the infamous or the incorrigible. Although he had very little use for politicians, except as a source of entertainment, he had been prevailed upon to enter the race for District Attorney on the Fusion ticket, a consolidation of both Republican and Democratic forces determined to defeat the scoundrels of Tammany Hall. Whether his faction — and they were factions divided not along party lines, but in practical matters — would be selected to represent the ticket depended upon the committee of eighteen. Matthew Bonner was indifferent to winning. What he cared about most was removing the Tiger from power, and if that required his name on the ticket, he was willing to do what was necessary.

All Bonners were raised to believe that wealth was a privilege to be enjoyed but not flaunted. Matthew Bonner lived by this creed and, in keeping with it, owned a conservative Federal-style home on Lexington Avenue, and maintained the family estate in Newport. The Bonner household did not lack luxury, but Matthew Bonner invested only in those possessions that gave him sincere pleasure. As his needs were few and his tastes restrained enough to please the most conservative old New Yorkers, his home was not ostentatious. He employed a housekeeper, a cook, a groom, and a live-in maid, but, a man who guarded his privacy zealously, he depended on dailies for the routine maintenance of his household. It was into this atmosphere that he had brought his young niece, Rachel, and it was in his dining room, under one of Pieter Aertsen's weary peasants, that she now sat drinking the last of her coffee from a Sevres cup.

"I don't believe anything like it has ever happened before. No one seems to know quite how to proceed. Mr. McNabb's turned it over to the Superintendent, but I'm sure he has an ulterior motive."

"No doubt." Matthew Bonner pushed away his empty plate and rose, lumbering over to the sideboard. "The man has a genius for self-preservation. Now there's a case study for you — the criminal mind at work."

Rachel leaned back in her chair, speaking to him over her shoulder. "I'm not interested in the criminal mind, Uncle Matt. That's your arena."

"But think what a help you could be to me," he said. He poured two small glasses of Cointreau from an amethyst crystal decanter and returned to the table, setting one in front of Rachel. "You've managed to infiltrate Ellis Island. Why not Tammany Hall? You could keep your eye on that scoundrel Croker for me."

Rachel took one sip from her glass, set it aside, and shook her head. "I wouldn't call it infiltrating. I have a job, and I do it. Besides, all that conspiring about money at Tammany would be dreadfully boring."

"Rachel, money is only boring when you have more than enough of it. The question is, how much is enough? They don't seem to have answered that question down at the Hall yet. And I don't doubt that you do your job. I know you take it very seriously. It's just that I'm not sure you'd have gotten it had they known who you were. I've been taking a few lessons in politics in Mr. Plunkitt's office."

Rachel smiled at her uncle. "You're joking, of course."

"On the contrary, I'm very serious. There's a good bit to be learned at the bootblack stand."

"Uncle Matt, what kind of a public servant carries out his business on the street? The man doesn't even have an office of his own, though heaven knows he can afford one."

"A smart man, Rachel. A very smart man. That's why I've been going down to the courthouse to listen to him. There's a good bit of political wisdom to be gained from the likes of George Washington Plunkitt."

"Such as what? How to buy votes and steal the city blind?"

He leaned back, tilting his chair on its rear legs despite a groan from the wood. "Let me give you an example. Yesterday's talk was on why politicians shouldn't wear dress suits." He patted the breast pocket of his jacket and pulled out a scrap of paper.

"Plunkitt makes it all very simple. He says that to make the voter in your district comfortable — and he emphasizes that it's the only way to get his vote — you want him to feel he's your equal, or even your better. So, regardless your means, you must live like he does — and not the wealthiest, but the poorest of them." He slipped the paper back in his pocket. "It's good advice, you know. In fact, it's the very reason Tammany has been so successful all these years. They study human nature the way the rest of us study law and the stock market. If we don't learn what they already know, we don't have a hope of election."

Matt finished his liqueur and eyed hers. "Are you going to drink that? There's no point in wasting it." She pushed it across the table to him and waited for him to go on.

"I suppose that's what I'm trying to tell you. It might be better if no one at the station knew I'm your uncle. You must seem to be like everyone else — working girl or bluestocking. People may be suspicious of you otherwise."

"I really don't know what bearing my station in life has on how well I do my job, but you're probably right. If Mr. McNabb knew I was your niece, he wouldn't like it. As to Tammany, well, I'm afraid Plunkitt and Croker must remain your project, not mine."

"And maybe not mine," Matthew Bonner said. "Croker learned to fight on the streets, and, let me tell you, he's as ruthless as they come. Tammany Hall will not give up one more vote than they absolutely have to. Our Fusion candidates will scarcely have a tooth or a nail left, come election day."

Rachel patted her uncle's hand affectionately. "I have every confidence that however toothless you may be, you'll be installed as our new District Attorney on Inauguration Day. Just keep your mouth closed when you smile for the photographers.

"And now," she said, rising, "I'm thinking of writing up a case study of this girl, if I'm free to observe her for awhile. The Superintendent's assigned me to be her daytime companion, but I don't know how long she'll be with us."

"Not longer than a day or two, I'll wager. I'll make some inquiries in the morning, and try to find out who transported the victim. And where."

Rachel left her uncle spreading the evening *Times* out on the table in front of him. She pulled the pocket doors closed behind her. "He's finished."

Matthew Bonner was a creature of habit, as both his niece and his housekeeper knew very well. In his early forties, he had never married — a fact to which Irene Garrity attributed most of his idiosyncrasies. There was, between them, a warmth of affection which many, had they known, would have considered unseemly between a single man and his employee. Not that their behavior was anything but entirely proper, but Matthew's occasional unguarded glances in Irene's direction were no less telling than the way she contrived to find extra work to do on the nights when he was out late.

Irene had been with Matthew since the day that Rachel, at the age of seven, arrived on the 4:40 train from Newport to take up residence with an uncle she hardly knew. The train had also been carrying two caskets, bearing her parents, after a boating accident took their lives off the shore of Rhode Island. Irene Garrity, returning from a visit with her sister, a maid in the Bonner household, had been hastily enlisted as the child's traveling companion. Her concern for Rachel's well-being had been recommendation enough for Matthew Bonner, and he had hired her on the platform at Grand Central Station.

Although she had been hired as a nurse, over the years Irene had filled the role of mother, confidante, and friend. At Matthew's urging, Irene had stayed on in his employ, assuming the title of housekeeper and the role of friend and companion, long after Rachel had finished her schooling and entered Barnard. It was with Irene that Matthew had discussed the trials of raising an adolescent girl, and later it was Irene who listened critically to his courtroom summations and campaign speeches.

"Why don't you marry Uncle Matt?" a ten-year-old Rachel had once asked Irene.

"What a brazen question! A man of your uncle's station does not marry the help," she had said, turning away quickly to tidy Rachel's dressing table.

When asked a similar question, Matthew Bonner had cleared his throat and blushed to the roots of his very red hair. "I'm sure Miss Garrity has many handsome suitors, Rachel. What would she want with an old fireplug like me?"

Even at ten, Rachel had recognized the sting of self-doubt in those words. Despite his wealth and education, red-haired, freckled, portly Matthew Bonner was not the stuff of which women dreamed. An eligible bachelor, to be sure, in the right circles he could have found a wife easily. But Matt Bonner was not interested in society, and avoided the right circles and the peril of falling prey to those aristocratic daughters who were looking to secure their positions by marrying even more wealth.

What Matt lacked in looks, he more than compensated for with intelligence, warmth, and strength of character. Rachel understood Irene Garrity, even if her uncle did not, and knew that handsome suitors need not apply as long as Matt Bonner remained in her life. And so they had settled into a routine — a family of a different sort from those of Rachel's friends, but a family nonetheless.

Irene disappeared into the dining room, ostensibly to make sure that dinner had been all right. Matthew would allow as how it had been too good, patting his girth with an embarrassed smile. Irene would admonish him that a man of his stature should look prosperous, and besides, there was nothing wrong with a man having a little muscle on him. He would invite her to sit down, and mention an interesting article he'd read in today's *Times.* And there they would stay — in the dining room — for the better part of the evening. Rachel could hear them laughing, even as she ascended the staircase to her own room.

Although she had been working at the station for some time, Rachel had, at first, come home so tired at night that it was all she could do to eat dinner with her uncle and drop into bed. Guiding the detained women through their daily routine, climbing and descending endless flights of stairs to carry documents and escort women and children to detention areas had left her feet sore and her back aching. But now, after six months, she had built up her stamina and grown accustomed to the endless hours on her feet. Finally, she could begin to pursue her real interests at Ellis Island. She had only recently begun to keep a journal of her observations, hoping, at some point, to translate them into an article for *Survey* or *Outlook,* or perhaps later to use them as a basis for her master's thesis. She withdrew a small notebook from the pocket of her skirt and took a seat at her writing table.

An hour later, Rachel had filled six pages of her journal with a description of the day's events, beginning with her encounter with Teresa Bastitelli.

"While most immigrant women seem to help and support others in their own group, the Italian women are less compatible. Southern Italian women — those from Sicily, Calabria, and Apulia — will stay together, advise and support one another, but are apt to be ignored by the better dressed and more prosperous women from the north. The resulting tension can be considerable.

"I have also observed that the Southern Italian women, like the Slavic women, are also more likely to be shy and frightened of the immigration process than their Northern sisters. Occasionally their fear translates into acts of random violence, as in the case of Teresa Bastitelli. Once she realized she was to be reunited with her husband, she came along as docilely as a kitten.

"Irish women, on the other hand, generally convey the impression of greater independence of spirit, although this may be because even the most backward Irish speakers also speak some English, and many speak it quite well, while the Italians and Slavs know little more than a few words learned aboard ship. Certainly a knowledge of the language must boost their confidence in their own ability to manage their affairs in the United States.

"As to the matter of Maggie Flynn, I hope to be able to study this case in depth, as the subject of violence among women has barely been scratched on the surface. Although she is now resistant to confiding in me, I have hopes that she will come to trust me, and I believe that the Superintendent shares my goal."

Rachel set down her pen and sat back in her chair to think about Joseph Hannegan. He was a fine-looking man with a dark, meditative cast. She would not have described him as handsome, but his black hair and startling blue eyes, straight sloping nose, and carved features gave him an intense and somewhat formidable appearance.

Rachel had never personally dealt with the superintendent before, but she knew that he had a reputation for honesty and integrity — two character traits treated variously by other employees at the station as admirable or insufferable, depending on their own disposition toward their jobs. McNabb, and to a lesser degree Commissioner Fitchie, had made it plain that they considered him an interfering troublemaker. But Rachel admired his courage of conviction, despite the fact that it went hand in hand with a quick temper. She had witnessed that today.

She had sensed that he harbored a certain sympathy for Maggie Flynn. Joseph Hannegan was Irish. While he had no discernible accent, there was a lilt to his speech — a gentle rising and falling inflection and an occasional idiom that betrayed his background. And yet there had been no talk at the station about his bias for his kinsmen, and certainly there would have been talk had he regularly interfered with deportations or Special Inquiry hearings in Irish cases. Perhaps he simply finds the girl attractive, Rachel thought, and wondered why the idea brought with it an unsettling disquiet.

Left alone, finally, Maggie Flynn cried herself to sleep. It was not a peaceful slumber, instead riddled with dreams that recalled the day's ordeal.

She stood at the rail aboard ship. An inspector was reading out their names. The young man from Galway answered to his. "That's me. I'm Dylan Moran."

The boarding inspector made a check mark on his clipboard and pinned a numbered tag to Dylan's jacket. "I've been wearin' long pants for awhile, now," Dylan said. "I believe I can be trusted not to get meself lost."

"Everyone gets tagged before landing," the inspector said. "Leave it where it is, now. If you lose the tag it'll go a lot harder for you getting through."

Behind her, the crowd from steerage was growing restive, pushing her hard against the rail and fairly lifting her off her feet. She gripped the railing, a cry of fear lodged in her throat. Where was Cormac?

"Numbers one to seventy prepare to land. One to seventy only, come forward."

Maggie checked her number. Seventy-three. Across the deck, Cormac picked up his bag. His number was sixty-seven. Maggie elbowed through the crowd and clutched at his sleeve. "Wait! What if we get separated?"

"I'll find you." He shook her off and strode down the gangplank.

The young man from Galway hovered in the background, watching her, as he had throughout the trip. He guided her back to the rail to watch their fellow passengers disembark for Customs — Maeve Daly, a tiny figure cloaked in a black wool coat, who was terrified she'd be turned back for her arthritis; Rosaleen Donnelly, trying to hide that she was in the family way; James Boyle, who said he was a carpenter. Cormac said he was a cutpurse.

"Seventy-one to one hundred forty," the inspector called.

"That'll be us," the young man said, and reached for the small basket trunk at Maggie's feet.

"I can manage it," she said, taking it from his hands.

He passed her the trunk, but gripped her wrist tightly. "Promise me," he said in a voice so low she had to strain to hear him, "Promise me you'll be careful." His words reverberated in her dream. *Promise me, promise me, promisemepromiseme-*

promiseme . . .

Then they were on the ferry. Cormac was waiting for her on deck, leaning back against the ship's rail.

"Where's your friend?"

They'd had this argument before. "He's just watchin' out for me."

Cormac tossed his cigarette over his shoulder and into the water. "We've been over this a dozen times, Maggie. Ya knew when ya came along ya'd have to take care of yaself."

Maggie swallowed, but her throat was tight and the effort hurt. "I thought . . . well, I thought that . . ." *I thought, IthoughtIthought . . .*

Before her stood a palace, red and gold in the midday sun, and undulating in the waves of heat that billowed up from the pavement. Another gangplank was lowered. Cormac pulled her along, but the crowd pushed her back until all she could see of him was the hand that clutched hers. She shoved through the crowd, scrambling to reach him, and tugged at his sleeve.

"Please, I thought it would be different," she cried. "I thought ya'd change your mind. I can't go through with it." *I can't, I can't, Ican'tIcan'tIcan't . . .*

He pulled away from her and turned to

stalk up the gangway. When he reached the end, he rounded on her and held up his hands, as if to ask why she was making him wait. Maggie hesitated, set down her trunk, took a breath, and reached into her sleeve.

She bolted awake, confused, reliving it all again. But she was not on the ferry. She was there, in the big building on Ellis Island, lying on her cot staring out into the darkness. And it was over . . . almost. She had only to wait now, she told herself, listening to her heartbeat in her ears until it finally slowed to a regular rhythm.

There were no windows in the room, or she would have been standing at one, gazing out into the night, telegraphing her thoughts to Cormac Doyle. I'm sorry, she would have said to him. I've made a hash of things, and I'm sorry. But there on the cot, closed up and isolated, she had no faith that her thoughts would reach him.

They had all warned her about Cormac Doyle. She remembered well the day she met him at Lissadell. She had been pegging the bed linens to the wash line when he'd sauntered out of the stables, startling her and sending a lightning tingle from her toes to the roots of her hair. It was the way he moved with cocksure grace. Or the way he squinted his eyes, avoiding the smoke from the cigarette that dangled from his lips. Or it was the way the rusty waves that fought out from under his tweed cap caught fire from the sun. Or the brazen curl of his smile, or the way he stood with his weight on one foot, or . . . it was everything about him. From that day forward, Maggie Flynn could see no one but Cormac Doyle.

He'd been hired to manage the stables, he said, by Miss Constance Gore-Booth herself. He had met her in Paris, where she told him about her father's illness and her concern for the welfare of his estate. Cormac had been happy to have a job to come home to and, according to him, Miss Gore-Booth had been happy to place the administration of her father's considerable stables in his care. As Maggie was herself a servant at Lissadell, she went her way, happy in the knowledge that she would see this shining god, this Cuchulain, every day.

And so she had — sharing picnics with him at the water's edge, and allowing him to walk her back to town at the end of her day. He'd not set foot inside her gate, but would leave her down the lane from her croppy father's cottage to go the rest of the way alone. And that was just as well, as she'd heard her father speak with some suspicion about the new man at Lissadell.

She didn't know why, nor did she care, until the day the constables came to her home looking for Cormac Doyle.

Maggie rolled over, the squeak of the cot's springs carrying her back to Ellis Island. New York, America, so close she could almost reach out and touch the gray buildings she'd seen from the ferry. He was out there now, somewhere in the night shadows, and she was left alone. She needn't be afraid, she told herself. There was nothing here to harm her.

If only it weren't so dark. But the station was lighted with electricity and she, a poor croppy's daughter, had never seen it before, let alone known how to turn it on. She sat up, sliding backward until her back was against the wall, drawing her knees up to her chin. She was sitting thus when the door opened, and the silhouette of a man appeared in the light. He closed the door quickly, pitching the room back into darkness, but Maggie heard his breathing and knew that he had not gone away.

CHAPTER EIGHT

"Cormac?" Maggie whispered. "Cormac, is it you?"

There came no answer, only steady breathing, and advancing footsteps. A man. She could smell him there in the dark and knew that whatever he was there for, it was not good. She scrambled further up the cot, poised to crawl over the end, but before she could get up he was upon her, pulling her to her feet with a vise grip to her upper arms. She cried out, but he covered her mouth with his own, shoving her backward. She lashed out at him, feeling her nails rake into his skin, before his hands slid down her arms to her wrists. He jerked them hard behind her back, clasped them in one of his great paws and pushed her back onto the bed. She kicked out at him then, but he was straddling her, pulling up her gown and fumbling with the drawstring of her drawers. She heard the fabric tear as he whipped the string from its casing. He pulled her up and wound the drawstring around her wrists until she felt as though the flow of blood to her hands had stopped. Then he shoved her backward again.

She tried to pull loose, but her own weight, and his on top of her, held her bound hands behind her. "No," she cried. "Please, no —"

He pushed his mouth against hers so hard that she felt her lips would split. His breath tasted of whiskey and spice, nauseating her. His hands were inside her drawers, tugging them to her ankles. She cried out — a small, thin wail of fear — but his hand came down over her mouth, pushing so hard she thought her teeth would break away from her jaw. Reflexively, she brought her knees together and tried to twist away from him, but he was too strong. He pried her knees apart and entered her with a thrust so hard she felt her membrane tear away in a searing streak of pain.

In a moment it was over, leaving only a warm rivulet of blood and semen running down her legs. He pushed himself off her and stood up in the dark. She couldn't see his face, only the vague silhouette of his body and the flash of a white handkerchief as he cleaned himself up and rearranged his clothing.

"If you tell anyone about this," he whispered, "I'll kill you next time. You understand me?"

When she didn't answer, he returned to the bed, clamping his hand over her throat. "Answer me. Do you understand me?"

She nodded her head and whispered, "Yes."

He rolled her onto her side and pulled the drawstring loose from her wrists before crossing the room. He eased the door open a crack, and pressing back into the shadows fumbled with his pocket watch, tilting it toward the light. He pushed the door closed again, turning back with a reminder.

"Don't make me kill you," he whispered, before jerking the door open and slipping out of the room. The lock clicked behind him.

Maggie didn't know how long she lay there. She knew she was sobbing and held her knuckles against her bruised lips to stifle the noise. She had never been with Cormac in that way. In spite of their illicit meetings, in spite of running away from Ireland together, they had agreed that the pleasure of loving one another could wait — should wait — until their wedding night. She would be his, and only his, he'd said. Now she was ruined. She would never go to her bridal bed the unspoiled girl she should have been. And she would never again think of the act — that act — as love.

At length a key turned in the lock. Maggie drew a sharp breath and held it, as a woman's figure appeared in the door and paused a moment before closing it again. She waited until the door was locked again, then dragged herself off the cot and fumbled in the dark for a chair. When she had found one, she jammed it under the doorknob. She felt her way across the room to the makeshift washstand they had provided for her and taking her towel, shoved it up between her legs. "I'll kill you," he had said. And Maggie believed that he would.

"The newest man in my service is John Litchfield." George Rockwell thumbed through a file folder. "He came on . . . let's see, two months ago, transferred in from the Buffalo station. Some of the watchmen and gatemen may not know him. I don't know about the matrons." He slammed the drawer of his filing cabinet, locked it with a small key and returned to his desk.

"But if one of the doctors on my service treated that man, there's going to be a record of it somewhere." He pointed to a heavy oak chair opposite his desk. "Sit down, Hannegan."

Joseph ignored the chair and paced the length of the room. "There wasn't time for records, George. They had to get him to a hospital right away. Tell me something," he said, pivoting on his heel. "What are his chances? It was an abdominal wound."

Dr. Rockwell shook his head. "I can't make a prognosis without seeing the patient, but in general, abdominal gunshot wounds can be very difficult to treat. Allowing for the blood loss and the time it would take to get him to a hospital, and considering the likelihood of peritonitis in an abdominal wound, I don't give him much chance."

Joseph resumed his pacing. "None of the hospitals have treated him. Suppose he died on the way. What would they have done with him?"

"You say a police cruiser conveyed him?"

"That's right."

"I suppose they might have taken him directly to the morgue. But don't forget, they could have just taken him to a local physician after he was shot. I'd keep checking the hospitals if I were you. If they took him to a private physician, he might have treated Finnegan in his office and be waiting until he's stronger to move him to the hospital. I'll check around on my service and let you know when I find out who treated him. I'd like to know myself."

Rockwell removed the cap from his ink-well and inserted his fountain pen, dropping the lever and lifting it again. It made a little sucking sound as the pen drew in ink. "From what you're telling me, he should have tried to stop the bleeding before transporting him. Of course, I don't know the medical details, and God knows there was no place in here to treat him. This is precisely why we need that hospital out there finished," he said.

"McNabb's sitting on it, as usual. Probably has his hand in the contractor's pocket." He reached for a stack of charts on his desk, flipped one open and signed the top form, setting the folder aside and reaching for the next one.

Here was an idea Joseph hadn't explored. "What would he have to gain by not getting the job done?"

Rockwell shrugged. "Prolong the job, charge more for the labor? Contractor probably doesn't pay his laborers what he charges the government. Have you been out there? They're mostly Italians and none of them speak English. They're probably happy to get the work, even if they're getting half the normal wage."

Joseph sighed. One more outrage to add to the list. The man's capacity for malfeasance was astounding, and yet no one could ever produce proof. What he didn't think of, Albert Lederman did. "I'll look into it," he said, although he had no idea where to begin.

Rockwell wiggled his jaw with his hand. "Think I've been chewing tin cans in my sleep. When I sleep, that is. Mostly I lie awake wondering what we're going to do when the first epidemic comes."

"All right, George, you've made yourself clear."

Rockwell grinned. "Good. How many ships do we have today?"

"Three." Joseph pulled an index card out of his pocket and read its contents to Rockwell. "The *Liguria* and the *Victoria* out of Italy, and the *Teutonic* out of Liverpool. The *Liguria* should already be in."

Rockwell grunted and pushed himself away from the desk. "Going to be a busy day. I'll let you know if I find out anything."

Rachel took Maggie's breakfast tray and carried it to the watchman outside the door. The girl hadn't touched it. When Rachel arrived, she was still lying on her cot, the blanket pulled up tightly around her in spite of the heat in the room. She must have cried most of the night, Rachel thought, because her eyes were red and puffy with lack of sleep and her whole face seemed to be slightly swollen. She had not yet said a word, just lay on her side staring at the wall.

Rachel returned to the room and began to tidy up, waiting for Maggie to make the first overture. Her towel was missing, and a peek into the chamber pot showed it not only full but tinged pink with blood. And that explained a lot — her tears, her silence, even the swelling in her face.

"Oh Maggie, is it time for your monthly? How inconvenient for you." She waited, but when the girl said nothing, she went on.

"I'll have to get you a doily belt and some pads from the medical service. While I'm gone you can get dressed and when I get back, I'll escort you to the ladies' room. I can ask one of the doctors to examine you if you're having much pain."

"No!" Maggie sat up abruptly. "No, I won't need a doctor. I'll do as you say."

Rachel left her and met Joseph Hannegan coming down the hall, carrying the girl's basket trunk. "She's dressing, Superintendent. I need to go down to the medical service."

"Good," he said, "I'll walk with you. I'd like to see if you recognize the doctor who attended to the victim." Rachel took the girl's case in to her, glad that Maggie would have fresh underclothes to change into, and rejoined Hannegan in the hall.

"Have you located him at the hospital?"

Joseph shook his head. "Rockwell thinks he may have been taken to the closest private physician and that he'll appear somewhere sooner or later. It's certainly possible. That's why I want to talk to the attending physician."

When they reached the medical division, Rachel went to a nurse privately with her request. The nurse returned in a moment with a basin containing a Turkish towel, a tin of tooth powder and a toothbrush. She quietly folded the towel back to reveal the doily belt and pads.

"She should have been given those things last night," Joseph said, pointing at the toothbrush.

"I'm afraid I didn't think about her teeth. But there's no harm done. She didn't eat her breakfast anyway, and I don't think she ate much of her supper last night."

They walked on to the end of the corridor and onto the registry floor. The first ship was in and the doctors were finishing their line inspection, standing at the head of the stairs to observe the gait and carriage of the examinees. Rachel was always amazed at how much they could detect in the few minutes they had to observe their patients as they climbed the stairs encumbered by packs and bags too precious to be left in the baggage room.

The air was dense with an unpleasant odor — a mixture of bodies gone too long without bathing and the increased perspiration of fear. For too many of the immigrants, this was the moment of reckoning. They came to America undernourished and overworked, and both conditions often left their mark in physical infirmities. How bitterly ironic, Rachel thought, that the very conditions they came to America to alleviate might prohibit them from having the opportunity.

Four doctors stood at the head of four lines of immigrants. Most of them appeared to be Italian, and the majority of those were men. "Birds of passage" the immigrant inspectors called them — men who left their families behind in Italy and came to work for a year or two before returning home with American dollars in their pockets. Many of them returned to suffer the separation again in order to provide for their families, and some to stay permanently, this time bringing wives and children with them to take up residence in Little Italy. If they had nothing else in common, the one thing they shared was fear. She could see it in the apprehensive curl of their fingers around the metal rails that separated one line from the next, and the white-knuckled grasp of baskets and gunnysacks as they watched the front of the line trying to gauge how best to stand or move to present themselves as the image of health.

At the head of the first line, a woman held a writhing child in her arms as the eye man attempted his examination, reaching for the lids to turn them back with a buttonhook. *"Dovete essere calmi,"* the mother crooned to him. "Be still, Carlo. Be still."

She clamped the terrified child's arms to her body and turned him to face the doctor over her shoulder while he completed the examination. In spite of the boy's tears, his mother laughed out loud with relief — a hearty peal of joy that made Rachel smile just to hear it — as they were waved on to receive their medical certificates before taking their place in a registry line.

In the second line, a doctor was instructing a man in broken Italian to walk to the end of the line and back. The immigrant's dark gaze flickered left and right, as if calculating the chances that he could break and run, but seeing none he seemed to sag and stumbled back to the head of the line. The doctor took his chalk and scrawled an L on the immigrant's brown wool jacket before waving him to the side to be directed by the gateman.

"No, no!" the man cried and bent to pull off his shoe. *"Vedete?"* he said, jerking off his sock and pointing at his left foot. "It is only a small thing, you see?"

"Move on," the doctor said, as the gateman escorted the man, taking him by the arm and pulling him away. He would be taken to an examination room, where another doctor would more thoroughly evaluate his physical condition. Perhaps they would find only a blister or an ingrown toenail, conditions easily treated and allowing him entry.

"Do you see him?"

Rachel turned her focus on the medical team. "No. I don't think he's here."

"Let's go on to the examining rooms, then."

Rachel followed Joseph off the Registry floor and back to the medical examination rooms. The waiting area was full. Joseph called each doctor out of his examining room, and Rachel passed on each in turn.

"No. No. I'm afraid not him either. He's not here, Mr. Hannegan."

"You're sure he was with the hospital service?" Joseph said, as they returned to Maggie's room.

"Oh yes. He was wearing the khaki uniform."

"Tell me what you remember about him."

"Not much. I only saw him for a minute. Brown hair, spectacles. I have the impression that he was quite tall, although I don't know why since he was crouching down when I saw him. And very thin, I think. But I couldn't swear to it."

"I hope you won't have to," Joseph said.

When they reached the witness room, Rachel left Joseph waiting in the corridor with Watchman Archer while she went in to see if Maggie was dressed. She gave the girl the doily belt and pads. Maggie turned them over in her hand, examining them curiously.

"I don't know . . . I'm not sure how —"

"Here," Rachel said, taking them out of Maggie's hands. "Let me show you. The pads, you see, are disposable. They've become quite popular here in America, because they don't have to be washed. Come along and I'll take you to the bathroom."

When they returned, Joseph Hannegan was waiting for them. He motioned to Rachel to take a seat, but Maggie remained standing, her hands crumpling her skirt into a wrinkled wad.

"Have ya come for me, then? Am I to be taken to the constable?"

Joseph shook his head and clasped his hands behind his back — a perfect posture of authority, Rachel thought.

"Not just yet. I need to ask you some questions, and this time I want the truth, Miss Flynn. Why did you shoot Michael Finnegan?"

Michael Finnegan. The name rang in Maggie's ears. At first, she couldn't think of what it meant. Who was Michael Finnegan? And then she remembered.

"I've told you, I've nothing to say about the matter, Superintendent. I shot him — I did, and I admit it. But I've nothing more to say to you. Please, just turn me over to your constables."

The Superintendent rubbed his face briskly with his hands and blew out a deep sigh. "I can't do that, Miss Flynn. I wish I could, but they don't want you."

Maggie eased slowly down onto the cot. "They . . . they don't want me," she repeated, unable to comprehend what he was saying to her.

"We have no proof of the commission of a crime yet. Finnegan hasn't appeared at any of the hospitals, or the morgue, and he hasn't sworn out a complaint. Frankly, I'm at a loss as to just what to do with you. I can't deport you and I can't hand you over to any of the authorities. But I will get to the bottom of this, Miss Flynn. I promise you that. And when I do, you'll wish that you had been more straightforward with me."

Maggie lowered her head, staring at the coarse fabric of her skirt. "But what am I to do? Who will help me?" she whispered.

"Who will help you? You won't even help yourself. If you would just cooperate with me, tell me why you did it. Did something happen aboard ship? Did he hurt you? Did he violate —"

The dizziness came over her suddenly. She felt the blood drain from her skin, heard a loud pounding in her ears. The matron was at her side, pushing her head down between her legs. She took Maggie's hands in hers, slapping them lightly. At length, Maggie felt the dizziness pass. She lifted her head and brought the room back into focus. The Superintendent was still standing over her, but he had come closer, and his drawn brows reflected his concern. The matron brushed her hair back from her forehead and blotted her damp face with a handkerchief that smelled like lilacs. If only she could stay like this — safe, protected, cared for.

"Maggie, is that what this is all about?" the matron said. "Did Finnegan rape you?"

But she would not open the door to that memory. She wanted to be left alone to wait. She wanted the questioning to stop, because lies didn't sit easily on her tongue. "No, he didn't hurt me. You'll have to believe me when I tell ya I had my reasons. That's all I can say."

She needed help. The constables were not coming for her. It had all been a mistake — a terrible mistake — and she didn't know what to do. She glanced up at her companions, both studying her with skeptical expressions. They wanted to help her, she thought, but they were the last people who could. She mustn't tell them about the shooting, and she couldn't tell them about last night.

What would they do if she did tell them about it? Would they even believe her? And what would he — that dark, faceless brute of a man — do to her? He would come back, rape her again, and this time he would probably kill her.

"May I ask one thing of you?" she said.

Joseph folded his arms across his chest. "What is it?"

"I'd like to speak to a priest."

CHAPTER NINE

Father Aloysius O'Gara reminded Rachel of a terrier. Short and muscular, with a purposeful gait and the air of a street ruffian, he exuded fierce determination. He wore a black cassock with a wide streak of dust down the left side and a tear in the left sleeve, and looked as though he'd just left off street brawling after his opponent had gotten the better of him. His complexion was pitted with scars — measles, perhaps, or acne. A thick shock of straight, sandy hair crept out from under his black biretta over his right eye. He tossed his head, as if to shake it out of his way, but it was soon back tickling his forehead. His appearance did not inspire Rachel with confidence.

Of course, Rachel herself was high church Episcopalian, where a rector without dignity would likely find himself a rector without a church. Father O'Gara would not have fared well at Calvary Church. Uncle Matt would like him though, she thought, recalling her uncle's recurrent objections to "chilly clerics and their frozen faithful." And he would remind her that Father O'Gara served in a poor parish where he had to be at least as doughty as his parishioners, and probably a little bit tougher. It was the Plunkitt principle in action.

"Right this way, Father," she said, directing him to the witness room door.

O'Gara carried a small black bag with him. Archer rose and pointed to his chair. "I'll have to ask you to open that, Father," he said.

Father O'Gara laid the bag on the chair and opened it to reveal the contents: a white surplice and purple stole, a crucifix, and a breviary. Archer made a cursory visual inspection and, satisfied, waited for the priest to close the bag before unlocking the door. Rachel introduced the priest to Maggie before taking leave of them.

"I'll be back when you're finished, Father," she said and closed the door.

"The Super was looking for you, Miss Bonner. He said he's putting a call in to Father Grogan."

"I'll go tell him that Father O'Gara was already here."

She found Joseph Hannegan in his office

carefully perusing a large stack of mail. Sometimes as many as three hundred letters came into the station in a single day. Many of them went to detained immigrants themselves — letters from family members anxiously waiting for them on the other side of the harbor, letters from lawyers handling deportation cases — but a substantial minority still fell to the administrators to manage. These were often personal pleas from new Americans desperately seeking intervention on the behalf of a sister, a child, or an aging parent. Sometimes they came through the many immigrant aid societies who worked on the island. Sometimes they came from family members themselves. It was a burden Rachel would not have liked to carry. She wasn't sure she had the heart to turn anyone away from the Golden Door and wondered how Hannegan faced it day in and day out, and he the son of an immigrant himself.

Joseph looked up when she knocked on the doorframe. "Come in, Miss Bonner. Take a seat."

Rachel remained standing. "I only came by to tell you that there's a priest in with Maggie now. I went down to the missionaries' room to look for Father Grogan and found another priest already there. Father

O'Gara is his name. He went right up to the girl."

"Al O'Gara? That's odd. He knows Father Grogan has this mission. What's he doing here?"

"He didn't say, but I assume he came to see someone, probably someone in detention or deportation."

"All right. Well, if you see him again, ask him to come by my office before he leaves." Rachel turned to go, but the Superintendent stopped her, gesturing at the chair in front of his desk. "Wait. Sit down for a minute. I'd like to talk to you."

When Rachel was seated, he went on. "What do you make of the Flynn girl, Miss Bonner? What do you think is going through that empty little head of hers?"

Rachel thought about it for a moment — not that she hadn't thought it over many times in the last twenty-four hours. But Maggie's demeanor this morning had been entirely different from the previous day, and Rachel wasn't sure it could all be put down to her menstrual cycle. At length she said, "To begin with, I don't think her head is empty at all. I think it's full of secrets. She's made it clear enough that there's more to the story than what we're seeing, but she's not going to tell us. She's protecting him, I think."

"Protecting her victim?"

Rachel nodded slowly. "I hadn't realized it until just now, but yes, I think she's protecting him — his family, his reputation — or someone else. But that doesn't make sense, does it?"

Joseph sat back in his chair and studied Rachel thoughtfully for a moment. "I'm not sure. Protecting him, eh? I don't know. Perhaps it does."

Joseph saw Rachel out of his office, closing the door behind her, and returned to his desk. He opened a lower desk drawer and took out a plum and a jackknife, dropped into his chair, and propped his feet on the open drawer, thinking about the matron who had been sitting across the desk from him only a few minutes earlier.

Something was different about Rachel Bonner. He had to admit she was pretty, with shining dark eyes and hair as rich a brown as his golden oak desk. But many pretty women came through the station, some so exotic and beautiful that photographers like Louis Hine could hardly wait to photograph them. Her beauty was not extraordinary. He sliced neatly into the plum and carefully pulled back the skin, eating it in large thin leaves.

He'd guess she might be in her early twenties — twenty-four at most — while most of the other matrons were at least a few years her senior. But it was not only youth that set her apart. Some of the other women had slight accents that betrayed backgrounds not unlike his own, but her speech was flawless. And she had a cultivated, self-possessed manner about her — the way she held her chin up when she spoke and the way her hands, at rest, lay gracefully in her lap. Her hands. That was it. The fingers, long; the nails, neatly trimmed, each the exact length of the others and with a high, natural gloss. No calluses, burns, rough spots. Rachel Bonner did not cook, wash her own clothing, dust, or mop, or do any of the chores that most women at the station did.

He gazed down at the peeled fruit in his hand — the sweet, soft part. The juice ran between his fingers. He always ate the skin first, liking the way its tart bite made the meat all the sweeter. She wore the same clothing as the others — simple serge skirts and plain white shirtwaists — but their quality was superior and in their tailored cut clung perfectly to her slender figure. He was fairly sure she didn't wear a corset, as her small waist didn't have the pinched appearance of whalebone and tight lacing. He liked the natural look of a woman without a corset. He particularly liked it on Rachel Bonner. And that, he thought, is enough of that. The United States Treasury Department did not pay him to think about women without corsets.

He could see the harbor outside his window — a distant view of barges chugging into port, and the gray-blue silhouette of the city beyond it. A ferry from the Battery made its way toward the station. It would be carrying missionaries, families eager to greet a newly arrived member, and probably reporters, as the investigation of the Boarding Division was drawing considerable attention from the press. Well, that was McNabb's problem now, and well deserved at that.

McNabb had told him he would be called into the investigation as a witness in the Sapelli matter. He had already given his statement to the U.S. Attorney, but when the case went to trial — if it went to trial — he would have to appear in court. Sapelli had been arraigned the day before. According to the *Times*, the shipping line had disavowed any knowledge in the matter, and claimed that Sapelli had acted entirely on his own in offering Joseph a bribe. Joseph doubted this very much, if only because Sapelli had worked for the line only one month, and Joseph had been hearing whispers about the questionable practices of the Boarding Division for some time. The liner's refusal to cooperate would make it very difficult for McNabb's committee to get to the bottom of the problem. No doubt McNabb was counting on that.

Joseph took a bite of his plum and followed the progress of a Cunard steamship as it moved out of the harbor and toward the open sea. So many problems plagued the station. After Powderly appointed him, Joseph had made a list on a long lined pad of all the conditions that he felt needed correcting. The list had taken up three and a half pages. Joseph kept it in his center desk drawer as a reminder of why he was there. In three months, he'd only managed to check off two entries, having dealt with them to his complete satisfaction.

There was always an immediate problem, often an emergency, to take up his time. Maggie Flynn was just the latest in a long line of incidents that McNabb had used to keep him busy and out of the way. Well, it wouldn't work this time. He was going to dispatch the Flynn problem quickly and get back to his own job. He would not be kept out of the Boarding investigation.

Joseph tossed the plum pit into his metal wastebasket, wiped his hands on his handkerchief, and pulled open his middle desk drawer to retrieve an envelope. There had been a letter in Maggie Flynn's little trunk. He'd almost forgotten about it. He and Matron Bonner had searched the case before turning it over to the girl, but had found nothing in it that might explain her actions. Nothing but the letter, and that had seemed unimportant at the time. Still, he had set it aside in his top drawer, intending to study it more closely later. He took it out now and turned it over in his hands.

It was addressed to Miss Maggie Flynn in Drumcliffe, County Sligo, Ireland. He folded back the torn flap and pulled out a single folded sheet.

"Dear Miss Flynn,

"I am informed that you are interested in a position as a domestic servant in the United States and am herewith forwarding money for your passage on August 10, on the Cymric *out of Londonderry. You will receive an annual salary of $300 as well as room and board. After two years' service, you will also receive passage home and one month off. I will expect you to*

report to work immediately upon your arrival in New York.

> *"Sincerely,*
> *"Emmaline Westcott."*

But Miss Flynn had not reported for work, and the station had not had any inquiries about her from Mrs. Westcott, nor anyone else. Joseph picked up the telephone and had the switchboard connect him with Central. When he set it down again, he wore a perplexed scowl. Mrs. Westcott was not on the telephone line, although now almost everyone of a certain social standing was connected. He studied the letter, noticing for the first time that the handwriting was rough — not the neat, Spencerian script he might expect from a well-to-do woman seeking a servant. And the paper was cheap and thin.

He turned over the envelope and studied the return address with a deepening frown. 207 Rivington Street, New York, New York. Probably an employment agency, as Rivington Street was a neighborhood that produced domestic help, not hired it. But recruiting labor from abroad was a violation of the Contract Labor Laws. Although domestics were excluded, he wasn't sure that Emmaline Westcott would know that, and it might give him a bit of leverage in getting information out of the employment agency.

He folded the letter and returned it to its envelope, tucking both into the pocket of his jacket. Somewhere out there he had to find answers to the riddle of Maggie Flynn, and Rivington Street seemed like a good place to start.

Father O'Gara had already left Maggie when Joseph reached the witness interrogation room. Joseph did not go in, but went directly to the missionaries' room and caught him on the way out.

"I'm afraid I can't talk now, Joe," Father O'Gara said, continuing down the corridor. "I need to get back to the church in time to hear confessions."

"I'm going that way myself, Father. I'll walk with you and we can talk about the girl on the ferry."

O'Gara stopped, tossed his hair out of his eyes and pulled a battered pocket watch out of his cassock. "I can't tell you anything about Miss Flynn that she can't tell you herself. Nor can I tell you anything that she won't tell you herself. Besides, I almost forgot," he said. "I agreed to see the brother of a parishioner before I leave. He's a detainee. If I go now and then catch the next ferry, I should still just make confessions. Don't let me keep you, though. It could take me longer than I expect." He was gone with a billow of his cassock and a wave, leaving Joseph to ponder what Maggie Flynn had told the priest that he was afraid he might betray.

CHAPTER TEN

The sun hovered low over New Jersey's farmlands when Rachel left the station. She stood at the ferry rail and watched the slow, smooth progress of shadows spilling across the harbor, spreading like an ink stain over the surface of the water. It had taken her weeks to reach this point, where she could stand at the rail of the ferry without fighting a wave of nauseating fear. Had traveling to Ellis Island meant more than traversing the harbor, Rachel would never have seen the inside of the Great Hall. She had sailed the open waters of the Atlantic to Europe a few times, but that had been on steamers so large and commodious that she never had to set eyes on the water if she chose not to. Ferries and barges were another thing altogether.

The summer had been beastly, each morning bringing a renewal of the heat that would broil the pavement and boil the air.

A trickle of perspiration slid down between her breasts. She was wearing her coolest shirtwaist — a fine cotton lawn with a low neckline — but it wasn't cool enough. She took off her boater and let the breeze off the water blow through her upswept hair and cool her neck. She didn't envy the immigrant women who had made the trip earlier in the day, many wearing heavy shawls and woolen vests.

She gazed across the water at the island of Manhattan, watching the sun catch on the dull granite buildings and smelt them into a warm gold, as if the hand of a great alchemist were at work. New York — America's crucible. They came here expecting to live as they had lived in their villages at home — to wash their laundry in the East River and hang their pastas outside to dry in the sun. But New York changed them. With the help of missionary societies and settlement houses they soon learned the American way of life. However necessary the process might be, no one was left unscarred.

Rachel tried to imagine what it might be like to have her world turned upside down, for that was the reality of America, that nothing in their lives would ever be the same. Often that was to the good. America offered them opportunities, education, and citizenship. But in return, America asked them to change their way of life, and sometimes their most fundamental beliefs. It wasn't always a good bargain.

What had Maggie Flynn expected from America, and would she ever get the chance to find out for herself? Aside from the girl's time with Father O'Gara, Rachel had spent most of the day with her, and at the end of it knew little more about Maggie than she had when she came on duty that morning.

Rachel had taken her the latest *Harper's* and *Delineator* to alleviate the boredom that presented a constant problem at the station. Maggie leafed through them listlessly, as if only to please her, before setting them aside to lie on her cot, her knees drawn tightly to her chest. She denied having menstrual pain and was adamant in her refusal to see a doctor. A Mrs. Meahan, from the Home for Irish Immigrant Girls, had been in to see her, but with no more success than the Superintendent or Rachel herself.

"She doesn't seem to want our help," Mrs. Meahan commented to Rachel. "Although it's plain enough that she's frightened. I can't do anything for her but try to find her an attorney, but I've warned her that no one will take her case if she won't tell us the truth."

By afternoon Rachel had resigned herself to Maggie's silence and spent the rest of the day making notes in her journal. It was not until she was preparing to leave that Maggie spoke to her again.

"Must ya go?" she asked.

"Well . . . yes. My shift ends in a few minutes. I have to report in to the head matron and catch the four-forty ferry."

Maggie sat up, her complexion chalky and her posture rigid. "Will I be alone again tonight?"

"There won't be a matron with you, if that's what you mean. There wouldn't be much point, would there, with you asleep?" Rachel narrowed her gaze. "I hope you're not thinking of trying to leave us, Maggie. There's no way off the island."

When Maggie didn't answer her, she picked up the girl's untouched dinner tray, left an uneaten bowl of stewed fruit on the table and carried the rest to the door. "I'll be back in the morning. Have a good night," she said.

She closed the door and waited while Watchman Archer locked it. Before she turned away, she heard something bump the door and jar the knob. She hoped that the girl wouldn't try anything foolish in the night.

Rachel started at a short burst from the ferry's horn. They were pulling in to the Barge Office — a gray stone building located on the Battery's outer wall. It looked like a medieval castle, with turrets and rotundas, and the harbor as its moat. A central tower and flagpole climbed high above the rest of the building. On top of it, an American flag snapped in the wind. Even as she watched, it was being lowered before the sun could set upon it.

On the dock, some of the second night shift were already gathered in a cobblestone courtyard waiting to board. They had been preceded, an hour earlier, by the first night shift — watchmen, matrons, and custodians — who had taken over the duties of the day-shift employees. By having two day shifts, and two night shifts, the station was never left unattended and operations continued in a smooth rhythm. Remarkable, Rachel thought, considering the hundreds of employees involved in the daily grinding of the bureaucracy.

To the left of the knot of employees, Rachel noticed a young man lounging against a street lamp, hands in his pockets and legs comfortably crossed, watching the night shift with considerable interest. When the ropes had been tied off and the gangplank

141

pulled up, his attention turned to the ferry. His gaze swept over each of the passengers waiting at the rail. Rachel wondered if he might be waiting for an immigrant. Maybe no one had told him that this ferry was reserved for station employees and missionaries. At length, he pushed away from the lamppost and ambled toward the boat. If he tried to board, someone would stop him and explain the protocol for meeting passengers to him. Rachel headed for the train, digging into her bag for the fare.

"Beggin' your pardon, Miss, but are you the one who took the girl away yesterday?"

Rachel stopped abruptly and turned back. He was talking to Cora Bainbridge, the day-shift head matron, but Cora was shaking her head. She pointed to Rachel. The young man thanked her and hurried to Rachel's side.

"That would be you, then? Are you the lady who took the girl away?"

Rachel studied him carefully. Brown hair, a scattering of freckles over his nose, no facial hair. An unremarkable face. He stood five feet seven, maybe eight inches. His breath smelled of peppermint.

"May I ask what your interest is?"

He shrugged and smiled disarmingly. "I met her on the boat. I just wanted to see that she's all right."

"She's all right, Mr . . ."

"Dylan. My name's Dylan."

"Did you also meet the victim, Mr. Finnegan, on the ship?"

"Can't say that I did, ma'am. We were jammed down there in the steerage, ma'am, and we were wearin' each others' shoes, it was that tight. What's to happen to her now?"

"We're waiting for the marshals to take her into custody, Mr. Dylan. Did she tell you anything about Michael Finnegan? Or why she was coming to America?"

Dylan scratched his head and shifted his feet. "I'm thinkin' she said she was comin' to a job with a fancy society lady, but I can't be sure."

"I see. Well, I'm sure the Superintendent would like to talk to you." Rachel dug into her pocket, producing her journal and a small gold pencil. "Give me your address, Mr. Dylan, so he can get in touch with you."

Dylan backed off a pace. "I'm movin' around right now. Lookin' for work, ya know. When I find a job, I'll be lookin' for a room close to my work."

"All right. Is there someone else he can contact? A friend here in the city, or a relative?"

Another backward pace. "Oh no, no one like that. I'm all alone. Will ya carry a message to her for me?"

"I . . . I suppose —"

"Tell her not to worry. Tell her it will be all right. We'll take care of it. And thank you, ma'am," he said, turning to hurry away.

"Wait! Mr. Dylan?"

But he had already disappeared into the shadows. Rachel rushed through Battery Park after him, but by the time she reached State Street he had vanished. She returned to the ferry breathless.

The captain stood at the rail waiting for late passengers to make a last-minute dash for the boat. He sucked on a cigar the width of Rachel's thumb, talking around it in a garbled voice. "Can't stay away, Miss Bonner?"

"I need to go back to see the Superintendent," she said.

The captain shook his head. "Not there." He pulled the cigar out of his mouth and gestured with it toward the street. "Brought him over an hour, hour and a half ago. Is it an emergency?"

Rachel hesitated. "It might be. I'm not sure."

The captain rounded on his heel to face his passengers. "Anyone there know where the Super lives?"

The passengers exchanged murmurs and headshakes until a charwoman stepped forward. "I do. My Enda and his Da are that close. He lives on Bleecker Street just below Washington Square. If you're wantin' the number, I can't help you. But I can tell you what the house looks like."

Rachel produced her journal and pencil. "Go ahead," she said.

Joseph turned off Second Avenue onto Rivington Street, passing one of the many small synagogues that freckled the Lower East Side. Just what the devil had become of Father O'Gara? He'd waited through one ferry, but the priest had not reappeared. He'd catch up with O'Gara eventually, if not at the station, then surely at St. Joseph's. But what had he been doing at the station in the first place? Most parish priests routinely left the immigrants on the island to the ministry of Father Anthony Grogan and his staff at Our Lady of the Rosary Mission.

On his way out, Joseph had stopped in the baggage handler's office. "I need to see a piece of yesterday's baggage off the *Cymric*," he said. "Michael Finnegan, number sixty-seven." The chief baggage handler went off to check on it, returning after some time with a puzzled expression on his face.

"I've checked everywhere, Superintendent, but I ain't got any bags for number sixty-seven."

"Could it have gotten mixed up with someone else's luggage?"

The handler pulled on his chin. "Not likely. Never happened before. I'll put my men on it and we'll go over every piece in the baggage room, but I ain't expectin' no surprises."

"Well, please try. It's very important. And if you do come across it, have it sent up to my office, will you?"

He'd left the office then, taken the ferry across to the Battery and boarded the Second Avenue train for Rivington Street. All around him was the detritus of new construction as the proposed subway began to take shape. As if the East Side needed more bedlam in the street.

Joseph did not make many excursions into the old neighborhood, and he never did so willingly. It held few happy memories for him. One glance told him that nothing had improved. In fact, if anything, it might be worse. He skirted a pile of furniture, pots and pans on the sidewalk, and closed his ears to the keening woman who sat on top of them lamenting her eviction. There was nothing he could do for her.

Signs hung everywhere — COAL, ICE, WOOD; ROOM TO LET; SHOE REPAIR. Signs in Hebrew, signs in Italian. Picture signs for those who couldn't read. Garments hanging on outdoor racks fluttered ghostlike in the breeze. Bedding on the fire escapes, trash in the gutters and trampled down on the sidewalks. Men lounging in the doors of bucket shops. It all added up to an atmosphere of chaos — shifting ground and constant upheaval, as if the street where you went to sleep at night might not be the same street when you woke up.

Even now, at dusk, the pushcart peddlers were still out, although most of them were shutting down and moving off to store their carts overnight. Their season was too short to make a decent living, and they needed to wring every ounce of light from the days when they could work. He shouldered between them, scarcely able to see more than the next rack of coats or pile of rags. To his left, a greengrocer and his wife were carrying their fruit stand inside. An apple fell out of the bin and rolled to an abrupt stop at his feet. Joseph stopped to pick it up under the watchful eye of the grocer's wife. He set it back on top of the bin, receiving a suspicious scowl for his trouble. The apple would be sold for cheap as bruised fruit. He knew all about bruised fruit. There had been a time when he was happy to get it.

He had come to the Lower East Side at the age of ten, the son of a poor croppy who'd been evicted from his tenant farm in County Mayo. He'd stood at the end of Delancey Street looking with horror on the masses of people, assailed by the odors of strange foods, rotting garbage, urine and excrement. A dead dog, covered with maggots, lay in the gutter as children played around it. Joseph had picked up his sister and turned her away, distracting her with the crimson awning of a shoe repair shop and the strings of sausages in the window of Schneider's Butcher Shop. And then they had followed their parents, and Dennis's good friend, Seamus O'Neill, to the dark apartment on the fourth floor of a rear tenement whose only recommendation had been that it had running water on every floor — cold water, in the hall, dripping into a dank and scummy sink of black zinc. Tompkins Street — two blocks from the East River. So close he could almost smell the longshoremen sweat.

"Suspenders! Suspenders here! You need some suspenders, mister? Hold up your pants good. You see."

"How's business?"

The peddler shrugged, his thin shoulders rising and dropping under a long black vest, gray with age and three sizes too large for him. "Some days iss good, some days ain't so good." He grinned, his smile a dark cleft where once there might have been teeth. "You buy today, we eat good on the Sabbath."

Joseph produced a quarter and waved off his change. He took his suspenders and turned away, embarrassed by his own generosity. The peddler stared at the coin in his hand as if he had never seen one before. Joseph had only gone a few steps when the peddler caught up with him.

"Better quality . . . the best," he said, dangling another pair of suspenders and yanking the first pair out of Joseph's hand. "Those ain't so good."

Joseph made the exchange and hurried away. No, nothing had changed. Work and food might be hard to come by in the old neighborhood, but pride was always in great supply. He stood on Rivington Street, but it could have been Delancey, or Orchard, or Hester. There was a depressing sameness to them all, and a desperate feeling about them, as if the store awnings of scarlet, blue, and yellow could make them cheerful places to be. But bright colors did not make up for too many people and too little food, money, even air to breathe. And that was the real reason that he never came back to the old neighborhood. It suffocated him.

He crossed the intersection at Essex, glancing up at the block numbers. On the fire escape above, a dozing woman sat on a three-legged stool and nursed her baby while a toddler beside her cradled a rag doll. On the corner, three boys lounged lazily against the window of a fish market and watched him through hooded eyes. Gang members. What streeter, he wondered, falling back on the gang parlance of his youth. He couldn't recognize them, didn't know the signs anymore. But there had been a time in his youth when it had been very important to him. At twelve, he'd wanted nothing more than to run with the Whyos, and maybe move up later to Tammany Hall.

Two years in America had taught him a lot. He'd seen the ward bosses, with their thick cigars and gold pocket watches. True prosperity lay in politics. Tammany was the quintessence of power in New York, and Joseph had his eye on the prize. But Dennis and Fiona Hannegan had their eyes on their son and their backs turned firmly to the Tiger. Dennis had kept his belt handy and his son in school, while Fiona went to work as a daily to bring in the extra money that would take them off Tompkins Street.

At sixteen, Joseph helped his father move their few belongings to the west side and into a marginally more prosperous neighborhood. Two years later, he went to work on the docks as a night watchman, studying on the job and attending day classes at City College. He barely remembered those years, existing on four hours of sleep caught where he might. He had packed his mind with class work, shutting out everything else until the day when, finally, diploma in hand, he went to work for the immigration service. Things had just begun to turn around for the Hannegan family when Fiona discovered she was carrying the baby who would take her life. How she would have loved the boarding house, and how she would have hated Moira being chained to it.

Joseph did not enjoy revisiting his youth. His first experience with a whore had taken place five blocks from where he now stood. Seamus O'Neill's oldest child and daughter, Doreen — a girl of considerable passion and even more experience — had entertained most of the boys on the block at one time or another, while her mother sweated in the laundry and her father chased Fenian dreams. It had been a wild and heated afternoon from which fourteen-year-old Joseph had emerged, his desire and curiosity satisfied, but haunted by sadness and guilt.

He had never been able to look Doreen O'Neill in the eye after that day. Her memory still caused him pain. And he thought that his one liaison with her had been the first crack in the glossy lacquer on his friendship with Liam. Not that Liam was in the dark where his sister's virtue was concerned. On the contrary, Liam thought Doreen should do whatever it took to get out of the Lower East Side, an attitude he applied to himself and his brother Kevin as well. That had been at the center of their first real argument. Joseph thought Liam should put a stop to his sister's behavior. Liam was too busy moving up in the world to concern himself with it.

Joseph stopped in front of Goldfarb's bakery window. More than anything else, he hated the smell of the tenements — cabbage and fish, mildew and sweat boiling in the suffocating heat of the summer, when not a trace of air whispered down the air shaft, and steeping in winter's smoky damp. The bakery had been a godsend. There he would stop in the early morning, gulping in air fragrant with the scent of fresh bread, hoping to exchange the stagnant odors in his lungs and the taste on his tongue. But the senses, he discovered, have a long memory. His hair and clothes smelled of the tenements and no amount of lye soap would scrub it away. Even now the smell flooded his memory and made him gag. Mother of God, how he hated the tenements.

At the corner of Attorney Street, he came to a confused halt. He'd been so consumed with memories that he had forgotten where he was going. He took Maggie Flynn's letter out of his pocket and checked the address — 207 Rivington Street. Another block or so, almost to the Irish section. A dark priest was hurrying toward him, cassock flying in the wind, one hand clamped on his head to keep his biretta in place.

"Buona sera," he said, nodding at Joseph.

"Good evening, Father." If he didn't hurry, there would be no one in the employment office to question about Emmaline Westcott. He crossed Ridge Street and moved to the other side of Rivington, following the numbers as they ascended the block of tenements almost to the corner of Pitt Street.

But he needn't have worried that the office might be closed. Joseph stood in front of a red brick tenement house, its staircase flanked on one side by a tailor's shop, and on the other, by a grocery window hung with cheese and sausages. There was no employment office at 207 Rivington Street.

CHAPTER ELEVEN

Above him, the first glimmer of light in the dusk appeared behind open windows. Joseph stepped back into the street and followed the rows of windows and iron fire escapes to the fourth floor. Five front apartments were illuminated.

Someone was frying onions. Well at least it wasn't cabbage, a vegetable that would, in adulthood, never cross his lips again. He drew in a deep breath and ascended the staircase, stepping into the hall, where the odor was stronger yet and the day's heat had gathered to linger in the stillness. Nevertheless, he was pleasantly surprised at what he found there — scrubbed floors and the dim glow of a gas lamp to illuminate the narrow entry. The housekeeper cared about her job.

He followed the cramped hallway to the first door on his right and gave it a sharp knock. Behind the door, the metallic clatter of a lid being dropped onto a pot was followed by heavy footsteps. But the door was opened by a small boy — not more than four — who struggled with a broom in his right hand and a dirty piece of cardboard in his left. His mother was three paces behind him. She glanced up at Joseph and gasped, before hurriedly shooing the boy back into the room.

"Si?" she said, her dark eyes widening. She twisted her apron in scarred hands. *"Avete un problema?"*

Joseph hadn't thought about his clothing. The cut of his suit would speak for itself to anyone living in a working-class neighborhood. She would suspect he was an official, possibly a detective. Policemen were not beloved in a neighborhood where petty thievery and gambling were tools to sustain life.

"It's all right," he said. "I'm from Immigration. *Immigrazione.*"

She gasped again, glanced back into the apartment and made to close the door. "No!"

"Wait," he said, shoving his foot against the door. "Please. I am looking for Emmaline Westcott. Does she live here?" He searched his mind for a fragment of Italian he could use, but came up wanting. "Emmaline Westcott," he repeated.

The woman in the doorway stared at him, focusing carefully on his mouth as he pronounced the name. "West-cott," she repeated slowly. "West-cott?"

"Yes, exactly. Emmaline Westcott. Does she live here?"

The woman glanced behind her, as though help might be forthcoming, but there seemed to be only the child in the apartment. Her husband, if there was one, was not yet home from work. If she had any boarders, which was likely, they were not there either.

"Non conosco l' inglese."

"Are you the housekeeper?" Joseph saw no recognition in her eyes. He pantomimed sweeping and washing the floor. "You?"

"Si," she said, after a moment's thought. "Housekeeper." She followed this with a lengthy explanation in Italian, most of which eluded Joseph. But he had the impression that her husband might be the agent who rented apartments in the house. And he thought he understood that her husband worked late. At length, he shrugged and backed away from her.

"Thank you. *Grazie.*"

There were other apartments he might try. But surely if there were an Emmaline Westcott living in the building — which he now seriously doubted — the housekeeper would have at least recognized the name. He would have to come back, and bring with him someone who could translate Italian and wouldn't frighten the housekeeper.

The Sixth Avenue El rattled over Rachel's head and blew hot breath down the back of her neck as she descended the staircase to Eighth Street. She consulted the notes in her journal and turned back five blocks, following the charwoman's directions past the park to a house on Bleecker Street.

In her teenage years, Rachel had spent considerable time in the compact, hardy brownstones that bordered the north side of the park. The Rhinelanders, Stewarts, Coopers, and deForests all lived in the comfort their prominence suggested. Nowhere in the city was the contrast of class more starkly evident than in Greenwich Village, where old New York families on the north side stubbornly clung to luxurious homes and traditions in spite of the surrounding decay. It had all been a fashionable area in its time but, outside the northern blocks, had become run-down, even squalid in places and dotted with the industry of box factories and garment sweatshops.

Nevertheless, the Hannegan house was well kept and exactly as the charwoman had described it. It was smaller than the brownstones of a later time, with a stucco front and narrow shoulders, its expanse spread vertically through four floors. Rachel rang the bell and waited, contemplating the ROOM TO LET sign in the window. Was the Superintendent merely a boarder in the house? But the charwoman had said that her husband was a friend of Mr. Hannegan's father.

"Have you come about the room then? I'm afraid I'm getting dinner on, but if you're willing to wait, I'll be free to interview you after I get the potatoes in the oven. Come along."

Rachel got only a glimpse of the young woman's face before she turned and moved down the hallway and through a door to the left, leaving the front door open for Rachel to follow. Rachel stepped tentatively into the hall, stopping next to a hall tree to wait for the woman to return.

She hadn't considered the possibility that the Superintendent might be married, or that she might be arriving at an inconvenient time of the day. She took a hesitant step backward. Maybe she should just leave. But before she could decide, the young woman stuck her head back into the hall.

"Please, come in. You can wait here in the parlor. I won't be a minute."

"No, I . . . I'm afraid you've misunderstood. I'm looking for your husband."

"Yes, so am I. I suppose he'll come along eventually, though Lord knows I don't much care for what I see out there right now, if you know what I mean."

Rachel stared at her, perplexed. The young woman came forward and guided her by the arm into the parlor, to a place on a heavy mahogany Empire love seat. "Now if you're not lookin' for a room, what is it that brings you here?"

"I . . . well, I wanted to speak to your husband — the Superintendent. I work at the immigration station, and I've —"

The woman leaned back against the doorframe and let go a musical laugh, as though someone were running through the treble keys on a piano. "I'm sorry," she said. "You must think I'm daft — that remark about looking for a husband." She offered her hand to Rachel. "I'm Moira Hannegan. You're looking for Joseph. He's my brother."

Rachel was surprised at her feeling of relief, but it was short-lived. Out of the corner of her eye, she saw another woman — frail and delicate in appearance — hovering in the hallway.

"Can I help you with something, Miss Dove?"

Miss Dove stepped into the parlor door. "I'm sorry to interrupt, Moira. I just wanted to tell you that I won't be home for dinner tonight. I have . . . an engagement."

Moira's eyes sparkled mischievously. "An engagement, Miss Dove? Would that be with a man? And what shall I tell my brother when he comes in looking for you?"

Miss Dove's cheeks colored, the same soft rose as her dress. "Go on with you, Moira," she said, feigning a brogue. "He'll not be lookin' for me tonight."

Moira laughed in delight and added a layer of brogue of her own. "Why, Miss Dove, I believe you're makin' fun of me! And who might this engagement be with, if you don't mind me askin'?"

"A friend from the Historical Society, and that's all I'm goin' to tell you, Moira Hannegan."

"Well, I won't be tellin' Joseph about this. It would break his heart."

Miss Dove rolled her eyes and shook her head before moving down the hallway and out the front door. Moira turned back to Rachel, her eyes still glittering.

"She's shy as a lamb when Joseph is in

the house, but get her alone and she's a different woman. I tell her she ought to go into burlesque. But you didn't come here to be entertained, did you? Just let me get these potatoes in the oven, and I'll be right back."

Rachel studied the room covertly, not wanting to be caught in the appearance of prying. Most of the furnishings were inexpensive reproduction pieces and looked as if they might be secondhand. But they were highly polished and carefully arranged to their best advantage. A marble topped lyre table next to the love seat held a china pitcher so fragile it looked as if the tiniest vibration might shatter it. Rachel turned it over to read the mark. Belleek. It was good that they didn't live under the El, she thought as she replaced it.

In the corner stood a sewing cabinet, open, with a black Singer machine waiting for a foot to pump its treadle, and across the room the brass pedals of a small rosewood piano anticipated the same. There was a pair of pressed oak Morris chairs, a camelback sofa covered in fading blue brocade, and a glass-fronted bookcase chocked with volumes, which she couldn't resist inspecting. Descartes, Plutarch, Cervantes, Fielding, Dostoevsky, and Milton. The books were arranged in collections of philosophy, fiction, autobiography, and poetry. Two volumes on etiquette and deportment intruded on the otherwise scholarly display.

On the wall hung a vivid watercolor in a heavy frame. Rachel moved closer to look at it. It was primitive, but somehow engaging — bright green hills, dotted with sheep, and a small gray cottage in the distance. The perspective was slightly off, but the artist had a good eye for detail.

"Miss Dove painted that," Moira said from the doorway. She balanced two thin teacups in her hands, crossed the room and set them on a low table.

"She did it from a calendar picture of Ireland. For Joseph, after he repaired the sewing machine for her. Of course, it is my sewing machine . . ." Moira shrugged as if her meaning were clear.

"I took a chance on milk," she said, handing Rachel a cup. "Is that all right?"

Rachel indicated that it was, and returned to her seat.

"She's an excellent seamstress," Moira said, picking up the conversation where she seemed to think they had left it off. "She can turn the prettiest French seam."

What Rachel knew about sewing would fit into a thimble. Irene had tried to teach her but soon gave it up as a lost cause. Moira went on extolling Miss Dove's many virtues until she realized that she was rambling and stopped self-consciously. She ducked her head and took a quick sip of her tea.

"I'm sorry," she said, "I don't get many chances to talk to other women — except Miss Dove and Mrs. Shapiro — and really we haven't much in common. I miss it."

Rachel waited for her to continue her awkward soliloquy, hearing an echo of her own occasional loneliness. "Miss it?"

"Well, miss my school friends. I'll go back some time, but not now. Joseph and Dad need me here, to run the boarding house."

Rachel had a question poised on the tip of her tongue, but Moira answered it even before she had decided to ask it.

"Nursing school," she added quietly, and took another sip of her tea, effectively closing the subject. She set her cup aside and turned her full attention to Rachel. "Ah well . . . tell me about working for my brother at the station. Is he a tyrant?"

Rachel laughed. "I don't think so. I don't usually have much contact with him. But I learned something today. . . ." She hesitated, not knowing how much she should say, sensing that the Superintendent might prefer to keep the business of the immigration service private.

"He asked me to keep him informed about a matter at the station, and I think I have some interesting news. But perhaps I should keep it until tomorrow," she said. She suddenly felt self-conscious and intrusive, and set her cup down with embarrassed resolve. "I really shouldn't have come here disturbing you."

"But I'm sure he'll be here soon. Don't go," Moira said. "Let me get you another cup of tea."

"No, I really think I should —" Their argument was settled with the opening of the front door.

The Superintendent seemed surprised to find her there but not altogether unhappy about it. Her appearance, he said, was fortuitous, in fact. He needed her help. Would she mind waiting long enough for him to change out of his uniform?

"My mother was a bridget," Moira said, picking up their conversation as though it had not been interrupted, "but she wanted more for me than this." She glanced around the boarding-house parlor with a critical eye. "She wanted me to have an education."

Moira kept herself well-informed. She and Rachel quickly moved on to discuss Carrie Nation, prohibition of alcohol, and women's right to vote. She was keenly interested in the new Fusion ticket for the coming city elections. She was just warming up to her subject when the Superintendent reappeared in the doorway.

He wore a collarless shirt under a brown wool vest and slightly shabby tweed trousers. A soft wool cap dangled from his hand. "I hope you'll forgive my appearance, Miss Bonner, but it suits my purposes for the moment.

"If Dad is asking for me, I'll be home in a bit," he said to his sister.

"You will come back, won't you?" Moira said plaintively, standing at the front door as Joseph and Rachel descended the steps. On impulse, she turned before she reached the sidewalk and hurried back up the stairs.

"Tomorrow," she said. "There's a tea for the Fusion ticket. I wasn't going to attend it, but if you'd like —"

"I'd love to go," Moira said, then laughed at her own eagerness. "You must think me a pathetic creature."

"Not in the least. I didn't want to go alone, and now I won't have to. We'll meet and go together. Let's say 2:45 in Union Square."

Moira agreed, and called out an afterthought to her brother. "It's dinnertime, Joseph, and you're keeping Miss Bonner from her supper."

"I'll take care of it, Moira."

He stood at the foot of the steps, studying Rachel with a pensive expression. She waved at Moira, as he took her elbow and turned her south toward Prince Street, automatically stepping to the outside of the walk.

"We'll need to catch a car across town," he said. "You do speak Italian, don't you?"

"Well, yes. I can usually make myself understood, but I'm not as fluent as I'd like to be."

"It'll do," he said, turning her south toward the streetcar stop. He explained about the letter and the trip he'd already made to Rivington Street. "It's a small Italian pocket between the Jewish section and the Irish strip along the East River. The housekeeper doesn't speak much English, and I don't speak Italian. I want to find out what she knows, if anything. Afterward, we can stop for a bite of supper if you'd like."

"It's not necessary, Superintendent. I can get something when I get home."

"And have my sister nagging at me for the next three days? It would be favor to me if you'd just let me get you dinner and be done with it."

Rachel had received more gallant invitations, to be sure, but she accepted nevertheless. He was, after all, her supervisor at work. Besides, although the invitation sounded grudging, she sensed that there was a grain of sincerity in it — if only a sincere desire to discuss Maggie Flynn.

The crosstown streetcar was noisy and crowded. Joseph guided Rachel toward the back, seating her in the only available place, next to a portly businessman who studied the evening edition of the *New York Times.* He grunted at Rachel and turned away, as if she might ask for a section of his paper. Joseph stood next to her, his feet planted apart for balance. Across the aisle, a young woman tried to comfort a tired, crying child.

"Bowery," the conductor shouted and rang the bell.

The businessman folded his paper and scrambled over Rachel, nearly bowling over the woman and child in the aisle. Joseph took the young woman's elbow to steady her, pulled her back and let the businessman pass. The young woman smiled gratefully and lifted the child to her shoulder before following the man down the aisle.

Rachel slid over on the seat to make a place for Joseph, but he relinquished it to an older woman staggering under a string bag full of groceries and an armload of piecework. She dropped into the seat with a groan, piled her load on her lap, put her head back, and fell to snoring loudly. Joseph grinned over the woman's head. Something in his smile made a laugh bubble up in Rachel's throat, but when the woman slumped over onto her, he reached across and tapped her shoulder, leaning over the seat.

"Let's get off here at Clinton," he whispered. With his help, she clambered over the snoring woman, leaving her collapsed on the seat to continue her nap.

"We're going to 207 Rivington Street," he said. They walked down Clinton one block to Rivington, turning east toward Pitt. Beside them, barricades lined the sidewalk and the last of the subway laborers shouldered picks and axes for the walk home. They called out to one another in Italian, in voices as dark and rich as their native wines, and sent furtive glances in Rachel's direction.

Rachel smiled to herself. It was just as well that the Superintendent did not understand Italian, or he might have felt compelled to defend her honor, and the men doubtless would have been embarrassed had they known she understood them. But after all, they were not saying anything that other men had not said about her, even if it had been framed a little more poetically.

"We'll be putting up with this for some time to come," Joseph said, gesturing at the construction site.

"But who will want to board an underground train when they can ride on top of the ground and see where they're going?"

"Plenty of people, if it will get them where they're going faster. Besides, the Beach subway was fairly popular, for all that it carried passengers only a few blocks."

"Beach subway? To Coney Island? Where is that?"

Joseph grinned and pointed at the street. "Down there, but somewhere on the west side, I believe. And not beach, but Beach — named for its inventor. It was a great pneumatic tube that carried a car through it. Quite popular in its day."

"I've never heard of it."

"Nor had I, until one of our boarders, Miss Dove, told us the story at dinner. She's quite an expert on the city's history."

As they turned onto Rivington Street, Joseph seemed to withdraw into himself. He walked, she noticed, at a faster clip, his hands balled into fists, arms swinging purposefully at his sides. His expression did not invite further casual conversation.

Rachel had not spent much time on the

Lower East Side, except to visit settlement houses as an undergraduate, but she had heard other social workers speak of it with a mixture of affection and despair. Now she looked about her with interest. In her part of New York, neighbors rarely saw one another, unless it was by appointment or while out strolling in Gramercy Park. But here, neighbors leaned out of their windows, shouting to one another across the narrow expanse of fire escapes and alleys, while their children made mischief in the streets below. Young lovers met in the recessed doorways of shops, clutching at any private place for an intimate moment alone in a place that knew no privacy. Still, in a city where human stamina was tested to its limit, these narrow streets pumped with vigor. Impoverished though its residents were, it was only a poverty of things, not of spirit. No doubt any one of these people would have gladly traded places with her, but that, she thought, was only because they had not experienced the starched life of privilege.

Rachel was neither foolish nor romantic enough to believe that their lives were better than hers. But she did think that they were warmer. Closer. The rich, she theorized, had developed their conventions to keep their fellow men at arm's length and their institutions intact. In their slavish fidelity to custom, they dressed alike under the guise of propriety and fashion, and behaved alike, behind the pretense of etiquette, and anyone who deviated in the slightest soon found himself a pariah. Perhaps what frightened the rich most about the poor was their refusal to allow caste to dictate their conduct. Despite the teeming throngs of people who flocked to tenements all over the city, they were individuals starkly different from one another in appearance and manner, politics and religion.

One such individual was sauntering toward them now. He might have been seventeen and wore a dandified suit of large brown checks and a derby hat cocked over his brow. Both suit and hat were shiny with wear and grime. He twirled a scuffed cane with a curved brass neck in his left hand, and tipped his hat to her with his right — a burlesque of the society man about town. It was a harmless pose and conveyed a jaunty optimism that typified, to her, the attitudes of the tenements.

"Do you know," she said to Joseph when the boy had passed, "that in Uganda, only the upper caste are permitted to use walking sticks?"

"Fascinating," he said, but the word carried little conviction. "If you're referring to that one, that cane of his is probably a weapon."

"Weapon?"

"There's a blade hidden in the shaft, Miss Bonner. It's called a sword cane."

Rachel glanced uneasily over her shoulder at the young man in the checked suit. He had stopped to talk to a younger boy on the street. The boy was backing away, shaking his head, as the young dandy advanced upon him. He was still twirling his cane, but he had lost much of his charm.

CHAPTER TWELVE

"They are all rented by families, all Italian, except one. She isn't sure who's actually living there, if anyone is at all," Rachel said. "She hasn't seen anyone but the man who rented the flat."

"When was that?"

Rachel turned back to the housekeeper, a Mrs. Parrillo, who gazed at a stain on the ceiling and counted back on her fingers before launching into another stream of Italian.

"She thinks it's been a month, maybe six weeks. She remembered because she went away with her children to a summer retreat — probably a settlement house farm — and when she came back, the house was a mess. She was washing down the front door when the man came to rent the flat."

"What did he look like?"

Joseph listened to the exchange, watching Rachel's face as she blinked uncertainly. She followed up with a question — no, a verification, Joseph thought, of what Mrs. Parrillo had told her. When Rachel turned to him, the perplexed expression on her face remained.

"He was a policeman. At least I think that's what she said. *Poliziotto, si?*"

"*Si,*" the woman confirmed. She held up her hand, rising on her toes to indicate that he had been two inches taller than Joseph. His hair was red, she said. And his skin very white. His eyes, she remembered, were blue.

"And very fair in complexion," Rachel repeated. "He doesn't sound Italian, does he?" She turned back to Mrs. Parrillo with a question. Did this man speak Italian?

"He only spoke enough Italian to make his needs known. But if he were a policeman, he might have to know a little Italian, wouldn't he?"

"Yes, if his beat is in an Italian area he might. Did he pay for the room?"

At the question, Mrs. Parrillo stepped back into her doorway, as if to protect herself, or the money the man had paid her. He had paid for three months, she said, and it was perfectly legal. She had done nothing wrong, had she? If the man didn't use the flat, what difference? She hadn't rented it again. He had paid the rent, and she was holding the flat for him. Besides, he had the key.

"Where is the flat?"

"On the fourth floor, in the back."

Joseph stepped away from Mrs. Parrillo's door and walked down the hall, past the stairwell to the back of the building. There was a back door, with a window that looked out into a barren courtyard holding a privy and several ash cans. The rear of another tenement, facing onto Delancey, was visible across the alley. Joseph returned to the waiting women.

"If he came and went by the back door, she might not see him. I think we should have a look at the flat."

"Shall I ask her for a key?"

"No. I think we'll be able to get in and I'd prefer that no one else know we were here. Thank her, and tell her we're leaving."

Mrs. Parrillo seemed relieved that the interrogation had not come to trouble. She smiled, nodded, offered them coffee. Rachel extricated them as gracefully as possible and followed Joseph to the front door. He opened it, closed it again, and put a finger to his lips. In a second, the housekeeper's door closed.

Joseph moved forward quietly with Rachel close behind. They ascended the stairs lightly, past flats exhaling the odors of garlic and strong cheese, infused with a dank smell of mold from the hall sink, and another smell Joseph knew too well. Somewhere in a wall on the second floor, a dead rat was decomposing. Most of the doors to the flats stood ajar. Behind them, babies cried and loud voices carried on musical conversations in Italian.

On the fourth floor, Joseph knocked on the door of the rear left flat. After several tries, he dug in his trouser pocket and brought out a small, folding knife. "I learned a few things on Tompkins Street," he said. He probed the keyhole with a narrow blade and quickly had the door open. A faint scratching noise came from the dark interior of the flat. Rachel stepped back with a quick gasp. The movement was not lost on Joseph.

"Are you all right? Maybe you'd better wait out there."

Rachel moved back another pace as a gray shadow darted across the door. She took a deep breath. "Yes, I'll be all right," she whispered, and glanced around the hall. "And anyway, I'd rather not wait out here alone."

Joseph went in first stamping his feet, reached back and took her hand, pulling her into the room. He pushed the door around until only a crack of light sliced through the darkness. He would have liked to have kept her hand in his — soft and smooth as it was — but let it go, and felt in his pocket for a box of matches. He took one out and handed the box to her, struck the match on his shoe and cupped his hand around it to contain the light.

The flat was the typical tenement configuration. The hall door opened directly into the kitchen and led, to the immediate left, to a small back room. Another door off the kitchen led into the front room — the only one with windows. A stagnant, smothering heat surrounded them. Joseph peeked into the back room, then led her through the kitchen to the parlor.

There was nothing of value in the apartment. A kettle on the stove, and two chipped cups beside it. Two cots with straw mattresses. A kerosene lamp. Cigarette butts littered the floor, along with several empty bottles of cheap whiskey. He picked up one of the bottles and studied the label. Irish whiskey.

"Shall we light the lamp?" Rachel asked, reaching for the glass globe.

"No. It can be seen from below. We don't want to warn them off."

To their right, a thin cotton curtain covered a narrow recess in the wall. Joseph gently pulled it back.

"Oh!" Rachel jumped backward as a rat scurried between Joseph's feet. She dropped the box and matches spilled over the floor. Joseph kicked at the rat reflexively and watched as it ran under one of the cots.

"Are you all right?"

Rachel had wrapped her arms across her waist, as if they might protect her. Even in the dim light, he could see the fear etched in her face. "I . . . I'm sorry," she said. "I dropped them. It startled me and I . . . I'll pick them up."

She stooped down and began sweeping the matches into her hand. Joseph shook his match out and crouched beside her. In the darkness, their hands touched.

"I'm sorry."

"No, it's all right."

The dark seemed to heighten his senses. She smelled so clean — of glycerine soap, and a hint of lilac toilet water. He had a glimpse of himself, burying his face in the hollow of her neck, and felt a twist in his gut that momentarily paralyzed him.

"Do you have the box?" she asked.

He shook off his confusion. "No. Yes, here it is." Together they held the box and dropped the matches back in. He wondered if she, too, had felt the electricity between them.

"We'd best make sure we have them all," she said, and struck a match against the box. In the light of the flame, the bones of her face seemed even more fragile, her skin as delicately translucent as a piece of Belleek.

"I don't see any others."

He cast about, willing himself to look away from her face. "No, that's all of them, and I think there's only one rat. It's gone under the cot. Stay close to me and you'll be all right."

He took her arm and guided her toward the closet. She struck another match illuminating, in its quick flare, two battered cases on the floor — one, a scuffed brown leather, and the second, a carpetbag lying half-open on its side. Joseph squatted down.

"Bring the light closer," he said.

He felt through the carpetbag quickly, finding only clothing — men's clothing, he thought. A celluloid collar, a tobacco pouch, and straight razor confirmed it.

He moved on to the valise, laid it out on the floor and popped the locks. In the semi-dark, his fingers swept over a soft-bristled shaving brush and a tin of tooth powder. A wool cap and a glass bottle, too small to be whiskey. He held it to the light to read the label. *Allen's Cocaine Nasal Tablets — for Catarrh, Asthma, Hay Fever, Prickly Heat and Skin Eruptions.*

"Cocaine and whiskey. Now there's a bad mix," he said. As Rachel replenished the light, he shoved the bottle back into the case, and pulled out another one, taller and made of heavy glass with a cork stopper. Diamond Ink. Joseph pulled out the stopper and smelled the liquid. It had no particular odor and was, very likely, what it said it was. There wasn't much left anyway. He stoppered the bottle and put it back into the case.

"What is that?" Rachel said, pointing at a corner of deep red under a flannel nightshirt.

Joseph pulled out a book and turned it over to read its title. He handed it up to Rachel.

"*Discours sur l'origine de l'inegalité,*" she read. "Rousseau." She opened the book and flipped through it quickly. "The text is in French. How odd," she said, handing it back to him.

Joseph took the book by its covers and shook it, but nothing fell out. He closed it and laid it back in the case. There was nothing much left to search — two pairs of woolen socks, a fountain pen and three sheets of folded paper, a pair of sleeve garters and two linen shirts. He pushed it all back into the case and snapped the locks, returning it to its upright position. Her hand squeezed his shoulder.

"Superintendent, there's something else," she said, reaching past him to pull a shirt out from under the carpetbag. She handed him the match and held the shirt up by the shoulders. "Look at — Oh!"

He was leaning toward the bag when she cried out, but before he could turn he was thrust head first into the closet, his skull slamming against its back wall. Sprawled against the back of the closet, he struggled to right himself in the dark, fighting a nauseating dizziness. Either he had blacked out from the blow, or the match had been extinguished. He heard the shuffling of feet and a muffled cry, followed by the sound of tearing fabric. Joseph heaved himself to his feet. "Miss Bonner, are you all right?"

Her voice came out of the dark. "I think so."

"I'll be back," he said, stumbling in the dark. Memory took over as he navigated the darkness through the kitchen until he found the doorknob. In the hall, the same smells and noises persisted, as though nothing out of the ordinary had occurred. Joseph flew to the stairs and peered down, but no one was descending below him. He raced back to the flat, almost colliding with Rachel at the door. In her hand, she held a rag covered in red stains. She held it up, but he didn't give her time to speak.

"The roof," he said, darting toward a dark staircase that ended at a heavy door.

Rachel took one glance back at the flat, stuffed the rag into her pocket, gathered her skirt and followed him up.

By the time she reached the roof, he was already on the next one. The glow of a three-quarter moon outlined two male figures beyond him. As she watched, they crossed from a third roof to a fourth. She hiked up her skirt and strode across the six-inch fissure between the buildings, hurrying after Joseph. Below, in the street, the noise had increased as neighbors left their suffocating flats to sit on their steps and gossip. A crescendo of boys' voices reverberated between the buildings, and the sound of a stickball game registered dimly on her consciousness.

She was on the third roof when, in the distance, a door slammed. Joseph leapt ahead of her, little more than a dark shadow suspended in the air before his feet hit the top of the next building. He raced toward the stairwell door, calling back to her, but she couldn't hear him. She moved as quickly as she could, ducking under clotheslines, skirting washtubs, pigeon coops, and abandoned bedding.

She stopped at the roof's edge and looked down at the top of the fourth building, several feet below her. This time a wider gap, perhaps as much as three feet, separated the tenements. She took a deep breath and stepped up onto the concrete ledge.

"Dammit to hell!" Joseph yanked on the door but it didn't move. He reeled away, turned back, and landed a kick on the lock, but to no effect. He skirted the perimeter of the roof, peering down over the side until he reached the rear of the building. Below, a door slammed back against its hinges.

Rachel edged her way along the ledge until she could see them from her higher perch. They darted between the children in the street, around a messenger on a bicycle, past a bootblack stand and between two men carrying groaners of beer.

"Over here," she called, but Joseph still peered down at the alley below. She waved frantically at him, pointing down at the street. He turned and sprinted across the roof, running the length of the front wall but apparently unable to spy them. Rachel yanked her skirt up around her knees and started forward over the ledge. Her foot had barely touched concrete when he spun around again, looked down, and raised his arm. A loud crack shivered through the air.

Rachel flinched and felt her footing slip before she plunged into the breach between the buildings.

Chapter Thirteen

She thought the scream had caught in her throat, like a nightmare from which she struggled to escape, but knew she must have cried out when Joseph's face appeared above her. "Jaysus, Mary and Joseph, what have you done, Rachel girl?" he said softly.

Rachel peered up into his face, her thoughts as frozen as her tongue. The only thing keeping her suspended in the breach was her grip on the ledge of the fourth building. Her face burned where it had scraped brick in the fall and her arms ached in their sockets. She was dimly aware of a throbbing in her knee where it had hit the building ledge on the way down.

Joseph was down on one knee now and reaching for her. She felt his hands wrap around her upper arms and his quiet strength flow into her. "Rachel," he said calmly, "I want you to let go and grab my arms."

186

"I can't," she whispered. "We'll both fall."

"No! We won't. Don't I have you good and tight? One hand at a time. First your right."

She gazed up into his face above hers, his eyes lost in the shadows. He nodded his head in reassurance. She had to do it, had to trust him and believe that he could hold onto her. She closed her eyes and gripped the ledge even more tightly, willing every ounce of her strength into the fingers of her left hand.

"That's the girl," he said, when her right hand moved onto his arm. "Now the left."

The left hand was easier, with the right clutching at the knot of muscles under his sleeve. And then it was over. He didn't warn her, but pulled her up and she was in his arms, safe on the rooftop, before she had a chance to draw another breath. She buried her head against his shoulder and felt her body tremble before he gathered her in his arms. "You're safe now," he whispered into her hair.

She relaxed against him, allowing herself to enjoy the protection of his arms until her knees grew steady again and her shivering stopped. "Thank you," she said, pulling back to look at his face. "I'm sorry. You might have gone after them if —"

He caught her against him, and this time she heard a tremble in his voice. "What could you have been thinking? I told you to stay there."

"I didn't hear you. I could see them running, and —" She broke off, suddenly aware of the hard knot pressing into her shoulder.

A gun. He carried a gun. It was secured in a shoulder harness under his vest. That was the sound that had startled her, causing her foot to slip. She slid her hand across his chest and felt the smooth wooden stock under her fingers. He caught her hand and pulled it away, took her elbow, turning her, and guided her to an overturned washtub.

"I thought they might stop if I fired a warning shot," he said, gently seating her on the tub. "I didn't expect you to leap into the fray quite the way you did." His wry smile quickly gave way to a frown.

"You're a bit scraped up." He pulled a handkerchief out of his pocket, squatted next to her and dabbed at her cheek. "You'll need some iodine on that."

Rachel winced at his touch. "A little cool water will help. But my hands —"

Joseph took them and turned them over. A streak of dark clouds had obscured the moon. "I can't see them in this dark," he said. He stood up and looked around the rooftop. "Not a lantern anywhere. I'll have to go down over there," he said, pointing to the other roof, "come up here and unbolt the door from the inside. Don't try to follow me this time."

She watched him nimbly leap over the gap between the two buildings. When he was gone, she pulled up her skirt. She could feel, more than see, that the knee was bruised. Her stocking was torn and stuck to the skin where a wide abrasion had wept and bled. She plucked at it carefully, inching it over the worst part of the wound. The stocking could not be saved. She tugged off her boot and pulled the stocking down over her toe, using it to blot the oozing knee, but her thoughts were not on her injuries.

He'd smelled good — of bleached linen and a spicy sweat, a hint of shaving soap and tobacco. His clothes were rough, but his arms were strong and warm about her, nothing like the tentative embraces of the few sleek suitors she'd ever had. Still, he had gentle hands with a touch so light that his handkerchief had barely grazed her cheek. She closed her eyes and still felt the lingering warmth of his breath on her face. She didn't hear him behind her until he cleared his throat.

He'd brought her a dampened handkerchief, and she pressed it to her face while he took her ankle in his hand and gently rotated it. "Give me your stocking," he said, "and try to clean up that knee."

He carefully cut off the top of the stocking with his knife, leaving enough to cover her foot inside the boot. This, he laced loosely in case her ankle swelled, before he moved on to study the bruise on her knee. She hadn't pulled her skirt down, though modesty surely demanded it. But she trusted him, and was struck again by the gentleness of his touch. Her breath caught in her throat as, for a moment, she thought he might kiss her knee. Instead, he lifted the hem of her skirt and dropped it over her legs, stood and brushed his hands together.

"It may weep for a while. Perhaps you should stay home from the station for a few days. I can assign someone else to the Flynn girl."

"It will be fine," she said, surprised at the plunging disappointment she felt as he dispelled the moment of tenderness with an efficient tone. She tucked his handkerchief into her pocket. "I'll launder it and return it to you at the station," she said, rising. He reached out to steady her, lest her knee give way, but she stepped out of his grasp. Her hand went to her cheek. "I must look a mess."

Joseph dismissed the idea with a wave of his hand. "It's barely noticeable." He led her to the rooftop door. They descended the staircase into another tenement, this one not as well kept as Mrs. Parrillo's. The roof leaked and a dank pool of water lingered in a depression in the linoleum floor.

"Watch your skirt," Joseph said. They descended to the first floor before he spoke again, turning her toward the front door. There he waved her back and preceded her through the door, checking up and down the street before allowing her to exit. "In case they are still out there," he explained.

On the street, activity had picked up as neighbors finished their suppers and escaped the sweltering heat of their buildings. Men were off to local saloons and meetings of their societies. Women took up customary places on their front stoops to mend, gossip, and watch the children play in the street. They called greetings and jokes to one another, suddenly silenced at the passing of strangers. Rachel was conscious of it all, though her companion seemed to look past them, watchful for the two men who had accosted them in the apartment.

"They're long gone," he said at length.

"Did you get a look at them?"

"No. It was too dark to see their faces."

Joseph swung across to the street side and guided her back in the direction they had come, taking it more slowly in consideration of her knee and ankle. "Well, what have we learned? It's not the home of Emmaline Westcott, we know that," he said. "They could have killed us both, or at least injured us very badly, but they didn't. There was something in those bags they wanted. But what?"

They lapsed into silence as Rachel reviewed in her mind what little she remembered. And it was very little — an elbow, shoving her away from Joseph; the shirt, torn from her hands; the scuffling, as another man pushed Joseph into the closet; and finally, footsteps running back through the kitchen and into the hall.

They had covered six blocks before Joseph stopped in front of a shining plate glass window lettered in gold paint: Koenig's Bar and Grill. "You must be hungry. Do you like German food?"

"Um — yes, but you don't have to —"

"German it is, then," Joseph said. He grabbed hold of the brightly polished brass handle on the door and swung it open, waiting for her to precede him. A beaming bald man in a bright white apron met them at the door and led them past several tables of customers to a booth near the back of the restaurant. The air smelled of hops, and bleach and starch from the crisp white table linens. When they were seated, Joseph pulled off his cap and felt his head, coming away with fingers smeared with thick, sticky blood.

"Your head!" she said, rising quickly. "We need to leave right now. You've got to get home and get some ice on that."

"Sit down, Miss Bonner." He glanced sideways and back at her. "People are looking at us. We already look like we've been brawling. Let's not call further attention to ourselves. Please, sit down."

Rachel complied, but not without another murmur of protest. When their waiter appeared, Joseph ordered beer and wiener schnitzel for them both. "No cabbage or kraut. And you can bring the beer right away," he added. A moment later he held a frosted stein against his forehead, while Rachel sipped tentatively from hers.

"What we know, then," he said, "is that the flat is not inhabited by Emmaline Westcott. There were no women's things in those suitcases. Irish whiskey bottles point in the right direction. And at least one of them is literate."

"In French," Rachel reminded him.

Joseph sighed. "None of it makes any sense. I don't know a single Irishman who can read French, not to mention philosophy. *Discourse on the Origin of Inequality,* wasn't it?"

"Yes. Have you read it, Superintendent?"

Joseph picked up his napkin and swiped at a red streak on his hand. "In English. Society as the source of vice and oppression. Not an unusual conviction for a tenement dweller. What is unusual is finding someone in a tenement who can, and would, read it. Especially in French. I'm beginning to doubt that this has anything whatever to do with Michael Finnegan and Maggie Flynn."

"But it does," Rachel said slowly. Suddenly, she reached across the table and squeezed his hand. "I just remembered . . . I've been wondering why it seemed familiar. I've seen that book before." She glanced down and quickly withdrew her hand. "Have you gotten Michael Finnegan's bag yet?"

"The handlers can't find it."

"Because it isn't there. It's in that apartment on Rivington Street — or it was, anyway. And that book belongs in the leather valise. I know, because I put it there."

Rachel left half her wiener schnitzel on her plate, but finished her beer. She gazed across the table at Joseph finishing his dinner and experienced a brief but arresting awareness of the intimacy in watching him eat. There had been a moment, when he was inspecting her knee, when she thought he might kiss her. She would have complied, even felt her own spark ignite, until his mention of the station reminded her that he was her superior, and that a kiss on a moonlit evening might prove very awkward the next morning.

They had spent the meal talking about the book in the suitcase, and how she came to think that the case belonged to the mysterious Michael Finnegan. If it was true, and they both believed it was, then someone had removed the suitcase from Ellis Island. But who? And why?

The waiter appeared, setting a small dish of cloves on the table before whisking their dishes away. Joseph pinched up a clove and dropped it on his tongue. He pushed the dish closer to her. "I wonder if anyone else was traveling with them," he said. "It seems stupid now, but I never thought to ask her."

Rachel reached for a clove but stopped, her hand in midair. "What have I been thinking? I completely forgot!"

"Forgot what?"

"The reason I came to see you this afternoon. There was a man waiting for me at the Barge Office. He wanted to know about Maggie. He had made the crossing with her, he said, and he just wanted to know if she was all right. His name was Dylan and —"

"First or last?"

She thought a moment. "I don't know. I assumed it was his last name. It was the only name he would give me. I tried to get an address to contact him, but he ran away."

Joseph was listening with renewed interest. "Did he say anything else?"

"Well, he denied knowing any Michael Finnegan. He just said he had met Maggie aboard ship. But wait, he did say one other thing. Something very odd. He said, 'Tell her not to worry. Tell her it will be all right — we'll take care of it.' I wonder what he meant."

CHAPTER FOURTEEN

Joseph eyed his missal, trying in vain to follow the Gospel as Father O'Gara read it. But Father O'Gara was a mumbler, and unless a parishioner found a seat in the first five pews, he was likely to get little out of the Gospel and less out of the sermon. It was the twelfth Sunday after Pentecost, and the Gospel was the parable of the Good Samaritan. O'Gara was, apparently, finished reading, as the first five rows took their seats and the rest of the church followed suit.

The heat in the church was oppressive, the still air thick with the odor of melting wax. After years of high Masses, a heavy veil of incense lingered over the altar like unanswered prayers. Beside him, Moira fanned herself with a small holy card she kept in her missal — the Blessed Mother, a commemorative card from Fiona's funeral. On the back, Joseph knew, were the vital statistics of his mother's life — dates of birth and death, names of husband and children — compressed into four lines that said nothing about the sacrifices she had made for her family, her heartache, the things that made her laugh or cry. It didn't reveal how she'd taken the edge off the household, softened his father's stern, unyielding dictums with reason and compassion, encouraged her children to reach for more than Dennis's remote dream of a free Ireland. It angered Joseph, that little card intended to commemorate a woman who was so much more than a few vital statistics. And it didn't even offer up much of a breeze.

On Joseph's other side, Dennis stirred in the pew, pulled out a handkerchief and mopped his face, removed his spectacles and wiped behind his ears. Even now, he was probably thinking about the next Clan na Gael meeting — how they would raise money to pour into Ireland, or how they might politically maneuver a little support from Bourke Cockran or some other Irish American politician. They'd had another argument just this morning, after Dennis's despondent announcement that a large Boer convoy had been captured.

"Why, Dad, do you let something that's going on in Africa spoil your day?"

Dennis had thrown down the *Times,* fuming. "Because their victory is our victory. Now is the time to strike, don't you see? The Boers are twisting the Lion's tail, and the more they twist it, the better it is for us. British troops are still shipping out to Africa in droves. There's hardly anyone home to mind the store, let alone to mind Ireland. If we can hit them now, while they're concentrating on the Boers, we have the best chance of succeeding."

"And what is it that you think you can do from America, Dad?"

Dennis turned away, pouring himself a cup of coffee from a pot on the sideboard. He'd kept his back to his son, as though he hadn't trusted himself to look Joseph in the eye. "You've never taken the oath, Shosav. Until you do, there's nothing more to be said."

There was plenty more to be said, Joseph thought, but not much point in saying it. Because Dennis would never be made to see that he owed his loyalty to the country that had fed and clothed his family for twenty years. They had not always lived well in America, but they'd never been on the verge of starvation here, as they had been in Ireland. It was an argument they'd had time and again without any resolution. There would not be resolution this time, either. Joseph had no plans to take the oath of the Clan now or ever.

Father O'Gara had finished his sermon and returned to the altar. Joseph stood with the others as O'Gara genuflected before the altar and began the Creed. Joseph studied the priest's back, reflecting on what he knew about Aloysius O'Gara.

He had come to the United States a very young child, had grown up in Boston and bore the scars of a tough neighborhood and a rough-and-tumble life. In an odd way, it suited the priest, whose parish was just west of the fifteenth ward. Most evenings, when he wasn't visiting the sick or sitting in on a Sodality meeting, Al O'Gara could be found in one of the many pubs along Christopher Street, dispensing the Word over a pitcher of beer. And many were the nights, so it was said in the neighborhood, that Father O'Gara delivered a truculent husband into the arms of a wife who was worried that his pay envelope would be empty by the time he got home with it. Somewhere in the distance the altar bells tinkled. Joseph dropped to his knees mechanically.

Dennis Hannegan approved of Father Aloysius O'Gara, a rare and remarkable endorsement from a man who thought that by and large priests should stick to teaching catechism and organizing church fairs. Joseph sometimes wondered what O'Gara had done to win his father over.

"Ecce Agnus Dei, ecce qui tollit peccata mundi."

Moira tapped him on the shoulder, motioned for him to sit back and raise the kneeler so that she could get out of the pew for Communion, fixing him with a quizzical expression as she passed. His attention had wandered so much during the Mass, Joseph wondered if he should stay to hear the next one. It wouldn't do any good. He wouldn't be able to concentrate. He had too much on his mind. Rachel Bonner, for instance.

It had been a long time since he'd passed the evening with a woman other than his sister. Rachel Bonner evoked a longing in him that was not wholly new, but had never before had a face. He smiled bitterly to himself. A typical Irish bachelor, wanting a woman and drinking to forget. And that was what he had done. At her insistence, he had put Rachel Bonner on a streetcar, instead of seeing her home, then returned to the boarding house to finish off half a bottle of whiskey before going to bed. But he had not forgotten her.

His thoughts returned to the rooftop now,

to watching her as moonlight spilled back across the roof and the last cloud drifted away. She'd taken off her stocking and gathered her skirt above the knee. The glistening whiteness of her skin reminded him of marble and an ancient Greek sculpture of Aphrodite he'd seen at the Metropolitan Museum. But her skin, he knew, would not feel like marble. It would be warm to his touch and soft under his fingers, like fine Swan-skin. He'd cleared his throat reflexively, a reaction to a stirring deep within him.

Rachel turned, her lips parted in surprise, but she made no move to pull down her skirt. In the moonlight, the abrasion on her cheek looked bright and angry. He had dampened his handkerchief in the sink downstairs and crossed the roof, extending it in his hand. She took it from him and pressed it to her face.

"Thank you," she said. "It feels so cool."

Joseph dropped to one knee in front of her, took the stocking from her other hand and let it drop its full length. He took out his jackknife and sliced it across the ankle, handing the upper part back to her. "Give me your foot," he said.

He cradled her slender ankle in his hand, conscious of the delicate bones under the skin, and the soft round calf of her leg above him. He brushed a piece of loose gravel from the rooftop off the sole of her foot. "Your face looks better," he said. "Try to clean up the knee."

While she pressed the damp cloth to her knee, he rotated her ankle gently in the socket. "Is it sore?"

"No. Just my knee."

He slipped the piece of hosiery over her foot, following it with her boot. "I'll lace it loosely," he said. "You may have a bit of swelling yet."

When the boot was laced, he peeled the handkerchief back and studied her knee. A scarlet bruise had started to swell on one side of the joint. He touched it tenderly, then caught himself. This had to stop, he'd thought, before he found himself kissing her, or worse, kissing the strawberry bruise on her knee.

Father O'Gara's voice brought him back to the present. *"Dominus vobiscum. Ite, Missa est."*

Joseph rose with the others and filed out into the center aisle of the church. Moira and Dennis were quickly waylaid by friends. Father O'Gara had left the sacristy by the side door and, still vested, stood in front of the church greeting his parishioners. Joseph was waiting to speak to him when a heavy hand clapped him on the back.

"Didn't expect to see you so soon again, my friend."

Joseph turned to find Liam O'Neill, his face wreathed in a shining smile. "How are you, Liam?"

"Right as rain, Joe. *Conas tá tú?*"

Liam O'Neill spoke perfectly good, unaccented English except when it suited him to do otherwise. In the pub, at church, around Seamus, Dennis, and their cronies, he lapsed into burlesque Irish or, worse yet, Gaelic. Joseph found it intensely annoying.

"And were you able to buy your voters jobs?"

Liam assumed a wounded expression, but it soon cleared into another broad smile. "All perfectly legitimate, Joe. I told ya', my Tammany days are behind me. Truth is, Mr. Croker and I didn't see eye to eye on a few little points. Boss Croker doesn't much care for rebels."

"I thought Croker was in Ireland."

"Most of him, sure, but his hands are still in New York. Ah well, it's just as well. I have the pub, now. I just slake their thirsts, and that's enough to keep me busy."

Not only were they keeping him busy, Joseph thought, but they were making him rich. Liam wore a double-breasted suit of light gray tweed with a vest two shades lighter, a crisp blue striped shirt with a red bow tie and a black bowler hat. The suit was as fine a fit as the best New York tailor could produce. Liam O'Neill had always had a taste for quality — in clothing, in food, in women. As if to prove Joseph right, Liam turned to Moira, sweeping the hat off his head in a gesture that would have been comical, coming from anyone else.

"Shame on you, Moira Hannegan," he said.

"And for what am I to be ashamed, Liam O'Neill?" Moira asked, mimicking Liam's brogue.

"God didn't put you on this earth to outshine the sun."

Moira laughed and rolled her eyes, looking pleased in spite of herself. Liam had been pursuing Moira resolutely, if sporadically, for years. He'd appear on their doorstep on a Sunday afternoon with a bouquet of lilacs or daisies, insist that she take a stroll with him or join him in a hansom cab ride, returning her to their door promptly at six. And that would be the last that she'd see of him for weeks, until the notion to court her struck him again. At first she had taken his overtures seriously, but after repeated episodes, Moira had developed the appearance of studied indifference to him. Only Joseph knew the truth, that Moira was far from indifferent. Liam had been turning up more often lately, and the character of his attentions seemed to have grown more serious.

"I'm goin' to marry her one day, Joe, you'll see," Liam had said. "When I have enough money, when I can give her the life she deserves, I'll be back with a ring."

Dennis would approve the match without question. While Joseph wanted nothing more than for his sister to have the life she deserved, he profoundly hoped it would be with someone else. Liam was like a boy with a hoop and a stick, tapping Moira only often enough to keep her spinning. He loved Liam as only a brother might — conscious of his flaws but willing to overlook them. Until it came to his sister. When he prayed, and Joseph privately admitted that was all too infrequently, it was for another man to come along — someone with charm equal to Liam's and the integrity his friend so obviously lacked. But Liam was the only sun on Moira's horizon right now, and in his light she was like a flower opening its petals to receive his warmth. What he did for her was grand. It was what he might do to her that worried her brother.

The crowd around Father O'Gara had cleared. Joseph left his family basking in Liam's glow and joined the priest at the church doors.

"Joe," Father O'Gara said, "I'm sorry I didn't get up to see you on Friday. I was running late and had to get back to hear confessions."

"It's all right, but I'd like to talk to you now, if you don't mind."

O'Gara shifted his feet and adjusted the maniple that hung over his left arm. "I don't have much time, Joe. I'm saying the next Mass, too."

"All right, then I'll come straight to the point. I need a favor from you, Father. I suppose you heard the girl's confession?"

Father O'Gara frowned. "Yes," he said warily. "But you know very well —"

"I'm not asking you to break the seal. But I do want you to try to convince her to tell me what happened out there."

Father O'Gara blew out a long sigh and gazed across the churchyard at Dennis, Moira, and Liam. At length he said, "I'm not sure I can help you, Joe."

Joseph stared at the priest and tried to suppress his rising frustration. "You're not helping me, Father. You're helping her. Do you want her to go to jail?"

Father O'Gara crossed his arms, slipping his hands into the sleeves of his alb, and rocked back on his heels. "You can put your mind at ease, Joseph. I don't think that will happen. If you give it a few days, it will sort itself out. Just let it go."

"Father, a few days or a few weeks, this problem will not solve itself. Don't you understand that I have to follow the law? At the very best, I have to deport this girl. And the worst — well, I don't have to tell you what the worst is, do I? Get your oil ready for last rites and keep your stole at hand, Father. It could happen to her, make no mistake."

Father O'Gara reached for the door handle. "I've got to go prepare for the next Mass." He pulled the door open and stepped into the dark nave.

"But Father —"

O'Gara's features receded into the shadows. "I'll make you a promise, Joe. If it goes that far, I'll stop it. I can, and I promise you I will."

Now just what the hell did that mean?

CHAPTER FIFTEEN

"Well if you won't come walkin' with me, I'll just have to walk with you, I suppose. But you can't take these now, can ya?" Liam O'Neill pushed a small bouquet of violets, perfectly matched to the sash of her dress, into Moira's hands.

"They're lovely, Liam."

Joseph stood at the parlor window, just out of sight, and watched them on the front steps of the boarding house. Moira pulled a few stems out of the bouquet and folded them between the rows of lace and pin tucks on her bodice, securing them with one of her hatpins. "Now, how do they look?"

"Like shriveled weeds. I tell ya', you have to stop showin' up the sunshine and flowers. It's not good for the morale of the other women of New York."

Moira dismissed this with a wave and handed the remaining flowers to Dennis, who sat on the front stoop beaming on the couple. "That tongue of yours is so coated in flattery, a sincere word couldn't find its way out of your mouth."

"And your ear doesn't recognize one when you hear it. I'm tellin' ya', Moira, I'm comin' for you one of these days, and it's goin' to be soon." He turned and winked at Dennis.

"When my hair is gray and my teeth are a memory? Thank you, but I'll not be waiting around for you while you build your houses of straw and castles in the air."

She turned to her father. "I don't know what time I'll be back, Dad. But since it's Sunday, the boarders know to take their supper out tonight anyway. I've left sandwiches in the icebox for you and Joseph."

"Don't worry about us," Dennis said. "Stay out as long as you like."

She adjusted her hat and pulled on a pair of gloves, speaking to Liam over her shoulder. "Now, if you're walking with me, you'd best come along. I don't want to be late."

"And what are we goin' to be late to, may I ask?"

"To tea."

"You're choosin' tea over me? Now I am hurt," he said.

Moira laughed. "Not just any tea. A political tea. For the Fusion ticket, but maybe I shouldn't be telling you that."

"Nothin' I'd like better than to see old Croker tossed from the Hall. Come along, then. Go have your tea with all those stuffy birds, Moira *Aroun,* but when you're fillin' your cup with cream, think of me."

Joseph watched them stroll, arm in arm, down the street. When they had turned the corner, he picked up his tools and the stepladder and joined his father outside.

"Liam was here. You just missed him."

"I saw him."

"Well, why the devil didn't you come out? He asks about you every time I see him."

He passed his father on the steps, opened the ladder below the parlor window and climbed up three rungs. "He's just blowing hot air, Dad. Besides, I saw him at church this morning, and at dinner several nights ago, remember? We said about all we have to say to each other then."

Joseph carefully tapped the grip of a screwdriver against the window until a piece of the broken pane chipped loose and fell into the parlor. He took a pair of pliers from his pocket and plucked at the edge of a remaining piece of glass, pulling it free and dropping it to the ground below.

"Why do you encourage him? Don't you know he'll just bring Moira to grief?"

Dennis tapped his crutch against the step and gazed down the street, as though Liam and Moira were still visible. "You can't even give him a minute of your time anymore. Why, Shosav? What's happened to ya'?"

"It's my fault, is it?" Joseph laid a slab of broken glass on the stoop and began teasing out the smaller shards that remained in the frame.

"He wants to see ya', but you run the other way."

"And you keep encouraging him to come back, even if I don't want to see him. Even if he's bad for Moira."

"She loves him, Shosav." Dennis shifted his weight off the stump of his severed leg. When he was settled, he took out his pipe and dug into his tobacco pouch. "You'd better make your peace with him. He's goin' to be around a lot, whether you like it or not." He struck a match to the bowl and drew several times on the pipe.

"Not if you tell her you disapprove of him."

"And why would I do that? He's like a son to me."

"Maybe more than the son you have, isn't that what you're really saying?"

"You sound like a whinin' schoolgirl, Shosav, and I just don't understand it. You were like brothers and now you want nothin' to do with him."

"It's not that I want nothing to do with him, Dad. I understand Liam — maybe better than you do. Yes, we were like brothers. Still are. But Cain and Abel were brothers, too, and look where it got them. I'll see him every night of the week and drink myself half to death in that pub of his, if that's what you want. But I want Moira to have nothing to do with him. He's no bloody good for her, and that's the truth. Do you want her to end up like poor Cecilia?"

"Don't bring Cecilia into this, Shosav. You know I never approved of the way Seamus treated his wife, but what could I do about it? Didn't I talk to him until I was all out of talk? Seamus was always pullin' the devil by the tail. He never could keep a job for long."

"Never could, or never would?"

Dennis shrugged. "Does it matter? Liam's different. He's got a good head on his shoulders and he's makin' a good livin' for himself. She'll never have to work. She'll have a cook and a daily, and the time to shop for fancy clothes."

"On Tammany money."

"Jaysus, Mary and Joseph! Sure they drink at the Ballyglass, and why wouldn't they? And why wouldn't he take their money, like any other payin' customer? He's got a good business for himself and he'll be able to give Moira the things she deserves."

"Happy lives are not built on fine china and big houses, Dad. He'll give her those things, all right. And leave her at home with them while he goes out drinking and gambling and whoring."

"You just won't give him a chance, will ya'?"

"I gave him plenty of chances, Dad. I gave him a chance to help Doreen before she ended up strangled in a brothel. I gave him a chance to search for Kevin, and God only knows what's happened to him, missing from the age of twelve."

"He's gone west. Sure Liam's right about that."

"And what if he's not? What if he's right here, in New York? What if Kevin's in trouble and needs help? Did Liam lift a finger to find his own brother? Too busy at the Ballyglass. Too busy taking care of Liam. And once he has her, he'll be too busy to take care of Moira."

Joseph dug the tip his screwdriver into the frame, trying to loosen a tenacious piece of putty, but it slipped, putting a deep gouge in the window frame. "Bloody hell," he muttered, attacking it with the pliers.

"You make him sound like the devil himself, but he does a lot of good. Saved two families from a tenement fire and found a third one a place to live and decent clothes to put on their backs. But you wouldn't know about that, because you'll never hear a good word about him."

"There's nothing good to say about any O'Neill, Dad. Cecilia was the only decent one in the lot of them — except for Kevin, and he was too young to judge. And now we'll never know, will we? Make Moira into an O'Neill and the best you can hope for is that Belleek and Waterford will bring her happiness, because Liam never will."

Dennis pulled his crutch up under his arm and struggled to his feet. "I won't listen to another word of this, Shosav. They love each other, and I'd trust him with my own life. When he asks for my blessin' on the marriage, he'll have it."

The glass in Joseph's pliers splintered. He hurled the tool to the ground and wheeled around on the ladder. "You give him your blessing to marry her. Go ahead, but I warn you, I'll never forgive you for it. Maybe that doesn't matter, though. Once she marries Liam O'Neill you'll have the son you always wanted. And God help you all."

■ ■ ■ ■

"The tea is sponsored by the Republican Women, although of course it's for the Fusion ticket, so there will be women of every political disposition there. Now if only we could vote," Rachel added.

They stood outside the Metropolitan Club. Rachel hadn't told Moira where the tea was to be held, but had instructed the cabbie to let them out at the corner of 59th Street. With the bruise on her knee still fresh, the walk of the last block was slightly uncomfortable, but it gave Moira time to take in the marble facade, columns, and main gate.

"Mr. Morgan's club? You mean it's here?" Moira said. She glanced around nervously, smoothed her dress and touched her hat. She started to unpin the violets, but Rachel stopped her.

"No, leave them. They're lovely with your dress." Rachel linked their arms and gently led her through the gate and into the courtyard. "It's very pretty, you know. And in perfect style."

"Miss Dove helped me make it," Moira said. "But are you sure it will be all right?"

They were met in the grand central hall

by a steward who gave Moira a quick but thorough inspection and seemed satisfied.

"The Fusion Tea?" Rachel said.

"In the Ladies' Dining Room, miss."

"You see?" Rachel whispered. "The steward thought you looked just right." She led Moira through a corridor, following the soft buzz of teatime chatter to the dining room. But Moira shrank back at the door.

"I can't —"

"Of course you can." Rachel took her wrist and gently pulled her into the room.

Moira stood in the doorway, her lips slightly parted. "Heavenly day, I've stepped onto a wedding cake," she whispered.

Rachel understood what she meant. It was a lovely room — the white plaster walls covered in lacy bas-relief of flowers, cameos, and columns. The customary tables had been removed and replaced by dainty damask chairs in small groupings. At the end of the room stood a low table, covered in starched linen, bearing several large, silver tea services. A china platter was stacked with petits fours, iced in pastel colors, like small gift boxes waiting to be opened. Beside them stood a silver platter of strawberry tarts and three cut-crystal cake stands, each bearing a layer cake. Three carefully unobtrusive waiters, who might have blended into the plaster had it not been for their shiny black hair, served tea and pastries to women in immense, flowery hats and, here and there, a man with a bowler tucked under his arm.

Rachel had been to the club many times since her debut. In fact, it was in this very room that she had decided, at the age of eighteen, that she must find something more worthy to do with her life than make endless rounds of luncheons, teas, and shopping tours with companions whose principal interests lay in who had joined or left the ranks of Mrs. Astor's four hundred. She'd entered Barnard College that fall, while her fellow debutantes went on to make "good" marriages and form the roster of the next four hundred.

"Come along and we'll get some tea," she said to Moira. "And I shall introduce you to some of the women." Rachel wound her arm through Moira's and turned her toward the tea table, just in time to see Mrs. Bradley Martin flying in her direction. She wore a dress of dove gray and a matching hat topped with a nest of feathers. Her stout figure was even more pigeon-breasted than the fashion. She swooped down on the two young women, her gloved talons wrapped around the arm of a short, florid gentleman.

"Oh Lord, here comes the UnderAstor." If she'd known that insufferable woman was going to be here, she'd have thought twice about coming. Why wasn't she in Europe or, better yet, sinking on her yacht in the middle of the Atlantic?

"Rachel, my dear, it has been too long."

"Hello, Mrs. Martin. How is Cornelia?"

"The viscount and countess are quite well, thank you. They're traveling at the moment."

Rachel could barely hide her amusement. Viscount indeed. The fourth earl of Craven and viscount of Uffington was little more than a crude farm boy looking to upholster his title with someone else's wealth. Cornelia Martin's parents had more than enough, and her mother was thrilled to barter a substantial portion of it for her sixteen-year-old daughter's place in British society. Rachel considered them all proof conclusive that neither rank nor money conveyed refinement

"In fact, I'd like to introduce you to a dear friend of theirs — Captain Arthur Vine. Captain Vine is the former British attaché. He's come back to us for the America's Cup. You might recall seeing him at Cornelia's wedding."

The attaché made a small, stiff bow.

"Wonderful to meet you," he said, gazing over her head and around the room.

Mrs. Bradley Martin turned an appraising eye on Moira. "Aren't you going to introduce your friend, my dear?"

Rachel turned to Moira first, deliberately flouting convention. "Moira Hannegan, this is Mrs. Bradley Martin and Captain Arthur Vine."

Mrs. Martin did not miss the snub. "Hannegan? An Irish name, isn't it? Is she, perhaps, a relation to your Miss Garrity?" she asked, with a malicious little smile.

Rachel felt the small, upswept hairs on her neck tingle. "Irene is fine, and thank you for asking. As to your question, Miss Hannegan is a friend of mine. We share similar interests."

"Ah, I see," said Mrs. Bradley Martin. "You've met at the immigration station, I suppose. I must say I'm surprised you have the stamina to come out on Sundays, working all week as you do. Six days, is it?"

"Yes, Mrs. Martin, six days a week, just like ninety percent of the working world. But I don't suppose you know a great deal about work."

The older woman gave her a superior smile, failing to recognize that Rachel had not meant it as a commendation. She turned to Captain Vine as if she were an actress and her script required an aside.

"Our Rachel is a reformer, Captain Vine. She works at the Ellis Island Immigration Station, you know. Her uncle, Matthew, is quite the freethinker, but we're fond of him anyway." This captured Captain Vine's interest.

"In what capacity are you employed, Miss Bonner?"

"As a matron. I translate occasionally, but mainly I work with the detained women. Actually, I work under Miss Hannegan's brother, who is the Superintendent. And we have found that we share an interest in politics — especially in the Fusion ticket."

"Ah," Mrs. Martin said, sweeping her gaze over Moira with undisguised distaste. "And you a bridg— that is, an Irish woman. One would think that you, of all people, would be supporting Tammany Hall."

Moira stiffened. "We are not all scoundrels and thieves, Mrs. Martin. Nor are we all uneducated laborers just looking for fair treatment, and going where we must to find it."

"Mmm, I see. Quite," Mrs. Martin said, dismissing her. She had aimed and fired her most pointed remarks and was ready to move on to a new target. "If you'll excuse me, I should be visiting with the other guests. We get over to the States so infrequently now."

"Quite," Rachel said. "Don't let us keep you."

"A pleasure meetin' ya, ma'am," Moira said, affecting her thickest accent. "If yer hirin', I might like to come 'round to apply for a position. A day maid, ya' know. What do ya pay?"

Mrs. Bradley Martin colored darkly. "Really, Rachel," she spat. "You might think about Matthew's reputation before you bring just *anyone* into the club. Come along Captain Vine."

Captain Vine, however, did not follow. Apparently relieved to be set free of her, he lingered with the young women, tugged on his celluloid collar and gazed into the crowd. At length he turned to Rachel.

"Your work sounds quite interesting, actually. Is it not dangerous?"

Rachel thought back to Teresa Bastitelli, for a moment. "Not really, not when you try to understand the women and their fears. You must remember that many of them are separated from their companions and families. They don't know what will happen to them, and they don't speak English, so they feel powerless. It can

222

become tense at times, but I wouldn't say dangerous."

"But what about the shooting, Miss Bonner?"

Rachel felt herself stepping onto shifting ground. The Superintendent had said the shooting was not to be discussed, and yet she couldn't very well deny that it had happened when Vine obviously knew about it. His expression was attentive and expectant. "Shooting, Captain Vine?"

"Of the anarchist. You must know about it," he said, rather impatiently. He glanced at Moira, then lowered his voice and leaned toward Rachel. "A young Irish woman shot her companion on the dock."

"Yes, I am aware of it, although it doesn't involve me."

"But you must know something about it, unless shootings are everyday occurrences at your station. Did they catch the other man?"

This struck a discordant note. "I assure you, Captain Vine, shootings are hardly common. In fact, I can't recall another one. And now if you'll excuse us, I haven't introduced Miss Hannegan to any of my friends, and I believe Mrs. Martin is looking for you."

Captain Vine accepted the rebuff and

returned to his stiff bow. "A pleasure to meet you ladies. I do hope we'll see each other again."

"Quite," Moira quipped, adding under her breath to Rachel, "Bloody crumpet stuffer."

"I'm sorry," Rachel said, when they were out of earshot of Mrs. Martin and her captain. "It was selfish of me to ask you to come. I had no idea that old vulture would be there. She has no more interest in politics than she has in . . . in. . . ."

"Good manners?"

Rachel laughed. "Exactly. The truth is, I didn't want to come here alone. I don't fit in with these women, and I never have. But since I am here, I suppose I must do what I came here to do — talk about my uncle's views and why these women should try to influence their husbands to vote for him. Since most of them take their political views from their husbands in the first place, it does seem as though we are all wasting a perfectly good Sunday afternoon." Rachel shrugged. "But waste we must. Come along, and I'll introduce you to the least free-thinking women in New York."

"Well, most of them are cordial enough. I've a feeling that Mrs. Martin resents you for some reason."

"The resentment is mutual, I assure you.

It goes back a few years, to my debutante season," she explained.

The season she was to come out, Mrs. Martin had taken it upon herself to shepherd Rachel through the round of luncheons, dress fittings, and balls. Irene Garrity was the closest thing Rachel had to a mother, but she was not good enough for Mrs. Bradley Martin. As Matthew Bonner had no sisters or cousins to step in, Mrs. Martin had felt it her duty to relieve Irene of the pleasures of Rachel's season, making made it clear that there would be no Irish housekeepers fiddling with the wrong fork or spoon in the Ladies' Dining Room of the Metropolitan Club.

"I didn't make it easy for her," Rachel concluded, "and I've never regretted it."

Moira sat quietly during the return cab ride, gazing out the side window of the hansom at Brooks Brothers and Paul J. Bonwit, Lord and Taylor, and Arnold Constable. Rachel could only guess what she was thinking, and privately berated herself for poor judgment. The abrasion on her knee stung, but her conscience smarted more. She had embarrassed Moira, although it had not been her intention. Hoping Moira would enjoy the afternoon, she had not counted on the appearance of Mrs. Bradley Martin, self-appointed doyenne of New York society. Moira could not have felt equal to the occasion with the imposing Mrs. Martin to suggest to her that she was not. Rachel longed to reassure Moira that in the company of ladies she stood head and shoulders above the regular members of the Metropolitan Club. But to do so would be to invoke Shakespeare's Gertrude who "doth protest too much." Better to keep silent than to add injury to Mrs. Martin's insults.

"Do you know that the National Council of Women is going to be meeting in Buffalo during the Exposition?" she said.

"Yes, I read about that. Wouldn't you like to be there?"

"I would, but even if we can't be, we can still let Miss Anthony know how we feel. She's coming through New York on her way to Buffalo, and there's to be a rally at City Hall. I know I made a mess of this today, but would you consider going with me anyway? I'd really like to hear what she has to say."

"I'll meet you at City Hall with my placard in hand." Moira put a reassuring hand over Rachel's. "Miss Bonner, let me explain something to you. When you're Irish, you get accustomed to the slights. Even in nursing school it was difficult, with some of the other girls thinking I had no right to be there. A few of them even doubted that any hospital would hire an Irish nurse. I've always thought the 'No Irish Need Apply' stories were very much overstated, and I still do, but what I've learned is that they don't need signs. They let you know in other ways. Most of those women were very gracious. There are Mrs. Martins everywhere to test our patience and our manners. We just put on our social armor and prepare to do battle."

Rachel liked the expression. Her social armor.

CHAPTER SIXTEEN

Joseph sat at his desk the next morning, the copies of witness statements before him. He had separated them into two stacks as he read — one of *Cymric* passengers, the other, station employees — hoping, somehow, that they would provide him with a complete picture of what had happened both on the ship and the morning of the shooting. Instead, they had raised more questions.

Rosaleen Donnelly said that Maggie Flynn and Michael Finnegan were lovers on their way to America to marry. He was a bit standoffish with the other passengers, she said, but affectionate toward the girl. Maeve Daly thought they were both very much in love, but Maggie had confessed to her that they were not planning to stay in America long. Mrs. Daly thought they should be married before they took a wedding trip. John Boyle didn't like Michael Finnegan. "Secretive" was the way he had described him. When not with Maggie Flynn, he'd spent most of his time with another man. They didn't mix in with the others much, he said, didn't join in games of Forty-five or the endless discussions of Home Rule and Irish politics. Boyle did not know the other man's name. After all, weren't there almost a thousand people in steerage?

Some of them had seen only the result of the shooting — Finnegan lying in a pool of blood on the dock, Maggie with a small gun in her hand. Johnny Cullen had seen her pull the gun out of her sleeve. Kathleen O'Brien had heard them whispering just before they landed. She thought Maggie was upset and Finnegan was angry. But absolutely no one thought that Michael Finnegan had mistreated Maggie Flynn either aboard ship or after landing, and not one of them had the slightest idea why the girl had shot him.

The statements of Ellis Island employees were no more enlightening. Before the shooting, the groupers and gatemen had been busy herding the aliens toward the Great Hall, helping lone women with baggage, answering questions. Afterward, it was all they could do to establish order, and after all, the police and the doctor were on the scene so quickly they had not needed to do more than that. No one could identify the doctor. The two watchmen who had detained Maggie Flynn said she had come with them docilely, all the while abstractedly watching as the doctor and cops worked over Finnegan's body.

Joseph picked up another affidavit, this one from one of the station's janitors. Joseph knew that Fotis Apostolou spoke a very broken sort of English. Nevertheless, his recollections were clear and factual. More to the point, Apostolou had helped the doctor and the cops load the patient into the police cutter.

Joseph dropped the statement on top of the employee stack and placed a call down to the Chief of the Janitorial Division. "Send your man Apostolou up to me at once." He dropped the receiver onto the phone box and sat back in his chair. Finally, someone might be able to tell him something he didn't already know.

"They've come for the Flynn girl."

Over the shoulder of Julius Conrad, Chief of the Deporting Division, Rachel could see two police officers. One looked down at his feet. The other had his back turned to her and softly jingled a pair of handcuffs in his left hand while he rocked on his heels. Rachel stepped out of Maggie's room and closed the door.

"Did the Superintendent order her released to them?"

Conrad glanced back at the cops, but neither of them met Rachel's gaze. "They say he called the Police Commissioner's office to have her picked up."

But he'd said nothing to her about it, which Rachel thought was decidedly odd. In fact, she hadn't seen him yet this morning, but surely he would have come to tell her if Maggie were being moved. "And you verified this with the Super?"

"No, but —"

"Ma'am?" The officer with the handcuffs had turned around and faced her. "We're on duty. We don't have time to go over our orders with everyone in the place. We need to get the girl and be on our way." He started to push past her, his hand almost reaching the doorknob. Rachel stepped into his path.

"Lock the door, please, Mr. Archer."

The watchman hesitated a breath — too long for Rachel. She pulled out his key ring, on its retractable cord, and turned it in the lock. The men stared at her, their jaws hanging in astonishment. Archer, after a moment's indecision, took his place next to her and crossed his arms.

"Now," she said, "if you'll come this way I'll take you to the Superintendent's office. I'll take care of this, Mr. Conrad," she said, turning to the Deportation Chief. "I know you have a full schedule this morning."

The men lingered a second longer before following her down the corridor past the Registry Room and into the Superintendent's office on their right. Joseph was at his desk, poring over witness affidavits. Rachel delivered the policemen with a perfunctory explanation and returned to the witness room to check on Maggie.

He had called the Commissioner's office — that much was true. But that had been two days ago. No one had contacted him since then to inform him that Michael Finnegan, or his mortal remains, had been located. Joseph rose and walked around to the front of his desk.

"And where is Finnegan now?"

"In the morgue, sir. Died of a gunshot wound to the stomach, they say. I'm told there was a score of witnesses to the shooting."

"Yes. You'll need their statements, I suppose. I have them right here, but I'll have to have them copied and sent to police headquarters. Where will you take the girl, Ludlow Street? She should go to a federal jail."

The cops glanced at each other before one of them gave up an answer. "Ludlow's full, sir. With the Tombs not yet rebuilt, it's going to have to be Blackwell's Island."

Joseph supposed he should feel relieved to be turning the girl over to someone else to worry about. But he didn't. He still had too many unanswered questions. At the top of his list was why the girl was being picked up by city cops instead of federal marshals. And he wasn't sure how a girl like Maggie Flynn was going to fare at Blackwell's Island, home to whores who'd as soon cut your throat as shag you, and every other kind of criminal from petty thieves to child molesters and murderers. Maggie was going to be eaten alive there. Still, he couldn't very well refuse to let her go. She had committed a very serious crime, and a man was slabbed at the morgue because of her. She had brought this on herself.

"Well, Officer . . . what is your name?"

"Mackey, sir."

"All right, Officer Mackey, I'll have to fill out a couple of forms for you to sign before I can release her to you. Have a seat," Joseph said, pointing to a pair of chairs in front of his desk. "I'll get those forms and be back in just a minute."

Joseph left the two cops in his office and hurried next door to McNabb's office. The Assistant Commissioner was tied up with Boarding Division hearings this morning, and the office was empty. Joseph removed the forms from the filing cabinet and turned to leave, but hesitated in the doorway. Something about this was decidedly odd. He pushed the door around, leaving only a crack through which he could see the corridor, went to McNabb's desk and picked up the telephone.

"Central?" he said. "Ring up the New York City Police Morgue."

When he hung up the phone, he had more questions than answers. One thing was certain. No one was removing Maggie Flynn from his custody until he was satisfied that all was in order. Joseph emerged from McNabb's office just in time to see the cops hurrying through the door to the southeast stairway. Fotis Apostolou was standing in the hall.

"Wait a minute!"

"Can't wait," one of them called over his shoulder. "We'll be back for her."

The cops darted out of sight, leaving the door swinging behind them. Joseph hurried up the hall. "I think don't like I remember them," Fotis said.

"Remember them?"

"*Neh,* these police," Fotis said. "They take man."

Joseph stared at the janitor for a second before Apostolou's remark made its impact. "Stop them!"

Both men lunged for the stairwell, Joseph preceding Apostolou by several steps. The door below had just slammed its frame, reverberating in the narrow enclosure. Near the bottom, Apostolou vaulted over the railing and hit the door, emerging in the front vestibule. A crowd of newly landed immigrants was moving through the main entrance. Apostolou fought his way against the mob past a gateman directing passengers to the baggage room. Behind him, Joseph grabbed the grouper.

"Come on," he said. "I need your help."

Mackey was already in a cutter working on the engine while the other cop cast off their line. He leapt into the boat and pushed off the dock. The engine fired to life.

"Hold it," Joseph yelled. "You two — stop right there."

Apostolou raced across the dock, stopping only long enough to pull off his shoes. He was on the edge, poised to dive when Jo-

235

seph's arm shot out to stop him. "It's all right, let them go. You can't stop them now anyway."

"I swim good," Fotis protested.

Joseph pointed at the cutter. It was already in the ferry slip, and another ferry was moving in to dock. "I'm afraid we're too late."

"They say 'no,' they not the cops pick him up. But I know was. I am very good remembering." Fotis Apostolou took the seat that Joseph offered him.

"Other thing," he continued. "The boat — not harbor police."

"Yes, I noticed that myself. And you're absolutely sure that they are the same officers who picked up the victim?"

"*Neh,* very sure, Superintendent."

"How about the doctor? Would you remember him if you saw him?"

Fotis scratched his chin, where a blue shadow of stubble was already appearing. "I think yes. I do remember doctor. Tall and thin. With *to moustaki* and hair starts here," he said, brushing his hand back from the top of his crown to indicate a receding hairline.

"Was he wearing a uniform?"

He was. According to Apostolou, he was dressed in the khaki uniform of jodhpurs and stovepipe boots worn by the medical service. George Rockwell had interviewed every physician in his service and reported to Joseph first thing that morning. No one admitted to having treated the gunshot victim on the dock or known where the victim had been taken. Rockwell acknowledged, however, that occasionally a new doctor in the Marine Hospital Service was sent to the station to observe. Although it was unlikely, one of them could have slipped past him, especially if he had just arrived when the shooting took place.

Joseph picked up the typed copy of Apostolou's statement and read back through it quickly.

"So you packed the victim's suitcase. Where did you put it?"

"I move to door. Then I help police and doctor."

"And after that, where did you take the suitcase?"

Fotis frowned. "I don't take nowhere. Gone when I come back. I think a baggage handler has pick it up."

"We can't find it, Mr. Apostolou."

Fotis's frown deepened. "This is bad thing."

Joseph sighed. "It's a mess, that's what it is." He glanced back down at Apostolou's statement.

"If you helped them load Finnegan onto the police boat, that certainly gave you plenty of time to remember their faces." He tossed the statement back onto his desk impatiently and gazed toward his window, speaking as much to himself as to the janitor. "But where did they come from? And where did the doctor come from?"

"This doctor — I see him before," Fotis said.

"Before? Here at the station?"

"No, not at station every day, every day. That morning only. He take break, smoke cigarette."

Joseph sat forward with renewed interest "I want you to tell me everything you remember, Mr. Apostolou. Every single detail."

When the janitor had finished his story, Joseph thought that he knew more. He just wasn't sure what, exactly, he had learned. The janitor had told the same story that everyone else had, of seeing the girl pull out the gun and shoot her companion. He had seen the boat arrive with two policemen in it, although he was no longer sure it was an official harbor patrol boat. But he was absolutely sure that they were the same two cops who had appeared at the station this morning. And he had seen the doctor, just a few minutes before the shooting, taking a break to smoke. The janitor had been sweeping around the powerhouse and kitchen when the doctor appeared, coming from the northwest side of the island. Apostolou thought that he had been down at the water cooling off. He had deduced this from the fact that the doctor was putting on his jacket as he walked toward the Main Arrivals building.

And that was entirely possible. All the staff took breaks between arrivals and many of them went outside to smoke since, after the fire in 1897 burned the original station to the ground, smoking was now prohibited inside. While the northwest seawall was not the most convenient place to go to cool down, it wasn't out of reason either. But it was an odd place to go to smoke, as the incinerator was there and the odor of garbage could be suffocating. It was also a very secluded spot, which meant that there might not be another witness to corroborate Apostolou's statement.

Joseph had called the police morgue from McNabb's office. They had no record of receiving Michael Finnegan. However, they did have two unidentified knifings and a gunshot wound to the chest, all of which had come in yesterday. A bullet in the chest could have been mistaken for an abdominal wound. And if these cops had been the ones to pick up Finnegan in the first place, they would have recognized the body. They probably wouldn't have known the victim's name, unless he had been able to tell them. But his condition might have been too grave. He might not have been conscious. But why had the cops run away this morning? For that matter, why did they deny having picked up Finnegan in the first place?

Joseph reviewed what he knew — the doctor no one could find but who might be an observer, the police who had arrived in an unmarked cutter and run away without waiting for their prisoner, the body in the morgue which might be Finnegan if every witness had mistaken a chest wound for an abdominal wound. Irregularities, any one of which, taken individually, might be plausible. Together, they shaped up to something else.

CHAPTER SEVENTEEN

By the end of the day, Joseph Hannegan was in a very bad temper. He had spent the remainder of the morning and most of the afternoon testifying before McNabb's investigating committee as to what had occurred with Ernesto Sapelli. The committee was made up of four men — McNabb, Chief of Registry Lederman, Registry Inspector Crater, and Commissioner Thomas Fitchie, who had returned early from his vacation to sit in on the hearings. Joseph had never been sure whether Fitchie was truly corrupt, or merely weak and incompetent. The hearings had not clarified the matter for him.

One thing he knew — the apples at the top of the barrel were rotten, and they were slowly spoiling all the rest. Not every inspector, clerk, or privilege holder at the station was corrupt. But in an atmosphere where graft and coercion were allowed, even encouraged to proliferate, it was hard for the most upright of men to keep their jobs without sacrificing their integrity. Powderly's appointment had given Joseph a special immunity to the pressure. McNabb knew very well why Joseph had been given the job of Superintendent. Joseph thought that McNabb must expend a good bit of energy trying to outwit him. The truth was, Joseph did spend a lot of his time trying to maneuver around the Assistant Commissioner. It was like a champion chess game, with all the station's employees and immigrants as pawns. But he didn't much care for chess.

"Now let me see if I understand you correctly, Superintendent," Fitchie had said. "You're saying that Mr. Sapelli's offer of a bribe is not an isolated incident."

"That is correct, sir."

"And on what do you base your opinion? Have you been offered bribes by other stewards or ship's representatives?"

"I am not a boarding inspector, Commissioner."

"Then how are you in a position to know?"

"Commissioner, I have received numerous reports and complaints from passengers who were approached by steamship employees and told that they could buy citizenship papers allowing them to land without

242

going through inspection. I have made it a point to inform Mr. McNabb, and I assumed that he had kept you apprised of the complaints."

McNabb glared at Joseph, but addressed himself to Fitchie. "I have read Mr. Hannegan's reports and made some inquiries about the complaints, Commissioner, and have determined that they are without foundation. There seemed to be no point in bothering you with unsubstantiated rumors."

"I see," Fitchie said, shifting in his chair. "Well, Mr. Hannegan, as you well know, ninety percent of the complaints we receive are from disgruntled immigrants who don't like the way we handled some aspect of their landing. They'd like nothing better than to create a few problems for us if we so much as detain a family member or try to treat their sick. I'm afraid I can't take these reports too seriously. Now if you have information from station employees —"

McNabb sat forward attentively. "Yes, Hannegan, how about that? Do you have affidavits from other inspectors or interpreters?"

Here, of course, was the quandary. There were honest inspectors on the island — plenty of them — but most of them could not afford to jeopardize their jobs by coming forward with information. And their jobs would be in jeopardy, for McNabb could be ruthless if he felt betrayed. Joseph had tried to convey, subtly, that he would protect their jobs, but he could not risk divulging Powderly's purpose for him unless he was certain that he could provide irrefutable evidence of McNabb's collusion in corrupt practices. Both McNabb and Fitchie had powerful friends. If Joseph's position were to become public knowledge, it could cause Powderly problems in the Treasury Department. At the very least, there would be an outcry in the press and no one, not even Joseph, wanted that.

He had come to realize that no outside observer, no matter how close, could ever understand the complexities of managing hundreds of aliens every day. The press only heard about, only cared about, the hard cases — the split families, rejections, and deportations. Never mind that the great majority were passed through the station quickly and helped, as much as possible, by a great bureaucracy which, fundamentally, did have their best interests at heart. If there were anything on which he and McNabb agreed, it was that station problems had to be handled internally and with delicacy. So far, McNabb had managed to outwit him, but one day he would slip up. Joseph would be waiting for him.

"No," Joseph said, "I don't have any affidavits from inspectors."

He had lost this round, but the match was far from over. Meanwhile, he still had to deal with the problem of Maggie Flynn. Only one thing had gone right today. He had found Rachel's Mr. Dylan. His name was Dylan Moran, and his destination had been a familiar address — 207 Rivington Street.

"Right in here, Maggie," the matron said, gently pushing her into the Superintendent's office. Mr. Hannegan was waiting for them, seated behind his desk, flipping through piles of typewritten pages.

"Deportation orders," he said, setting them aside. He pointed to one of the chairs in front of his desk. "Have a seat, Miss Flynn. I asked Miss Bonner to stay late today while I talk to you. I hope I will not have detained her without cause."

Maggie perched on the edge of the chair, keeping her back ramrod straight. She mustn't let them see how frightened she was. She couldn't eat, couldn't sleep. She had begun to doubt that she would ever leave this place. "Isle of tears," she'd heard Johnny Cullen call it, and so it had been for her. She waited for the Superintendent to continue.

"All right, Miss Flynn," Joseph said. He rose from his chair and walked around the desk to stand in front of her, his arms folded across his chest. "We'd like you to tell us about Dylan Moran."

Maggie waited for him to go on. When he didn't, she said, "I don't know anyone by that name, Mr. Hannegan."

The Superintendent did not like her answer. He flexed the muscles in his jaw and glared at her. "Miss Flynn, I have had a very long day and my patience is at an end. We know that Moran traveled with Finnegan, and we know that he is concerned about what has happened to you. Now, I want you to tell me who he is and where he's gone."

Her heart leapt. "He's worryin' about what's happened to me?" But that did her no good, of course, if she didn't even know who he was.

The matron took the seat next to her. "He met me at the ferry, Maggie, and asked me to bring you a message."

"But I don't know him, Miss Bonner. I swear I don't."

246

The Superintendent sighed impatiently and rubbed his face with his hands. "Describe him, Miss Bonner." She did.

The young man from Galway. Of course! "Ah," she said, "now I know who you're talkin' about. But I never met him before we got on the ship. He was travelin' in the steerage. I talked to him a little now and again. Is he in trouble?"

"What did you talk about?"

"Mrs. Daly. She was worryin' about her arthritis, and whether it would keep her from comin' through. He said he thought it would be fine. There are ways to get around those things, he said."

"For example?"

Maggie glanced over at Rachel. "I . . . I don't know. He didn't tell me."

They stood over her, watching her every move and analyzing every word that came out of her mouth. Give nothing away, she told herself, and stared down at her boots, concealing her face as best she could. But the Superintendent had said the young man from Galway — Moran, was it? — had been traveling with Cormac. It couldn't be true. She would have known. He would have told her! And yet . . . something nagged at her. *Promise me,* he had said to her on the ship, and again in her nightmare. Why had he warned her to take care of herself unless he had known that something would happen?

Her mind went back to the ship and the way Moran had lingered in the background, always close, haunting her like a spirit or a guardian angel. The air between them, Cormac and Dylan, always seemed charged with some spark, some tension she couldn't quite fathom. She'd thought Cormac was jealous of the young man from Galway who seemed to admire her, but she knew now that there was something else between them, something she hadn't understood then, and didn't understand now. She glanced up into the expectant faces of the matron and Superintendent.

"Is he in trouble?"

The Superintendent tapped his fingers on his desktop. "Quite probably, yes. But not as much as you are, Miss Flynn. The police came for you this morning."

"Yes?" Maggie leaned forward, her pulse racing. "Am I to go with them?"

Hannegan frowned. "No. I sent them away."

He'd sent them away. Her last hope of escaping this place. Maggie felt her throat tightening. I will not cry, she told herself and managed a single word. "Oh."

"But surely you don't want to go with them. Do you know what's waiting for you out there, Miss Flynn?"

Maggie could only shake her head. She felt the Superintendent's patience snap. He took her by the arm and pulled her out of her chair, briskly walking her to the window behind him. Beyond them, the city had fallen into darkness. The moon, as they watched, faded behind an ominous bank of leaden clouds.

"Look out there, Miss Flynn. Do you see New York?" She nodded silently.

"We have a prison here, Miss Flynn. It's called Blackwell's Island. I'll be escorting you there myself. It's as bad a place as ever you'll see. Rats and whores, murderers and thieves —"

"Superintendent —" He cut off the matron with a wave of his hand.

"Believe me when I tell you, you've never seen the like of it in Drumcliffe, Maggie. Think of the worst person you've ever known. Make him ten times worse, then multiply him by hundreds. And those," he said, "are the guards."

"The guards," she whispered. "Men?"

The Superintendent spared her no mercy. "Some of them, yes, and not New York's finest."

She felt the floor tilt under her feet and her knees begin to give way. He caught her before she could fall and guided her into a chair. *Cormac, I tried, I tried.* But she could no longer hold back the tears. They came a flood, as if some outside force of nature were acting upon her. She let them overtake her, wracking her with sobs, streaming even from her nose and mouth. They didn't understand, couldn't understand.

Above her, the Superintendent watched her with a surprised, helpless expression. How very like a man. Faithless creatures, they were. The matron emptied her pockets on the desk before coming up with a handkerchief for her. Maggie took it gratefully, blew her nose and wiped her eyes with the back of her hands.

"Maggie girl," he said softly. "Don't throw your life away. Tell me why you shot him, and what Dylan Moran has to do with it."

Maggie mutely gnawed on her thumb. Miss Bonner pulled her hair back away from her face, gently, the way her mother might have, and the weight of missing her family descended upon her in fresh tears.

"You have to help yourself, Maggie," the matron said. "There's no one else to do it for you."

"I can't," she cried softly. "If I must go to

prison, then I must. There's nothing else for it."

They let her cry until there were no tears left in her, and waited for her to tell them what she could not tell them. At length she stood up, smoothed her skirt and squared her shoulders. "Please, take me back to my room now."

Rachel returned to Joseph's office when she had seen Maggie settled back in her room and gotten her a dinner tray. The Superintendent had been too rough with her. He'd been trying to scare the girl into talking, Rachel knew, but his efforts had miscarried. She was more withdrawn than ever. Rachel could have cut her own tongue out for reminding Maggie that she had no one to help her. It had only seemed to harden the girl's resolve.

She found Joseph standing next to his desk, a stained rag in his hands. It had come from her pocket. "The shirt," she said.

He glanced up at her and back down at the rag. "The shirt we found in the flat on Rivington Street. They tore it when they grabbed it away from me. I'd forgotten about it."

Joseph walked over to the window and held it to the light. The stain was scarlet —

a deep, rich red, like the color of fresh blood. "Well, divil my soul," he said, softly.

"Sir?"

"It wasn't blood at all, Miss Bonner. This is an ink stain."

"But why would his shirt be covered with . . . Oh! I see," she said. "Red ink looks like blood."

"But it doesn't stain like blood," Joseph said slowly. "Blood turns a rusty brown when it dries. And this is bright red. Do you know what that means?"

Rachel dropped into the chair, staring at him. "It explains a great deal, doesn't it? Her unwillingness to help herself. Her refusal to talk about why she did it. She never shot him at all. It was —"

"All a ruse, Miss Bonner. Michael Finnegan is alive. In fact, I'd wager one of those two men who knocked us about the other night was Finnegan himself."

Rachel nodded. "And the other one was probably Dylan Moran."

Moran, she thought. She had wanted to tell the Superintendent something about Dylan Moran. What was it? She'd thought of it this morning, but then he had been in the Boarding Division hearings. She'd been thinking about Moira and the Fusion Tea.

"Superintendent," she said, sitting forward

suddenly. "Do you know a Captain Arthur Vine?"

Joseph glanced absently at her over his shoulder, then returned his attention to the rag. "British attaché, wasn't he? Never met him."

"Does he have any contact with the station?"

"Not that I know of. Why?"

"Because he knew about the shooting. He asked me about it at the Tea."

"Well, it has been in the newspapers, Miss Bonner."

"But no mention was made of Moran, was it, sir?"

"No one knows about Dylan Moran but you and me, and Maggie Flynn."

"On the contrary, Superintendent. Captain Vine asked me about 'the other man.' He may not know his name, but he knows there was another man involved. Do you suppose he's connected with this somehow?"

Joseph tossed the rag on his desk and sat back down, gazing over her shoulder with a preoccupied expression. After a moment, he shook his head. "Arthur Vine is friend to no Irishman. He even dislikes John Redmond, the Irish M.P., and many think he's more Sassenach than Gael. No, I don't think he'd dirty his hands in anything involving the Irish. Perhaps he was just testing the waters with you, Miss Bonner. Trying to find out more about the shooting, maybe looking for something he could use to make us — that is, the Irish — look bad."

"Perhaps," Rachel said, although she was far from convinced.

Joseph picked up the rag and turned it over in his hands. "There must be a plan to get her off the island, but I don't see how. It would take a lot of men, unless. . . ." He looked up at Rachel and went on slowly. He seemed to be trying out the words, seeing if they made sense, and deciding that they did. "Unless they planned to have the police remove her."

But Rachel was not thinking about the police. She was remembering her conversation with Captain Vine. " 'The one who shot the anarchist' — that's the other thing he said!"

"What are you talking about, Miss Bonner?"

"Captain Vine referred to Maggie as 'the one who shot the anarchist.' He called Finnegan an anarchist. Isn't that strange?"

Joseph sat very still. "On the contrary, Rachel," he said softly. "It's the first thing about this incident that really makes sense."

It was all beginning to come together. Like an Impressionist painting, it was difficult to grasp the whole if they just looked at the paint daubs individually. But standing back, looking at them all, the picture began to take shape. If an anarchist wanted to get into the United States, if he had no choice but to travel by major steamship line, and therefore be processed through Ellis Island, what could he do to avoid inspectors who might well recognize his description, even if he traveled under a false name? He could be shot, and taken away to a hospital before he ever entered the Great Hall. And if he had a traveling companion, his suitcase might be picked up by that companion and carried through processing, to be returned on the other side of the Golden Door. Indeed, it made a great deal of sense.

CHAPTER EIGHTEEN

Joseph set the telephone back in its cradle. "I caught Jenkins on his way out. He says there are no lookout orders posted at the Barge Office. He hasn't seen one in months."

"Is that possible?" Rachel said.

"Possible, but not probable." Joseph pushed away from his desk. "Let's make a visit to the Boarding Office."

Downstairs, all was quiet. Despite the fact that Joseph frequently stayed at the station into the evening, he was always struck by the stark silence of nighttime, so unlike the daytime pandemonium. Baggage handlers and registry clerks were gone. The railroad waiting room, always a lively hub during the day, yawned like a dark and empty cave. Across the corridor, the Boarding Office was dark. He unlocked the door and threw on the light.

"Where do we begin?"

Joseph surveyed the office in disgust. On the right, a bank of filing cabinets lined the walls, their tops shingled with brown folders waiting to be filed. Likewise, the Boarding Chief's desk was scarcely visible under heaps of papers, envelopes, and files. The only clear space in the room was the clerk's small desk, neatly arranged around a large black typewriter.

"No wonder the Boarding Division is in such a confounded mess," he said. "The only thing they seem to keep up with are their bribes."

He picked up a folder on the desk and flipped through it. "Cattlemen's certificates for the last three months. Unfiled." Another file held reports on detained cabin aliens for the week. "The Information Division should have these every day. How are we going to keep up with all these people if no one ever reports them?"

Rachel had begun perusing the folders on top of the cabinets. "I might as well file these as I go. At least that will put a little order to the place," she said.

They worked for an hour, Joseph stabbing the silence with the occasional oath as he detected another duty left undone. "Some of these reports go all the way back to April," Rachel said. "Citizens' certificates."

"Let me see those."

She handed the file over to him. They appeared to be in order, but then, that was hardly surprising. They were simple enough to falsify. "I'd wager that better than half of these are fabricated, but it would take months to prove it. I'll hold onto it anyway, just in case I run out of work," he added with a sardonic smile.

Rachel managed to put the files to rights fairly quickly, but the task of clearing the Boarding Chief's desk was considerably more involved, if only because the clutter had to be separated before it could be organized. "It's a one-man job," he said, dropping a torn envelope into the trash. "When I get it all separated, I'll probably need your help going through it, though."

Rachel took a seat at the clerk's desk and rolled a sheet of paper into the typewriter. "I can't, for the life of me, imagine how they learn to do this quickly," she said, carefully poking at the keys. "The letters are arranged so randomly."

"I understand that originally the keys were laid out in alphabetical order, but they came together too quickly and jammed. With this arrangement, the typist has to reach around on the keyboard, and that slows the process down."

They lapsed back into a silence punctured only by the occasional clack of a typewriter key. At length, even that stopped. Joseph looked up to find Rachel slumped over the desk, her head cradled on arms folded on top of the machine. She had been at work for almost fifteen hours now. McNabb had taken the station's launch to the Battery, and the ferry would not be back until time to pick up the late engineering shift at 11:30. Joseph let her sleep.

She looked so vulnerable. Several tendrils of hair had come loose from their pins and straggled down the nape of her neck. Even in the poor illumination of the overhead fixture, they shimmered with red lights, as though an unseen artist had coated each strand separately with a wash of burnt sienna. Something about the ivory skin of her neck made her seem particularly young, and in response to it, he felt a formidable obligation to her, as though he had been charged with her safekeeping. Her near fall between the buildings was almost a physical memory, as if something fine and irreplaceable had almost slipped through his fingers and shattered at his feet. Even now he felt his heartbeat quicken at the thought. She gave a deep sigh in her sleep, almost as though she knew what he was thinking. He forced his attention back to his task.

He had the papers on the desk separated now and began filing them in folders, stacking them in piles and composing, in his mind, the terse note he would leave for the Boarding Chief. What he had discovered — mounds of letters and telegrams warning of possible criminal or anarchist activity in the United States, or headed in that direction — was enough to justify firing the Boarding Chief. But Joseph knew that McNabb would find a way to protect him, especially now, with the spotlight focused on the Sapelli scandal. A disgruntled former Boarding Chief could be very dangerous to Edward McNabb and his cronies.

The letters in one folder alone spanned three months and, as far as Joseph could determine, not one of them had spawned a lookout order for inspectors in the Barge Office, the very people most likely to encounter, potentially recognize, and stop someone trying to enter the United States illegally. Lookout orders should have been posted in the division offices and instructions given to all boarding inspectors to check them regularly. In fact, copies should have been typed and circulated among all the immigrant inspectors frequently, not hidden away under a mound of papers on a desk. That they were here, instead of someplace more accessible, was damning evidence in itself. At its worst, it enabled undesirable foreign nationals to slip into the country unnoticed. At best, it was careless and sloppy.

Here was a telegram from the American Embassy in Rome warning about a man traveling with two women and suspected of importing them for immoral purposes. They sounded suspiciously like Alfredo DeLuca and his apocryphal daughters. Joseph set the telegram aside with considerable satisfaction. Even if Hanrahan legitimately believed DeLuca's story, and Joseph was under no illusion that he did, had the Boarding Chief been doing his job, inspectors would have been obliged to watch for the procurer instead of helping him to enter the country.

He picked up another letter, this one from the British Foreign Office, dated August 4, 1901, and signed by one of the undersecretaries to Henry Petty-Fitzmaurice. It followed up on a previous warning regarding one Cormac Doyle, Irish anarchist, approximately six feet in height and weighing some fourteen stone. Auburn curly hair, possible facial hair. One identifying scar, on the neck below the left ear lobe, diagonal and approximately three centimeters in length. Thought to be traveling with another conspirator.

"Well, well," Joseph said, "Michael Finnegan, I believe I've found you."

Rachel roused herself at the sound of his voice and stretched gracefully. "Have you found something?"

"Yes, I believe I've found Michael Finnegan. His real name is Cormac Doyle."

Joseph handed Rachel his keys. "The kitchen will be locked by now, I imagine. Whatever you can find will do," he said. "There should be something left over from lunch or supper."

Neither of them had thought about eating until long past the hour for supper, so intent were they on trying to find Vine's anarchist. Now that they had him, or believed they did, they were free to relax. The late shift ferry would arrive in about an hour, but neither could stave off their hunger any longer. Rachel had offered to find them something to eat while Joseph put away the files he had taken from the Boarding Office.

He watched her leave, then set aside the letter from the British Foreign Office and dropped the rest into a deep desk drawer, turning the key in its lock with a sense of profound satisfaction. He thought he had it all now — all the necessary evidence to confront Maggie Flynn with the truth and get to the bottom of where Cormac Doyle might now be hiding. He would need Rachel Bonner for it, though. She, better than he, could make the girl see reason. He was too apt to lose his temper.

Joseph pulled out his pocket watch and checked the time: 10:17 p.m. He'd been on the job for almost sixteen hours. He leaned back in his chair and raised his feet to his desk, shoving aside a pile of his own papers and a small, green leather notebook. Tomorrow, the Boarding Chief would find a note requiring him to report to the Superintendent immediately. He wouldn't, of course. Joseph could see it in his mind's eye — how the Chief would, instead, go to McNabb, demanding to know what was going on. He had been assured of McNabb's protection; of that, Joseph was certain. McNabb, who was a master of diversion, would charge into his office hurling accusations of . . . what? Infringing on the Chief's privacy? No. This was government property and, in theory if not in fact, the Boarding Chief was responsible to his immediate superior, the Superintendent. No, it was more likely to be a charge of obstruction of justice. McNabb would claim that Joseph was interfering with his investigation — perhaps that he had removed evidence from the Boarding Office. Joseph would enjoy the moment of confrontation. He would present the file of citizens' papers and follow it up with the file of warning letters and telegrams that had been ignored. And McNabb would begin tap dancing around charges of dereliction of duty and misconduct. It should be quite a show.

His own office must be in perfect order, of course. Which it wasn't. Joseph squared his papers into a neat stack, discarding anything unnecessary, and positioned them carefully on the corner of his desk. But the green notebook was not his, nor did he know where it had come from. He flipped through a few pages, stopping at a sketch of a woman in foreign dress. She wore many layers — dress, vest, skirt, apron and headscarf, each heavily embroidered and fringed. Colors had been noted to the side of each garment. The sketch was titled *Woman from Pirin, Bulgaria,* and below it a notation: "The Bulgarian dress is remarkably like the dress of the Greeks of the northern regions."

Joseph turned to the front of the notebook and found Rachel's name. He vaguely remembered her taking it out of her pocket and setting it on the desk earlier in the day. He turned a few more pages. Irish women, she had written, generally convey the impression of greater independence of spirit.

The entry was dated August 19, 1901, the day Maggie Flynn had arrived. After that, most of Rachel's entries concerned Maggie and her well-being. She had talked very little, and what she had told Rachel were merely descriptions of life in Drumcliffe, her neighbors, the town gossip, and family stories. He flipped to the back and read the most recent entry.

"I am struck by the primitive way of life in small town Ireland, as Maggie describes it. The adjustment to New York must be enormous. I would very much like to discuss this with Irene and Moira.

Moira handled herself remarkably well at the tea yesterday. It is amazing what one generation of Americanization and education can achieve. A lesser woman would have been intimidated by the money and prestige in the room. Although she was initially self-conscious, she soon overcame her apparent misgivings and gave Mrs. Bradley Martin a good dose of the Irish sharp tongue."

It took a moment for Joseph to absorb

what he had read, that she was writing about Moira, his sister. It came over him with embarrassing disquiet. He had trusted her. She evoked in him some sense of his own worth as a man, or so he had believed. And wasn't he just the fool? He closed the journal with a snap, pitched it onto the desk and walked to the window, throwing it open to alleviate the sudden heat generated by his gathering anger.

Her words resounded in his mind — *handled herself remarkably well.* As if his sister might be an animal to be observed by some female Darwin, her behavior recorded to be analyzed later. Clearly the Bonner woman had nursed misgivings about Moira's ability to handle herself in social situations. The tea had been a social experiment and the investigator pleasantly surprised at its outcome. But that, of course, was because of Americanization and education, the goal of every social worker.

Mother of God, how he hated reformers, with their polite criticisms and sanctimonious ways, and none of them having the faintest idea what an immigrant's life was really like. They marched in, this infantry of social workers, armed with suggestions for improvement but ever mindful that one could only expect so much because, after all, they were dealing with foreigners who hadn't the benefit of Americanization and education. When it came down to it, they were as xenophobic as the rest of America. They just covered it up better than most.

Rachel felt the coldness of his manner the moment she stepped through the office door. He stood, his back to her, gazing at the harbor beyond. He didn't turn when she pushed open the door carrying a dinner tray.

"Well, there wasn't much to choose from. I've reheated some of the stew from dinner," she said.

"I seem to have lost my appetite."

"Oh." She set the tray on his desk and waited for him to make a move. When he didn't, she busied herself grouping two place settings of silverware. "Perhaps if you try a few bites —"

"Spare me your suggestions, Miss Bonner. I don't need you to tell me when to eat."

"Yes, of course." She continued setting their places, arranging the bowls on opposite sides of the desk in anticipation of an intimate meal, but her own stomach was churning now. When she had everything arranged, and he still had not left the window, she pulled a chair up to her side of the desk but remained standing.

"I suppose we'll wait to interrogate Maggie until tomorrow? That really seems best, since —"

He turned on her then, meeting her gaze with wintry composure. His pale blue eyes froze her on the spot. "*We* will not be interrogating anyone. I am considering reassigning you, or rather, returning you to your former duties with the detained women."

Rachel clasped the back of the chair. "But what about Maggie? You said that you wanted me to convince her to talk to me. I think she has begun to trust me, at least —"

"Maggie Flynn trusts no one," he said sharply. "Perhaps she's right."

Rachel shivered, and crossed her arms, tucking her hands beneath them. The room felt cold, with a gusty wind coming in the open window. A fly buzzed past her, grazing her hair. She swatted at it and shuddered when its persistent drone grated on her nerves.

"Please, sir, tell me why I'm to be taken off of Maggie's case. I'm afraid I really don't understand."

Joseph's gaze bore into her. "I suspect there are many things you don't understand, Miss Bonner. Not the least of which is Miss

Flynn." He opened a desk drawer and withdrew a fly swatter, slapping it down on the desk so hard that one of his papers skidded across the surface. "I'm thinking now that I should have found an Irish matron — someone who would understand her better."

The injustice of his remarks stunned her. She kept her arms folded, lest her balled fists act with a will of their own. It wasn't fair. No one could have gotten through to the girl. She had done her best to win Maggie's confidence, but he'd said it himself — Maggie Flynn trusted no one. Nevertheless, they had developed a friendship of sorts. Through her talk of Drumcliffe, her family, and friends, Rachel had learned a good bit about Maggie Flynn. That she had come away from those conversations more perplexed was hardly surprising. The Maggie of Drumcliffe was vivacious and funny, telling stories of Mary Feeney, the local gossip, and her brother Jerry's antics in school. The Maggie of Ellis Island was a sad, withdrawn shadow of herself.

"Does it matter so much that I'm not Irish? It doesn't seem to matter a whit to Maggie."

"I didn't think so," he said, turning away from her to follow the progress of the fly.

The air whistled through the screen on the fly swatter, but the insect was too quick for him. He flexed his jaw. "But I've changed my mind. No one wants to be treated as a zoo animal, Miss Bonner."

He smacked the swatter on the desk with such force that she started and took an involuntary step back, watching as he lifted the insect on the edge of the swatter and dumped it into the wastebasket. Clearly, he was in a very bad temper.

"Perhaps," she said, carefully, "we should wait to discuss this until we are both more rested."

"There is nothing to discuss." He tossed the fly swatter on the desk. "I am ordering you off the case."

Rachel left the Superintendent's office with her head high, before she might say something that would lose her job, or worse, before she started to cry. She carried the tray bearing her lone bowl of stew grasped carefully in her shaking hands. Tears of rage and frustration pooled on her lower lashes as she hurried down the hall and into the stairwell. Her throat constricted so that she could barely swallow, never mind speak. In the stairwell, she leaned against the wall and tried to gather her thoughts. What had changed? In the time between leaving the

Boarding Office and returning from the kitchen, something had gone very much awry between them. She looked down at the stew, cooling into a greasy pool in the bowl, and suddenly wanted to be rid of it, as if it were responsible for their discord. She hastened down the steps to the first floor.

The baggage room was empty except for a charwoman mopping around the main staircase and a night watchman whose heels rapped the floor like a gavel as he crossed the room on his way to the watch clock station near the stairs to the southwestern tower. "See you in a while, Sadie," he called and waved to the charwoman.

"If yer lucky," she said, not looking up from her task.

Rachel followed him into the corridor, past the Information Bureau and the Council of Jewish Women. At the watch clock station, he inserted a key into a small metal panel near the door, opened it and removed another key. This he inserted into a cylinder which he carried in a leather case attached to a strap over his shoulder. He turned the key, removed it, returned it to its place, and locked the panel.

"Good evening, Matron," he said, with a tip of his hat, when he passed her.

She nodded a greeting and hurried on her way outside and over to the kitchen building. She left the tray at the door and retraced her steps. The late ferry would not arrive for another half an hour, but she had nowhere to go where she could be alone, and the last thing she wanted was to make polite conversation. She stopped in the Matrons' room only long enough to collect her hat and purse, exiting the station by the side door.

Outside, the wind had picked up. The air felt fresh and damp, and cooler than it had been in weeks. The sidewalk was wet. Rachel vaguely remembered a shower, sometime in the early evening, while she was still closed up with him in the Boarding Office. Nothing had been wrong then. What had happened to turn him so completely against her?

She reached the water's edge of the northeast bulkhead without purpose. The gentle lapping of the waves fueled her slight nausea. She turned away, but could not have gone far without running into it again. That was the nature of an island, she reminded herself caustically. And the station was, indeed, an island — a world unto itself, constantly overrun by visitors who never stayed. They went forward or they went back, and even if they were detained, it was only to hover on the edges of station life, like ghosts not yet departed for the nether-world.

When she first came to the station, she'd made the mistake of becoming too attached to the detainees, especially the children. She had grieved when they were returned to their countries, sometimes leaving behind a loved one, always clutching the thin fabric of their dreams in tatters as if they might somehow be mended. This was not why she had come to Ellis Island. She had come to help, to make the way smoother and easier. But finally she had learned that part of her job might be to make the way back less painful, to offer some bit of hope or re-assurance, or maybe just a fresh handker-chief for their tears. Joseph Hannegan had made her feel that all her effort was for naught.

She was more than competent in her job, even if he would not admit it. Few matrons had the knowledge of several languages and the ability to find their way around in a few more. Even the head matron occasionally came to her for advice, and Rachel sus-pected that the Superintendent knew it. There was something frigidly personal in his anger, a very intimate hostility. Rachel swallowed against the throbbing ache in her throat. She wanted Joseph Hannegan's approval — perhaps more than she had ever wanted any other man's — and he had withdrawn it.

"Stay where you are and turn around slowly."

Rachel stiffened with an involuntary chill and did as she was told. Behind her, on the walkway, a watchman stood backlit by the glow of a street lamp. "Identify yourself," he said.

Rachel swallowed, relieved to find the tension in her throat had lessened. "I'm a matron here at the station. Rachel Bonner."

The watchman advanced across the grass until he was too close for her comfort. He carried a nightstick in one hand and a battery lantern in the other. In the light of the lantern, his skin looked blotchy and red, his uniform slovenly — wrinkled and stained with a flesh-colored spot on his collar. Greasepaint?

"You're no matron. I know all the matrons here." He raised his lantern and studied her face before taking in the rest of her with a slight smile. "Some of 'em," he continued with a wink, "real good."

A second chill went through her. "I'm a day matron and I believe I have a right to know who you are."

"Watchman Cain, and you got no rights until I say you got rights. Look here, sister, if you're a day matron, what are you doing still here at this hour of the night?"

Rachel sent him a withering glance and summoned up the same chill voice Joseph had used with her. "I am not your sister. Nor am I required to explain myself to you."

Cain smiled sardonically, reached into his pocket and dropped something on his tongue. He raised his lantern and gestured toward the harbor. "Well, sister, you can explain that to me or to the marshals. Don't matter much to me."

Rachel looked out at the water. With the assistance of his light, she could see something floating perhaps twenty feet from the bulkhead. She hadn't noticed it before. "I don't even know what that is, but I can assure you I have nothing to do with it."

Cain eyed her skeptically. "Funny coincidence — you here, and him out there." He stepped closer to the water's edge and directed his light on the floating object.

"Him?" Rachel followed him, not wanting to get too close. She thought she could smell whiskey on his breath.

It was coming closer now. Every lap of the water moved it forward a few feet toward the bulkhead. "What is — Oh my God, we have to help him! Do something!"

Cain glanced around nervously, but made no move despite her repeated urging. She couldn't do it — no, she couldn't! But she must. She pulled up her skirt and started for the water. "If you won't help —"

Cain grabbed her arm and pulled her back. "There's no help for him, sister." He aimed his beam over the water again. "He's coming our way. No point getting wet. The water will carry him on in. I'll stand watch on him while you go up to the station and bring help," he said. Rachel was already running toward the Great Hall.

Chapter Nineteen

Dr. James Morton was a meticulous man who spent far more time in his examinations than the other medical inspectors and had the reputation of slowing the process to a standstill. He had, thus, been shifted to night duty where his primary focus would be treatment rather than examination. Most of the time, Rachel admired his thoroughness. Tonight, she regretted it deeply.

She leaned against the wall, feeling the cool tile on her back, and breathed through her mouth, but only as often as absolutely necessary, as the very air tasted of death. The Superintendent had asked her to stay to take Cain's statement, write out her own, and take notes on the doctor's findings. There had been an undertone of cruel insistence in the request. "The life of the reformer can be bleak, Miss Bonner. Of course, if you're not up to the task —"

"I'll stay," she said crisply, searching in

her pocket for her journal. It wasn't there, and she didn't know what she had done with it, but its absence struck a dissonant chord in the back of her mind. Nevertheless, the Superintendent had provided her with a pad and pencil.

They had placed the body on an examination table in one of the medical rooms, and while waiting for the doctor, Joseph dictated a preliminary description of the victim's clothing. "Brown trousers and a brown herringbone tweed jacket. One pocket appears to be torn off. White collarless shirt. One shoe missing, the other, a black ankle-length military boot. Trouser pockets are empty. Are you getting all this, Miss Bonner?"

In answer, she held up the pad for his scrutiny. She felt slightly faint, but stubbornly clung to the reality of the examination room, unwilling to let him see her discomfiture.

"Ah, taking notes are you? Good." Dr. Morton went to the sink and washed his hands. "Sorry to be late. Setting a broken arm. One of the men fell out of a top bunk. Treat the living before the dead, of course."

He took a hand lens from a cabinet and leaned over the body, examining it, it seemed to Rachel, an inch at a time and calling out his findings. "Moderate bloating and early decomposition. Nails still intact. . . ." They rolled the body onto its side.

"Look at that," he said. "He may have drowned, Mr. Hannegan. But he had help. See there? That's a bullet wound to the stomach, although you can scarcely tell. The fish have been feeding on the body. Looks like the bullet went clean through him. He must have been shot at close range."

"What about the facial discoloration?"

"Probably postmortem bruising. He may have bumped up on some pilings somewhere, or been hit by a boat or two. They wouldn't have seen him. The body would have sunk initially, then surfaced later."

"Is there any way to tell how long he's been dead?"

The doctor hesitated. "No definitive way, I'm afraid. But I've seen a good many of these cases — some drownings, some fatal injuries in the water. Sometimes they're unrecognizable. This fellow isn't. I'd guess about three days."

Was this how her parents had looked? Bloated, blanched? Had her mother's face been bruised beyond recognition? She didn't remember, didn't know if she had ever known. She remembered their caskets, sitting before the main altar in Grace Church. Uncle Matt had hold of her hand, squeezing it so tightly it hurt, but even at the age of seven she had recognized unbearable grief in his stricken face.

Sometimes she dreamt about them, swallowing water, searching for each other in the cold deep. Calling her name. She had never thought about what happened to them afterward. How long were they in the water? Had the fish . . . ?

"What about this scar?" Joseph asked.

"Probably from a knife fight or at least something with a very sharp edge, like a straight razor. The cut was very clean. You can see that the margins were even. It may be the only way we can identify him — or was he carrying any identification?"

"No. Nothing. But I believe I already know who he is. Miss Bonner?"

With effort, Rachel pushed herself away from the wall. "Yes?"

"I want you to bring Maggie Flynn here. Take a watchman with you." Joseph turned to Cain, lingering eagerly in the background. "Go with Miss Bonner and bring the girl here."

"Superintendent, please. Don't subject her to —"

"I have no choice, Miss Bonner. I think we both know who this is. Bring the girl —"

"Fine." Rachel cut him off. She turned on

her heel and marched out of the Medical Division, trusting Cain to follow her. Behind her, she heard the Superintendent call out to her.

"Don't tell her anything, Miss Bonner. Just bring her here."

Maggie slept very little now, always waiting for something to happen. For the first time in her life, she thought she understood the agony of Purgatory — waiting to go to Heaven, with little prospect of ever getting there. Reunion with Cormac would be Heaven, but Ellis Island was a mere Purgatory. Superintendent Hannegan had made it clear enough today that Hell was a place called Blackwell's Island.

The sound of footsteps outside her door alerted all her senses. He was back. But he would not rape her again, even if she had to kill him. They'd locked her up here for one murder. What difference did another one make now? She reached down under the cot and brought out the empty chamber pot, creeping softly across the room to stand behind the door just as the key turned in the lock.

"Wait for me here, Mr. Cain." Matron Bonner pushed the door open, casting a light from the hall across the empty cot.

"Maggie?"

"Behind you, Miss Bonner." She crept out of her hiding place, the chamber pot in her hands.

The matron stared at her for a long moment. "What were you planning, Maggie? Surely you don't think you can get off the island, even if you disarm me or the watchman."

"No," Maggie said. "Of course not." But she couldn't explain herself further, and understood how it must look to the matron. "But why are you here? Shouldn't you be home in bed by now?"

"Normally, yes. Have you a dressing gown, Maggie?" Rachel went to Maggie's trunk, rummaged through it and pulled out a shawl. "This will do," she said, and dropped it around the girl's shoulders. "Put on your boots, please. Mr. Hannegan needs to speak to you."

Maggie did as she was told. But what could he want at this late hour of the night? She felt a little flutter of hope in her breast. Perhaps they had finally come for her.

A watchman was waiting for them in the hall. Maggie shrank back at the door. "It's all right," the matron said. "Go ahead of us please, Mr. Cain."

"But —"

"Ahead of us," Miss Bonner insisted. The watchman reluctantly complied. Maggie allowed the matron to draw her out of her room.

"Where are we goin'?"

"Just to see Mr. Hannegan," Rachel said, gently pulling her along.

They passed into a great room divided by metal pipes and rails. Maggie hadn't been there before. "This," Rachel said, "is where the immigrants come to be processed. It's the Registry Room. And down here are the medical lines and the examining rooms." She guided Maggie past the lines and into a divided hallway. Light spilled from a room at the end of the passage and an unpleasant odor assailed her.

"Is there an animal. . . ."

The matron ignored her question, but slowed her pace. "Maggie, remember that I'm right here with you," she said. "And Mr. Hannegan is waiting for you." She led Maggie into the room and stepped aside.

It was a stark room worse, even, than her own. Pale green tile and bright lights that hung low on cords beneath metal shades. Mr. Hannegan was waiting there, watching her face intently with those penetrating blue eyes of his. Behind him stood a man in a khaki uniform, but he was not, she thought,

Cormac's doctor.

She took a deep breath, gasped and covered her mouth and nose. "Is someone sick?"

The Superintendent's expression remained impassive. "Come in, Maggie. It's all right," he said. "I need to ask you a question."

He nodded at the other man, and they both stepped aside, revealing an examining table. Maggie took a step forward, glanced at the Superintendent and took another step. She knew that he was still watching her, but she could not take her eyes off the table. What was on it? Slowly, she moved closer, until she stood next to it.

A body? But so grotesque, so inhuman. Swollen and gray, bruised. Rusty hair matted and filthy, with tangles of weeds caught in the curls.

She felt the blood drain from her face, and her knees soften, as if her senses had recognized it before her mind could take it in. It couldn't be him, she thought, even as she sank toward the floor.

The smell of ammonia brought her around quickly. Her body was in control and she could only follow its demands. She sat up abruptly and vomited into a basin the matron shoved under her chin. Rachel bathed her face with cool water. "Better?" she said.

Maggie nodded, scattered and grasping for what had caused her to faint. The odor of death brought it back. Cormac, dead and gone from her forever. She tried to stand, but her knees would not hold her.

"It can't be," she whispered. "I didn't hit him. I shot . . . I shot into the air. I couldn't have hit him, could I?"

The Superintendent helped her into a chair, turning it away from the body. He squatted at her feet and took her hands in his. "It is Cormac Doyle, isn't it?"

Her answer came in a thin, high whimper that seemed to come from someone else. Her ears were ringing. She couldn't hear what they were saying to her — the questions he was asking, the consolations they must be offering her. She was dimly aware that the matron was rubbing her back, and yet she could not say that she felt it, because she couldn't feel anything at all. They stepped back, as if expecting something from her. She gazed up into their faces and wondered what they wanted of her. At length, she stood and pushed the chair aside, drawing up next to the table where he lay.

She longed to touch him, to wind her

fingers through his curls, and yet her hand would not go there, as though her body refused to acknowledge what her mind knew to be true.

"Cormac," she whimpered, "I didn't want to do it. I told you. Why did you make me do it?" She forced herself to lay the tip of her finger to the scar on his neck, and felt his cold, waxy flesh. It did not feel real or human and, somehow, that made it easier to bear.

Somewhere a clock ticked mechanically, reminding her of the hours and days and years ahead that she would have to live without him. Throughout her lonely incarceration on Ellis Island, she had clung to some hope that he would be restored to her. Even as she'd seen it receding, she had reached out to clutch it more tenaciously. She'd held fast to her dreams of a croppy's cottage of her own and a man who would come home to her at night smelling of a day's sweat but not diminished by his work or ground down under the heel of the landlord, for Cormac would never be that. She turned away.

"Take me back to my room, please," she said. "There's nothin' left for me here."

Dr. Morton pressed a bottle of laudanum

into Rachel's hands. "You can give her this to calm her and help her sleep. But beware of giving her too much, or with too much regularity. We would not want her to become dependent upon it." Rachel slid the bottle into the pocket of her skirt.

"We won't be giving her any until after I've questioned her, Doctor," Joseph said.

"Superintendent, I am opposed to this," Rachel said. "She is in no condition to be questioned right now. We need to give her time —"

Dr. Morton was quick to agree. "She's had a bad shock, Superintendent. Give her a little time to recover."

"I'd like to, but I'm afraid I can't. If I don't act now, she may never tell us the truth. She's a naive girl, Doctor. She doesn't seem to understand the consequences of what she's done. If I spare her now, I may not be able to keep her out of the executioner's hands. Which do you think is better?"

Joseph construed the doctor's brief hesitation as agreement. "We'll keep the body here until Dr. Rockwell arrives this morning. Will you make the necessary arrangements to have him moved to the city morgue?"

Dr. Morton agreed that he would, and left Rachel and Joseph standing in the hall outside the witness interrogation room. When he was out of earshot, Joseph turned to Rachel.

"Let us be clear about a few things, Miss Bonner. I am only allowing you to be here because Maggie needs a woman with her now. I still intend to replace you on the case if any matron is required further. I imagine Miss Flynn will now be moved to Blackwell's Island.

"I have taken note of your opposition to questioning her, but I am going forward with it. Her situation is now infinitely worse than it was yesterday. Cormac Doyle, whom you and I have been calling Michael Finnegan, has now turned up dead. He was shot in the stomach, just as witnesses described Maggie shooting him." He held up his hand to stop her obvious objection and went on.

"No, I don't believe this is the result of the shooting on the dock, but we have absolutely no way of proving that. Dr. Morton cannot swear to a time of death, and neither of us actually saw the men who attacked us on Rivington Street. Once I turn her over to the marshals, they will undoubtedly prosecute her for murder. We must get the truth out of her immediately, while she is unguarded enough to tell us what this was all about. You may not like it. I confess that I don't like it myself, but that is the way it must be." He opened the door and strode in ahead of Rachel, offering her no opportunity to argue with him.

Maggie sat on her cot, knees to her chin and her folded arms covering the rest of her face, as though she would have spun a cocoon around herself had she been able. Her chest shuddered in little sobs and she gasped for air. Rachel took a seat next to her, stroking her hair and softly shushing in her ear.

Joseph pulled up a chair and straddled it in front of Maggie, taking the girl's hands in his own. He didn't like what he was about to do any more than Rachel did. Perhaps, in fact, it pained him more, for to him she was not just a laboratory specimen. She could have been Moira, or Doreen O'Neill, or any one of dozens of the young women he had known who were too quickly captivated by men with sweet tongues and grand ideas.

"Maggie from Drumcliffe, it's time to talk to me," he said, gently squeezing her hands. "You didn't kill Cormac Doyle. I know that as sure as I know my own name, but I can't prove it without your help. Miss Bonner and I want to keep you out of jail, but we must have the truth from you if we're to do that.

Let me tell you what I think happened, and you can tell me if I'm correct." Maggie shivered and let Rachel wrap a blanket over the shawl around her shoulders.

"Cormac Doyle," Joseph began, "is wanted for crimes in Ireland. The Brits are saying he's an anarchist. He was escaping to the United States, but he knew it was risky for him to try to come through the immigration station. So he conceived of a plan — that you would appear to shoot him, so he'd be taken off the island before he ever got into the Great Hall. He put a bladder of red ink under his shirt, and when you discharged the gun, he punctured it, so witnesses would think that you had hit him. Dylan Moran picked up his suitcase and carried it as his own, then met Doyle when he cleared the station and got to New York. But he had help on this end, didn't he? He couldn't have gotten away with this without someone to carry him off the island. The police who picked him up were supposed to take you with them, as if they'd arrested you. They didn't expect our officials to get to you first, did they?"

Maggie shook her head. "I thought the constables would come for me, but they never did. Cormac said if something went wrong, they would come back to get me.

Why didn't they?"

"They tried, but they were recognized by one of the janitors and it scared them away, Maggie. I'm sure they would have tried again, when the time was right. But I wouldn't have let you go, because the crime is not in their jurisdiction."

Joseph dropped Maggie's hands and pushed his chair back a bit, rising to pace the room. "That is, essentially, what we know, Maggie. But if we're to find Doyle's real killer, and exonerate you, we will have to know a great deal more. Do you understand that?"

She nodded her head a fraction, as though she understood but had not made up her mind what she would do about it. Joseph waited, letting the full impact of what had happened settle on her.

"I met Cormac at Lissadell," she said. "Do you know it?" Joseph did not.

"I worked in the manor house. He came as a horse trainer. He had been living in Paris."

"Paris?" That might explain the book.

Maggie nodded. "He met Miss Constance Gore-Booth there. Her father owns Lissadell, but he has been very sick. Miss Gore-Booth hired Cormac as a horse trainer and sent him to Drumcliffe."

"Paris," Joseph repeated, finally realizing the full import of what she was telling him. "Where he met Irish exiles, I suppose. Did he join the Irish Republican Brotherhood?"

"I think so, yes. At least, I know he was a Fenian."

"Excuse me," Rachel said. "What is a Fenian?"

"A fighter for Irish independence from England," Joseph said. "The name comes from Fianna Éireann, a legendary band of Irish warriors led by Finn MacCumhaill. The British look upon them as criminals. They sent us a warning about him. I found it last night." He turned back to Maggie.

Maggie shook her head. "He was doin' somethin'. The constables were after him in Ireland. He wouldn't tell me what he had done wrong, only that it was important for Ireland, and that he was comin' here because of it. If we wanted to be together, I had to come with him, you see. My father would not allow me to see him again after the constables went lookin' for him. And he needed my help. Someone had to pretend to shoot him."

"And it couldn't be anyone associated with the IRB, because that might arouse suspicion," Joseph supplied. "It had to be someone who was completely innocent, and it had to be very carefully planned in advance. The doctor and the police in the harbor were all a part of the hoax."

"They were."

"But who helped him? It had to have been other Fenians."

"Yes, but Cormac never told me. Only once did I hear a name, well, overhear it actually, and I don't know where the man is. Cormac was talkin' to someone down at the water one evening. I went to find him to walk me home, as he always did. I heard him mention a name."

"What was it, Maggie?"

She hesitated a fraction of a second before answering him. It was the one name Joseph dreaded to hear. "John Devoy," she said.

CHAPTER TWENTY

Rachel waited on the dock with the second-watch night matrons for the 7:40 ferry. She thought she must be bruised, and that when she undressed, she would find her body covered in great purple mounds of battered flesh. In the last twenty-four hours, she had ridden a wave of emotions that must surely represent the gamut of human experience. She had felt the warmth of Joseph Hannegan's esteem, and its sudden, cold withdrawal; the horror of unnatural death and with it, the anguish of untapped memories and dark fantasies. Rage, pity, disgust, and fear, each dealing her a blow in turn throughout a long and very black night. She couldn't take much more.

"Miss Bonner."

Rachel steeled herself to turn around, knowing that the final blow might yet be dealt. The Superintendent held her journal balanced on the tips of his fingers, as if he were offering up a sacrifice. "This is yours, I believe."

She snatched it from him and thrust it into her pocket. "How did you acquire it, if I might ask," she said.

"Don't you remember? You left it in my office yesterday, on the desk."

"I remember very little of yesterday, and I am trying to forget last night," she said. But now the dissonant chord struck again, and with it, a slowly emerging comprehension. "You read it?"

Joseph faltered momentarily. "I didn't realize what it was at first. It was on my desk. If you were concerned about guarding your privacy, you should have been more careful with it." The deep color in his face betrayed the inadequacy of his justification.

"Thank you for returning it to me," she said stiffly. "You may be sure I will be more careful in the future."

She turned away and gazed out at the harbor, willing the ferry to arrive, but it was still only a speck on the horizon. His hand was on her elbow. "I'd like a private word with you," he said, turning her away from the dock. She wriggled loose of his grasp, but after a brief hesitation, fell into step with him. They walked toward the end of the island and around the ferry basin toward the hospital construction. When they were out of anyone else's hearing, he stopped.

"About your relationship with my sister, Miss Bonner. I'll come straight to the point. Moira is not a lab specimen for you to study. She was under the mistaken impression that you were her friend."

"But I am. I admire —"

"Please do not insult my intelligence. Among other things, you wanted to see how she handled herself at tea. Well, you have your information now, and I will not permit my sister to be used for any more of your social experiments. Please stay away from her."

And there was the final blow, a slap as surely as if he had used his open hand. She reeled back a step before recovering her self-possession. "You have no right to prohibit me from seeing your sister. Moira is a grown woman and perfectly capable of choosing her own friends without the help of her older brother. We will continue to be friends until I hear otherwise from her, not you. Furthermore, Superintendent, I do not understand your innuendos about zoo animals and lab specimens, so if you have something else to say to me, please get on with it and be direct."

Joseph's expression darkened, causing a

tremulous feeling in the pit of her stomach. "All right, let me be perfectly clear, Miss Bonner. I do not like social workers. You do more harm than good with your studies of 'the Irish' and 'the Italians,' as though we can all be neatly fit into one category or another."

He paused, just long enough for her to interrupt him. "I am sure I haven't the faintest idea what you are talking about. I would remind you that we all, including you, refer to the immigrants by country. They are Irish and Italian, and if you are trying to tell me that there is no difference between them, then frankly, Mr. Hannegan, you have taken leave of your senses. And if classification treads upon your delicate sensibilities, then you are living proof of what all social workers know — that children of immigrants are haunted by their background."

His blue eyes blazed, reminding her of chips of broken glass, but his words were even, and all the more disturbing for their dispassion. "On the contrary, Miss Bonner. I am not haunted, as you say, by my background, nor is Moira. When she told me that you were Matthew Bonner's niece, I should have realized that you must have an agenda, that someone of your society could not possibly be interested in my sister as a friend. What, exactly, did you expect of her? Did you think she'd order up a bucket of beer, or that she might tell a story or two about the little people? Well, you and your elegant friends have had your fun observing the specimen outside of her native habitat. It will not happen again."

"You know absolutely nothing about me. And aren't you doing precisely what you accuse me of, assuming that someone of my 'society' could not be interested in having your sister as a friend? Tell me, Mr. Hannegan, just which one of us is guilty of snobbery?"

Before he could answer, she left him and marched back to the ferry slip. The 7:40 had arrived and she boarded immediately, shouldering her way past the disembarking day-shift matrons and watchmen, to take up a position at the rail on the port side. He boarded behind her and remained at the starboard rail.

As if Moira had to be protected from her. As if her efforts at the station were not genuine. He hated social workers. Well, where would the city be without them? How many immigrant women had learned American ways thanks to social workers? How could they expect to assimilate if they never became Americanized? She made these arguments to herself over and over until the Barge Office came into view. But even as she clung to the mooring of moral outrage, she felt herself drifting on currents of self-doubt.

Could he be right? Had she treated Moira as a social experiment? After all, she knew how Moira would be received by Mrs. Bradley Martin, but she hadn't expected the old biddy to be there. Nevertheless, Mrs. Martin was only one of many society matrons who believed that some institutions should be preserved for the privileged. Why had she taken Moira to the Metropolitan Club, when they might just have gone to tea?

She'd enjoyed Moira's company, and gloated privately when Moira refused to let Mrs. Martin belittle her. But it should have been Irene, not Moira. At eighteen, she'd sat by impotently while Mrs. Martin barred Irene from the club. Now she'd had her revenge, but at what price? It had given Irene no satisfaction, and now might cost her Moira's friendship. And what was worse, she knew she had sacrificed her own integrity.

When the ferry docked at the Barge Office, Rachel waited until the Superintendent had gone ashore and disappeared across the park before she left the boat. She could scarcely lift her feet to make the walk to the Third Avenue El, and almost wept with gratitude when she fell into a seat on the train. She had the car almost to herself, but it gradually filled as they moved uptown through stations at Fulton and Franklin, Chatham Square, and beyond. By the time they reached Houston Street no seats remained, but they took on only three young women, shop girls obviously absorbed in the search for amusement.

"Pl-eease, Nora," one of them pleaded, "it's the last Coney Island trip of the year."

"I can't. How many times must I tell you, Minnie? I have other plans."

"What's more important than Coney Island? Your Ma won't care. She likes us."

Rachel watched them with an interest calculated to divert her from her own inner turmoil. Nora had turned away from her friend, giving Rachel a clear view of her heart shaped face and wistful green eyes. She wasn't happy. Minnie nudged the third girl with her elbow.

"Mr. Carnegie VanAstorBilt said he's gonna take her to the Palm Court one day." Nora's brows twitched together as Minnie went on without noticing. "Mayayay-be," she said, "he's going to ask the question."

Minnie hugged herself and bounced up

and down on the tip of her toes, as if she could hardly contain her excitement. "They could get married in Grace Church, like Cornelia Martin, and go to Venice for their honeymoon."

Nora wheeled around on her friend with manifest impatience. "Stop it, Minnie! I've told you before, real life is not a Laura Jean Libbey novel. Princes don't marry their upstairs maids, and owners' sons do not marry the hired help!"

"Then why do you go on seeing him?" Minnie snapped.

Nora bit her lower lip and stared at her friend. "I don't know," she said quietly.

Rachel followed the three girls off the train at 23rd Street. Nora hurried down the stairs ahead of the other two, but she needn't have rushed, as Minnie's attention had flitted on to a new subject.

"The Barn Stormers are giving a racket next week. I can't wait! But I don't suppose Nora will grace us with her company for that, either," she said, raising her voice pointedly. Rachel left them to turn down Lexington Avenue.

Owners' sons do not marry the hired help. Rachel knew Nora was right. The phrase had an uncomfortably familiar ring to it, and an unreasonable anger boiled up inside of her: *someone of your society could not possibly be interested in my sister as a friend.* But it wasn't true. She wasn't like that. She hadn't been raised by the most egalitarian of men to look down upon anyone as her inferior. She had been born into a family of means, it was true, but had she ever expected special privileges at the station? In fact, she'd gone to great pains to conceal her background and fit in with the other matrons. If she always declined their invitations to rackets and day trips, it was simply because she didn't share their interests. Wasn't it? Her step slowed and the weariness of hours on her feet overtook her. She mounted the stairs at the Gramercy Park house propelled by sheer will.

Irene and Matt were in the dining room having a last cup of coffee. Their heads almost touched as, together, they reviewed a menu for a dinner party he was giving. Rachel watched their backs from the door for a moment.

Sunlight spilling through the window caught on a few streaks of silver in Irene's hair. Irene was aging, Rachel realized with surprise. And Matt's hair was no longer the vibrant, deep red it once had been. In fact, it was more gray than red at the temples. Irene leaned forward, her soft waves grazing his shoulder, but she pulled back instantly in a smooth, practiced manner that suggested she'd done it many times. His hand came up, as if to catch her at the waist, then dropped back into place at his side. The gesture somehow filled Rachel with rage.

"Well, isn't this a domestic little scene," she said from the door. They turned in surprise.

"Rachel?" Irene started toward her. "Are you all right?"

"I'm fine, Irene." She tossed her boater on the table, went to the sideboard and poured herself a cup of coffee. Her hands shook as she sloshed cream into the cup and onto the saucer. "It's just that I'm wondering why you two must play at marriage when you could have the real thing."

Irene colored deeply and glanced over at Matthew. His mouth hung open in astonishment. He cleared his throat. "Rachel, really —"

"I'll order you some breakfast," Irene said, hurrying toward the door.

"No! I don't want breakfast, and I don't want you to leave, Irene. I want to know the truth." She turned and leaned back against the sideboard, eyeing her uncle.

"Why have you never married Irene, Uncle Matt? Isn't she good enough for you?

Is it because you're afraid she won't fit in at the Metropolitan?"

Rachel had rarely seen Matt Bonner angry. He was angry now. "How dare you embarrass Irene, or me, this way, Rachel. What's come over you?"

"Common sense, I suppose. I've been watching this go on for seventeen years, praying that the two of you would come to your senses. How long have you been in love with her, Uncle Matt? Fifteen, sixteen years?"

He smoothed his tie and looked away, but Rachel didn't wait for an answer. She turned to Irene. "How many suitors have you had in the last seventeen years, Irene?"

"Rachel, this is hardly the time —"

"How many?"

Irene sighed and glanced at Matt. "In for a penny, in for a pound, I suppose," she said. She turned back to Rachel. "Two."

"A beautiful woman with only two suitors. How odd. Why didn't you marry one of them?"

"Because I wasn't in love with them. You're tired, Rachel. Let me have Alma draw you a warm bath."

Rachel felt the ropes slipping their mooring, taking her into undercurrents she now knew had been circulating beneath the surface of her life since the day she walked through the door of Matt Bonner's house holding Irene Garrity's hand. "I don't want a bath. I don't want breakfast. I want —"

But her ropes had not slipped. She had cut them with deliberation and without forethought, and now they could not be mended. Whatever the reason for their pretense of employer and housekeeper, it was not any of her affair. She had unmasked them without purpose, and in so doing, had set them all adrift. They could never go on facing one another day after day as if this had not happened. She had asked a question that would have to be answered, and the enormity of what she had done reverberated in the silence. She carefully set her cup back on the sideboard.

"I'm so sorry," she whispered, and ran from the room.

CHAPTER
TWENTY-ONE

Joseph slammed the door and tossed his hat at the hall tree. He missed, but didn't stop to pick it up. He headed straight down the hall and up the stairs to the second floor, where the men's bedrooms were located. As he turned into the hall, he saw Moira in the back bedroom changing Mr. Kessler's sheets.

"Joseph?" she called, "I was getting worried about you. Are you hungry?"

"No," he said, and kept walking down the hall.

"But —"

"Not now, Moira."

He strode to the door of the front bedroom and threw it open with enough force to rattle the bookcase behind it. A basin of water, bar of soap, and razor sat on the bedside table. Dennis was sitting on the bed in a Balbriggan undershirt and drawers, strapping on his prosthetic leg. He glared at his son over the rims of his glasses.

"You might knock next time."

Joseph went straight to the wardrobe and yanked the doors open, pulled out a clean shirt and trousers and tossed them on the bed. "Put them on. We're going out," he said.

"I haven't even shaved yet. What's the matter with you, Shosav?"

"There's nothing wrong with me, but there must be something wrong with you, old man. What could you be thinking, putting your own son's job at risk?"

"Sure I haven't the slightest notion what you're blatherin' about."

Joseph picked up his father's shoes and hurled them at his feet, stalked to the corner and grabbed up his crutch. "Spare me your lies, Dad. My job has never meant anything to you. Never mind that it pays most of the bills around here. Never mind that I work for the United States government."

"Joseph! What on earth is going on?" Moira stood in the door, her arms full of dirty sheets. "What are you shouting about?" She turned to Dennis. "Dad, what's this about?"

Dennis shrugged. Joseph raked his hand through his hair and lowered his voice. "It's got nothing to do with you, Moira. Stay out of it."

Moira took in the clothes on the bed and the crutch in Joseph's hand. "Are you going somewhere?"

"We are indeed. We're going to see John Devoy."

Dennis shook his head. "Now, son, I think we can clear this up without involvin' John."

"And I'm to trust you, am I? Forget it, Dad. I want to hear it from the horse's mouth."

"Hear what?" Moira said. She dropped the sheets outside the door and stood with her hands on her hips. "What does John Devoy have to do with the station?"

"You want to explain it, Dad? No, I suppose not." Joseph turned to his sister. "John Devoy and his merry band of rebels used the station to bring in a Fenian wanted by the British. Dad was right in the thick of it. How else would they have known about procedures at the station? But they have their own spy, Moira. Your father and mine, the rebel hero, Dennis Hannegan. If McNabb gets wind of this, he'll have my job and be raising a toast to me at Mickey Condron's before the day is out."

"Dad?"

Dennis reached for his shirt and slipped his arms into it, studying the buttons attentively. "He's makin' more of it than it really is, Moira. We had to get the man in somehow. There just wasn't another way." He glanced from Joseph to Moira. "It's important to the cause."

"Oh, Dad." Moira went to the bed and picked up his trousers, squatted at his feet and slipped them onto the artificial leg. "How could you jeopardize Joseph's job that way?"

Dennis picked up his watch from the bedside table and wound it thoughtfully. "It didn't go as smooth as we planned it," he admitted.

"Indeed not," Joseph said. "In fact, there's a young woman from Sligo under detainment at the station. She's eighteen years old and never been outside of Drumcliffe in her life, until now. She's probably going to be moved to Blackwell's Island and charged with murder."

"Murder?" Dennis took off his glasses and stared at Joseph. "Well, we'll have to clear that up right away. There was no murder. Not really."

"On the contrary, Dad." Joseph relished the moment, and the look of alarm on his father's face. "Cormac Doyle turned up on the station bulkhead early this morning with a gunshot wound, and he was dead as your cause."

Moira convinced Joseph to give his father time to finish his morning routine. She set a mug of coffee on the kitchen table in front of him. "Can't you wait until you've had a bit of rest? You've been up all night. You can't be thinking straight, and you're as cross as a bag of cats."

"I'm thinking straight enough," he said.

She filled the big iron kettle at the sink and started it heating on the stove, took the milk jug from the icebox and poured two sips into his mug. "He didn't do it to hurt you, you know. He did it for the Clan."

"Now would not be the time to be defending him to me, Moira. I'm not of a mood to hear it." Joseph slipped a cigarette out of a pack in his pocket and struck a match to it. It tasted hot and made him cough, but he drew deeply on it anyway.

"Didn't I do just as they asked? When Liam went to the Whyos, Dad took his belt to me and made me swear to stay in school. And didn't I do it, and work bloody nights to help out around here at that? And how does he thank me for it? By sneaking around behind my back and undermining my job. He knows how bloody hard I've worked to get where I am. He knows Powderly trusts me, and McNabb would like nothing better than to catch me in the middle of a scandal, but that doesn't stop him. Nothing stops him when it comes to that bunch of god-damned fanatics."

Moira gathered up the sheets, dumped them into the kettle and fetched a dolly stick and washboard from behind the curtain below the sink. "I'm not taking his part, mind you," she said, "but I understand him. You know, Joseph, I remember almost nothing about Ballyglass, but I do remember what it was like to be cold and so hungry I couldn't sleep, and curled up against you in the night to try to stay warm. Bad as it was on Tompkins Street, it was never like that."

Joseph stubbed out his cigarette. "I'd just as soon not visit the past. Where is this leading, Moira?"

She rotated the dolly stick between her hands, raising it up and down every third or fourth turn. The sheets sloshed and spattered water up on her apron. She pushed her hair back out of her eyes with her forearm and looked at him.

"Just this. He came from a place that should have been his own, where he should have had the right to work and a way to feed his family. His own country, Irish as he is,

311

but he had no rights. And he comes here, to a place where the Irish are the scourge of the city — as reviled as ever a Negro was in the South — and even in the worst of jobs and the worst place to live, he's better off than he ever was at home. Do you blame him for being angry? Can you blame him for wanting things in Ireland to be better for all those brothers and sisters and cousins he left behind? Even a country that hates him treats him better than his own."

"This country does not hate him or any other Irishman, Moira. When they come here to work, and live a clean, sober life, no one is better liked than the Irish. Too many of them don't, and that's the problem."

Moira turned her attention back to her task. "You may be right, but I'm telling you the way he sees it. The child whose mother rejects him will go back again and again searching for her love. He'll protect her and do everything he can to help her, and all the while he'll be asking himself what he's doing wrong because she doesn't love him. But he won't give up, Joseph; he'll just keep trying. That's Dad, and Ireland is his mother."

Moira poked at a pillowslip and lifted it out of the kettle, slopping it over to the sink. Joseph could see the steam rising off of it, but if it burned Moira's hands, she didn't seem to notice. She picked it up and scrubbed it against the washboard.

"And that leg of his doesn't help. He feels impotent, don't you see? He can't work and he has twenty or more good years ahead of him. He wants to make his mark somewhere, and Ireland most of all. He wasn't thinking about your job, or about that girl. He was thinking about how he was changing things in Ireland, that's all."

A silence fell over the room, relieved only by the rhythm of Moira's work on the washboard. Joseph finished his coffee considering what he had left unsaid between them — that he'd tried to please the old man all his life, walked the straight and narrow, gotten a good job and promising future, and yet it was Liam, who gave not a tinker's damn for anyone but himself, who was his father's white-haired boy. But Moira would not have listened to him, probably wouldn't listen to him about the Bonner woman either. He took his mug to the sink, rinsed it, dried it and set it up on the shelf, and went to meet his father at the door.

"Will you slow down?" Dennis asked. "I'm havin' a hard time keepin' up with you, son." Joseph slowed his step only enough

313

that Dennis could, with effort, stay abreast of him.

"Liam's comin' to dinner tonight," Dennis said companionably. "You'll be there, of course?"

"I don't know where I'll be. Out trying to keep Maggie Flynn out of Blackwell's Island, I expect. But I'll be making no great effort to dine with Liam O'Neill, I can tell you," he added.

Dennis opened his mouth, but seemed to think better of a rejoinder when he noticed his son's expression. They caught a cross-town car and met the Second Avenue El at 8th Street. At first, Dennis had refused to give him John Devoy's address.

"Fine," Joseph said. "I'll find it out for myself. Seamus will give it to me if I tell him I want to take the oath. In fact, it's better that way, if I go without you."

Dennis had slapped a slouch cap on his head. "Come along, then."

They rode the el in silence for forty blocks, before Dennis leaned toward his son confidentially. "You can't compromise us, Shosav. You must promise me that. John'll be wantin' you to take the oath and join the Napper Tandys before he tells you anything."

"I'm making no such promises. I won't be

joining the Napper Tandy club or any other wing of Clan na Gael. I'm an officer of the United States Treasury Department. I've already taken an oath, and it overrides yours." Joseph turned in his seat so that he could look his father square in the face.

"You forget, Dad, that I have powers of arrest. I'm warning you, if you refuse to answer my questions, I will use them."

Dennis crossed his arms on his chest, stared straight ahead at an inexplicable hat covered with miniature frosted fruit on the woman in front of him, and said no more to his son until they alighted at East 99th Street. "Let's get it done," he said and strode out ahead of Joseph, moving as fast as his artificial leg and crutch would go. When they reached Devoy's building, Dennis made one last appeal.

"I know you're angry, son. And I can't even say that I blame you much. But if you want help from John Devoy, you'd best keep your tongue in check. He's a hard man, Shosav. He's had to be."

They climbed to a second-floor flat and knocked at a door in a dark hallway. A woman's voice questioned them from behind the door. "Who is it?"

"Dennis Hannegan, Kate. I need to speak to John right away."

A small, square woman opened the door. "Oh," she said, taking in Joseph beside his father. She sent a wary glance toward the front room. "And who's this with you?"

Dennis removed his cap and took a step into the flat. "It's all right, Kate. This is my son, Shosav. He's at the immigration station. Kate McBride, John's sister," he said over his shoulder to Joseph.

Her hair was wiry and gray, like strands of steel twisted and roped into a bun at the nape of her neck, and when she looked at Joseph, her thin lips formed a noncommittal line. "John's in the front room," she said, and pointed them through a kitchen where the unpleasant smell of cabbage lingered heavily.

Joseph had met John Devoy before, at weddings and funerals his father had insisted they attend. He hadn't liked the man much then. His opinion did not alter now.

Devoy was black Irish, like Joseph's own family, with silvering hair and eyes of piercing blue. His beard was still as black as a winter sky, and thick and rough as the steel wool they used on the pots in the station's kitchens. A coarse thatch of eyebrow hovered low over his eyes, and lent him an angry appearance, even on the rare occasions when he was not, in fact, angry. This was not one of those occasions. He was squinting over an old edition of *The Irish Times* and threw it down in disgust when Joseph and Dennis entered the room.

"Redmond and his blasted United Irish League are hurting us almost as much as the bloody Brits, Hannegan," he shouted. "They're no better than collaborators. Good to see you, Joe, lad," he said, and rose to extend his hand.

He was a stocky man, built square like his sister and barely taller than Joseph's shoulder. His hand was dry and calloused, his handshake hard and uncompromising. He pointed them to chairs, picked up a black lacquer ear dome and fitted it into his ear. "You'll have to speak up for me, lad. Are you finally going to take the oath, then?"

"We've come about another matter, John," Dennis said hastily. "Shosav's had some news about Doyle."

Joseph glared at his father, annoyed at the way his own role had been so deftly transformed from adversary to ally of Clan na Gael. But he also recognized effective diplomacy when he saw it, and judging by Devoy's expression, diplomacy might well be needed. His eyes had narrowed and his features had the studied vacancy of a man who had trained himself to give nothing

317

away unintentionally.

"What have you told him, Hannegan?" Devoy asked evenly.

"Nothing, John. The girl must have told him what she knows. He put the rest together."

"Doyle is dead, Mr. Devoy," Joseph said. "He washed up at Ellis Island early this morning with a gunshot wound. The doctor thinks he's been dead twenty-four to forty-eight hours, but he can't say for sure that it wasn't longer."

Devoy registered no shock, but listened, turning the ear dome carefully in Joseph's direction. He stroked his beard and nodded his head, as though this information might not be news to him. "I suspected as much," he said at last. He didn't deny knowledge of Cormac Doyle, which would have been foolish after all, and Devoy was no one's fool. But he said nothing more, waiting for Joseph to continue.

"You and I both know that Maggie Flynn didn't kill him, although she may be prosecuted for it. I'm here to help her."

"What makes you think you can?"

"I know Doyle left Ellis Island alive and well. I want Moran to come forward and tell the marshals the truth."

"Moran can't help you without jeopardizing the operation, and we can't afford to do that. There must be other ways to save the girl."

Joseph shook his head. "I can't think of any. There were too many witnesses to the shooting, and the doctor can't place the time of death recently enough to exonerate her. She can tell her story, but who's going to believe her?"

Devoy frowned, but nothing in his posture indicated concession. "Sometimes there have to be sacrifices in war. The girl may have to be one of them."

Joseph stared at him, struggling to give voice to the incomprehensible. "You'd let an innocent girl be condemned to death for a crime she didn't commit, when you have it in your power to save her? When it was you who set events in motion in the first place?"

Devoy rose slowly from his chair and stood gazing out his window. "Do you know how many innocent women and children died during the famine, Joe?"

Joseph stirred with a rising impatience, but, when Devoy turned he saw in the older man's expression the wound that would not heal. "Almost a million people died during those five years, Joe, and the Brits stood by and watched. Their children and grandchildren would do the same today. That is the yoke we're under. If the girl had to die to save so many others, don't you think she would? Wouldn't any true Irish man or woman?"

"Then at least let's give her the choice. She has a right to that."

Devoy turned away. "It can't be done, Joe. Don't you think I would save her if I could?"

Reluctant as he was to believe it, Joseph knew that Devoy was telling the truth as he saw it. Here was a man who clung to his vision past all reason. And why wouldn't he? He had given his entire life to it, choosing celibacy and loneliness because he could not ask a wife to live as he did. What a terrible joke it would be to find, at the end, that his sacrifices had been for naught. And Joseph believed that the future held exactly that anticlimax for Devoy and men like him. He could not allow Maggie Flynn to be sacrificed on their altar of futility.

"Then I want to know everything about the operation. Perhaps I can find the killer myself."

Something in the older man softened. He returned to his chair and readjusted the hearing aid. "I can tell you nothing," he said. "Unless you take the oath."

It always came back to the same thing.

What angered Joseph was not that these men were irrationally devoted to their ideals, but that they expected everyone else to embrace them with the same fervor. Never mind that it meant forfeiting one's own integrity.

"I've already taken my oath, Mr. Devoy, and it's to a government much more powerful than your band of rebels. My oath states that I will protect and defend the United States. That means that if I have cause to believe that someone is not acting in my government's best interests, I am required to take action to stop them. I can do that, Mr. Devoy. I can call on the resources of the United States Treasury Department to put a stop to your organization's activities once and for all. And I will do it if I have to."

Devoy was on his feet. "You have no right to come in here demanding information and threatening me. I don't know what your father may have told you —"

"My father has told me nothing, and believe me, it makes him no hero in my eyes. The truth of the matter is that I'm going to find out who killed Cormac Doyle. I'm not going to sit by and let an innocent girl be executed for you or your cause. Now you need to ask yourself which way is better

— to cooperate with me and start giving me the information I need, or to let me start turning over rocks and finding out for myself. But you had better be prepared, because all kinds of ugly things are going to crawl out from under them."

Devoy thrust out his jaw. His solid form seemed even more rigid and immovable, but at length the changing color in his face betrayed him. "Ask me your questions. I'll answer what I can," he said.

Joseph took a seat. "Let's begin with Dylan Moran," he said.

Devoy glanced up at his sister, standing in the kitchen doorway, and gave her a brief nod. She disappeared into the kitchen, returning seconds later with a young man at her heels who had been hiding in the room behind the kitchen. He leaned against the kitchen door and crossed his legs, jamming his hands into his pockets.

"Ya wanted me, didja?" he said. He pulled a peppermint out of his pocket, unwrapped it and popped it into his mouth.

The familiar smell of peppermint took Joseph back to the tenement on Rivington Street. "Dylan Moran, isn't it?" he said.

Chapter
Twenty-Two

"And who mightcha be?"

"I'm the man you clouted on Rivington Street."

Dylan pushed himself off the doorframe, and shot him an easy grin. "Well, if I'd known ya were a friend, I'd have taken you down to the local for a slug."

"I'm not here as a friend, Moran," Joseph said, sending Devoy a warning glance. "I'm here to find out what happened to Cormac Doyle."

Moran's gaze shifted to Devoy and back to Joseph. "Don't know, but I'll go bail he's asleep in a trollop's bed. He'll come round when he sobers up."

"I didn't say I was looking for him. I said I'm here to find out what happened to him. He's dead, Moran."

Moran turned back to Devoy, whose expression confirmed it. He fell backward, grasping the doorframe, and stared at Joseph as if he couldn't take it in. "Yer sure?"

"Maggie Flynn identified him early this morning."

Moran raked his hand through his hair and turned on his heel, pacing off a four-foot square, agitated as a man trapped in a cell. "Goddammit, he should have waited for me! Why didn't he wait? He knew better. He knew it was dangerous."

His gaze roamed over the room's dusty trappings, as if Cormac Doyle might be hiding behind the hulking walnut sideboard or under the sagging springs of the rusty iron day bed. "Stubborn bastard, too smart by half. 'I'm a cat, doncha know, and I've still got eight lives left' he'd say to me. Always takin' the chances, gamblin' against God. Damn ya, Cormac! If ya were here, I'd shootcha myself!"

"Whisht!" Kate McBride grabbed him by the arm and shook him. He stared at her without comprehension, but it put a blunt end to his anger. The grief that would be so much deeper and darker, Joseph thought, would come privately later. He eased out of Kate's grasp and dropped into a straight chair, elbowed his knees and covered his face with his hands. At length, he crossed himself. "God rest his soul," he said. "He was the best friend I ever had."

Silence hung over the room like a black crepe drape. Joseph waited a respectful moment before withdrawing a small notebook and pencil from his pocket. "Is there family in Ireland that we should contact?"

Dylan shook his head. "There might be somewhere, but he never talked about them except to say that his da' was hung for Phoenix Park. The girl was the only other one. Whatever you might be thinkin', Cormac did love her."

And this, Joseph thought, was what Fenian rebels brought to the ones they loved. Doyle's father had been a rebel himself, and an assassin, who'd left his son a legacy of bitterness and betrayal. And here was poor Maggie with a murder charge on her head, all for falling in love with the wrong man. He wanted to jerk his father out of his chair and shake him senseless. This is what you'll bring us to, he shouted in his mind. This is what your precious Ireland will do to us. Moran interrupted his thoughts.

"Maggie — how is she?"

"Grieving and frightened, as well she might be. She'll be charged with murder, unless the lot of you come forward with the truth."

"No!" Devoy leapt out of his seat, and his compact body seemed to loom over the rest of them, as though his small stature were an illusion hiding a much larger presence. He stood with his feet apart and his fists doubled, ready to take on any man foolish enough to challenge him. "We will not compromise this operation for a slip."

"But she'll be charged with murder, John." For the first time, Dennis looked truly disturbed. Joseph locked his gaze with the older man.

"I thought we had settled all this, Mr. Devoy. I'm going to clear Maggie Flynn's name, whether it means compromising your people or not. As I see it, you have two choices: you can tell me what in hell is going on, and we can work together, or you can try to keep the truth from me. But I will use every bit of my authority as an agent of the federal government against you. I can have you deported, Devoy, and I won't think twice about doing it. It's up to you."

Kate McBride had not missed a word of the exchange. Standing in the kitchen door, she wrung her hands like a sopping rag. "Listen to him, John. You'll have nowhere to go. If they send you back to Ireland, you'll be arrested on the spot. Do you want to die in Kilmainham Jail?"

"If that's what it takes," he said, his gaze never breaking with Joseph's.

"Well, if you won't think of yourself, then think of me." As if this might not be impetus enough, she added, "Think about all the men out there relying on you."

Kate McBride's dour features were etched with anxiety. Devoy glanced at her and away again. Shoving his hands in his pockets, he turned his back on the rest of the men. "Tell him, Moran."

Dylan leaned forward, elbows resting on his knees. "Two nights ago, it was. We'd had a clamper over the girl. He loved her in his way, ya see, but he had a roving eye. He was all for visiting a trollop. I didn't like it, said I wouldn't go and he could just go alone. Well, he grumbled about it, but finally he gave in, so I went out to buy us some food and a bottle. While I was gone, Cormac received a note. It was signed by Mr. Devoy, here, or at least that's what it said. It said there was a rescue on for the girl and told him to take a ferry —"

"The Communipaw ferry," Devoy supplied, turning back around.

Dylan nodded. "Right. To New Jersey. He was to come alone. There wouldn't be room for me. When I got back, I found the note." He pulled a slip of paper out of his pocket and handed it over to Joseph.

There was nothing remarkable about it —

just a plain sheet that could have been purchased in one of hundreds of stationers' stores around New York. The message was printed, and said just what Moran had reported, that Doyle should take the 9:00 Communipaw ferry to New Jersey. He would be met on the other side. Joseph passed the note over to Devoy, but Devoy waved it away.

"I've seen it," he said.

"And does this look like your signature?"

"It does."

Joseph turned the note over and held it to the light. The letters in the body of the note barely showed through, but the signature was deeper and had left an impression in the opposite side of the paper. "It was traced," he said.

"If I'd been there, I would have followed him. He shouldn't have gone alone — he knew better — but I suppose it was seein' Mr. Devoy's name and all. Anyway, I did go down to the ferry, but I was too late and the last boat was gone. Cormac must have caught it. I knew he wouldn't be comin' back that night, seein' that the ferry had quit runnin' for the night, but I thought sure he'd be back in the mornin'.

"That's the last I saw of him. When he didn't come back by the next night, I came here lookin' for him. Mr. Devoy thought it best for me to stay here. Mrs. McBride went to the flat and brought back my things. And here I've been ever since, waitin', hopin' that Cormac would show up."

It made sense to send Doyle to New Jersey. The immigration station was far closer to the Jersey coast than to Manhattan. But how could he have believed that they could get Maggie out of the station when she was locked in the witness room and there were watchmen and gatemen everywhere? Whoever had shot Doyle had put him in a boat and dumped him when he got close to the station. They would probably never know whether or not Doyle was alive when he went into the water. The body sank, as Dr. Morton had explained, then began to rise sometime later as it floated toward the island. It was not coincidental, Joseph thought, that Doyle's wound was exactly like the one scores of witnesses had seen Maggie Flynn deliver on the dock.

"Why did you come here in the first place?" Joseph said.

Moran glanced at Devoy, who shook his head. Joseph reached into his breast pocket and brought out his identification from the Department of the Treasury. Kate McBride sent Devoy a mute plea.

"All right," he said. "But it must go no further than this room."

"I can't make that promise."

The older man's expression darkened. "You'll leave me nothin', will you boy?"

"I'll give you as good as you gave Maggie Flynn, if that's what it takes."

Devoy blew out a long, silent whistle, but finally began. "Doyle was in charge of receiving guns shipped from the States. It was a small operation, exclusively Napper Tandy — received by a man in Liverpool who sent them on to Derry. Moran, here, picked them up in Derry and took them to Lissadell, where Doyle was stockpiling them."

"Was the landlord part of this?"

Moran shook his head. "Not the old man. But Constance Gore-Booth seems to be leanin' toward our side, even though she's a Protestant. Cormac and I met her in Paris when we were there with the IRB. It's the perfect place, doncha' see? A Protestant big house right on the water. She set up Cormac as horse trainer on her father's estate. It gave him the freedom he needed to move guns with the horses and feed. It was a grand plan," he added wistfully.

Devoy returned to his seat. He loosened the cuffs of his shirt and methodically rolled them back as he spoke. "Our man in Liverpool is in jail, and you know Doyle's end. Moran was the only one known to both men on that side of the Atlantic, but more to the point, he was the one that no one in the States knew about. When our man in Liverpool was arrested, and Doyle went on the keeping in Drumcliffe, he knew there was a stag in the operation."

Dennis's gaze went to Moran, still elbowing his knees and watching Devoy. Joseph knew what his father was thinking, but warned him off with a frown, and turned his attention back to Devoy. "Who knew about the operation?"

"I've been over this a dozen times myself, lad. Six men sit on our executive board — the Napper Tandy club, that is. Myself, your father, Tom Clarke, Dan Cohalan, Seamus O' Neill, and Pat McCartain."

McCartain. Another stroke of the artist's brush, another dab of color to clarify the image. What better way to fool onlookers than to send a doctor to do a doctor's job? If he'd been stopped, who better to talk knowledgeably with other doctors about wounds? And that suggested they'd probably also sent real New York cops — off duty, but with genuine uniforms and badges that no one would question. Brilliant.

"You had to set up this operation in advance. Did your cops know who Doyle was and why he was here?"

Devoy shook his head. "Once they take the oath, they follow orders. They don't ask questions." He said it proudly, but the virtue of blind obedience was lost on Joseph.

"Who found the flat for Doyle and Moran?"

"Cohalan," Devoy said.

Joseph turned back to Moran. "Did you stay on Rivington Street?"

Moran shook his head. "Not after you'd been there. He found us another flat."

"And where was the second flat?"

"Forsyth Street, number thirty-four."

Joseph glanced over the notes he had taken, but his mind was elsewhere. At length he reached into his pocket and brought out a dollar.

"I haven't eaten in almost twenty-four hours," he said, turning to Dylan. "Moran, why don't you go down the street and get us some sandwiches and beer. I believe I saw a pub down the way."

It was an obvious ploy, and Devoy picked up on it as Joseph thought he would. "It's too much for Kate," he said. "Go for her, won't you lad?" Moran took the money and left without a backward glance.

"As I said, they follow orders," Devoy added when the door had firmly closed behind Moran. Joseph, however, waited until Moran appeared on the street below before continuing his questions.

"How much do you know about him?"

"He was Doyle's second in command. He had great grah for Doyle. You saw how he took the news."

"I saw how he seemed to take it."

Devoy waved his hand impatiently. "I spoke to Cormac Doyle myself. He was convinced the leak came from the States. Moran came along to help provide cover for him and get him through the station."

"But he's the obvious choice for informant, the only one on the Irish side who escaped the notice of the constables."

Devoy met his gaze steadily, his eyes a coldly blazing blue. "I don't like stags, Hannegan. I've had two in my operation, and never a worse betrayal than Henri LeCaron. It pains me to say this but I am convinced the leak came from here."

He shifted in his seat and stroked his beard. Joseph felt him hovering on the edge of further disclosure. "Besides, there is something else," he said slowly. "The Lissadell operation is not the only one we have in place. Guns on the western coast are not very useful to men in the eastern counties. There is, or was, a second operation in Dublin. The shipments came in through the port of Glasgow. Most of them went out of Dublin on fishing boats. Last week I got word that our man in Glasgow is in Barlinnie prison."

Dennis sat forward abruptly. "Not Dublin too, John."

Devoy confirmed it. "It's a matter of time until the Brits round up the men on the east coast unless they get my warning first. Neither Doyle nor Moran knew about the Dublin group. The leak is here, in the States, and we've got to find it or a half-dozen men. . . ." He let his words trail off, as if contemplating the setback was more than he could bear.

"All right, let's assume you're correct and you have a stag in your organization. Who made the shipping contact in Liverpool?"

Devoy's gaze shifted to Dennis, and a bitter smile flashed across his face. "Don't you know, Hannegan? Your father."

They stood below the station on 99th Street while a train thundered over their heads. Dennis leaned heavily on his crutch. Seams of fatigue and worry scored his face. "My hand and my word, son, I had no part in tippin' the constables."

Joseph found himself at a loss for words. On all the earth, Dennis Hannegan would be the last person to betray his cause. It was a measure of how far apart they had grown, that Dennis could think his son would even suspect him. "I know you didn't, Dad," he said softly. "And so does Devoy. It will be up to the two of you, though, to find out who did."

Before Moran returned, they had agreed that Devoy and Dennis Hannegan would have to trace the movements of every man on the executive committee on the night Doyle was killed. "Your people will give you far more cooperation than they would ever give me," Joseph said. "We need hard-and-fast alibis for every one of the men on that committee. Anyone who looks even slightly suspect must be investigated very carefully. In the meantime, I suggest you give Moran something to do that will keep him far away from your investigation. To my way of thinking, he's still the most likely suspect."

When Dennis had excused himself to go down to the privy in the alley, Joseph had one final direction for Devoy. "It will be up to you to investigate Seamus O'Neill. It can't be left to Dad." Devoy had agreed without question.

Dennis hobbled toward the stairs up to the platform. "I can't believe that any one of us on the committee is a stag. I've known every one of those men for years, worked side by side with 'em on hundreds of operations and not one of them ever compromised."

"Things change, Dad. People change. Even you. You can't hold your stout like you used to, for example. Get a little too much and you might forget yourself, start thinking everyone's your friend —"

"Confound it! I didn't, I tell you."

"Don't be scalding me with your abuse. It was just an example."

Joseph followed his father up the wrought iron staircase, instinctively putting his hand on the older man's back, ready to catch him if he should lose his balance. He was keeping his composure only with great effort. Hard experience had taught him that when both of them were in a temper, they might as well be speaking different languages.

He should have been able to depend on his father at least to get answers from Devoy. The old rebel had bucked at having to reveal one more piece of his plans than he thought was absolutely necessary. Over Moran's sandwiches and beer, Joseph had tried to pull it out of him inch by inch.

Where had the guns come from? Devoy had declined to answer. How were they shipped? Again, Devoy had refused to give out the information.

"It's not something you need to know," he said. He locked his gaze with Joseph's. "I'll give you this. Moran's sworn, of course. I'll put him to watch the dealer and the shipper."

Joseph made a hollow protest, but capitulated easily. "I'll accept that for now, but if I need the information later, I expect you to give it to me."

Devoy rose with the other men. "What will you do now?"

"While you're working on your end, I'm going to interview the employees at the Communipaw ferry. My position at the station should give me some influence with them. Maybe one of them will remember Doyle and who he met. Whoever killed Doyle is probably your informer, but we can't be absolutely sure. I'll let you know what I learn."

When they reached the platform, Dennis dropped onto a bench to wait for the train. His breathing was labored, an indication of how difficult getting around on the crutch was for him. But he refused to use the chair except at home. "Can't take the blasted thing on the train," he complained. "Can't get around old women on the sidewalk." Joseph thought it was more than that — a reluctance to surrender another inch of his independence. It was one of the things he admired about his father.

"What I don't understand," Joseph said, taking a seat beside his father, "is how Doyle could have believed they could rescue Maggie from the station. Surely they knew she was under guard."

"I don't know what they knew, Shosav. You didn't tell me about the girl, so they couldn't get any information from me." There was a moment of tense silence between them, Joseph trying on several versions of what he wanted to say — that Dennis had no right to pass on information about the station, that whatever was told to him was told in confidence. Dennis derailed him before he started.

"But don't forget, everyone knows about the *Catalpa*."

"Everyone but me, I suppose," Joseph said. "What is the *Catalpa?*"

Dennis leaned back expansively, beaming at his son. "Whalin' ship. Back in '76, there were six Fenian prisoners in a penal colony in Australia, ya' see. Friends of Devoy, and he was determined they weren't to live out their days there. So he brought together a crew, bought the *Catalpa* and sailed it to Australia with John Boyle O'Reilly. They rescued the Fenians and brought them back here to New York. Say what you will about John, he's not afraid of the grand deed. Even now, he's plannin' —"

Dennis stopped, staring down at the toe of his shoe for a moment, the truth of his momentary slip clouding his face. It was enough that he saw, now, how easily secrets came to be divulged. Joseph smoothed it over.

"So I suppose if he could do that, a rescue from Ellis Island seemed like a small thing to Doyle."

"I suppose it did," Dennis said quietly.

"So who is Henri LeCaron?"

"British informer." Dennis stood up, gazing down the track at the oncoming train. He stuck the crutch under his arm, hobbled to the edge of the platform and back again.

"His real name was Thomas Beech, and Devoy believes he was responsible for the death of his friend Pat Cronin. Cronin was murdered when Beech testified in London that there were other spies in the Clan ranks. Some of the other brothers thought he was talking about Cronin, and soon after, poor old Pat turned up dead. It all happened years ago, but Devoy's never gotten over it. It'll be the devil's own cure for the traitor when you find out who he is."

Dennis paused to adjust his crutch. He opened his mouth and abruptly closed it again, pressing his lips in a thin line.

"What aren't you telling me, Dad?"

The older man paused a breath and shook his head. "I'd be careful how I talked to John Devoy, son. He won't let anyone, even you, get in the way of Clan business."

"If you're telling me that Devoy is a dangerous man, I figured that out for myself a long time ago. But I can't let it stop me. I have as much obligation to protect the people coming through that big gate out there in the water as I have to protect the rest of us, and I couldn't sleep nights knowing that girl was facing execution because of the likes of John Devoy." And you, he silently added.

When they were finally on the train, Joseph surrendered to the exhaustion he'd been keeping at bay. He laid his head back against the seat and listened to the rails clattering under his feet. He had called McNabb from the station in the early hours of the morning to report finding Doyle's body. It would be transported to the city morgue today, and the U.S. Marshals would follow to pick up Maggie. It might be best, he'd suggested to McNabb, to wait to move the body until evening, when activity at the station would be minimal, to forestall the attention of the press. Likewise, it would be best to delay bringing in the marshals until the body had been removed, separating them into two ostensibly unrelated events. McNabb concurred, as Joseph knew he would.

"I want you there when they pick up the Flynn girl, in case the press gets wind of it," McNabb said. "This is your responsibility."

Joseph wanted to keep Maggie out of Blackwell's Island as long as possible, although he knew he couldn't retain her indefinitely. There was only one way to bring McNabb to the same conclusion.

"I haven't had any sleep in twenty-four hours," he said. "I'm afraid you'll have to manage remanding her to the custody of the marshals. You can handle the reporters. They'll probably have questions about the Boarding investigation anyway, and I can't answer those." It worked.

"She'll be here when you get back," McNabb growled and hung up the phone. Joseph had smiled to himself. Sometimes McNabb made it just too easy.

But he was not to be underestimated.

Keeping the Assistant Commissioner in the dark about the Flynn investigation was essential. If he had any idea that Dennis Hannegan and his cronies were involved in the Doyle murder, McNabb would descend on Joseph like a rat on a corpse, gnawing at him until Joseph had not a shred of integrity left. Even now, Joseph was hanging onto his principles with difficulty.

In theory, he believed he should tell the marshals everything he knew and withdraw from Maggie Flynn's case, perhaps even resign his job. In fact, there were other, more important issues at stake. It would be the height of arrogance to suggest that only he could do the job Powderly had assigned him. But the trust he had cultivated in other station employees would not be easily reestablished by someone else, and in the interim, McNabb would have free rein to do as he liked at the station. The stakes were too high to allow himself the luxury of leaving the job with his principles intact. But it was those very principles that made him vulnerable to Edward McNabb. He'd claim that Joseph had tried to cover up for the Flynn girl because his own family was involved in an attempt to deceive the United States government. And he'd have Lederman as a witness, testifying that Joseph had been unwilling to investigate. Worst of all, there was just enough truth in it to convict him.

CHAPTER
TWENTY-THREE

Rachel lay on her bed watching the vine of small pink rosebuds climb their pale green striped background. She had selected the wallpaper at age fifteen — a sentimental choice dictated by adolescent dreams of tormented heroes after the Heathcliffian model. It occurred to her now that Heathcliff really wasn't a very good catch. Good men did not taunt, abuse, or neglect the women in their lives. They loved them.

The way Matt Bonner loved Irene Garrity. But sometimes there were barriers to love, although Rachel was not sufficiently experienced in that kind of intimacy to quite understand them. It seemed to her that Matt and Irene stood on opposite sides of a glass wall and needed only to break the glass to come together as they were meant. She had ruthlessly shattered it for them, but instead of bringing them together, she had left them lacerated and bleeding where they stood.

She had awakened with a feeling of heaviness, as though the very air in the room would crush her. She would have to get up sometime. She couldn't escape back into sleep, filled as it was with nightmares. Irene was drowning, and neither she nor Matt could save her. Joseph Hannegan declared his love for Maggie Flynn. Moira stood over her, utensil in hand, declaring that this was an oyster fork. Nightmares born of the events of the day and all the more painful because they were rooted in reality.

The light of the street lamp outside her window projected on her wall the shadows of leaves that shimmered in the evening's breeze. Even as she watched, one detached from its limb and floated slowly out of sight, leaving behind no sign that it had been there but the diminished fullness of the branch. And so it seemed with her life, that people detached themselves one by one, eventually leaving her to stand bare and alone in the world. Her parents, gone at the age of seven; no grandparents to steady her, few friends remaining from her youth, and now Matt and Irene, whom she had willfully shaken until one of them was bound to fall. Moira Hannegan, for whom she felt a deepening friendship, would be cut off from her by her brother. She had become fond of Maggie Flynn, but Maggie might even now be on her way to Blackwell's Island.

Suddenly, Rachel had to know. She slipped out from under her counterpane and grabbed her dressing gown off the bedpost, tying it around her waist as she hurried down the stairs to the telephone. No, the night matron said, they had not taken the girl yet, although there were rumors that she was to be picked up in the morning. Rachel dropped the receiver into the cradle with relief and went to find her uncle.

Matt sat at the dining table staring straight ahead, a full plate of pork chops, potatoes, and asparagus in front of him, and a cup of coffee growing cold in his hand. The newspaper sat to his left, as yet folded just as the boy had delivered it. Rachel took a bowl from the butler's pantry and ladled green turtle soup out of a Havilland tureen on the sideboard. Her hand shook, and a bit of the soup sloshed over the side of the bowl.

"My behavior this morning was inexcusable," she said.

"Yes," he agreed. "It was." He set down his coffee cup, as if he could no longer bear the weight of the tissue-thin china.

Rachel snatched a napkin off the stack next to the tureen and mopped up the spilled soup. "I'll go apologize to Irene right now."

"Sit down, please, Rachel."

Rachel gazed into the mirror above the sideboard. Matt wasn't looking at her, but staring at some invisible point on the wall. Her heart grew heavy at the anguished stillness of his expression. She put the napkin down, and joined him at the table.

"She said 'No'," he said at last.

"You asked her?"

"I did. She said 'No.' "

"But why, Uncle Matt? She loves you."

"Apparently not," he said, turning to meet her gaze, and letting the full impact of his pain register on her.

"But you love her, don't you?"

"Does it matter? Why would she want me, Rachel? I'm forty-six years old and nothing to look at."

"And kind, and clever, and witty. She loves you, Uncle Matt. I know she does."

"You can't force love, Rachel, just because you want it to be that way."

"You were forced to love me," she said. "No one gave you a choice."

He smiled sadly at her. "It was no great chore learning to love that winsome little girl with the big eyes who stepped off the train all alone."

Rachel toyed with the spoon at her place, remembering how, as a little girl, she'd gaze into the bowl and laugh at her own reflection. Matt had shown her that, and explained how convex and concave surfaces bent the images they reflected. She must have loved her father, although she barely remembered him now, but she couldn't have loved him more than this man sitting at the table with her. Only as an adult had she realized the sacrifices he'd made. He was a young man when her father died, and must have felt very much at sea, faced with the prospect of raising his brother's daughter, and not even married himself. He didn't know the rules of child rearing, but operated on instinct, and on the way he, himself, would like to be treated. It was a good way to raise a child.

"Why haven't you ever married, Uncle Matt?" she said. "Wouldn't it have been easier for you — having to raise me, I mean."

Matt pulled his watch out of his vest pocket and wound it absently. "The first few years, I was . . . off balance, I suppose you could say. All I could concentrate on was my practice, and what I should be doing for you. There wasn't time in my life for a wife. And Irene was doing a fine job with you. I couldn't imagine anyone doing it better."

He slipped his watch back into the pocket and gazed down at his untouched plate. "And then, I don't know, really. Irene was here. I never met another woman who interested me."

"I'm sorry," she said.

"So am I." He pushed his plate away, picked up the paper and rolled it into a tight cylinder. "I'm going into the office."

"Tonight? Now?"

"I have work to catch up on, and the campaign is going to pick up speed after the committee of eighteen make their final selections. Assuming Seth Low is nominated, I won't have a free minute."

Rachel dipped into her soup. "Is there any doubt?"

"Considerable, actually." He stood up, smoothed his tie and buttoned his jacket. "Seth is behind right now, and there are too many contenders out there to be complacent. Tell Irene, if you see her, that I'll be home late."

"Wait," Rachel said. "I know I'm not in a position to ask favors, but I was wondering if you would consider taking on a new client. I'll pay you your usual fee."

"It's not a matter of money, Rachel, and

even if it were, I wouldn't take yours. I have a campaign to manage. Running for political office is a full-time job in itself."

Rachel swallowed back her disappointment. "You're right, of course."

She rose and returned to the sideboard, passing over the pork chops, but selecting a filet of sole and buttered asparagus. "Besides, there are plenty of good attorneys in New York. Who would you recommend?"

"Well, there's Frank Carroll, Charlie Orr. Both good men." He started for the door, but turned back. "Out of curiosity, what's the case?"

"Murder," she said. "The accused is Maggie Flynn, the Irish immigrant girl I told you about."

"But there was no body."

Rachel picked up an asparagus spear and nibbled on it. "Well, there is now."

She took her plate to the table, waited while he resumed his seat, then filled in the details up to the point when Doyle's body washed up at the station. "I just called the station. They haven't arrested her yet."

"Well, it's probably imminent," he said. "Depending on how quickly the body was sent to the morgue, I'd expect she'll be picked up in the morning. I'll need to talk to her as soon as possible. Let me try to clear my desk tonight."

"You'll take it?"

Matt stood up, swallowing the last of his cold coffee. "If that were you, in a strange country, abused by someone you'd trusted . . . well, I hope someone would help you. Yes, I'll do it."

After he'd gone, Rachel went looking for Irene. "She's in her apartment, Miss," the maid told her. "She's been feeling poorly all day and said she didn't want to be disturbed."

"I'll look in on her, Alma," Rachel said, taking the backstairs down to the first-floor basement. She rapped sharply on the door, but didn't wait to be invited in.

"Irene?" she called.

Her answer came from the bedroom to the left of the hall. "I'll be out in a minute."

A newspaper lay open on the desk in Irene's small parlor. The page said "Classified Advertisements." Beside it sat a stack of envelopes, addressed, stamped and ready to be sent out. Rachel picked them up and flipped through them. Orbach's, Siegel-Cooper, B. Altman, and several that looked like housekeeping positions.

"You're overstepping your boundaries, Rachel," Irene said quietly. She took the letters out of Rachel's hand, returned them to the desk, and laid the newspaper on top of them. "Some things are private, even from you."

Rachel drifted over to a settee nestled in the bay window that looked out at the garden and the carriage house beyond it. From there she could see into Irene's bedroom. A pile of dresses lay sprawled across the bed. It struck her, in a moment of irrelevance, that Irene had always worn the plainest of dresses befitting a nurse or housekeeper when she could have afforded much better, almost as if she were determined to remain in her place and give Matt Bonner no reason to think of her otherwise. She set the thought aside for closer examination later and turned to the subject of why they were there, and why a faintly familiar portmanteau sat next to her dressing table.

"Why are you doing this?" Rachel said.

"I can't stay here. How can I look at him morning and night? My refusal hurt him —"

"And I've hurt you both. I'd give anything to go back and start yesterday over again."

Irene took a chair across from her. "Least said, soonest mended. Some things can't be undone. I'd have thought you'd learned that by now."

Rachel's composure dissolved, flooding her with anger, both at herself and at the victims of her unwitting cruelty for allowing themselves to be hurt by her. "You're absolutely right, Irene. I should have learned it, but apparently I haven't. At least I'm not running away from what I did. I wanted to, but here I am, facing you and wishing I were standing in front of a firing squad instead. You're running away — not from something you did, but from something you feel. Why won't you marry him? I know you love him. Tell me that you don't."

"I'll tell you no such thing, Rachel Bonner," Irene said. "But we don't all love in the same way, or for the same reasons. I've stayed here long past the time I should have gone. He needs to be getting on with his own life, with his career, and I need to be getting on with mine."

Irene picked up a pillow and raked her fingers through the fringe, working through some knots and smoothing it before she replaced it on the settee. "I've never been comfortable having suitors call for me here. It seemed wrong for me to be going out with men when you needed me here with you. But there may still be a man out there in need of a wife like me. I'd like the opportunity to find out.

"Yesterday, I realized that you're a grown woman. You don't need me anymore. I'm thirty-nine years old, Rachel. It's time I started thinking about my own future."

"Uncle Matt is your future, Irene. Can't you see that? He loves you. He wants to marry you."

"Does he now?" Irene's steady gaze bore into her. "Or is he just too much the gentleman to allow you to embarrass me?"

Rachel looked away, but Irene went on. "He lives such a poor, plain life," she said. "Too kind to tell me that I've stayed too long at the party. Too shy, maybe, to find himself a wife when a housekeeper would do. If I leave, maybe it will force him out of that freckled shell of his. You'll be marrying soon yourself. . . ."

She didn't know why, but Rachel's thoughts went to Joseph Hannegan. He would hate what she had done. She'd proved him right. Social workers meddled where they didn't belong. *You do more harm than good,* he'd said. And so she had.

". . . because it's been a comfortable life for both of us," Irene continued, but Rachel was only half-listening.

Was it just a comfortable life? Had she so badly misread their feelings for one another? They had raised her together. Perhaps she had misinterpreted their bond, confused their solidarity in loving her with love for each other.

"He's given me every opportunity," Irene was saying. "I should be able to find a good position. He was always very generous with me, so I've saved up enough money to find myself a nice little flat. It will be the first time I've ever lived in a place all my own."

They needed time, Rachel thought. If only she could keep Irene here, under Matt Bonner's roof, she was sure she could change things between them. "Will you promise me something? Promise me that you'll wait until after the election to leave. You can mail those," she said, shifting her gaze to the envelopes on the desk, "anytime. If you leave now, he won't be able to concentrate on what he's meant to be doing. It might destroy his campaign."

"A professional like Matt Bonner? I hardly think so." Irene rose, picked up the stack of letters and squared them on the corner of her desk. "I have to go now, Rachel. I've given you and your uncle the last seventeen years of my life. Don't ask me for one day more."

CHAPTER
TWENTY-FOUR

Dinner was over when Joseph descended the stairs. He'd managed to get five or six hours of sleep and was feeling somewhat recovered from the ordeal of the night before. He could hear the women in the parlor.

"They're showing hems a bit longer in the back this year, Grace." This brought a muffled response from Miss Dove.

"Well, I didn't know you were making it until just this minute, did I? You know the new S line makes you lean forward a bit. I really think you can just raise that an inch or so in front. You want her to be in fashion, don't you?"

Joseph stood outside the parlor door for a moment, listening to the women. Here was a world he knew nothing about, a place as alien to him as a Jules Verne novel. He peeked around the doorway just in time to hear Miss Dove's exasperated answer.

She was kneeling on the floor, a row of pins clamped between her teeth. Moira stood on a footstool above her wearing a deep crimson dress that rustled as she moved. The neckline was cut low, adding the illusion of extra length to her already graceful neck. Mrs. Shapiro stood next to her, holding up a magazine for her inspection. Miss Dove snatched the remaining pins out of her mouth and glared at Mrs. Shapiro.

"If I turn the hem up enough to make a difference, it will throw the whole line of the skirt off. It has to taper off evenly, don't you see? If you'd told me before I cut the pattern, I would have made the necessary changes, but I'm not going to ruin the gown now trying to adjust it."

As lingerie saleswoman and resident modiste, Mrs. Shapiro would not be denied her say. "All right then, but Moira you must come down to the store and get one of the new S-shaped corsets. They're all the fashion these days."

"And look desperately uncomfortable," Moira said.

"With your waist, you don't need a corset at all." Miss Dove turned up the last inch of hem and sat back on her heels. "There," she said. "Step down and walk across the room, and let's be sure it won't drag on the pavement. Nothing will destroy a dress faster."

"What about shoes?" Mrs. Shapiro asked, flipping through her magazine.

"My brown Sunday shoes will do fine, I think." Moira lifted her skirt and stepped off the stool, glancing up to meet Joseph's gaze.

"Something new?" he said.

Miss Dove greeted him with her customary blush, but Mrs. Shapiro was not hampered by any such reserve. "Black kid, Mr. Hannegan. She ought to have black kid pumps to wear with this dress. Something cut low with this little curved heel that's all the fashion," she said, pointing to a page of ladies' footwear.

"I don't need new shoes." Moira walked across the room, modeling the dress under Miss Dove's critical eye.

Joseph had to admit that the effect of the new dress might well be spoiled by a pair of rundown shoes. He tucked several dollars into the little woman's hand. "Will you go with her, Mrs. Shapiro? Make sure she buys herself something nice. Don't the fashionable ladies sometimes match their shoes to the color of the dress?"

Mrs. Shapiro clapped her hand to her

cheek. "What a lovely idea! We'll look tomorrow, Moira."

Joseph listened to them plan, grateful to the other women for fussing over Moira. She'd had so little of that kind of pleasure in her life. He cleared his throat self-consciously.

"What's all this for, anyway? Something special?"

Moira turned with a graceful lift of her skirt, returning to the footstool for an adjustment in the hem. "Liam's taking me out to see Grace Dudley in *Florodora* and to dinner afterward."

He wished he hadn't asked, and he didn't feel better about it when Mrs. Shapiro gave him her assessment of the occasion.

"Mark my words, Mr. Hannegan, he's going to ask her to marry him."

Miss Dove shot her a furrowed brow, but Mrs. Shapiro seemed unaware of it. Moira glanced up, and he saw in her apprehensive expression that she, too, expected a proposal. For a moment their eyes locked — hers beseeching him for approval. He could not ruin this moment for her, despite his feelings toward Liam. He smiled.

"Well, I'll leave you ladies to it, then. I have to go out for a while, Moira. I may be late."

Behind him, Miss Dove excused herself and followed him into the kitchen. "Forgive me for intruding, Mr. Hannegan, but Moira put a pot of tea on to steep for us and we all forgot about it," she said, gathering cups and saucers for a tray. "I don't want her dragging her hem on the kitchen floor."

"Let me help." He opened the icebox and took out a jug of milk for her tray. "You'll want sugar, of course," he said, fetching a sugar bowl from the dresser.

Miss Dove turned to him tentatively. "Perhaps it is none of my affair, but I was wondering if you're feeling better."

"Feeling better? I wasn't sick, Miss Dove, just very tired."

"No, I didn't mean that exactly." She turned away to arrange her tray. "I must confess to a bit of eavesdropping. I unintentionally overheard Moira talking to Mr. O'Neill about your disagreement with your father. She was quite upset," she added, with a slight reproach in her voice.

"Yes, I know. Moira takes everything to heart."

"Exactly." Miss Dove turned to him, her gaze more direct. "Mrs. Shapiro and I are very fond of Moira, Mr. Hannegan. She has been so dear to us, making us feel welcome and a part of the family. Neither of us like to see her hurt."

"Nor do I," Joseph said. "I wish she could have been spared knowing about this particular incident, but there was nothing for it."

"No? Well what is done, is done. But since I have gone this far, I should like to say something else. You may not like Mr. O'Neill; I confess to having some doubts about him myself, but opposing their marriage is not the answer."

Joseph opened his mouth, but she did not let him interrupt. "Moira, herself, has told me about your opposition to Mr. O'Neill's attentions. Sometimes she needs another woman to talk to. In any event, a bit of counsel: when you speak badly of him, you force her to defend him, which merely draws them closer. She must be given the opportunity to see for herself that he is a . . . well, that he is not the man for her. Moira is a bright young woman and no one's fool. She will see it in time, if you let her. And now, I will leave you with that thought and return to the hem, before she comes looking for me."

He watched the door swing closed behind her, aware that he had been given very wise counsel. But now was not the time to dwell on it. He went out the back door to the little shed in the alley. In his quest for self-improvement, Mr. Kessler had succumbed to the bicycle craze a few years previously, passed through it relatively unbruised, and moved on to higher pursuits. The bicycle had found its way to the shed, where it had resided for several years now. Joseph took the bicycle lantern off the shelf, tested it and, pleased to see that it still worked, hung it on the handlebars. He got off to a wobbly start, but by the time he turned onto Macdougal Street he was feeling very much the master of his two wheels.

To his right lay the Negro section of Greenwich Village and the notorious Minettas, Street and Lane, of Stephen Crane novels; to the south spread the growing Italian district. But the Village was changing so rapidly, he could scarcely keep up with it. He passed Maria's, where Spaghetti Hour had come to an end, but the tantalizing aroma of Italian cheeses and sausages lingered. His stomach growled in response, and he realized he hadn't eaten dinner.

Dinner. Liam was taking her to dinner in the fashionable manner, after the theater. Not that Moira was one to be tempted by society and fashion. It was the man himself who seduced her, and Joseph saw no way to change that. If Liam asked her to marry him, and Joseph very much feared that Mrs. Shapiro was right, Moira would accept, and Dennis would bless the union. And he, Joseph, would have no choice but to stand by and watch her enter into a marriage that could only bring her misery.

Joseph turned off Macdougal and onto Spring, following it to Washington and turning south again. Perhaps he was wrong. Perhaps Liam had really left Tammany, as he claimed, and taken a new and more honorable path. But that was not the Liam he knew and had known all his life. That Liam would take the quickest route to wealth and stature, no matter how sordid the way.

He might make an appeal to Liam himself. If he really loved her, he might be willing to spare her the anguish that their marriage would surely cause. But if he was nothing else, Liam was fundamentally selfish. He might want to spare her, but he wanted to have her more. Nevertheless, Joseph could make one appeal. Despite all their years of friendship, he had never asked anything of Liam. It was time he did.

Joseph turned into the Communipaw terminal shortly before the eight o'clock ferry was due to depart, paid his penny, wheeled the bicycle on and parked it next to the rail. He withdrew his identification from the pocket of his jacket and, leaning against the rail, waited for the ferry to get under way. At length, the thrum of the engines swelled and the water in the slip began to churn. Once they were on the water, he sought out the pilot.

"Last Sunday, you say?" The pilot shook his head. "Only one of this crew works Sundays is Hackberry. Jake!"

He signaled to a man who was talking to a young couple at the rail. Hackberry clapped the young man on the back and broke away, coming toward them with a shuffling, old man's gait.

"Wife died a few years back," the pilot explained, as they waited for Hackberry to reach them. "Can't seem to get over it. Doesn't like to take Sunday off if he can help it. Lonely.

"This gentleman wants to ask you some questions," the pilot said when Hackberry had joined them.

Joseph presented his identification and introduced himself. "I'm trying to track down the movements of an immigrant. I know he took the nine o'clock ferry from New York on Sunday night."

Hackberry found nothing unusual in the request. After all, it was not uncommon for immigration agents to come looking for aliens on the lam. He combed his fingers through the wild white sideburns that encroached on his jowls. "Not much going on Sunday nights. Last ferry, you say? What's he look like?"

"Tall — maybe six feet, a hundred eighty or ninety pounds. Dark red hair, auburn I suppose the ladies would call it. He was wearing a belted brown herringbone sport jacket and brown trousers. Irish. Probably had an accent."

"Sure, I remember him. Big feller. Not very talkative. Standoffish. Stood over there, by the gate. First off, I remember."

"Was he traveling with anyone else?"

Hackberry shook his head. "Nope. Weren't more than fifteen people on that trip anyway. All by himself. Didn't talk to no one. I tried talkin' to him but he cut me."

"Did you see him get off the ferry?"

"Yup. Like I said, he was first off."

"Do you remember which way he went?"

Hackberry smoothed his mustache and thought for a moment. "I got off the ferry to use the facilities in the station and there he was, waitin' down by the door. Started to go talk to him again, but then a man came up to him. Saw them shake hands and then they went on out the door."

Joseph felt a surge of excitement. "The other man, did you get a look at him?"

"Nope." Hackberry shook his head. "Too far away. Eyes aren't what they used to be. He was a little shorter than your friend, but that's about all I can say about him."

"How much shorter?"

"Now you're getting too particular. Don't remember exactly. Couple of inches, maybe. Probably about your size, a little smaller."

"Was a carriage waiting?"

Hackberry laughed. "Sure! Half dozen of them out there in front of the station, all the time. Don't know if they got in one or not."

Joseph thanked Hackberry and gave him his business card. "Please, call me if you remember anything else."

As soon as they landed, Joseph wheeled his bicycle off the ferry and into the Jersey Central Railroad Station. It was not the first time he'd been in it, but he was always struck by its architecture. The warm, welcoming feeling of gabled roofs, arched doorways, and big clocks reminded him of the houses in fairytales he'd read to Moira as a child.

He glanced around the waiting room at the smattering of people in various states of discomfort. Here and there a family huddled together on a bench to wait for the next train. Some were probably immigrants from the station who had missed their connection or been misdirected. A few were tramps whose limited funds bought them a ferry ride to a roof over their heads and a wooden bench for a bed. Fall had begun to gnaw at the air, and warmer climates beckoned the clever ones who could escape the agents' notice long enough to grab a ride on a freight car. A cop circulated around the waiting room, tapping them on the soles of their shoes with his nightstick.

"Whaddaya think this is, a hotel? Where's your ticket? Don't let me see you in here again."

They'd roll off the benches and depart for the rail yard to await their rides. Joseph caught up with the cop when he'd finished his rounds. "This a joke?" he said. "You know how many people get off that ferry every day? You expect me to remember one?"

The cop was right. It was a ridiculous request, and would be equally ridiculous to look for the one cabbie, in hundreds, who might have picked up Doyle and his assailant, and would remember it.

"Nah, no pleasure boats around here," the cop replied to Joseph's next question.

"You're lookin' for somethin' small? Some of these companies on the waterfront," he said, gesturing toward the river with his nightstick. "Some of 'em keep launches for the high muckety-mucks to take 'cross the river to the city. Might try some of them."

Joseph thanked him and walked the bike outside. To his right, a narrow channel was jammed with barges and cargo ships, all carrying freight to be unloaded and sent overland to destinations in the west. Anyone navigating a small craft in those waters might not live to tell the story. Joseph turned to his left and found more wharves, but these were scattered and, above all, less congested. He pedaled across a grid of tracks and began following the water's edge past warehouses and shippers. All had docks, but none had small craft anchored at them. In the distance the silhouette of the station loomed over the water. In daylight, it would seem close. By night, it was a macabre presence as haunting, in its way, as the phantom Flying Dutchman.

They had to have left from here, or somewhere very close — the shortest distance to Ellis Island. Joseph thought. He rode as near to the water's edge as he could, down the piers and back again. At Warner Paints, he skidded to a stop at a small steam launch bobbing next to the dock and pulled his lantern off the bike. The launch was firmly chained and padlocked through a ring on the dock. By the look of it, the lock had been rusting in place for some time. Joseph gave it a tentative jerk, but it held fast. He aimed his light out over the boat, covered in a canvas tarpaulin. A dingy pool of water had accumulated in the crevices of the tarp. He remembered vaguely that it had rained the night Doyle's body washed ashore, but the water in the tarp was dank, with a greenish scum floating on top. If Doyle's assailant had used this boat, he'd gone to great trouble to put it back in its original condition and that, he thought, was most unlikely.

Canfield Lubricants had a barge anchored at their pier, and Beckel Textiles had several, but neither had anything small enough to be crewed by two, or even three men. Perhaps they had turned the other way, upriver. There were more opportunities to find pleasure boats above Penn Station, but if that had been their destination, Doyle would have been directed to take the Hoboken or Christopher ferry. Besides, the further north they went, the more river traffic to negotiate in getting to Ellis Island. And Joseph had no doubt that the station had been their destination. Whoever had murdered Doyle intended his death to look like the result of Maggie's assault. No, it had to be here, somewhere close to the Jersey Central Railroad Terminal.

Aiken Hydraulics. Certainly a manufacturer who would do business in the city, probably even kept their offices somewhere in Manhattan. A business that would ferry its management between the plant and its customers fairly regularly. A business that had a small, elegantly appointed boat with an overhead canopy to keep the sun off. Large enough for one person to pilot and several passengers to travel comfortably. Just like the one he was looking at.

Joseph dropped the kickstand of his bicycle, removed the lantern and shone it on the ropes by which the boat was moored. They were reeved in a metal ring on the dock, and none too carefully, as if it had been done in haste. No chains. No padlocks. A pool of water from the recent rain had accumulated in the stern of the boat. Joseph stepped over it and into the launch, shining his light to take in the layout. The engine was situated slightly aft of the center of the launch, its tall smokestack peeking above the canopy. Three bench seats covered in padded leather cushions divided the launch into discrete sections.

The assailant, he reasoned, would have sat in the stern to control the engine. Doyle would have situated himself in the bow, probably acting as lookout for the fictitious rescue mission. They would have moved well out into the water before the shooting, giving the murderer time to stoke the burner, and guaranteeing that the gunshot would not set up an alarm on shore. Joseph took the assailant's position and imagined himself facing the man he was going to kill. He raised his light as if it were a gun, shining it onto the smooth mahogany hull of the bow. Except that the wood was not smooth. In fact, it had a deep chink in it. Joseph felt his stomach clench. He took out his penknife and, climbing over the center seat, began to dig into the wood. In a minute, he had a bullet in his hand. He turned it over, studying the outer covering of copper that looked peculiarly unchanged, as if it might have been hammered into the hull instead of shot from a gun. He had never seen anything like it before. Carefully, he wrapped it in his handkerchief and sat down in the bow to think.

Doyle had to have been shot at close range for the bullet to pass through his body and into the hull, if indeed this was the bullet that killed him. But Doyle had not been stupid. He'd lived under the constant threat of exposure in Ireland and come to America in search of a stag. It hardly seemed likely that he would have let his assailant, who was supposed to be driving the launch, leave the engine to get as close as the shot required. And it was equally unlikely that, if this were a wild shot, he would have given the murderer a chance at another.

Joseph closed his eyes, imagining the force as a bullet slammed into his body. He let go of his natural instincts, allowing himself to slide off the seat onto the floor, and opened his eyes. Something hard and pointed pressed into his back. He rolled onto his side and shone his light under the bow. The anchor — and, caught on it, a piece of herringbone wool, possibly torn off when the murderer was trying to move the body. The murderer had not seen it, probably because, not wanting to call attention to himself, he hadn't used a lantern. Joseph added it to the collection in his handkerchief.

There should have been blood. He played his light out over the keel, but the dark mahogany finish of the interior conspired with the night to hide any stains. Instead, his light caught on the flash of metal. He pulled himself upright and clambered over the center seat, past the engine, groping under the bench in the stern. His hand closed around a small metal cylinder. He brought it out and trained his light on it. A brass tube about an inch long. A shell casing, but unlike any he had ever seen before. He took his revolver out of its shoulder holster, flipped back the cylinder and removed a bullet, laying it next to the one in his hand. This new cartridge was shaped differently, without the customary rim that held the bullet in the cylinder. He reloaded the revolver and returned it to his holster, sat back on his knees and stared at the casing, trying to make out what it could mean.

The murderer couldn't have used a rifle that, unlike a revolver, would eject a cartridge. A rifle was too cumbersome and difficult to hide. Doyle would have gone overboard rather than allow his assailant to shoot him like a clay duck at a carnival. Besides, why use something as unwieldy as a rifle, when a revolver would do the job? And more important, assuming that he had used a revolver, why would the murderer have emptied the cylinder while still on the boat?

Twenty minutes later, Joseph was pedaling around the channel toward the Penn Station ferry. He had known he would miss the last boat from Communipaw, had planned for it with the help of Mr. Kessler's bicycle. His hand went to his pocket, and the handkerchief, which now held the cartridge, as well as the bullet and the piece of fabric from the anchor. The latter, he was fairly sure would match Doyle's jacket, but he knew, instinctively, that it was the bullet and cartridge that would hold the real answers.

CHAPTER
TWENTY-FIVE

"You know that Irene is leaving?"

Matthew Bonner tapped his fist against the ferry rail and stared down at the murky water below. "I know. Next week. I'm helping her find a flat and I've told her I'll do all I can to help her find a position."

Rachel wheeled on her uncle in astonishment. "Why? Do you want her to leave?"

"I want her to be happy, and if that means she has to leave us, then I want her to go to a decent job and a good place to live. She deserves that."

"Of course she does. But I think you can stop her, Uncle Matt. She thinks you asked her to marry you because I embarrassed her. I know I did, and I could cut my tongue out. But you can still —"

"Miss Bonner?"

Rachel didn't have to turn to know who was at her elbow. She wondered how much he'd heard, and how much satisfaction he'd take in knowing that she had meddled in something that wasn't her affair. But turn she did, and met his gaze squarely.

"Superintendent."

"I'd like to talk with you for a moment," he said. "Before we reach the station."

Rachel had almost forgotten that he intended to take her off Maggie Flynn's case. This could present problems. He might not allow her uncle to see the girl, despite the fact that Rachel knew that in all of New York Matt Bonner was the best man for the defense. And then, of course, she would have to explain to Uncle Matt that she had been ordered off the case, and how would she do that when she didn't quite understand it herself?

Joseph's questioning gaze went to Matt, standing next to her. Rachel made the necessary introductions. "My uncle has agreed to take on Maggie's defense. I do believe she'll need an attorney, and as far as I know, she has none." She braced herself for what might come next, but he surprised her.

"I'm afraid she will indeed," he said. "Good to know that she'll be represented by someone with such a fine record." Matthew Bonner's record and reputation were well known. Still, Rachel felt unaccountably pleased that the Superintendent was aware of them.

"In fact, that is what I wanted to discuss with your niece," Joseph continued. "I don't think we have much hope of preventing an arrest, unless you have some legal trick to pull out of your hat. All we can do is try to prepare Maggie for what is about to happen. Miss Bonner has filled you in on what we know?"

"She has," Matt said. "But there are too many gaps, Superintendent. If we have any hope of saving the girl, we must find out something about this Doyle and what his business was in America. We have to have some inkling of who wanted to kill him. Now, I've worked with one or two private investigators in the past and they've been most helpful —"

"Mr. Bonner," Joseph said, before Matt could continue. "I'm going to ask you to hold off contacting any investigators for a little while. I have some information I'd like to look into first."

"All the better. It will give my investigator a place to begin."

"No, sir, it will send my sources into hiding, and if that happens, we will have no chance at learning what we need to know. I'm asking you to allow me time to investigate the matter myself."

Matt seemed quite taken aback by the suggestion. "Forgive me, Mr. Hannegan, but are you really the best man for that job? A private investigator has both the resources and experience to pursue the information. It is not a job for amateurs."

Joseph shifted his weight and glanced out toward the water. Rachel had never seen Joseph Hannegan embarrassed, and yet he seemed acutely uncomfortable now.

"I have resources of my own," he said slowly. "I can't compromise them at the moment."

Matt's jaw hardened. "If you're trying to protect your own, or someone else's job, I would remind you that the consequence of this crime is very likely a death sentence. Are you really prepared to take responsibility for this girl's life?"

Joseph stiffened. "You may be sure I am not protecting anyone at the station, sir. If it becomes necessary to save her, I'll hold nothing back. But I believe I can get the information you need before any private investigator can get near it. If I didn't think so, I wouldn't suggest it. Send in your man, and you risk forfeiting the only opportunity we have to save Miss Flynn. Give me two weeks. If I haven't found the answers, I'll give him everything I've learned and he can take the investigation from there. Are we agreed?"

Matt's ambivalence expressed itself in the drumbeat of his fingers on the ferry rail. At length he said, "I don't know you, Superintendent, except for what my niece has told me which, by and large, has been favorable. But she knows how a case for the defense is constructed and the duress we will be under. I'll leave the decision to her. Rachel?"

Joseph flushed to the very roots of his hair and looked away toward the station. Although she was rather enjoying his discomfiture, she believed that his concern for Maggie was sincere, and the likelihood of his forestalling investigation for any but the most creditable reasons unlikely. She waited until he had turned back to meet her gaze and inclined her head a fraction. "Perhaps you could give him a few days," she said.

Matt's skeptical expression dissolved to a guarded confidence. "All right, Superintendent. But remember that preparing a good defense takes time. I will try to delay going to trial as long as possible, but right now, it seems inevitable. If your sources fail you, I'm trusting you to come forward with what you know, no matter who may be compromised."

"I confess, gentlemen, that I am completely to blame in the matter," McNabb said. A crowd of reporters clustered around him on the sidewalk to the left of the ferry slip. Joseph stepped onto the dock and melted into the edge of the crowd, while Rachel and Matt entered the station.

"I should have taken control of the investigation myself instead of leaving it in the hands of a subordinate, but I must admit that I had apparently unwarranted confidence in his ability to handle the situation. In fact, I expect to be making a full inquiry into the way this matter was handled, and do whatever is necessary to rid the station of complacence and incompetence." Joseph groaned silently. The rat was sharpening his teeth.

"Since the deceased's body was discovered," McNabb continued, "I have taken over the case myself, and I can assure you that the witnesses' statements are in the hands of the authorities and they are proceeding with their investigation."

The man from the *Times* craned to see over the crowd of reporters in front of him. "Will the girl be arrested?"

"I expect that arrest is imminent, yes. We

must send a clear message to people coming into this country that crime will not be tolerated on Ellis Island."

Joseph stepped back a couple of paces. To his right, he recognized Georg Oberholtzer, one of the seasoned reporters from *Staats Zeitung* and one of McNabb's most aggressive critics. Oberholtzer was gazing at him intently. When he caught Joseph's eye, he raised a brow and jerked his head toward McNabb.

"*Schwein,* eh?"

"Exactly," Joseph agreed. "You might want to ask him about the Boarding investigation." There was a question sure to embarrass McNabb.

A delighted grin spread over Oberholtzer's face. Joseph eased backward out of sight.

"Mr. McNabb, have your boarding investigators stopped taking bribes since Ernesto Sapelli's arrest?"

Joseph left the Assistant Commissioner sputtering angrily at the reporters and hurried upstairs to the Witness Interrogation room. Watchman Archer met him at the door. "Mr. McNabb was here looking for you, sir, and if I may say so, he's in a foul temper this morning."

"Well, gird your loins, Archer, because it's going to be a lot worse when he finishes with that mob outside," he said. "If he comes back looking for me, under no circumstances should you let him in here. Knock on the door and I'll come out."

He found Maggie sitting on the cot, her hands folded meekly in her lap. Matt Bonner was talking to her. "There is nothing I can do to prevent the federal marshals from arresting you right now," he said. "But once you have been arraigned, I will request bail and your release into my custody."

Maggie perked up a bit at that. "And will they give it to me?"

Matt's glance went to Joseph, then to Rachel. "I don't want to give you any false hope, Miss Flynn. Very likely not. Murder is a capital crime and treated very seriously in this country."

"But I didn't do it!"

"We know you didn't," Bonner said, gesturing at Joseph and Rachel. "But we must still prove it, and that means you must tell me everything."

Joseph went to Maggie and took her small hands in his. "I'll be leaving you in Mr. Bonner's hands now, Maggie. You can trust him completely. He's here just to help you," he said. "If the marshals don't bring a prison matron with them, Miss Bonner will accompany you to Blackwell's Island and see that you're. . . ." Here he hesitated. See that she's safely locked away? That she's not mistreated? But that would only serve to heighten her fears. He turned to Rachel with a mute plea for help.

"I'll want to make sure that you have everything you need, Maggie," she said. "I know a few of the matrons, and I'll make sure that they understand your situation."

Joseph sent her a grateful nod and turned back to Maggie. "Watch yourself, now, in the jail. Cooperate with the guards and keep to yourself, will you? And what I told you about the Blackwell's Island?"

She nodded slowly, her eyes large and green as Connemara marble. "I wanted to scare you, Maggie girl. That's all. I'll be coming to see you, and so will Miss Bonner. We'll have you out of there soon, I promise you." He squeezed her hands lightly and chucked her chin. "You've plenty of mettle, Maggie Flynn. And don't you worry, we're going to find out who did this to Doyle, and to you."

Clan na Gael could be damned.

"Is he in there?"

"He, sir?"

"Hannegan. Don't play innocent with me, Archer, unless you're prepared to find other employment."

Watchman Archer blanched, to Edward McNabb's deep satisfaction. He had never liked Archer much anyway. Too damned smug. If there was one thing McNabb could not tolerate, it was the righteous. But he did enjoy bullying them. Even now, Archer was calling Hannegan out of the girl's room.

"Good of you to put in an appearance, Superintendent," McNabb said, with elaborate courtesy. "Come to my office, if you don't mind." He did not wait for a response, but marched down the hall trusting Hannegan to follow.

Albert Lederman was waiting for them, lounging comfortably in a leather chair in front of his desk. Good. A shrewd observer, he was the ideal second in any duel of wits with Hannegan.

"Sit down," McNabb said, but Hannegan remained standing, staring him down, his icy blue eyes filled with undisguised contempt. Well, he would not shrink from this self-styled plaster saint, especially when he knew very well that he had the upper hand for a change.

"I want to know just what you were thinking, detaining that young woman here at the station. She should have been turned over to the authorities long before now."

Hannegan sighed and rubbed his face briskly. "To do what with? They would have had to release her. We had no body, and no proof that a crime had been committed, McNabb. They would have put her on the street without so much as a 'Fare you well' and she would not have been cleared through the station. Are you suggesting that we just toss immigrants out into the streets indiscriminately? At best, if they had been on the job, they would have just returned her to our custody. What was the point of that?"

"The investigation was not our affair in the first place."

"I would remind you that you were the one who insisted that it was our affair first and foremost. When I wanted to release her to the marshals, you demanded that I undertake an investigation personally. I was opposed to it, but I did it anyway. And now here we are, and you are accusing me of what? Incompetence? Malfeasance?"

"A preliminary investigation," Lederman interposed. McNabb stood aside and let the Chief of Registry take the lead.

"I recall the conversation very well, Hannegan. Mr. McNabb asked you to make a preliminary investigation and write a report before turning the girl over to the federal authorities."

McNabb recognized his cue. "That's right, Hannegan. Where is your report?"

"I don't recall your requiring a report." Hannegan turned away, averting his gaze to the window. "Besides, there is nothing to report."

Lederman stirred a fraction in his chair, drawing McNabb's glance. The Registry Chief sat forward and raised a single eyebrow, alert to something McNabb himself had missed. McNabb invoked his most sarcastic tone.

"Nothing to report? A body floats up to our bulkhead, is examined by one of our doctors and identified as the victim of a shooting that took place in our jurisdiction, and you say there is nothing to report? Apparently, you are even more incompetent than I imagined, Hannegan. Commissioner Powderly will not be pleased."

Hannegan turned back from the window, his eyes glittering maliciously. "Commissioner Powderly will doubtless be distracted by the far more damaging and pervasive corruption of the Boarding Division than by a single incident among immigrants. And speaking of that, had Boarding been on the job in the first place, none of this would have occurred."

McNabb clutched at the advantage slipping from his grasp. "What the devil are you talking about? One thing has nothing to do with the other."

Hannegan smiled. "On the contrary. You wanted a report? Well, you're not going to like what you hear, McNabb. The victim's name was Cormac Doyle. He was wanted by the British for anarchy. They sent us a warning, complete with the information that he was traveling on the *Cymric,* but no one in Boarding bothered to post a lookout order. If they had, Doyle would have been picked up at Customs and the shooting would have been averted."

Blood pounded in McNabb's ears. He'd known this was a bad idea, putting Hannegan on the girl's case, and now it was coming back to plague him. Those incompetents in Boarding would be explaining themselves from now till kingdom come.

"You'll want to bring this up in the investigation, of course. Dereliction of duty," Hannegan added, as if he would not know the charge. The insufferable cheek!

"You have the documents to prove this?" McNabb demanded.

"Of course."

"Where?"

"Under lock and key."

"I want them," McNabb shouted, pounding his desk. "Have them in my office in half an hour."

Hannegan remained impassive. "You will have them when the investigation reconvenes, McNabb, and not before. Or I can send them to Washington and let Powderly serve you with them himself," he added, a hint of amusement in his voice.

Really, this was too much. McNabb's glance went to Lederman. The Chief of Registry gave him a short nod. McNabb straightened the papers on his desk, grasping at his little remaining dignity. "All right," McNabb said. "Have them at the next hearing.

"As to the girl, a complete report, Hannegan. In writing. You have forty-eight hours. And I expect you to take full responsibility for obstructing the investigation into the murder of Cormac Doyle. I warned you about pedestals. Yours is starting to rock."

When Hannegan had gone, McNabb fell into his chair and raked his hand through his hair. Panic had seized him. "We've got to stop him! That lookout order might just be the straw that breaks Powderly's back. If there hadn't been a murder, but . . . confound it, can't those people in Boarding get themselves straight? First Sapelli and now

388

this. Powderly will be on the next train if he gets wind of it. And Hannegan's going to run right to him. How the hell are we going to stop him now? One thing will lead to another and soon we'll have people coming forward —"

"Calm down, for heaven's sake. We get the documents back. Besides, I don't think Hannegan will make good on his threat. He's hiding something himself."

This was what he liked about Albert Lederman. He was unflappable in the face of the worst. "Hannegan? Hiding something?"

Lederman nodded calmly. "Didn't you see the way he turned away? He was lying."

"About what? Something to do with us?"

Lederman balanced his chin on the tips of his fingers and studied the photograph of William McKinley on the office wall. "No, it's something that involves him. Something he's done, maybe, or neglected to do. Or perhaps he's gotten himself personally involved with the girl. He wouldn't have told us about the lookout order if he hadn't felt threatened. He would have just handed it over to Powderly and waited for the explosion."

McNabb heard his voice rising but was powerless to control it. "Well how are we going to find out? What good does it do us to know that he's hiding something if we have no idea what it is?"

"We watch," Lederman said, rising. "He'll give himself away. The noble can't bear to be hypocritical. I'll take care of it, and get the papers back while I'm about it."

McNabb sat back and let his panic recede. He could always count on Albert Lederman.

CHAPTER
TWENTY-SIX

Joseph kicked himself all the way back to his office. First, he'd let his temper get the best of him, and then followed it by that deadly hesitation. How could he have been so stupid? Lederman was like a predator on the scent of a kill, and in that momentary pause Joseph had opened a vein and poured out his own blood. Lederman would have his nose to the ground from now on, looking for that one damning piece of evidence McNabb could lay before Powderly. Powderly could never justify keeping him in his position if his integrity were rightfully challenged. And, unfortunately, Joseph thought such a charge might be perfectly justified, regardless the end he was working for.

He hadn't intended to reveal Boarding's dereliction on the lookout order, but McNabb had pushed him too far. They would be looking for it now, and his desk was the first place they would go. If they searched, they would find not only the letter from the British, but also the other papers he had removed from the Boarding Office — records of citizens' certificates and warning letters from other countries. Joseph went directly to his office and unlocked his desk, withdrawing the stack of documents from his bottom drawer and depositing them in a folder labeled "Missionaries" in his filing cabinet. It seemed a safe enough place for them, since McNabb would recognize that, in them, he had no proof that Boarding's negligence had caused any other real harm. But the letter from the British was another matter — a primary piece of evidence in Cormac Doyle's entry into the country. He slid it into an envelope and sealed it, considering what he should do with it.

He couldn't remove official documents from the station without being in breach of half a dozen laws. But anywhere he might lock the envelope away would be within easy access of Edward McNabb, and Joseph had no doubt that he and Lederman would be searching for it. It would have to be somewhere they wouldn't think to look, and that left him with only one place.

He called Rachel out of Maggie's room and led her into the stairwell away from witnesses. "I must ask you to put this in your locker, and keep it locked at all times," he said, handing the envelope to her.

She took it with an unspoken question in her gaze. "It's extremely important," he added. "I'll explain it to you later. For now, please just lock it away."

She seemed to understand the urgency of his request. Joseph watched her disappear down the stairs to the matrons' room and wondered what she would think if she knew he was compromising her position at the station. If McNabb found out, he'd exact his revenge on the weakest victim. But he had no choice. The letter was his trump card, the only thing that would keep McNabb and, more important, Lederman from sniffing out his father's involvement in the Doyle affair. Satisfied that he had done the only thing he could, he returned to his office and found a visitor waiting for him.

George Washington Plunkitt was a stout man of medium height who habitually wore a silk top hat. It was propped on his knee, the receptor of a jaunty finger-tapping tattoo as he gazed around Joseph's office.

Joseph circled around to his desk and stuck out his hand. "Senator Plunkitt? What can I do for you?"

Plunkitt shook his hand, adding a warm little squeeze before releasing it. "Good to see you, Joe lad. Good to see you."

"Always a pleasure, Senator." Joseph took his seat at the desk and regarded the politician thoughtfully. For all that the man was a greedy scoundrel, he liked Plunkitt. There was something engaging about him and his down-to-earth, folksy ways — a quality not lost on the voters, either. "But what brings you here?"

"The girl, of course, Joe. You know we always have a special interest in our Irish constituents."

"Well I wouldn't call the girl a constituent, Senator. She's only just arrived, after all, and it's not as though she can vote."

The Senator stroked his thick mustache thoughtfully. "Ah, but she could be, Joe, and that's the point. The wife and mother of future voters, and if those marching bluestockings have their way, a voter herself sooner than either of us might like. Besides, a number of my current constituents are very concerned about her. I promised them that I'd do everything I could for her. I have Howe and Hummel on call for her defense."

Howe and Hummel! If she weren't convicted by a jury, she'd certainly be convicted in the public eye merely by her association with her own attorneys. Joseph cleared his throat. "Actually, Senator, an attorney has already been retained for her."

Plunkitt sat forward. "Really? Someone from the Hall beat me to the punch, did they?"

"Not exactly," Joseph said. "He's not a Tammany attorney."

Plunkitt gazed at him, tapping the top of his hat in a hollow heartbeat of a sound. "Who then?"

Joseph struggled to suppress a smile. "Matthew Bonner."

The tapping stopped and Plunkitt's fingers went back to his mustache. He smoothed it twice, pulled his lip in and chewed on the edges of it, poked it back out, and gave the mustache another stroke. And then he broke into laughter.

"Delightful! 'Bully,' as our friend Mr. Roosevelt would say!"

Joseph couldn't help laughing himself. "I'm glad you're not upset, Senator."

"Upset? Why would I be upset? The boys down at the Hall will be jubilant. If Bonner's out fighting for the girl, he can't be campaigning, now can he?"

"You are a rascal, Senator."

Plunkitt tapped his hat, a happy staccato little rhythm. "Well, this is wonderful. Bonner's a fine attorney, if a bit of a prig. She'll be well represented. I'll be getting out of your way, then. I want to get on down to the Hall and give them the good news." He picked up his hat and started to rise.

But Joseph had another thought. "I understand Mr. Croker's ship is due in tomorrow."

"Yes, we're all looking forward to having the Boss back. With the elections around the corner, we are a ship without a captain, so to speak."

Joseph picked up a pencil and turned it over in his hands several times. "I'd like to ask you something about a friend of mine — Liam O'Neill. I understand he's left Tammany." Plunkitt watched him without expression as he went on. "I confess I was surprised. But I suppose the Ballyglass is keeping him pretty busy. It's a favorite of Tammany, isn't it?"

The Senator's expression became more guarded. "Some of the boys favor the Ballyglass, it's true."

"It's just that I didn't think O'Neill had that kind of money. It takes a good bit of chink to get a pub like that up and running. I haven't been inside, but I hear it's a nice place."

Plunkitt hesitated. "O'Neill is a friend of yours, is he? You surprise me, Joe."

Joseph sat forward, alert to the undertone

of suspicion in Plunkitt's voice. "Perhaps," he said, "friend is not quite the right word. O'Neill has been courting my sister, Moira. Between you and me, Senator, I'm concerned. I don't entirely trust him."

Plunkitt took his seat again. His fingers went back to the hat, drumming softly, slowly. "You have good instincts, young man," he said at length.

"Meaning what, Senator?" When Plunkitt didn't answer, Joseph strengthened his case. "Senator, this is my sister we're talking about. She thinks she's in love with him, and it wouldn't surprise me a bit if they announce their engagement before the end of the month. If you know some reason why Moira shouldn't marry him, I'd appreciate your being honest with me."

Plunkitt uncrossed and recrossed his legs, arranging the hat on the other knee. "All right," he said. "You've done us a good turn bringing in Bonner — not that I think you intended to, but that's okay — so I'll be frank with you. The Boss struck a deal with O'Neill. Now if you repeat this, I'll deny it, but he wanted O'Neill out of Tammany. The Murray Street building sealed the deal."

"He gave Liam the building?"

"Sold it, but for less than half the value, and I believe the Boss is carrying the mortgage himself. Kept it quiet, of course. Didn't want anyone getting ideas, you know."

Joseph tried not to let the shock show in his face. Croker was as tough as Tweed and twice as smart, and never a man to be intimidated by the law or public opinion. And yet, he had bought off Liam O'Neill. Why?

"I don't know if you heard about this," Plunkitt said in response to the unspoken question. "But O'Neill saved several families from a tenement fire. He was quite the local hero for a while."

"I heard something about that, yes."

"Well, the Boss got it from some of our boys at Engine 17 down on Ludlow that they thought somebody set that fire on purpose. There were sixteen families in that building. Thank God no one died. But one of the kids saw someone starting the fire up on the third floor. He claimed it was Liam O'Neill."

"Mother of God," Joseph said quietly.

"If there's one thing the Boss is always concerned about, it's Tammany's image. We know it's a little tarnished around the edges, but that's kind of like old family silver, if you know what I mean. This was a different sort of a thing, Joe. Oh, I could see why he did it. It got him plenty of votes, but it's no way to win elected office. You help the voters when they're down — find 'em jobs, decent places to live, help 'em stand on their own two feet — but you don't shove 'em into the gutter just so you can pick 'em up yourself. That's something else altogether. The Boss won't have anyone giving Tammany a bad name."

"Forgive me, Senator, if I step out of line here. I don't know Mr. Croker well, but they say he eats ground glass for breakfast. Why would he be afraid of the likes of Liam O'Neill?"

"Ground glass, eh?" Plunkitt chuckled. "I'll have to tell the Boss that one. He'll like it. Afraid?" Plunkitt shook his head. "Prudent, maybe. Men like O'Neill are hard to control. They're too grasping. . . ."

Joseph almost smiled at this. It might be the one word to expressly describe the whole of Tammany Hall.

". . . too volatile. O'Neill's the type to scale the ladder three rungs at a time, no matter who or what he has to climb over, if you take my meaning. A few years ago he was even nipping at my heels. Don't get me wrong, ambition is a good thing in a young man. But ambition without decency is a dangerous state of affairs. Boss Croker

399

might have had to work at controlling him. Between us, it was easier to get rid of him. Aye, there was many a dry eye after him in the Hall."

After Plunkitt left, Joseph remained frozen in his chair. Everything Plunkitt had told him only confirmed his own fears about Liam. He just hadn't wanted to believe them. He had wanted to find an explanation for Liam's wealth, some justification for Liam's behavior that would allow him to stand aside smiling when his sister walked down the aisle of St. Joseph's. What he had learned was infinitely worse than anything he had expected.

They had been close once. Liam had brought light and color into a desperate gray place and time. Liam had made him laugh with his imitations of the Paddys on the streets and in the bars, and his parody of the delicate ways of Miss Kittredge, the social worker. How many hours of his life had he spent running the streets with Liam O'Neill, stealing fruit from the vendor's cart while Liam charmed him with a risqué joke; peeking into the back windows of bawdy houses, hoping to catch a glimpse of a little bare flesh; sharing penny dreadfuls, pails of beer, and loaded dice? But that was the life of boys on the street.

This was different. A roiling nausea washed up his throat. Tenement fire. Women keening over a bit of broken crockery or the charred remains of a broom handle. Men with faces as gray and bleak as the ashes of their meager belongings. Shadows of them trudged through his mind, homeless, hopeless, grateful to have escaped with their lives. And grateful to Liam O'Neill for saving them from near destruction — destruction that Liam, himself, had caused.

This was a heavy knowledge to have to carry home to Moira.

A Black Maria hovered ominously next to the Barge Office, waiting for Maggie Flynn. Beside it stood a hansom cab. The drivers shot dice on a bench nearby and the horses grazed on a sparse patch of weeds. Joseph descended the gangplank with Albert Lederman at his heels.

"Your lady's carriage awaits," Lederman said, pointing at the Black Maria. He laughed and took off across the park with a wave. Damned vulture, Joseph thought.

He had seen the patrol boat anchored off the northeast pier when he boarded the ferry to the Battery. He had known they would come for her, of course, yet he'd hoped for an eleventh-hour stay. But only he could provide that, and now he wasn't sure he was strong enough to carry this much weight on his shoulders. He leaned against a tree and pulled out a pack of Duke cigarettes, studying the dark waves and deep-set, intelligent eyes of the woman on the package. She reminded him of Moira. He lit a cigarette, spitting a flake of tobacco off his tongue.

How would he tell her the truth about Liam? He would have to tell her sometime. Maybe not right away. Maybe she would come to her senses and never have to know. And what if he did tell her? She'd only see it as confirmation that Liam had left Tammany, just as he claimed. And the fire? She'd expect proof, but he didn't have it to give her, just a rumor heard and repeated. And when did you start believing Tammany politicians, she'd want to know. What would he say to that? He hadn't the faintest idea.

He was still trying to sort it all out when the patrol boat appeared on the horizon, chugging noisily and retching black smoke. Rachel and her uncle sat in the stern. Maggie Flynn hunkered between two marshals in the bow, looking like a wayward child disciplined for sassing the headmaster, not a murderess on her way to Blackwell's Island. They took her from the boat in handcuffs, and marched her off the pier, she with her head held high and her chin pointed defiantly at the heavens. One of the marshals opened the back door of the van and together they lifted her into the Black Maria, slamming the door closed behind her with a lonely clink of the lock.

Rachel and Matt climbed into the hansom. The van's driver waited for the two marshals to mount the seat next to him before cracking his whip on the pavement. The horse's head came up with a start and she took off at a trot. Joseph watched the carriage rock away into the waning light, black and apocalyptic as the banshee's coach-a-bower, and fancied he heard the howling of the dour fairy herself.

CHAPTER
TWENTY-SEVEN

A man in a brown tweed suit leaned over and spat, but the wad of tobacco fell wide of the brass spittoon, and within an inch of Joseph's foot. Joseph slid six inches down the mahogany bar, lit a Duke, and waved to a barman in purple sleeve garters. "Whiskey," he said.

So this was the Ballyglass. It had not been his original destination, and he didn't know why he'd come here, only that when he left the Battery he'd walked straight up Broadway without stopping, as though his feet had a will of their own.

"You see this?" the man in tweed demanded, recovering the six inches between them. His face loomed close enough to reveal a fresh tobacco wad tucked into his lip. He pointed to the small *Times'* headline: *Elaborate Precautions for Monarch's Safety.* Copenhagen, it said, was full of Russian detectives anticipating the Czar's visit and worried about anarchists who had him in their sights.

"Oughtta just shoot him and get it over. Kill each other in the streets, thas' what I say. Stop 'em all comin' over here at any rate, takin' over our banks, makin' money off the honest workin' man."

"Like yourself," Joseph suggested.

" 'xactly." He turned back to the bar for his glass and found it empty.

"Lemme have 'nother one," he said, holding his glass up to the bartender.

An angular, long-jawed young man in a pale gray suit had stopped just inside the door to roll a cigarette, causing a bottleneck of customers trying to shove past him to the bar. Joseph slipped into the middle of them and toward the back of the saloon, sliding in at the rail beside a portly man who was carefully studying the Gold Plated Watches page of a Sears Roebuck catalog. His attention fully engaged, he followed his finger horizontally across the page to the price, punctuating it with a soft "Hmph."

On the other side of the bar, three men were caught up in a robust dispute. One of them was Seamus O'Neill. Joseph was glad enough to escape the older man's attention.

"Look, I tell you it's got nothing to do with us," said a red-bearded man in a cocked derby.

"How can ya' say that, McManus?" Seamus slammed his mug of stout down on the bar. "Every red-blooded Irishman ought to be out in the streets protestin' it. Have ya' forgotten the country that gave ya' life?"

Before McManus could answer, the third man voiced a third opinion. "It's got plenty to do with us, if the voters say it does. My district's mostly Irish and they're gonna be at Carnegie Hall to hear him. Sorry, Seamus, but I think we need to be there to show our support for Home Rule."

For a moment, Seamus seemed stunned to silence. He cast a glance over the bar, catching Joseph's eye, but greeted him only with an angry shake of his head. McManus, however, was not ready to let the subject die. "Aaah, why should we give a damn about it? If they're not smart enough over there to either rise up or get on the next boat to America, they deserve what they get."

The third man glanced around warily. "I wouldn't be goin' around the district sayin' that. Not unless you want to find yourself beggin' on the street come January."

"America," Seamus spat. "Take a look aroundja, McManus. When's the last time you saw a green blade of grass or a sheep grazin' on the hills in Manhattan? Go on with ya'. Ya' can have yer bloody America," he said, pushing himself away from the bar.

Joseph braced himself for what surely was coming — Seamus afire with the zeal of republicanism, ready to bend his ear as though he shared the older man's passion. But Seamus turned away, heading for a table in the corner where a pair of b'hoys fondled a couple of empty mugs.

"Brian," Seamus called. "Get us up some stout here. On my tab."

With Seamus otherwise absorbed, Joseph was free to take the measure of the Ballyglass, or what he could see of it. Liam had plenty of custom, at least at this time of day.

It was long and narrow, with an elongated horseshoe bar in the center, a row of bentwood tables on either side and green octagonal tiles on the floor. A twelve-inch-wide shelf stacked with glasses stood in the middle of the horseshoe, in easy reach of the two barmen. The place seemed far bigger than it was — an optical illusion created by mirrored walls. The bar ended at the back wall in another bank of mirrors and shelves and a hinged section of counter that allowed ingress to the bar. Next to it was a door, and just as Joseph noticed it, Liam came through it, dapper as you please in a starched blue shirt and charcoal gray vest and trousers. A narrow cigar drooped from the corner of his smile.

As Joseph watched, Liam glad-handed his way down the bar, slapping this man on the back, clapping that one on the shoulder. By the time he reached the stout watch shopper, Joseph had memorized the routine. Like a series of dance steps, each gesture was choreographed — a part of the show.

"The divil my eyes," Liam said. He gave Joseph both the backslap and shoulder clap. "Is it yourself, Joe Hannegan, come to hobnob with the rogues and villains?"

"I found myself in want of a whiskey," Joseph said.

Liam slapped the bar. "A bottle and another glass, Brian. Come along, Joe, and I'll show you the place." Taking the glass and a full bottle, Liam led Joseph around the bar and through the rear door.

"This," Liam said, with a broad wave of his hand, "is the back room. We use it for parties and meetings and the like."

Joseph knew very well what the back room might be used for — prostitutes who arranged their visits to coincide with the nightly drink of the businessman on his way home. There were no couches in Liam's back room, however. Small tables and heavy wooden captain's chairs studded gleaming heart of pine flooring. With ornamented ceiling, brass chandeliers and sconces, the room was almost as fancy as the bar in front. "Rented for a meeting here tonight," Liam added.

A door on the far wall led to the alley outside and allowed private exit and entrance to the back room. It was bolted with a heavy iron bar. A second door, on the wall to the left, stood open. Beyond it, Joseph could see a roll-top desk of burnished golden oak, a leather chair to its left, a mate in front, and a shining brass cuspidor at its feet.

"My office," Liam said, stepping aside for Joseph to precede him. "I was beginning to wonder if you'd ever darken my door."

While Liam poured two generous shots from the Monte Cristo bottle, Joseph inspected the office. It was not as flamboyant as the rooms outside but had a comfortable, prosperous feeling about it. In the center, a small scarlet Turkish carpet was spread over golden pine floors. Its gentle green walls were hung with bright sconces, art reproductions, and photographs of Liam with Richard Croker and other city government luminaries.

"They're good for business, Joe. That's

all," Liam said, anticipating Joseph's question. "I'm out of the Hall. Not runnin' again. One term as alderman is enough for me."

Liam pointed Joseph into the leather side chair and took his seat at the desk, leaning back comfortably. He rolled his sleeves halfway up his forearms and lifted his glass. "To your enemies' enemies," he said, touching his glass to Joseph's. It was a toast Joseph could raise his drink to.

"Spaykin' of which," Joseph said, lapsing into the brogue of earlier years, "I met one of the same at the station today. Senator Plunkitt was in to see me."

Liam smiled. "That old fox? He's no enemy of mine, Joe. I like the old devil."

Joseph took a sip of whiskey, measuring Liam over the rim of his glass. "He is a likable scoundrel. But I didn't get the idea you left Tammany on good terms."

Liam looked offended. "By my soul, I did indeed. I wasn't cut out for politics, you see. Croker knew it and I knew it. We parted friendly enough." He hooked a thumb toward the front room. "Most of the men out there are from the Hall."

Joseph tossed back the remainder of his shot. "I have to admit I didn't believe you'd left them until I ran into the Senator." A shadow flickered across Liam's face. "What with your buying the pub and all," he added. "It must have taken a bit of chink."

"Aye, the pub has done me no harm," Liam agreed, sidestepping the implied question. "But I confess to missin' the old days, you and me runnin' the streets as we pleased."

He poured another whiskey for each of them. "Those were the days, with a rag on every bush."

"That was you, not me, Liam. You were the one with colleens to spare. I just got your leavin's." Joseph rotated his shot glass between his hands. "I'm here to tell you that Moira's not one of your trollops to be dallied with and tossed aside."

Liam stared down into his drink for a long moment, before openly meeting Joseph's gaze. He laid his hand on his breast. "I swear to you, Joe, before the Man above, Moira is different. I'm comin' for her soon, and I'll be puttin' her in God's pocket."

"Do you love her?"

"Never loved anyone more, Joe, and that's the truth."

Joseph set his glass on the desk, leaned forward and stared squarely at Liam. "I want a promise from you, Liam. For old times' sake, if you must. I want you to promise me that if you're suppin' with the devil, you'll stay away from her."

Liam nodded his head a fraction and looked away. "Why do ya' think I haven't come for her yet?" he said quietly. "But I'm about to change all that. I have the Ballyglass now, and a few investment properties. I've got one foot in your world, and I'm leanin' in. This time next week, I'll be a businessman straight up and legitimate as you please."

Joseph wasn't at all sure it was the answer he wanted to hear.

He left the Ballyglass with the ambivalent feeling that had so often shadowed his relationship with Liam O'Neill. He wanted to believe him, but knew Liam too well to invest what he said with much credibility. No matter what he had, Liam would always want more. He could tell himself today that he had reformed, even believe it himself, but tomorrow, when the opportunity for larceny presented itself, Liam would find a way to justify it. Providing for Moira would become the perfect excuse. And even if Liam walked the path of honor for the rest of his life, Joseph knew that he could never face his brother-in-law without recalling, with haunting clarity, that Liam had set fire to a tenement house for his own glory. Even now, his stomach pitched with the same fetid nausea that had plagued him after Plunkitt's visit. The effects of the whiskey on an empty stomach had done him no good either.

He'd almost forgotten the original errand that had brought him in this direction. Surely there would be gunsmiths near the Tombs site and the courthouse. That should have been his first priority. The clock was ticking for Maggie Flynn. There would be time to sort out Liam and Moira later.

Out on Murray Street, business traffic had slowed, leaving a few street arabs to perform and panhandle for those made more magnanimous by a stop at the local pub on their way home. But if the streets were emptier, the park in front of City Hall festered with new life as the gangs and toughs came out to work their mischief. Even now, a few beat cops were moving in with their nightsticks at the ready to break up the packs and send them on their way. Joseph turned north, following Broadway up a block to turn east on Chambers and cross to Centre.

The first gunsmith he found was closed. Joseph checked his watch. 6:20 p.m. Later than he'd thought. The second had locked up and was cranking in his awning. No, he didn't have any idea what it was, he said, stealing a quick look at his watch. Joseph thanked him and walked on.

On the corner of Centre and Thomas, he found a third shop. It was a narrow little place, scarcely wide enough for a small display window and a door, both bordered in neat stripes of gold paint. In the window, a matchlock musket lay nestled in a swath of maroon velvet. Joseph lingered in front of it and concentrated his attention on the reflection of a man on the other side of the street. A thin man in a pale gray suit, who had stopped to roll another cigarette. Joseph watched him lick the paper, roll it, and poke it in his mouth before disappearing around the corner.

A light was still on in the back of the shop. He tried the door and, finding it locked, rapped sharply on the glass. A man appeared in the door to a back room. Joseph held his identification up to the window. In a moment the door opened.

"I'm sorry," Joseph said. "I know you're closed but I need some help with an identification. Would you mind taking a look at something for me?"

The smith had a long, lugubrious face and narrow shoulders, which seemed, oddly, to fit the character of his little shop. "What is it you need identified?"

Joseph took out his handkerchief and opened it, displaying the bullet and cartridge. "This," he said. "Have you ever seen anything like it?"

The smith led him over to a glass case, switched on a green shaded lamp and pulled out a magnifying lens. "May I?" He took the bullet and casing, laying them side-by-side on a green felt mat under the light.

"Copper jacket. Rimless cartridge. About a thirty caliber." He set the lens down. "Just let me check on something," he said, and disappeared into the back room. He returned shortly with a catalog. "Hah! Found it."

He set the catalog on the counter in front of Joseph, who found himself looking at a pistol the likes of which he'd never seen. It had a long barrel and a peculiar square extension where one might reasonably expect to find a cylinder. Its handle looked remarkably like that of a common kitchen broom.

"You are looking at the firearm of the future. Called a Mauser Military Pistol, sometimes called a Broomhandle. Fire it and it automatically reloads from an internal magazine. Ejects the cartridge like a rifle and the next bullet springs into the chamber ready to be fired. Faster than a traditional revolver. Gotta admire German design," he said.

"Do you carry them?"

The smith shook his head. "Only seen one up close. They haven't made their way over here much yet. The factory's filling orders for Europeans, mainly police and military."

Police and military was a vast territory. "Where did the one you saw come from?"

"Another gun dealer. He bought it from a British officer who took it to South Africa with him to fight the Boers. I've got an order in to the factory, but I'm not expecting any for another few months. You interested in purchasing one?"

"I'm afraid not," Joseph said. He wrapped up the bullet and cartridge and put them back in his pocket. "I'm looking for the person who owns the one this came from." But he already had an idea just who that might be.

By the time Joseph left the gunsmith, the sky was dark and the street mottled with murky yellow pools from the street lamps. He turned north, heading for the Grand Street streetcar that would carry him across town to the Sixth Avenue El. The vermin were out, creeping from their holes along Bowery and the Mulberry Bend, lounging

in the doorways waiting for an easy mark —
Five Pointers mostly, king rats in the world
of scum. Easy enough to pick out, dressed
as dandies and perfumed like strumpets.
Even the proximity of police headquarters
and the Tombs did not keep the neighborhood safe from them, or from the whores
and trimmers who called out to him from
darkened thresholds.

"Need a girl, mistah? Gotta dollah?" One
of them stepped out of the darkness, fon-
dling her barely concealed breasts and lifting her skirts to reveal her garters, and little
else. He elbowed past her without comment.

"Doncha like girls, mistah? I gotta boy at
home."

Joseph felt sick with revulsion. This was
what Doreen O'Neill had come to before
she died. He could never forgive himself for
the part he had played in it, or her brother
for allowing it to happen. He tossed her a
quarter. "Go home to him, for God's sake,
and take care of him."

She let out a howl. "With a quatah?
Who're ya kiddin'?" She scuttled after him.
"Big spendah like you oughtta have whatcha
want. Whatcha want, honey?" Joseph stared
ahead and kept walking.

But the woman had not given up, turning

her assault on the next passerby. "Ya look like you could use a woman, mistah. I can fix ya' up just fine, anything ya' like. C'mon, honey, I gotta room just upstairs here. Hey, you got no call to shove me around!"

Joseph glanced over his shoulder. The woman stood on the sidewalk, one hand on her hip, her other fist in the air. She was screaming obscenities at a man on the sidewalk — a spectral blur in a pale gray suit.

CHAPTER
TWENTY-EIGHT

He had a shadow. When the gray specter had followed Joseph onto the Grand Street car, he'd left little room for doubt. But when he boarded the el, although he'd chosen a different car, it had been confirmed. The man in the pale gray suit was watching him.

He had done nothing about it, but allowed the shadow to stay on his heels all the way home. Better the devil you know than the one you don't, his mother would have said. If he lost him, or frightened him away, someone else might come in his place — someone who didn't roll cigarettes and wear a pale gray suit. Someone more deft at making himself invisible. But who had sent him? Devoy? Moran? The Brits? The stag? Or even, Joseph thought, as he gazed up at the altar, Father O'Gara?

Father O'Gara was delivering a sermon in his characteristic mumbling monotone. Didn't they teach priests to preach at the seminary? Joseph should have been listening to the sermon and paying attention to the Mass, but if he couldn't hear most of it, and couldn't understand what he could hear, what was the point, after all?

Dennis had said the Clan sometimes met in the basement of St. Joseph's Church, a fact that explained his father's benevolent attitude toward Father O'Gara. He wondered just how much Father O'Gara knew about the Clan's activities — how much he had overheard, learned in confession, or learned from his own participation in the organization. Although the church officially frowned on it, dissident clergy were hardly unknown in Catholic parishes both in Ireland and America.

Father Aloysius O'Gara was in a position to know far more than anyone might think. He didn't have to be on the executive committee of Clan na Gael to hear their confessions, or the confessions of any of the men who had taken the oath. Joseph remembered too well the day when, at the age of nine, old Father Kelly had called him by name in the confessional. Despite the screen, O'Gara would doubtless recognize the voices of some of his parishioners, and that might well give him information about Clan activities. But why would he betray them, unless it was because he didn't believe in what they were planning and hoped the Brits would stop it? His appearance at the station to hear Maggie's confession now struck Joseph as altogether too coincidental, and the cryptic remarks he had made afterward began to take on new importance. But if Father O'Gara was the stag, it meant that he was probably also a murderer, and the very idea went against everything that Joseph believed in.

When Mass was over, he left his father and Moira chatting with other parishioners and found the priest in the sacristy removing his vestments. "My Sunday off, Joe," he said. "I'm going to see my sister."

"Then I won't keep you long, Father. I just have a few questions for you." O'Gara's expression became guarded.

"I already know about Doyle and Moran — how they got him through the station and why he came here. What I want to know is why you were there."

O'Gara turned away to hang his alb in a large wardrobe. "They asked me to take her a message. They knew I might be the only one who could get in to see her."

"What was the message?"

The priest turned back around, picking up his biretta — a cue to Joseph that he intended to leave. "Just that they were going to get her out. They were going to send two policemen to pick her up."

"They did. It didn't work, because she was supposed to be remanded to federal authorities."

"Yes, I heard about —"

They were interrupted by Father O'Gara's young curate, who would be saying the remaining Masses of the day. O'Gara seemed relieved. "We'll be getting out of your way, Father," he said, leading Joseph out the side door of the sacristy into the sunlight.

"I'd like to stay, Joe, but Agnes will be pacing the floor. She's very punctual." He stuck out his hand. Joseph took it, and held it.

"One more question, Father. You knew what they were doing?"

The priest frowned and eased his hand from Joseph's grasp. "Yes, I knew."

"And yet you let them meet at St. Joseph's?"

O'Gara arranged the biretta on his head, the characteristic shock of hair drooping over one eye. "I'm sorry, Joe, but that's two and I'm late," he said, and was off without a backward glance.

Joseph mulled over the conversation as he

walked home. O'Gara had probably known about the gun running and yet he had done nothing about it, even giving it a sort of imprimatur by allowing them to meet in the church basement. How did he live with himself, a priest whose very vocation required him to love all men?

Joseph detested that kind of hypocrisy, and yet he now found himself in a similar position. He had told Rachel Bonner that he disliked social workers and warned her away from his sister. But if he had any hope of saving Maggie Flynn, he needed help. He was balanced on a tightrope, and McNabb was gathering up the net below. Everything he had done at the station could be twisted to appear that he was protecting his father and the Clan, and Joseph had no illusions that McNabb would accuse him of just that. And who at the station could be trusted, when McNabb openly rewarded corruption and betrayal, and if that failed, dangled job security over the heads of his employees? There was only one person who, he was sure, would put the life of Maggie Flynn ahead of her own job. Thus, by midafternoon, he found himself standing, hat in hand, in front of a red brick house on Lexington Avenue, gazing up at the graceful balustrades that bordered the porch.

The maid looked him over carefully. He smoothed his tie, and wished that he'd thought to wear something better than the gray tweed suit that must look so coarse to her. "I'm Miss Bonner's supervisor at the immigration station," he explained.

"But Miss Bonner is out for the afternoon," she said. Her thin eyebrows drew together, telegraphing the message that this was not the usual way of gentlemen callers. She glanced backward, into the foyer, as if someone might tell her what to do. "I could tell Miss Garrity that you're here."

"If you would," he said, although he had no idea who this Miss Garrity was. She opened the door wider, indicating that he should step into the foyer, and left him to hurry down the hall.

The house was not what he had expected — no heavy portieres or dark Turkish carpets, no ornately flocked wallpapers. The foyer, and the broad hall it led to, were papered in the palest silver blue stripe. The woodwork was painted white to match the marble flooring and the wide, curved banisters of a staircase that ascended from the hall. To the right of the door, a full-length mirror reflected the elegant appointments of the entryway. A simple Chippendale chest squatted to the left reflecting, in its high gloss, a silver salver on top. Joseph dropped a business card in the salver and turned back to see the maid coming toward him.

"If you'll follow me, sir?"

He did, past a set of closed double doors flanking the hallway and was ushered through the next door on the right — Bonner's library. A woman waited for him, standing behind a desk of the same warm maple as the paneling and shelves.

"Shall I bring tea, Miss Garrity?"

"If you will, Alma. And some of Mrs. Coffey's coconut cake." She watched Alma out the door before turning to Joseph. Her face was young, and quite beautiful, but her pale hair sparkled with a few streaks of silver.

"I'm Irene Garrity, Mr. Hannegan," she said. She extended her hand cordially. "Rachel has spoken so highly of you. I'm glad finally to have the opportunity to meet you."

He took her hand, realizing that he had no idea what to say to this woman. He hadn't an inkling of who she was — aunt? friend? or maybe Bonner's mistress?

She seemed to read all this in his puzzled expression. "I am Mr. Bonner's housekeeper," she said, smiling.

He glanced down at the desk, where she had been working on the household books. But in Bonner's library? Perhaps he didn't understand social convention as well as he thought he did.

"Please," she said. "Have a seat." She took her own, behind the desk, and waited until he had made himself comfortable in one of the large leather wingbacks in front of it.

"Rachel and her uncle were going to the jail to visit Miss Flynn after church," she said. "But I expect them back shortly, and I assume this must be important, so please make yourself comfortable. It shouldn't be too long a wait."

"Thank you. Please forgive me for intruding on your work, or on your Sunday afternoon."

Irene laughed. "It's no intrusion, I assure you." She gestured down at the open books on the desk. "I'm terrible with numbers. Rachel or her uncle always seem to have to straighten it out. A penny forgotten here, a nickel added there, and suddenly you're in a great amplush, aren't you?" She pushed the books over to a corner of the desk, as if to emphasize that he was not disrupting anything important.

A great amplush. A fix. Not an expression Joseph had expected to hear in the library of a house on Lexington Avenue. "You're from Ireland, Miss Garrity?"

"Many long years ago, indeed I am, Mr.

Hannegan. I came to this house as Rachel's nurse when her mother and father were killed."

"I wasn't aware that she had lost her parents."

"They drowned in a boating accident."

A guilty vision of Rachel, hovering in the corner during the examination of Doyle's body, floated unbidden to memory. Irene rose and walked to the marble mantel over the fireplace, picked up a photograph and brought it to him. A small girl in a white middy dress gazed solemnly at him through dark, sad eyes. "She was only seven years old, and a disarming little thing. Her uncle thought a photograph would cheer her up."

She retrieved the picture and returned it to its place. "It took a good deal more than that. But Matthew Bonner is as fine a man as you'll find anywhere, and he's been a good replacement for her father." Irene took her seat behind the desk again. She was comfortable in this room, as though she were mistress of the house.

"But no mother?" he asked, knowing quite well that he was treading the bounds of courtesy.

Irene Garrity didn't seem to mind. "Only me," she said. "But she's grown into quite a lovely young woman, despite being raised by an Irish housekeeper." She gave him a self-deprecating smile. "I don't mind telling you, she kept me on my toes."

Alma was setting out the tea tray when Matthew Bonner appeared in the door of his library. "Why, hello, Mr. Hannegan," he said. He shook Joseph's hand, waved him back into his chair and took the other one. "Do you have something for me?"

"Not yet," Joseph admitted. "But I believe I may be close. I actually came here in the hope of seeing your niece."

"Didn't Rachel return with you?" Irene said.

"She did. I left her picking dead leaves off the plants on the porch. Just a minute and I'll call her."

"No need, sir," Joseph said. "I'll see her outside." He left them in the library and found his own way down the hall and onto the porch. Rachel was bent over a pot of chrysanthemums, but straightened up when the door opened.

"Oh! Superintendent, what are you doing here?"

She wore a suit of pale, buttery gold, and a matching broad-brimmed hat that framed her hair and brought out its red lights. Her blouse, of the same soft color, was as sheer and delicate as angel's wings. With a faint

428

flush on her cheeks, she might have been an emblem of the season. He felt all in flitters in his rough tweed suit, and suddenly at a loss as to what to say to her.

She blushed under his gaze, but drew herself up a little straighter and carefully folded her hands at her waist. "Forgive me. I did not intend to be rude. Please," she said, moving toward the door, "won't you come in? I suppose you'd like to talk to my uncle. He's —"

"No. I came to see you. I need to talk with you in confidence. We could. . . ." He glanced around. This was not how he had envisioned the meeting. He had imagined himself in full command of his senses and the situation. But he hadn't expected her to be bathed in autumnal gold, a shimmering amber ray of sun against the somber background of the city.

She waited, observing his discomfort with maddening aplomb. At length, she said, "If you like, we could walk in the park. I'll just get the gate key."

She disappeared, leaving him to gather his wits. He had to pull himself together before he lost sight of the reason he had come. But he was a man, after all, and no more impervious to her beauty than any other man. She could hardly fail to know it, when he had stammered about like a scabby-kneed boy. He took up a pose, lounging against the balustrade, balancing his hat on the tip of his finger, but he was no Liam, and dropped the affectation before she came out the door.

"It's just around the corner," she said, as he followed her down the stairs. She waited for him on the sidewalk, but did not take his arm when he reached her. She had removed her hat, and rotated the brim between her fingers as they walked.

"You wanted to speak to me confidentially," she reminded him.

"Yes," he said slowly. "First, I must apologize to you. When I asked . . . insisted, that is, that you stay in the examining room with Doyle's body, I had no idea how your parents died."

She stopped walking and gazed into the distance, her expression remote. "I don't suppose you could have known. I didn't mention it. Nevertheless," she said, "you might have given me a choice. I would not have stayed."

She turned away, watching the traffic of carriages on the street and swallowed several times, as if she were trying to ease a pain in her throat. "It was very . . . uncomfortable for me."

Joseph looked down at his feet, at shoes in

need of a good polish, and felt very much at a disadvantage. It was not a familiar feeling to him. In her brief hesitation and the understatement of her discomfort, she had given him a glimpse of her pain and he felt himself the tyrant that she must think him. He longed to put it right somehow, but he could not explain his behavior even to himself.

"You are quite right," he said. "It was thoughtless and inconsiderate of me. Please accept my apology."

She resumed walking, stopping at the wrought iron gate to unlock it. "There is something else, isn't there? You didn't come here to apologize for your behavior."

He pulled the gate open for her and followed her through. "No, I didn't realize I had behaved quite so badly. And yes, I do have something else to discuss with you."

CHAPTER
TWENTY-NINE

"Do you mind if we sit down?" Joseph said. He gestured to a bench along the path they had been walking. He had never been in Gramercy Park before, or any other place where people like him were routinely excluded. From the bench, they could see the statue of Edwin Booth. A robin perched on his shoulder, as if she were whispering secrets in his ear.

The leaves were beginning to fall in earnest. They seemed almost purposeful in their drift — a scarlet one here, a gold one there — as if a great hand were arranging them to their best advantage. "Are you comfortable?" he said. "Not too cold?"

"I'm fine," Rachel said. "And I don't think you asked me to come out to discuss the weather with you."

"No."

The gardeners had been raking the leaves. Neat little piles dotted the park, waiting to be burned. A squirrel rooted under one of them and came up triumphantly with full cheeks, scampering off to a nearby tree.

"Your housekeeper said that you've been to Blackwell's Island."

"Yes, my uncle and I went to see Maggie and take her a few necessities. After leaving her there yesterday, I wanted to reassure myself that she was all right."

"And how did you find her?"

Rachel picked up a stray leaf from the bench and rolled the stem between her fingers distractedly. "She seems to have given up. When she first came to us, she was rebellious, almost defiant. Now she just seems hopeless." She shrugged. "I don't know what to do for her."

"You must reassure her that we will solve the problem."

"When I'm not sure that we will? I don't want to give her false hope, Mr. Hannegan. Besides," she said, giving him a sidelong glance, "wouldn't that be interfering, Superintendent? After all, I'm neither an immigrant, nor poor. I am merely a social worker who does more harm than good. I cannot possibly understand her or the way she feels."

"Ah," he said. "Throwing down the gauntlet, Miss Bonner?" He stood up and stepped a few feet away from her, pulling a pack of Dukes out of his pocket. He fished out the one remaining cigarette. "With your permission?"

"You do not need it, Mr. Hannegan. You are my superior. You may do as you like."

He lit the cigarette and peered at her through narrowed eyes as the smoke curled up in sinuous streams and drifted away. "Not today, Miss Bonner. Here in the park, we are just. . . ." Just what? A beautiful woman and a man who finds her disturbingly attractive? An angry woman and a man who has been suitably chastised? She waited serenely for him to finish.

". . . acquaintances. Out walking a on beautiful day."

"Then we have concluded our business," she said, and started to rise.

"No! Not yet."

He had been putting off asking her for her help. Did he have any right, really, to bring her into this mess? What would he do if she declined? And why would she even consider consenting when he had told her, rather bluntly he now conceded, that he neither liked nor trusted her?

He crumpled the cigarette pack in his fist. "It is possible," he said, "that I was rash in my remarks. It may be that some social workers do more good than harm. The right woman, in the right place. . . ." His words drifted away with the smoke from his cigarette.

"Is that an apology, Superintendent?" she asked, her lips pressed together as though that might hide her amusement.

He glanced over at the statue of Edwin Booth, and wished he had a talent for acting. "Let us say I am offering you an armistice."

"Because you need something from me."

Joseph pitched the pack into a nearby trash bin, dropped the cigarette and ground it under his heel. "I need your help. I find myself in a bit of a predicament with respect to Maggie Flynn," he said, resuming his seat next to her. "Do you remember the name she heard Doyle and Moran discussing?"

"John . . . I don't remember the last."

"Devoy. He's a Fenian living here in New York, involved in an Irish fraternal group called Clan na Gael. It was Devoy who arranged the scheme to pick up Doyle at Ellis Island and hide him on Rivington Street."

Rachel picked off a leaf that had fallen on his shoulder — a proprietary gesture, he thought, but she carried it off as though she was not aware she had done it. "But why?"

"Doyle was here looking for someone — a

traitor, or at least so he would say — to the cause of Clan na Gael."

"What kind of a traitor? What had he betrayed?"

"Gun running."

He waited for her reaction — anger, horror, disgust — but her face registered nothing more than perplexed interest. "Clan na Gael is raising money to support an insurrection in Ireland. They have been shipping small quantities of guns to several ports for . . . I'm not sure how long. A year or two, at least. I believe that Doyle either discovered the traitor, or the traitor was afraid that he might and disposed of him first."

Joseph paused. "I believe I may be on the trail of Cormac Doyle's killer."

Rachel sat forward. "But that's wonderful news! It could mean immediate release for Maggie."

Joseph laid a hand on her arm. "It isn't quite as simple as it sounds, Miss Bonner. There are several problems, and this is why I've come to ask you for your help. Without it, I may not be able to prove her innocence."

"Then you must tell me what I can do." She leaned toward him, distracting him with the fresh scent of her skin and hair. But her glance went past him, over his shoulder to the path behind him.

"The Sunday walkers are coming out, Mr. Hannegan. If we sit here, we are bound to be interrupted. Perhaps we should continue walking?"

He turned around. A tall, slender couple was coming toward them, walking a long, lean hound of some type who bore his owners a striking resemblance. A few paces behind them, a lone man took a seat on a shaded bench and opened a newspaper. Joseph rose with her and took the path again.

She took his arm, drawing so close to him that the brim of her hat tickled his chin. He could feel the warmth radiating from her body, as if she were sunlight itself. "You were going to tell me what I can do."

"Yes. To begin with, my own father is a member of Clan na Gael. I'm sure you understand that if this should become public knowledge, I would be implicated in collusion with their scheme on Ellis Island. If McNabb were to learn about it —"

Rachel completed the thought. "He'd use it as grounds for firing you. Maybe even criminally prosecute you."

"Precisely. If anyone else at the station were to learn about this, I could be compromised. I trust you not to say anything to

Mr. McNabb."

"I'd sooner tell the devil," Rachel said.

He allowed himself a brief smile and waited while another strolling couple passed them and continued on the path. The creak of the wrought iron grate signaled more residents entering the park. Joseph glanced back. Behind them, the man with the newspaper had moved to a sunny spot. He sat on the bench, rolling a cigarette. Joseph stiffened involuntarily.

"Is something wrong?"

He shook his head. "Probably not. That man on the bench — do you know him?"

Rachel studied him briefly. "No. That's odd, though, since Gramercy Park is closed to everyone but residents, and I do know most of them. But he's probably a guest of someone, out for a stroll while his hosts take their Sunday naps." She giggled at this. Joseph flashed her a smile he did not feel, but neither did he want to alarm her.

He had been careless, expecting his shadow to return in a pale gray suit. But the man on the bench wore black with a homburg to match, and now Joseph realized he had ridden the el in the same car. Perhaps he had underestimated the man.

"So we must keep all this from Mr. McNabb at all costs," she said, turning back to continue their walk.

"Yes, but the other problem is this. Clan na Gael will protect their own, no matter what. I can expect only limited help from them. Even from my father. Should they learn who the killer is before I do, I cannot count on them to come forward with information to exonerate Maggie. They used her in the first place, although they apparently thought they could rescue her. But I have little doubt that they will use her again if it serves their purposes."

"How vile," Rachel said. "She's just a girl, and she's done nothing to them."

"But they would say that the good of Ireland is at stake, and all great causes require martyrs."

Rachel raised a skeptical brow.

"Believe me when I tell you that I know how these men think. They are zealots and fanatics, my own father included. They will help me find him, because it is in their best interests to do so, but I can't be sure of their cooperation when the time comes to turn him over to the authorities."

"And that is why you need me," Rachel said. "Of course I'll do whatever I can, but I'm not sure I understand what that is."

"I'll explain, but first, let me tell you what I know," he said.

He gave her the complete story as he knew it, ending with the bullet and cartridge he had found. "I took it to a gunsmith. The bullet is from a new and fairly rare pistol made in Germany — a Mauser. Not many people in the United States have them yet. They're being issued for military use in Europe. At least one officer carried a Mauser in the British campaign against the Boers."

He waited for her to recognize the implication of what he was saying. She didn't disappoint him. "Arthur Vine," she said quietly.

"Exactly. Vine was the British military attaché here for several years — long enough to make any number of contacts. And now he's back."

"For the America's Cup race, supposedly. But you think he's really back because of Doyle and Moran?" Joseph confirmed it.

"And you think that Vine shot Cormac Doyle?"

He shook his head. "I doubt it. It seems too risky to me. I think that Vine is the stag's — the traitor's — British contact. Vine is the one who has been receiving information and passing it on to British authorities in Ireland. But I think he gave the informant the gun that was used to kill Doyle."

"But how do we prove it? For that matter, it still doesn't give us the murderer, does it?"

"Not yet. I have to draw him out. But before I can do that, I have to meet Arthur Vine, or at least see him close enough to be able to identify him. That is where I need your help."

"Yes, I see. So the problem, then, is to be in the same place that Vine is so that you can meet him."

"Exactly. I thought perhaps you might invite him —"

Rachel shook her head. "I don't know him well enough, and I'm not on close terms with his hostess. In fact, I quite detest her and she knows it. It has to be somewhere else, at a public occasion of some type. Let me think about it. I'm sure I can think of something."

He had thought it would be easy for her, that her social calendar must be as full as all the society matrons' published in the *Times.* His frustration must have shown.

"My uncle's interest in society has always been a matter of convenience, Mr. Hannegan. We have never cultivated the four hundred for the sake of their company. Quite frankly, they are about as lively and intellectual as a room full of mummies. But

Uncle Matt does love the opera and symphony, and he must occasionally do business with banks. And of course, politics does toss one into certain arenas. So yes, we can contrive a meeting with Captain Vine, but it may take a bit of ingenuity."

CHAPTER
THIRTY

Joseph left his shadow in Battery Park the next morning. He'd picked him up immediately, lounging in the doorway of Rossi's corner grocery store on Bleecker. He was dressed as a workman in a slouch cap and collarless shirt, looking for all the world like a plumber or a carpenter on his way to work somewhere in lower Manhattan.

The shadow was more resourceful than Joseph had first imagined and that, he thought, made him more dangerous. But he could hardly have expected to board the ferry to the station, nor would he need to if his purpose were merely to follow Joseph's movements. But was that his only purpose? Joseph wasn't at all sure. He patted his breast pocket, satisfying himself that his pistol was firmly holstered next to his shoulder.

He had begun to wish that he hadn't

involved Rachel Bonner in his problems. John Devoy believed that women were as expendable as men when it came to his precious cause. If this shadow came from Devoy, then Rachel might well be in danger. Moran could be as fanatical, although he'd seemed to harbor more sympathy for Maggie than anyone else had. The Brits, he thought, would probably not harm a woman, unless they felt it necessary to protect themselves. He couldn't afford to forget that he was chasing after a murderer.

And to add to her jeopardy, he had asked her to hold onto a letter that he knew McNabb wanted desperately. He'd had no right to put her job in peril, not to mention her life. Joseph arrived at the station determined to rectify his mistakes and relieve her of any further involvement in either problem.

He was not surprised to find that his office had been searched. A man of precise habits, it was nevertheless rare for him to leave his papers so perfectly squared on the desk. And the inkwell had been moved from its customary place on the upper right corner of his blotter to the more common central position. He opened his drawers but found nothing missing, save an under ripe plum he'd left in the bottom left drawer. Joseph chuckled, wondering whether it had drawn Lederman's mouth when he bit into it.

It had to have been the Chief of Registry, after all, who had methodically combed his office for the letter. McNabb would never risk being caught, nor have the composure to play it off if he were. Lederman, on the other hand, would relish a cool duel of wits with him. In fact, he might enjoy it himself, he thought with some amusement. But his concern for Rachel sobered him immediately.

"She's in the immigrant dining room," the head matron said. "Is there anything I can help you with?"

"Thank you, no, Miss Bainbridge. I'll find her."

The dining room had been set early. Miles of white butcher's paper blanketed long expanses of refectory tables, and at each place lay a plate, knife and fork. The first group of women and children were already there — the detained, fed first and bustled off to their day room for safekeeping. The atmosphere was subdued, as mothers softly urged their children to eat foods that were strange to many, comforting to a few. Some wore heavy shawls over their heads and shoulders; others wore hats as common and fashionable as anything in lower Manhattan. Some still wore the hopeful look of the newly detained; others sat with lowered eyes and creases of worry plucking at their mouths.

"Ella, na fame me pirouni." A young mother reached across the table and smacked the hand of a little boy just before his fingers went into the bowl. She wore a heavy jacket of blue, cut in a keyhole front, and a long white skirt with ruffled pantaloons beneath. Over all this, she had wrapped a wide knit sash around her waist several times, arranged the end over one shoulder and tucked it into her waist at the back, creating a sling for her infant child. The child slept, his cheek pressed to her breast, leaving her hands free to attend to the needs of two boys who might have been a year apart in age. She put a spoon in the younger child's hand and showed him how to dip it into the bowl.

"I wonder, sometimes, how they manage it, coming all this distance alone with little children." Joseph turned to find Rachel standing beside him, bouncing a toddler on her hip.

"It requires courage, and a good deal of strength," he said. "May I speak to you privately?"

"Of course." She shifted the child to her other hip and followed him out into the hall.

He turned, and seemed surprised to find her still carrying the toddler. "You are not a nanny, Miss Bonner."

Her cheeks flushed, and a spark ignited in her eyes. He hadn't intended to antagonize her, but he did want to regain his footing with her. Soliciting her help had shifted the advantage. She might be his social better, but at the station he was still her superior.

"You are quite right, Superintendent. I am not a nanny. But I am in charge of the detained women, as you know, since you assigned me there yourself. I believe your words, at the time, were 'to see to their well-being.' The mother of this child was not able to eat a bite of her breakfast for chasing him about the dining room. That is not in the interest of her well-being. And now, if you'll excuse me, she has finished her breakfast and seems to be looking for him."

"Miss Bonner, I merely meant that you are not required to take care of the children."

She seemed somewhat mollified by his explanation. "But I am. These women need every ounce of strength just to survive the day, and they can't begin it on an empty stomach.

"Here," she said, thrusting a heavy, cream-colored invitation at him. "The New York Yacht Club, tomorrow night. It's a reception for Sir Thomas Lipton. Vine is bound to be there, since he's an admirer of the Shamrock."

"About that, Miss Bonner. . . . I have changed my mind. I will not require your help after all."

"Really," she said coolly. "Then you've found a way to meet Captain Vine?"

He hesitated a fraction, just long enough for her to jump to conclusions. "I see," she said. "You're afraid that it might encourage me to be even more 'interfering.' "

"No! It's not that, I assure you. I have come to appreciate —"

"I seriously doubt that, Mr. Hannegan." She turned away, her back and shoulders stiff, but shortly pivoted on her heel. "We will never get past this, will we? You will hold it over my head from now on. Believe me, I deeply regret having written in my journal about Moira, but it is not because of what you think of me. I'm fond of your sister, Superintendent, and I would never do anything to hurt her."

"Miss Bonner, the incident is forgotten," he said.

"Apparently not," she snapped, and

started for the dining room. He grabbed her arm and pulled her back, lowering his voice.

"It could be dangerous! I don't want you involved."

"A party at the Yacht Club? What nonsense!"

"Not the party, but your association with me. We are dealing with a murderer, Rachel."

"I am well aware of that. Maggie Flynn sits in a cold, dark cell because of him, and I'm going to do what I can to help her." She raised her chin defiantly. "You cannot prevent me from going tomorrow night, Mr. Hannegan. And if I have to follow Captain Vine myself, I will. Or, you can escort me and we can follow through as we had planned. It is your decision."

Why did every encounter with this woman lead to conflict? And how was it that she always put him at a disadvantage? Even now, he felt himself giving in to her, despite the fact that he knew he shouldn't. She felt it too. She glanced down at the invitation he still held in his hand.

"We'll need that to be admitted. Be sure you bring it with you. I'll meet you outside the Yacht Club at eight fifteen." She paused awkwardly. He felt her embarrassment and shared it, but grinned to cover his own discomfort.

"Formal attire. You needn't worry, Miss Bonner. I can manage it. But I want to go on the record as capitulating under protest."

"Duly noted, Superintendent," she said, and turned away.

"And Miss Bonner," he added, "I will call for you — say seven forty-five?"

She nodded and turned her attention to the toddler, tickling him with dancing fingers. He laughed, and her laughter rang out like a bell with his. Indeed, she was the most exasperating woman.

On his way back to his office, Joseph had to pass the excluded day rooms along the corridor. Here was Limbo, where men and women waited to return to a home so inhospitable that it would send them fleeing halfway around the world. Most of them would never understand why they had been rejected at the gates of Heaven.

There sighs, complaints, and ululations loud
Resounded through the air without a star,
Whence I, at the beginning, wept thereat.
Languages diverse, horrible dialects,
Accents of anger, words of agony,
And voices high and hoarse, with sound

450

of hands,
Made up a tumult that goes whirling on
For ever in that air for ever black . . .

Dante's first ring of Hell. He'd often thought the verse should be inscribed above the doors. Beyond the day rooms lay the Special Inquiry rooms. The Witness Room was now back in full use and all traces of Maggie Flynn were gone. She had become emblematic to him — an effigy of all the naive, the gullible who loved, believed, and placed themselves at the mercy of others. Ellis Island overflowed with them, and men like McNabb and his band of thieves were delighted to make use of them for their own gain. It had to be stopped. He veered off to make a quick circuit through the Registry Room.

"Why are so many people in line for haircuts?" Joseph asked a watchman outside the barbershop.

The watchman shifted his feet and glanced at the white-garbed barber, who had turned his back to work on the man in his chair. "I suppose they need them, sir," he said.

Joseph scanned the line of men who spoke among themselves in anxious whispers. One held a handful of change in his open palm and appeared to be carefully counting it with the help of several others.

"Italians?"

"I believe so, sir."

"Don't let them leave. I'll be right back." Joseph sprinted to the registry desks and seized the first Italian interpreter he could find, returning before the immigrant in the chair was finished.

"Ask this man what is wrong," Joseph demanded. The interpreter complied.

"He's worried that he will not have enough money after he pays for his haircut."

Joseph turned a critical eye on the man. His hair brushed the top of his eyebrows under his cap, and rested on the back of his collar, but neither were egregiously long.

"Tell him I suggest he wait until he gets settled in America and then get a haircut. He might need his money more for other things."

"He is afraid," the interpreter explained, after a lengthy discourse by the immigrant. "They've told him that he must have his hair cut, or he will not be allowed to board the train in New Jersey."

"Who told him that," Joseph snapped.

He did not need the translation. The immigrant pointed to the barber himself, and to his assistant who was sweeping hair into a corner of the room.

Joseph could scarcely contain his rage. "Tell him it is not true. Tell them all — every last one of them in the line. Make sure they all understand. If they're not all Italian, find some other interpreters but make sure the word goes out, do you hear me? I don't want to see one man in line here who does not have hair to his knees and a beard to cover his privates."

As the interpreter worked his way down the line, explaining what the Superintendent had said, Joseph turned his anger on the guard. "You are a watchman — do you understand what that means? You're not merely an observer here. You have a specific duty. You knew very well these men did not need haircuts. In fact, I suspect you knew exactly what was going on, so let me give you a warning. If I find that you, or any other station employee, is in complicity with any scheme to defraud these people, I will not only dismiss you, I will prefer criminal charges against you. Have I made myself absolutely clear?" The watchman nodded, but he wasn't intimidated.

"And tell both of them," Joseph continued, pointing to the barber and his assistant, "that I want them in my office the minute they close for the day."

The bets were on, and the money was all

on McNabb. The Boarding scandal and its phony investigation had made clear who was running the station and it was neither Commissioner Fitchie nor Joseph Hannegan. McNabb held all the power, and he had already gotten word out that Joseph's job might be on the line over the Doyle murder. One misstep, and McNabb would force Powderly's hand. Well, if that was the way it was to be, then Joseph would have to make the most of his time here while he could, and that meant keeping a keen eye on the privilege holders.

And so the day went, Joseph moving from one concession to the next. He spent extra time at the currency exchange, where the changing of money was too often at the disadvantage of the immigrant. Clerks were watchful and courteous to their customers as long as he lingered on the sidelines, but tomorrow they would return to their old ways. A Sisyphean job, Joseph thought, and wondered, not for the first time, why he had taken it.

CHAPTER
THIRTY-ONE

Mila Liberka married Albin Konopka at four o'clock in the afternoon in City Hall. The bride wore an exquisite black velvet vest, embroidered with gold and white beads in an intricate daisy design, over a white on white embroidered blouse and a scarlet skirt. Rachel Bonner was her only attendant.

Rachel had served as bridesmaid in more weddings than she could now recall. She had been eighteen or nineteen then, and the weddings, the first fruits of the debutante season. She looked back upon them now as rituals of convention — money marrying money to take up hollow lives on Fifth Avenue, which they then escaped to Tuxedo Park. But here was a wedding to give her satisfaction.

The bride had been detained at the station for a week, twisting the ribbons on her apron and weeping softly into her kerchief while her husband-to-be traveled from Chicago to meet her.

"No come," she sobbed on Rachel's shoulder. And the matron could give her no assurances, for too often they did not come as they had promised, having met another in their new home. But Albin had been faithful, if a little late in arriving, and the couple was escorted, as regulations required, to Manhattan for the ceremony at City Hall.

"For you," she said to Rachel, pushing a handkerchief tied with a ribbon into the matron's hands. Inside lay a silver stickpin. It had a cruciform shape and was intricately carved with crowned eagle's heads, hearts and bands of geometric borders. From each arm of the cross dangled four delicate chains ending in tassels. Rachel had seen it before. It was to have been Mila's gift to Albin.

"I can't possibly take this," she said, handing it toward the groom.

"She want you have it," he explained. "No friend, but you friend. You listen."

"But it was for you."

"I know." He smiled. "Iss O.K. I have Mila."

Rachel left them on the steps of City Hall, Albin studying a railroad schedule while Mila gaped at the bustling city around them. Rachel could have gone home, and was much inclined to do so, but then there was Maggie. She had promised Maggie that she would visit her as often as she could. Tomorrow night she would be dressing for the Yacht Club reception. This afternoon she was weary to the bone. But she had news, and if ever someone needed encouragement, it was Maggie Flynn. She waved good-bye to the Konopkas, stopped at a pushcart for a frankfurter, and turned toward the East River and the ferry to Blackwell's Island.

Although prisoners were not normally allowed visitors for the first month of incarceration, Maggie was a special case. She had not yet been tried, and almost any excuse could become a pretext for consulting with her on her case. No one questioned the niece of Matthew Bonner. They took her to a private visitation room — a cold, uninviting cranny with stone walls, a stark wooden table, and three scarred chairs. But it was no more depressing than Maggie herself, who toyed with the buttons on the stiff striped shirtwaist they gave all the inmates. Rachel cringed at her small, lonely figure and vacant expression.

"I believe we may finally be getting to the root of it all," she said. "I expect I'll know more after tomorrow night."

Maggie barely acknowledged that she had heard her. Where was the girl of two weeks ago, the girl driven by some inner fire who spat sparks in the Superintendent's face? Rachel wanted to shake her until Maggie lashed out with all the anger left in her. If the worst happened, if they were not able to find the murderer, she could not prepare for trial like this. She had to want to fight if Matt Bonner was going to fight for her.

"Maggie, listen to me." She waited for the girl to look up, and when she did not, Rachel took her chin in hand, as if talking to a child. "Look at me, Maggie Flynn, and listen to what I'm saying to you."

The girl lifted her gaze, but her green eyes were as dull as the water in the East River. "I want you to stop sitting there like a mouse trapped in your hole and fight for your own life. You should be angry, do you hear me? Angry! Cormac Doyle had no right to use you as he did and leave you in this predicament. He took advantage of you and left you to pay for it."

Maggie pulled away from Rachel's hand and swallowed, her fingers returning to the top button of her waist. "I came with him willingly, Miss Bonner. Ya can't blame him for that."

"I can and I do. He had no right to involve you in his dirty business —"

The old Maggie flew to her feet, eyes blazing. "The business of saving Ireland from the Lion is not dirty, and if that's whatcha think, I'll thank ya to leave and take yer help with ya."

"But you can't save Ireland unless you save yourself, Maggie."

The spark extinguished as quickly as it had flared. "There's nothing I can do. It'll be left to men like Cormac, not to fools the likes of me." She slumped back onto her chair. Whatever fire was left in the girl could not sustain itself, and Rachel had neither the time nor patience to keep stoking it.

"All right, then," she said, pushing her chair back decisively. "Crawl back into your hole and I'll go on my way. But I'll be back, Maggie. I won't sit by and see you hung as a martyr to Cormac Doyle and Clan na Gael. I'll come every day if I must, and push you and prod you and badger and harass you until you'll start helping yourself just to get me out of your hair."

A shadow of a smile crossed Maggie's face. "The Brotherhood should putcha to crankin' the Lion's tail, Miss Bonner. Then they might give up Ireland just to get a little peace."

Rachel laughed, relieved to see a bit of the old Maggie. "Is there anything I can bring you?"

Maggie shook her head. "Well, maybe one thing. Couldja get me another one of those doily belts like ya got me at the station?"

"We'll have you out of here before you need them again, I hope."

"I need them now."

"But you just had —"

Maggie turned her face away abruptly. "Yer right, of course. How silly of me."

"But if you're having your monthly still —"

A deep flush appeared on the girl's cheeks and the hand that had toyed with her buttons began to shake. She set it in her lap, folding the other one resolutely over it, but the trembling crept up to her arms and shoulders. Rachel sank back into her chair.

"Maggie, what is it? Are you ill?"

Maggie gasped, as if she would speak, but when no words came out, she shook her head.

"Then what is it?" A sick dread flooded the pit of Rachel's stomach. When the prison was full, as it was now, sometimes, she knew, the women prisoners were guarded by men. "Has someone done something to you, Maggie?"

When no answer came, she knew she would have to be direct. "Maggie, you must tell me. Did someone . . . rape you?"

Maggie bolted from the table toward the door leading back to the cells. Rachel reached her just in time to pull back the girl's skirts before a stream of vomit splashed at her feet. She waited until the retching had stopped before carefully dabbing at the girl's pale face with a clean handkerchief.

"Come sit down," she said, leading Maggie back to the table. She eased the girl into her seat and brought her own chair around next to her. Maggie's trembling had stopped, replaced by large, silent tears.

"Was it a guard?"

Maggie nodded.

"Then we must tell the warden immediately and get you a doctor."

Maggie gripped her wrist. "No!"

Rachel shook her off. "I can't sit by while a rapist guards a prison full of women, Maggie, and neither should you. He must be stopped and punished."

The girl's voice came out a bare whisper. "It didn't happen here."

"It didn't happen here? Then where, Maggie? On the ship?"

Maggie made no answer, but stared at Rachel solemnly. Rachel returned her gaze as, slowly, the horror of it became clear.

"Oh my God," she whispered. "The station."

Irene was gone. Rachel knew it the moment she opened the door to the Gramercy Park house. The note on her bed merely confirmed it.

I could not bear to say good-bye to you, dear Rachel, the note said. *You and your uncle have been the lights of my life for so many years. But lights burn out. Times change. Even people change. You will always be the daughter of my heart. This does not mean that we won't see each other, only that when we do, it will be different. I have taken a flat on the west side and will send two men for the remainder of my things by the weekend. Your uncle has my address. When I'm settled, I'll call you and you can come to tea in my new home.*

Rachel dropped the note on the bed and went looking for her uncle. She found him asleep, slumped over the desk in his library with a cold plate of beef and a half-full decanter of scotch at his elbow. The fireplace had burned down to a few lonely embers. She poured herself a neat drink and sat down next to the dwindling fire.

In her heart, Rachel still believed that he loved Irene, and that she more than returned his feelings. They were mired in confusion — Irene, afraid that he had offered to marry her for appearance' sake, because he was a gentleman, and Matt, sure that she had rejected him because she did not love him. Even if she accepted now, Matt might never be sure that Rachel had not convinced her to do so. If Irene came back, it would have to be because he brought her here on his own.

Rachel left her uncle in the study and took the backstairs to the servants' quarters. The fresh smell of starch lingered in the stairwell from the laundry to the right of the stairs. Rachel turned left, down a short hall to Irene's quarters. The door was standing open and her key sat on a table to the left of the door. Rachel pocketed the key and turned on the light.

Irene's furniture was all there. She would not take it. Matt Bonner had furnished the apartment for her, over the years replacing the serviceable furnishings that had been there with newer, finer furniture suitable for any one of his own rooms upstairs. Irene would not understand that it had been for her, as Matt had found excuses to remove the old. "The slats on that bed are ready to break," he would say, or "that old upholstery must be full of dust and germs. I can't have Rachel playing down there in unsanitary conditions." Rachel had known all along that she was only an excuse for him to do something nicer for Irene. But had Irene understood it?

She wandered into the parlor, as familiar to her as her own bedroom, for she had spent many hours there with Irene — hours which otherwise might have been painfully lonely for a child with neither siblings nor close friends. Irene had taught her to brew tea and tat lace, not that she'd ever done either very well. And they had studied there together, Rachel declining Latin nouns while Irene read books of law so that she might be a better partner in conversations with Matt. Three crates of Irene's books now stood in the corner of the parlor, waiting to be picked up and delivered to her new flat. Rachel pulled one out of the top.

Our Deportment, Or the Manners, Conduct and Dress of the Most Refined Society. Rachel took the book over to the settee and sat down, letting the dog-eared pages fall open where they would. She was twelve years old again and watching Irene as she set stacks of china on the dining table, on nights when Matt was at his club or had a social engagement.

"Now," Irene said, picking up the book, " 'Table appointments for breakfast, lunch and dinner.' "

In her mind's eye, Rachel watched as Irene practiced table settings until she no longer had to consult the book, and could set the table while still carrying on a conversation. When she had mastered that, she went on to study the arrangement of guests and the proper form of service.

"Be sure that you remove dishes from the right and serve from the left," she instructed the maids. "Tonight, we are using the Prince of Wales's Feather. Let me show you how it is done." She took a starched napkin from a pile and folded it in half. "You will need to press as you go with a hot iron," she explained, never allowing the maids to see what Rachel knew — that she had only learned this fold the night before, taken from *The Steward's Handbook*.

Irene had been a more diligent student of conduct, manners, and the proper way to run a household than she, herself, had ever been at Barnard. For Irene, every day was a test. Had she chosen the correct form for his dinner party invitation? Should service be Old English style or *à la russe?* And most important, was Rachel's conduct sufficiently ladylike?

"We never want to embarrass your uncle, Rachel," Irene would remind her. "He has a position in society to maintain." Even at twelve, Rachel knew that when she said "we," Irene meant "I." Hot tears sprang to Rachel's eyes.

Now she would have to take charge of the household. She would have to find another housekeeper, and perhaps a valet, although Matt had never wanted one. But no other housekeeper would do what Irene had done for him — helped him choose his clothes when, in fact, he had little interest in either style or fit; made sure they were kept clean and in fashion and good repair; worried over the smallest details of his dinner; and managed his household accounts as carefully as Morgan managed his bank. Beyond the routine expectations for a housekeeper, these were acts of love. And no one, Rachel knew, would ever love Matt Bonner as Irene Garrity had loved him.

CHAPTER
THIRTY-TWO

"It had to have been someone with a master key to the Detention and Special Inquiry rooms. A watchman, probably. She can't identify him?"

Rachel paced in front of the Superintendent's desk. "She thinks she may have scratched him on the face or neck, and she remembers the smell of whiskey on his breath, but it was too dark to see his face. She said he was a big man —"

"— but Tom Thumb would seem large to a girl her size. It's not enough. Even if she scratched him, the scratches would have healed by now. Sit down, please, Miss Bonner. You're pacing like a tigress in a cage."

Rachel took the chair in front of his desk. "Yes. I'm afraid you're right." She began toying with her watch, lightly tracing the filigree on the gold case with the tip of a fingernail. Joseph watched her intently.

She had been calm and surprisingly explicit in telling him about the rape, forgoing the usual veiled euphemisms to call it what it was. But he knew that beneath her collected demeanor, she was suppressing her rage with effort. Rachel Bonner was nothing like his idea of society women, women who chose a mould and poured themselves into it like so much porcelain clay. One did not cast a woman like this — intelligent, sensible, occasionally amusing, and often infuriating. Rachel Bonners were sculpted by the unique circumstances of their lives. They could not be relied upon to do the expected, but their artlessness made them infinitely more complex and interesting than their conventional sisters. Joseph found he was very much looking forward to spending the evening with her. It was a disquieting realization.

"There is something . . . ," she said, drawing his attention back to the problem. But she did not, at first, complete her sentence. She stared over his shoulder, slowly rising to walk to the window behind him and look down at the grounds below. "Do you remember the night Cormac Doyle's body appeared? I walked down to the bulkhead while I was waiting for the ferry. A watchman . . . what was his name? Something Biblical." She returned to her seat and closed her eyes, as if she were trying to picture the scene.

"He was walking watch on the perimeter and he challenged me, demanding to know what I was doing here. I remember that I was uncomfortable around him. He implied certain things about the other matrons. I didn't feel entirely safe with him because his breath smelled of whiskey."

"And you didn't report him?"

Her eyes snapped open. "If you recall, we'd had a disagreement. Then Doyle's body washed up on the island and you forced me to stay in the room while the doctor examined him."

Joseph flinched, and opened his mouth, but she cut him off. "On the whole, the watchman's breath seemed a fairly unimportant matter. But I remember something else about him. He had a smudge on his jacket collar — something oily, like greasepaint. I thought, at the time, that it was odd."

"Not odd, if he wanted to cover up scratches on his neck," Joseph said, rising.

He went to his filing cabinet and opened the second drawer, rapidly thumbing through a collection of folders until he found the one he wanted. He tossed it onto the desk and returned to his seat.

"Night watch," he said, riffling the pages.

"Here they are. Stop me if you hear a name that sounds 'Biblical.' Abbot, Atkins, Anderson . . ."

She stopped him at the Cs. "Cain! Watchman Cain. That's him."

Joseph wrote the man's full name on a scrap of paper. He returned to the cabinet and pulled a second file, marked Schedules, flipped it open and studied the top sheet for a moment. "He was on night watch the night Maggie Flynn arrived."

"But it still isn't proof."

"No," Joseph said wearily, "and we may never have proof."

"But we must find it! I can't tell Maggie that he's still out here. What about the other women? What is to stop him from harming someone else? A matron? A charwoman? Half of this island is pitch dark at night, Superintendent. The charwomen have to go to the laundry building. Do we tell them there is a rapist on the island, or just let them find out for themselves?"

"I can't make allegations without proof, Miss Bonner."

"Then we must get proof. Perhaps you could put me on night shift for a while —"

"No! You will not put yourself in harm's way."

Joseph slammed the file back into its

drawer. "I don't think we're going to be able to charge him with rape, but I may be able to find another reason to discharge him."

He returned to his desk and grabbed up the telephone. "Connect me to Night Division, please." He waited while the operator made the necessary connections.

"This is Superintendent Hannegan. I need a watchman's clock and records. The watchman's name is Richard Cain."

Joseph pulled off the leather case and cracked open the watch clock. Inside, a circle of printed paper, dotted with impressions, waited for replacement until the next shift. This was not good. The record should have been replaced at the end of the watchman's shift and checked during the day. But why should the Night Division be different than any of the others at the station — careless, lazy, corrupt? Just one more dereliction to add to an already prodigious list.

He took a hand lens and carefully checked the watch station impressions against the preprinted times on the paper. Apparently Cain had made his rounds on time last night. What was more important, the watch clock was working correctly. He set it aside and removed a stack of paper circles from the brown envelope Night Division had

471

delivered with the clock. Each circle was marked with the date and initialed by the chief of Night Division. It was a simple matter to find the disk for August 19 and track the watchman's movements.

Cain was on the second night watch, beginning at 7:30, and was assigned to the Men's Dormitory. He and a second watchman alternated watch clock service beginning at 8:00 p.m. Joseph could only hope that it was during his circuit of watch stations that he had decided to pay his sinister call on Maggie Flynn. If he had waited until the second watchman began his service, all hope of detection would be lost. But to have waited would have been a far greater risk. Better to do the deed when the other watchman was occupied with affairs upstairs.

Cain had begun the watch service with the eight o'clock circuit, which he had followed to the letter, leaving the eight-thirty circuit to his associate. At nine o'clock that night, Cain had begun a new circuit. Joseph traced his route on the paper circle: Station 1 — Men's dormitory, Station 2 — Eastern Hall, 3 — Women's dormitory, 4 — Western stairs. From there, he would have descended to the registry floor: Station 5 — Southwestern stairs, near Room 205, where Maggie Flynn had been detained. Station 6 would

be the Commissioner's office, and 7, the northeastern tower. But stations 6 and 7 were missing. In the time it would have taken Cain to walk that circuit, bringing him back to the eighth station at the northwestern tower stairs, he had been raping Maggie Flynn.

Joseph found Rachel in a detention pen on the Registry floor inspecting the knee of a little boy whose cheeks were stained with tears. The women huddled along the edges of the fencing, watching as their children ran in circles, playing some form of tag, a game which apparently knew no national boundaries. Rachel ruffled the child's hair and dispatched him to his mother.

"We need some recreational facilities for them, Superintendent," she said, as he walked up. "A few balls, some marbles, and jacks. I see no reason that we couldn't have a playground on the lawn."

"In due time, Miss Bonner. Let us get the hospital built first, shall we?"

"Certainly, I see your point. If we were to take, say two or three of those construction men off the hospital project for . . . oh, perhaps a week, it might just bring progress on the hospital to a standstill."

"You are relentless, Miss Bonner. Perhaps I should turn the management of the sta-

tion over to you."

She turned, as if to say she would accept it, but checked the apparent impulse. "I imagine you came in here to discuss something else?"

Joseph took her by the elbow and led her to the door, stopping only long enough to break up a donnybrook between a pair of young Irish brothers, an Italian child, and a Greek. "To be continued on the streets of the city very soon, I imagine," he remarked. He signaled to another matron to take over for Rachel, and to a watchman to let them out.

"I've got him," Joseph said. "I can't prove he raped Maggie, and I don't think we ever will, but at least I can prove that he neglected his watch that night. It will be reason enough to dismiss him."

"He'll only go somewhere else and do the same thing. If only you would transfer me to Night Division temporarily, I believe I might be able to draw him out."

Joseph shook his head. "I've told you, I will not put you in danger. Besides, the advantage of attacking Maggie was that he knew she could never identify him. They were in a totally dark room, and she had no way of recognizing anything about him. You could hardly hope to duplicate those condi-

tions, nor would it be worth the risk.

"I have his address. I can at least inform his local precinct to keep an eye on him. I've told Night Division to send him up to me as soon as he reports for work."

"It's not enough, Superintendent. After what he did to Maggie, he deserves prosecution."

"He deserves to be cas—" He stopped himself just in time, blushing in spite of her apparent composure. "But we have to keep our minds on the larger issues. The rape was heinous, but Maggie's conviction for murder would be a tragedy." To that, she reluctantly agreed.

Watchman Cain appeared in Joseph's office shortly after four o'clock. "You sent for me, sir?"

"I did, Cain."

Joseph did not invite him to sit down. Instead, he unlocked his center desk drawer and tossed several paper circles onto his blotter, watching as Cain's placid expression settled into a slight frown.

"I know what you've done, Cain."

"What I've done, sir?"

"The rapes," Joseph said, pluralizing the crime, for now he was sure there had been more than one. Cain's watch record showed numerous lapses. The division chief appar-

ently had not even noticed them. Or maybe he just didn't care.

Cain stumbled back a step, but kept his expression dispassionate. "I'm sure I don't know what —"

"I'm sure you do. Maggie Flynn, for one. A helpless young woman in trouble. You raped her between 9:20 and 9:30 on August 19."

Cain answered him with a sly smile. "And you have proof of this, do you?"

"Not proof of the rape, no. If I had, you would not be standing in front of me now, I assure you. You'd be peering out between iron bars on Blackwell's Island." Joseph picked up the paper circles and locked them back in his desk drawer, his gaze never leaving Cain's.

"But dereliction of duty is another matter. You skipped two of your watch stations that night, and it is not the first time you have done it." Joseph reached down under the kneehole of his desk and withdrew a small crate. He pushed it across the desk.

"The contents of your locker, Cain. Inventoried by myself and two watchmen — including your whiskey flask. Sign the sheet and take your things." He thumbed open his pocket watch. "The next ferry is due here in twelve minutes. If you are not on it,

I will have you forcibly removed from the island."

Cain hesitated only a moment. The balance of power was not in his favor. He scrawled his name across the bottom of the sheet and straightened up.

"You can't just fire me without a hearing. I'll tell 'em I was sick that night — feverish and throwing up. Clancy'll back me up there. That's why I missed those stations. Sick as a dog, I'll say. I'll go to Mr. McNabb. We ain't finished here yet, Hannegan."

"And then there is the matter of your intoxication on the job the night the body washed ashore. And the witness who will testify to it."

Cain laughed. "The matron? You think McNabb's going to take her word over mine? That little whore, out walking on the bulkhead all alone? Who was she waiting for, Hannegan? Maybe it was you." Joseph stepped around the desk.

"You know, Cain, I believe you're right. We are not quite finished," he said, and drawing back his fist, delivered a punch to the other man's stomach, followed by an upper cut to the jaw. Blood poured from the watchman's mouth. Cain staggered backward, lost his balance, and dropped to the floor. Joseph shoved the crate at him

just in time to catch his vomit.

"Take it and get the hell out."

Joseph stood at the darkened parlor window and gazed down the street toward Rossi's grocery store. A street lamp spread a thin light over the corner, but did nothing to illuminate the recessed doorway. Nevertheless, the flare of a match told him what he needed to know. His shadow was still with him.

Behind him, a familiar set of footsteps came down the stairs and crossed the floor to the parlor door. "Oh! Mr. Hannegan, is that you in the dark?"

Joseph turned. "It is, Miss Dove." He hurried away from the window before she turned on the light.

"I just came down to find my red thread," she said, switching on a small lamp next to the sewing machine. "For a quick repair to Moira's dress. My, how nice you look! Are you going out?"

"Yes, I have a function to attend."

She rustled in the drawer of the machine cabinet, coming up with the desired spool. "Here we are. Shall I turn the light back off, Mr. Hannegan?"

Joseph glanced back toward the window self-consciously, but she didn't wait for an

answer. Extinguishing the light, she stepped to the window and drew the lace curtain back an inch. "He's still there," she said.

Joseph cleared his throat. "He?"

"The man you were watching. I noticed him from Moira's window earlier. It's the third night he's been there, watching the house."

"I didn't realize anyone had noticed."

She dropped the curtain and turned to him in the dark. "Oh, just me. Selma Shapiro wouldn't notice if her own hair were on fire, she's so preoccupied with her silly fashion magazines. Moira's too busy, and Mr. Kessler isn't here enough. He's been following you, hasn't he? Would you care to tell me why?"

The answer was an emphatic no, but only in Joseph's mind. In fact, Miss Dove could be quite helpful to him if he took her into his confidence. "It has to do with a matter at the station, something I'm not at liberty to disclose," he said. "But tonight it is imperative that I evade him. I'm just not sure how to do it."

"You must leave by the back door."

"Yes, I'd thought of that. But even if I do, I'll have to come out the alley two doors up. There's still a risk that he'll see me."

Miss Dove waved him off. "I can take care

of that for you, Mr. Hannegan. Wait here just a moment," she said, and disappeared up the stairs. In a minute she came back down with Mrs. Shapiro at her side.

"He is standing in the doorway of Rossi's grocery," she said to her companion. "I simply must know if he's the masher who has been pestering me at the library, Selma."

"But Grace, you must call the police!"

"I can't. Not unless I know it's him. You wouldn't have them arresting an innocent man, would you? Be sure you talk to him, because the masher has a lisp. And get a good look at him so you can describe him to me."

"But what will I say?"

"Tell him you thought Mr. Rossi was open late tonight. Ask him if he knows of a grocery store that's still open. Use your imagination, Selma!"

The front door slammed. Joseph stepped back to the window in time to see Mrs. Shapiro glance back at the door before turning onto the street.

"Go now, Mr. Hannegan. Wait at the alley until she reaches the corner. Mrs. Shapiro will keep him busy for a few minutes."

Joseph grabbed her hands and squeezed them. "Thank you, Miss Dove. And please —"

"Don't worry," she said. "Selma needn't know a thing."

CHAPTER
THIRTY-THREE

She wore a gown of ivory satin, its bodice embroidered with gilt thread spun fine as angel's hair. The narrow sleeves clung to her shoulders by will alone, descending to a décolletage that barely escaped immodesty. And Joseph had neither breath nor words to tell her how beautiful she was.

She was pulling on her gloves when she entered the drawing room, trying to work them up her slender arms and over her elbows. "Irene normally helps me dress, but she's. . . ."

She stopped to fumble with a pearl button on her glove, frowning. "Oh, I am perfectly useless with my left hand."

He took her hand and fastened the button for her. She was not wearing her customary lilac scent — and when had he come to notice what was her custom? Instead, a deep, spicy fragrance surrounded them and seemed to flow into his veins.

". . . so anyway, Alma had to help me do my hair, which was more or less like having the help of a bird building her nest," she said, pushing a stray lock into place. She gave her left glove a last yank. "There. It will have to do."

It would more than do. No mortal woman could eclipse her. He adjusted his white tie in the mirror and cleared his throat. "I have a carriage waiting if you're ready," he said.

Miss Dove's scheme had worked perfectly. Just as Mrs. Shapiro reached the corner, Joseph had emerged from the alley, slipped across the street and down an alley on the other side that connected him to Houston Street. There, he'd quickly secured a hansom, directing the driver to turn evasively, first onto McDougal Street, then again on Prince, but no one had followed them.

Rachel picked up a capelet of silky fur and waited while he dropped it over her shoulders. "You look very nice this evening," she said.

He wanted to return the compliment, but could only grope for words in the vacuum of his mind. He had to get hold of himself. But she didn't seem to expect a reply in kind, and anything he might say now would sound like a hollow effort. He would tell her. But later.

"I think," she said, once they were settled in the carriage, "that you must be from Canada."

"Canada?"

"Yes. We can pass you off as almost anyone if you're Canadian. No one ever knows anything about them."

"Ah. I see. And have you come up with a biography for me yet?"

She opened her evening bag and withdrew a bracelet, a chain of daisies composed of diamonds and seed pearls. She passed the bracelet to him and extended her hand absentmindedly.

"Well, you're in pulp and paper. No one in New York knows anything about forests, and they care even less. I think we should stay with your Christian name, but we'll need another last name."

"Something Protestant and not Irish," he added, amused by her enthusiasm for fabrication. He fastened the bracelet in place, turning the clasp to the inside of her wrist.

"Exactly. How do you feel about Taggart?"

"Joseph Taggart. It's fine."

"Yes," she said. "I think so too."

On the way to the Yacht Club, Rachel constructed the necessary biography. He was from Vancouver because, as she pointed out, it was about as far from New York as they could get. He was attending the Cup races as an observer, although he was very much interested in organizing a similar race on Canada's western coast. He tried to follow, but was distracted, there in the close darkness of the carriage, by the way the streetlights played across her slender throat and cheekbones, and emphasized the slight cleft between her breasts.

"Are you listening, Mr. Hannegan?"

"Of course, you said I own a steam yacht. That way they won't engage me in discussions about halyards and . . . what was the other one?"

"Headsails. You needn't worry, these people are only interested in themselves. Keep the conversation focused on them and you'll be fine."

"I don't have any cards. What will I do if they ask me for my card?"

"Hmm." She tapped her chin with a gloved finger. "You lost your case on the train. In fact, you're quite put out about it. It was gold, of course, a gift from your late father. It's inconvenient not having cards, but the case holds such sentimental value that you're simply devastated at its loss. Bore them with the details and they won't ask for your card again."

"I believe I'm beginning to understand

the technique."

They fell silent for a moment. As they drew nearer to the new 44th Street clubhouse, he reflected on how different their worlds really were. "I suppose you are a member of the club?"

"Not me. My uncle is, hence the invitation, but he rarely participates in their events, and then usually only for business or political purposes. But he has a small yacht at the house in Newport."

"Your summer home?"

Rachel laughed and shook her head. "We do not live the leisurely life of an Astor or a Van Rensselaer, Mr. Hannegan. Our house in Newport is our original family home. My parents and I were living there when they drowned," she said, her expression growing more solemn.

"How often do you go back?"

"We used to go back in the summertime, but I never really enjoyed it. I'm afraid of water, Mr. Hannegan. I don't like boats."

"But you take the ferry every day."

"Because there is no other way to get to the station. I force myself, day after day, to walk up the gangplank and stand at the rail. It is not easy for me."

"No, I suppose not," he said.

"We are on the early side of fashionable,"

Rachel said as they drew up in front of the door. "But I think that's just as well. As soon as Captain Vine arrives and you've had a good look at him, we can leave."

He wondered, as he helped her down from the carriage, whether the Fusion tea was as much on her mind as his. Here he was, standing in front of a lacy limestone building, with a stunning beauty on his arm. A helluva place for Joe Hannegan from the Lower East Side, he thought. If they only knew, they wouldn't even let him in the servants' entrance. He glanced over at Rachel, who was shaking out her satin skirt, and remembered her words. *It is amazing what one generation of Americanization and education can achieve.* Well, she was about to put it to the test. He gave her his arm; she raised her chin and sailed up the red carpet.

The New York Yacht Club was not the nautical design that Joseph expected. It was, in fact, a good deal grander, with carved marble balustrades, gilded moldings, and ornamental cornices. It had a vaguely sacred feeling about it, an impression reinforced by the early arrivals who conversed almost in pantomime.

Joseph checked the capelet in the cloakroom for Rachel and returned to the lobby, stopping just short of the door. She was waiting for him at the foot of the stairs, her ivory train fanned out on the crimson velvet carpet, gazing at something on the balcony above.

If he had been asked to describe her, he might have likened her to a swan. Or a soaring dove, perhaps. A lily. A marble goddess. But they were all just pale reflections of her. She turned to him, standing in the doorway, and offered a tentative smile. And at that moment, Joseph Hannegan knew for certain what he had suspected from the first — that his heart was in desperate trouble.

"You see that man?" Rachel said, leaning over the balcony. "The one wearing the pince-nez, standing there in the door."

She took a sip of her champagne. "That's Peter Marié. He's listed in *King's* as a capitalist. In fact, he is a collector of snuff boxes and fans, and a dreadful amateur poet. But his life's real calling, Mr. Han—er, Taggart, is as a cotillion leader. He is indispensable to social occasions, rather like the Havilland or Sevres."

Below them, New York's aristocracy was streaming through the doors in lavish gowns, pearl studs, and diamond links. A fraternity of wealth at home with others of their kind. Joseph, on the other hand, felt very much at sea.

Rachel set her empty glass at the base of a marble column and glanced around for a waiter. They had positioned themselves on the balcony so that they could see the guests as they arrived and ascended the stairs to the reception. But how long could they linger there without becoming conspicuous?

"Don't worry," she said. "They think I'm something of an eccentric. I can do almost anything and they won't be surprised. In fact, it will give them something to gossip about over their Nesselrode pudding at the Waldorf."

"And why do they think that, Miss Bonner?"

She unfurled her gold fan, the ladies' favor for the evening, and examined the tiny emerald shamrocks on the fabric. "Probably Peter Marié's idea — copied from one in his private collection," she mused, before answering his question. "Because I have a job, Mr. Taggart. And because I don't care for absinthe, *tableaux vivants,* or artifice. Oh, and probably because I was raised by an Irish housekeeper." She snapped the fan closed again.

"The woman in the mauve gown is Mrs. Benedict Cross. Widowed at the age of twenty-seven — he was forty-two at the time. She has the largest and most explicit collection of pornography in New York City, I'm told. Unfortunately, I've never had the opportunity to see it." She turned back to Joseph. "Why, Mr. Taggart, I've embarrassed you!"

Joseph twirled his champagne glass between his fingers. "Yes, Miss Bonner, if that was your intention, then you have succeeded," he said. He bowed and nodded to a couple coming up the stairs before turning back to Rachel. She was staring down into the lobby at a woman draped in furs and wearing a diamond coronet who stood at the entrance as if waiting for a flourish of trumpets. Two men followed her like a pair of footmen.

"The one with the silk top hat," Rachel said quietly. "That's Arthur Vine."

"Who is that he's with?"

She compressed her lips and raised her chin a fraction. "Mr. and Mrs. Bradley Martin." Just as she said it, the woman looked up, narrowed her focus on Rachel, and turned sharply away.

"And I have been cut," she said. She turned to Joseph. "If we're going to get near them, it will have to be on the force of your charm, Mr. Taggart."

"Then we should be mingling, so that I can ply my craft, Miss Bonner."

She took his arm and gently guided him back toward the Trophy Room and up a short flight of stairs to the Model Room. He had been struggling to appear impassive and unaffected by the grandeur of the place, but the Model Room defeated him. Here was the nautical theme he'd expected in abundance. The room was dominated by three bow front windows that all but duplicated the bow of a Spanish galleon. Oriental carpets and warm woods, ornately carved beams and balusters and a marble fireplace that occupied the center of the wall with the stateliness of Victoria enthroned. Together they forced upon him the aesthetic poverty of his life.

"Overdone," Rachel said, but he could not agree.

They drifted toward a sailboat encased in glass, stopping along the way to refresh their champagne and exchange a few words with other guests Rachel knew. "From Vancouver," Rachel said.

Joseph shook hands with the man, and bowed to the woman. What did she say his name was? Sheffield? Shepard. Chairman of the Board of Trustees of City College.

"I assume your uncle is off campaigning

elsewhere?"

"He is speaking tonight to the Knights of Columbus."

"Ah, good thinking. He'll have to bring over at least a portion of the Tammany supporters if he hopes to win. Well, give him my best, will you?" Shepard said, and moved on.

"You see how easy that was?"

They studied the models on the wall next to the door — miniature hulls of boats identified by small brass plaques but which looked otherwise identical to Joseph. "This one," she said, "is like —"

He felt her stiffen and take a sidelong glance at the door as Mrs. Martin cruised into the room, her companions bobbing in her wake. The silk top hat was gone, leaving the men almost indistinguishable.

"The one with the very stiff posture," Rachel said under her breath. "I think he wears a corset." Joseph suppressed a grin.

"If I leave you now, she'll come over to talk to you. She's just dying to find out who you are, but she wants no part of me. And so," she said, with a lift of her skirt, "I repair to fix my hair." She was gone before he could protest, and no more than out the door before Mrs. Martin steered through the crowd in his direction.

"Have I missed dear Rachel?" she said, as her escorts floated up beside her. She turned a steely gaze on one of them. He stuck out his hand.

"Bradley Martin. I don't believe we've met."

Joseph accepted the handshake. "Joseph Taggart, Mr. Martin. A pleasure to meet you." Martin introduced the rest of his party.

Vine's handshake was limp. Joseph smiled inwardly, thinking what his father would have to say about that. He quickly inventoried Vine's features, committing them to memory as best he could. Sandy hair, but balding. About five foot six and slightly stout. Florid complexion. Very stiff, as if he had back trouble.

"Have you been abandoned, Mr. Taggart?"

"I certainly hope not, Mrs. Martin. I believe Miss Bonner will be back shortly." He saw, in the rapid flicker of her eyelids, that she would come right to the point.

"Are you visiting in New York, Mr. Taggart?"

"As a matter of fact, I am. I'm here for the America's Cup, of course." Mrs. Martin turned to her husband.

He took up the investigation. "And where

do you hail from, may I ask?"

"Vancouver, actually."

"Another subject of the queen, Arthur." Mrs. Martin giggled girlishly. It was most unbecoming in a matron of her age. Vine looked down at his shoes, clearly bored by the entire exchange. His straight posture was more than soldierly. He didn't seem to be able to bend. Rachel might be right about the corset, Joseph decided.

Bradley Martin, an otherwise anemic man with an exceptionally round head, had eyes of glacial blue. He narrowed them now, and Joseph saw in his gaze that he was not merely her lackey, but in full complicity with her. "Is it only the race that brings you to New York, or have you business here as well?"

"Oh, of course I'll try to do a little business while I'm here," Joseph said. "But my principal interest is in the Cup."

"Perhaps I can help you make some contacts. Just what is your business, Mr. Taggart?"

Joseph cleared his throat. "Pulp and paper."

"Don't know much about that industry. How is business?"

"Pressing," Joseph said with a slight smile. Vine quirked his upper lip in acknowledgment of the joke, but it was lost on the Martins.

Mrs. Martin adjusted her coronet with a plump, gloved hand. "Isn't Charles Hathaway in something having to do with paper?"

"Commercial paper," Martin said, glancing around. "I expect he'll be here tonight. I'll have to send him your way."

But the clock was ticking for Mrs. Martin, and she had not a moment to waste on the exigencies of business. "And how do you know our dear Rachel, Mr. Taggart?"

"Through her uncle, of course. Ah, I believe I see her coming now," Joseph said, gazing at a spot over Vine's shoulder where Rachel was watching from afar.

"Oh my, and I see someone I just must speak to about the cotillion for the Daughters of the King. Please excuse me, Mr. Taggart. Do give Rachel my best." Mrs. Martin heaved to port and set a course for Peter Marié, towing the two men behind her.

"Impeccable timing, Miss Bonner," Joseph said, when she had elbowed her way through the crowd. "One more minute and I would have been discussing business with Charles Hathaway."

"Hathaway? Oh!" She clapped her hand over her mouth. "I forgot about him. Well anyway, I did a bit of investigating while you were charming the Martins. It seems that Captain Vine is staying at the Plaza Hotel."

CHAPTER
THIRTY-FOUR

Broughams and hansoms lined up by the curb were still discharging their passengers in front of the club when they left. They caught a glimpse of Sir Thomas Lipton as he arrived. It seemed odd to Joseph that the club should be honoring their adversary.

"He's lost every time, but he is always the gentleman about it. The club wants to acknowledge his sportsmanship. Stiff upper lip and all that," Rachel said.

Joseph hailed a hansom and helped her into the carriage, giving the driver an address before joining her.

"May I smoke?"

"By all means. That's quite pretty," she said, looking at the engraved silver case he'd produced from his pocket.

"A gift from my father on my graduation from college," he said. He turned it over in his hand. "I rarely carry it." It was too precious to him, representing sacrifices that his father had made at a time when he could least afford it. But such disclosures were too personal to be shared. He lit a cigarette, shaking out the match and tossing it out into the street.

"May I try one?"

"You smoke, Miss Bonner?" His surprise was not feigned.

"No, but I'm curious. Other girls do it. Do you mind?"

He answered with a broad grin and struck another match. "You must draw on it," he said, "or it won't catch hold."

She did, her eyes growing wide. She opened her mouth and let the smoke spill out in a cloud. "Well!" she said. "I'm not sure I see the attraction of this habit, but perhaps I haven't given it a fair chance." She drew on the cigarette again, held the smoke and blew it out in a soft, steady stream.

"Irene would be shocked. 'All my hard work to raise you up a lady, and you've come to this,' " she said, mimicking the housekeeper. "She did her best. I've probably disappointed her terribly."

"She really did raise you, then?"

Rachel lifted her chin and met his gaze without blinking. "With as much love, and worry and exasperation as any other mother,

Mr. Hannegan." Her tone was one he'd grown too familiar with — challenging, defensive. He decided to leave the subject there. She took several more draws on the cigarette before handing it over to him for disposal.

"I do see where it has a relaxing effect," she said, laying her head back on the carriage seat and closing her eyes. They rode along quietly for a few moments before the carriage drew up to its destination. She opened her eyes and looked out the window, and then leaned forward to get a better look at the street. "That was quick. Where are we?"

"The Astor Hotel."

"Hotel?" she said, a slight note of alarm in her voice.

"You claim to be eccentric, Miss Bonner. Let us see just how unconventional you truly are. Besides, it would be a shame to waste a dress like that on those cadavers from the Yacht Club," he said. "And I don't believe I told you how lovely you look."

It was easiest to tell her there, in the dim light of the cab, where shadows concealed her blushing reaction and, more importantly, his own. But surely she heard the huskiness in his voice, perhaps even the hammering heartbeat that was pounding in his ears.

"Thank you," she said quietly.

He stepped down from the carriage and waited to help her, taking her elbows as she placed her hands lightly on his shoulders. And light she was, as though she were borne on invisible wings. Her hands lingered on his shoulders a moment longer than necessary. He leaned toward her, drawn by the warm, dark scent of her. She raised her face to his. But he could not do this. He could not kiss her, knowing he would face her over a desk in the morning and they might once again be at odds over a problem at the station.

"Shall we?" he said, offering her his arm. She took it, but the silence between them was heavy.

He took her to the roof garden, requesting a table along the front of the upper deck where they could look out over the city. At their end of the deck was a dance floor where couples whirled through a waltz to the music of a sizable orchestra ensconced in an enormous shell to the rear. From their table they could see most of the roof below, with its grand vine-covered arbors, fountains, and arches, and couples promenading from table to table between low palm hedges. Strands of white lights draped in scallops above them, and globe lights ballooned from the medallions along the roof's edge.

"I've never been here before," she said. "It's quite charming."

It was, in fact, a considerably less polished crowd than they had left at the Yacht Club, but the first theatergoers were arriving, bringing with them an atmosphere of exuberance. Behind them would come the chorus girls on the arms of wealthy men, and the actors and actresses who knew it did no harm to their reputations to be seen with young "dudes" named Kernochan, Whitney, and Jay.

Joseph seated her and took the chair across from her, placing an order for a split of champagne and a light supper with the waiter. "It's not Sherry's or Delmonico's," he conceded. "But the music is good, the food is acceptable, and the view is incomparable. It may not, however, enhance your reputation to be seen here with me. Most of these women do not move in your social circles."

The waiter had returned with their champagne. Rachel waited until he had filled their glasses and left before responding. "Social workers' reputations are often compromised, Mr. Hannegan."

"And why is that?" he asked, amused by her prim retort.

"Because we must go places that are not socially acceptable in order to do our jobs. Many a social worker has spent more time in bars and pool halls than any of her male friends."

"Following in the steps of Carrie Nation."

"Some, yes," she admitted. "But not all. We are not all as fanatical in our views of alcohol as Mrs. Nation." She raised her glass to him in proof.

"But if you are going to help people, then you must go where the people are who need your help. Sometimes they're in bars and pool halls." She took a sip of her champagne. "But of course, you probably think that's interfering."

"As a matter of fact," he said, "I do. But sometimes I suppose interference is justifiable — by the right person, who understands."

She leaned across the table toward him, her eyes shining with indignation. "Understands what, Mr. Hannegan? Exactly what is it that social workers do not understand?"

"Ah, that is the question, Miss Bonner. And the answer differs for everyone." He lit a cigarette and offered her one, but she shook her head.

"Let me give you an example," he continued. "When the woman comes from the Immigration Aid Society, we'll call her Miss Kittredge, and she, decked out in her warm coat with the fur collar, notices there's colcannon on the stove."

"Colcannon?"

"Potatoes and cabbage. And she says to the mother of the house, 'Where is the meat?' 'But we don't have meat tonight,' says mother. 'There's milk and butter in the colcannon, and more milk to drink with supper.' There was never butter or milk to be had in Ireland. 'But there has to be meat,' says Miss Kittredge. 'Your children will be malnourished without it.'

"And then she says, 'And the children aren't getting enough air. It's stuffy in here. Smoky.' But of course mother knows they're not getting enough air. At least they had that in Ireland — air to spare. But the gombeen man's not after them, and they're going to school, and she bought them both new shoes at the second-hand store last week. And when the landlord sees fit to build his tenement with ventilation, there'll be enough air. But until then —"

"You can stop now," Rachel said. "You've made your point."

Joseph smiled. "Which is?"

"That the social worker doesn't understand how much better off they are here than they were in Ireland. That the mother thinks she's doing pretty well by her children."

"Well, she did think so," Joseph said softly. "Until Miss Kittredge came. Many a night my mother cried herself to sleep after a visit from the social worker."

Rachel gazed down into her glass and bit her lip. He had upset her, although it had not been his intention. He had not foreseen that his teasing would take them this far. "I'm sorry," he said. "I'm afraid I've spoiled the evening."

"No, you haven't. I just feel so terribly sorry. Sometimes we forget how easy it is to make someone else feel insignificant."

Joseph studied her there, in the glow of the rooftop lights. All evening he had fought the way her lovely shoulders and slender waist stirred him. But this gentle kindness in her moved him to helplessness. "You would never do that, Miss Bonner," he said.

She glanced up at him, surprised. A warm breeze stirred the potted palms, their leaves rustling like taffeta dresses. Above, a diamond studded black sky stretched out over the city. He reached across the table and took her hand. "Would you care to dance?"

He took her in his arms to the tune of "My Wild Irish Rose," conscious of the warmth of her flesh and the fine layer of satin that separated it from his hand. He eased her closer to him, just enough that his jaw grazed her hair and her skirt swayed against his legs as they moved in concert. She yielded without resistance. He turned her, guiding her with a gentle pressure to her back.

"You are an excellent dancer, Mr. Hannegan," she said. "I'm usually a bit clumsy, but you make it very easy."

"It is all in knowing how to move your partner," he said into her ear.

"Yes," she said, a bit breathlessly. "I see that."

When the dance was over, their champagne was waiting for them at the table. Rachel took hers and walked to the wall at the edge of the roof to look down on the traffic below. Carriages and streetcars, pedestrians on foot all moved in an endless stream.

"Be careful," he said, joining her. "This roof is a good bit higher than your last one, Miss Bonner."

She smiled and continued to gaze down on the city. "It's what you notice about New York, isn't it?" she said. "All the people, always in motion."

"I wouldn't know. I've hardly been any-where else, except Ireland. And I don't remember it all that well, but it was nothing like New York, I can tell you that."

She turned to him. "What was it like?"

He shifted uncomfortably. "Surely you know, from what Maggie has told you. It's poor and sad and hungry. And angry. The Irish laugh a lot, and drink even more, but that's what you do when you live on a precipice. When you wonder if tomorrow you'll be eating grass like your grandfather, because the potatoes have the blight and the bloody Brits would sooner see you die than have to feed you from their pockets."

"That's what drives men like your father, I suppose."

Joseph took a deep swig of his champagne and leaned against the wall. "I don't know what drives men like my father. They come here with a chance to put all that behind them, to do something for themselves and their families, and all they can think about is Ireland. They leave their children to find their own way while they chase dreams that can never come true."

"Did your father do that?" she asked gently.

Joseph surprised himself with his answer. "Not entirely. My father has devoted a good many years to his lost cause, and we've all heard enough about it God knows, but he never put it before his family. Some of the others, though. . . . But you didn't intend to unleash another tirade, and I won't bore you with one."

Their waiter had returned, bearing Little Neck clams and a split of Chablis. Joseph guided her back to the table.

"So now that we know that Captain Vine is staying at the Plaza, what is our next move," Rachel asked.

Joseph looked at her, his oyster fork poised in midair. "We do not have a move, Miss Bonner. I want you as far away from this as possible. Arthur Vine is a dangerous man, and whoever is working for him is even more so. Your part in all this is to keep Maggie from losing hope. You may tell her, by the way, that Watchman Cain has been dismissed."

"Without charges against him for what he did to her?"

"Unfortunately, yes. My hands are tied there. As to Vine, I will have to draw out the informer somehow. I have an idea, but I'd sooner not spoil the evening by discussing it." He laid his fork aside. The orchestra had struck up "After the Ball" and he longed to feel her in his arms again. She saw him rise and did not wait to be asked.

Why are you single; why live alone? Have you no babies; have you no home? Joseph let the bittersweet lyrics run through his head, conscious of their irony. There would be no other night like tonight. How could there be, when they lived on so little common ground? *Many the hopes that have vanished, after the ball.*

They returned to a course of partridge and artichokes, served up with a bright Sauterne and small talk about the coming elections. They were just finishing when Rachel's attention was drawn to the roof below. "Look, isn't that Moira? And I suppose that must be her beau?"

Joseph had forgotten that this was the night that Liam was taking her to the theater. He'd been late coming from the station and had dressed hurriedly without seeing her. She stood now, her arm in Liam's, while they waited to be shown to a table.

"How beautiful she looks," Rachel said.

And she did, her crimson dress setting off her black hair and fair skin to their full advantage. Liam said something in her ear and she smiled. The maitre d' showed them to a table on the opposite side of the roof garden.

"Shall we invite them to join us?"

Joseph watched as they were seated and Liam moved his chair close to hers. This was Moira's night. He could not spoil it for her. And his affection for Liam was rekindled in the radiance of her smile. Liam had the capacity to bring joy into her life, as he had brought it to her brother's youth. Where, and why, had they taken such different paths? Perhaps they could converge once again in loving Moira. He had to give her that chance.

"No," he said. "I think they want to be alone."

CHAPTER
THIRTY-FIVE

Miss Dove was waiting for him when he got home. She sat in the parlor, calmly reading Dickens, her hair plaited in a long braid that trailed over the shoulder of her rose house-coat. She closed the book and pulled the lapels of her wrapper together modestly.

"I was waiting to speak to you," she said.

"Is Mrs. Shapiro —"

"She's fine, although I believe she thinks I have developed a nervous condition. His name is Billy Bell."

Joseph dropped onto a chair and loosened his tie. "She asked him?"

Miss Dove shook her head. "Oh no, she would never do that. His hair, by the way, is red, but he does not have a lisp. Of course, that was all a story made up for Selma's sake."

"Then how did you find out his name?"

Miss Dove colored faintly. The blush was becoming to her. "I followed him."

Joseph froze in his place and groped for something to say. But she did not give him a chance.

"You needn't look so concerned, Mr. Hannegan. It was perfectly safe."

"You don't know that, Miss Dove! He might be a very dangerous man. What could you have been thinking?"

Miss Dove regarded him placidly. "I had it all planned, Mr. Hannegan. It was really very simple. Would you care to hear about it?" Joseph nodded dumbly.

She set her book aside and folded her hands in her lap. "After Mrs. Shapiro returned, and we had sent Moira off with Mr. O'Neill, I watched him for a while, but he stayed where he was. Your father was out, and Selma had retired early, so I went through the house and turned off all the lights. He must have thought we were all going to bed, because soon after, he left."

She rose from her chair and walked over to the window, pulling the curtain back a fraction. Joseph watched her, amused as her enthusiasm overcame her normally shy demeanor.

"I had anticipated his decision and was ready. When I saw him turn onto Wooster, I left the house and followed him. He was on foot, thankfully. I don't know what I should have done had he taken a car." She dropped the curtain and walked over to the sewing machine, picked up the spool of red thread and returned it to the drawer.

"Where did he go?"

She turned to him with a hesitant smile. "Down Houston, across Broadway, to a . . . tavern, I suppose you'd call it, although that might dignify the place a bit too much. It was called Knickers — a reference, I suppose, to the Knickerbockers, although I doubt that any of them have ever darkened the door."

Joseph thought the name might well refer to something more brazen, but he did not say so to her. "You didn't go in, Miss Dove?"

"Of course I did. How in the world could I learn his name otherwise? There were women inside, although I must admit they were not of the best caste, but I was prepared for that possibility."

Joseph massaged his temples. He had not expected her to go so far. How many women was he going to put in danger before it was all over?

"Please do not look so worried, Mr. Hannegan. It was really very simple. I waited until he was ensconced at the bar before I made my entrance." She giggled nervously. "I must admit that I cut quite a swath through the men, shouting at him from the door all the way to the bar."

"Shouting at him?" Now Joseph was really alarmed. "What could you —"

" 'Johnny Kennedy!' I shouted at him. 'It is you, isn't it? Ten years gone, leavin' me with three mouths to feed and not a penny in the till,' I said. 'And here you are, big as ya please, drinkin' whiskey and consortin' with the likes of these . . . these strumpets, while yer children are sellin' matches on the street and cryin' for the father they never knew!' "

"That's quite the brogue you have, Miss Dove," Joseph observed drily.

It embarrassed her. "Forgive me, I meant no offense, Mr. Hannegan. But it helped me, you see, to assume another personality."

"Yes. Please go on."

"Well, at first the men in the place were angry, but when I broke down and wept, they turned on him. He, of course, denied that he was Johnny Kennedy, but I stood my ground. 'I'd know you anywhere, John,' I said. 'And those three red-haired children of yours look just like ya down to the last freckle.'

" 'But the name is Bell, ma'am,' he declared. He was at great pains to prove himself to all of us, you see. Finally, he found a friend — a policeman on the beat — who identified him. Billy Bell used to be a cop, Mr. Hannegan, but he is no longer with the police force. I would have liked to find out more about him, but I must admit, I was growing nervous that I couldn't keep up the act."

"Just how did you get out of Knickers, Miss Dove?"

Her face flamed. "I was growing desperate," she admitted. "If I capitulated too quickly, he might be suspicious. An irate wife would hardly give in so easily, after all. So I told them that Johnny Kennedy had a scar on his chest and asked the other men to check it. In private, of course. They took him to a back room, and while they were gone, I slipped out."

Joseph sat silently for a moment, listening to the hall clock tick away the hour. Was this a trait of women that he had thus far missed? First Rachel, concocting her preposterous story about Joseph Taggart, pulp and paper magnate, and now this, and from as unlikely a source as he could imagine. At length, he found his voice.

"You are a woman of remarkable resources, Miss Dove. I really don't know what to say. You should never have taken such a risk, but since it is done and over, thank you. You have been an immeasurable help."

She smiled, and he realized that her high color had transformed her. In the golden glow of the parlor lamp, draped in her rose-colored wrapper, she was really very pretty. "I must admit, Mr. Hannegan, that I have always had a yearning to act. I quite enjoyed myself tonight and would do it again any time."

"I hope, Miss Dove, that you will never have to."

Billy Bell. An Orange name, he thought, as he climbed the stairs to his bedroom. Devoy would never hire an Orange man and neither would Dylan Moran. But the Brits were another matter. Tomorrow night he would be following Arthur Vine. He could not afford to have Billy Bell tagging along. He would have to find a way to get rid of him.

Kate McBride opened the door to Joseph the next morning. She didn't seem to be surprised to see him.

"I'm sorry to be showing up on your doorstep so early, Mrs. McBride, but I must see Mr. Devoy. Is he alone?" Joseph said.

"In there." She pointed to the front room,

where John Devoy sat over a sheaf of papers, adjusting thick glasses on the bridge of his nose. He glanced up when Joseph came in, but looked down again.

"Let me finish my thought, before I forget it."

Joseph took a seat and accepted a cup of tea from Devoy's sister. He watched her retreat to the kitchen, where she sat at a small table bleached white from scrubbing, and rubbed kerosene into her hands. She patiently massaged the oil into the joints of each finger, her mouth moving silently as she worked. She had propped a holy card against a lamp on the table and seemed to be directing her silent prayers at it. Devoy noticed Joseph's interest.

"Rheumatism," he said. He folded his stack of papers and carefully inserted them into an envelope. "We both suffer from it, though Kate more than I."

Again, Joseph was aware of Devoy's booming voice, the result of his apparent deafness. "Never grow old," he said, affixing a stamp to the envelope. "When you're young, you think you never will. When you're old, you wonder how you could have been so stupid." He set the envelope aside and turned his full attention to Joseph, inserting the dome in his ear.

"So why are you here? Have you found him?"

"Not yet, but I'm getting close," Joseph said.

"Then what are you doin' here?" Devoy shouted. "Why aren't you out there findin' whatever proof you need, instead of here blatherin' with me?"

"Because I need your help," Joseph said. He glanced back at the kitchen, where Devoy's sister had completed her prayers. "First, I need to know what you've found out about the other men on the executive committee and where they were the night Doyle died."

Devoy shook his head. "Not enough. Cohalan was at a dinner at the Lawyer's Club. The *Times* reported on it, and several other people verified it. Pat McCartain was at the hospital until the wee hours tryin' to keep a patient alive. Tom Clarke and Seamus O'Neill were both at home, but no one can verify either one for me. But I can't believe it of either one of them, lad. I just can't believe it," he said, his voice drifting away.

Kate McBride appeared in the doorway, her small black pocketbook over her arm. "I'm goin' down to the grocer, John. Do you want cabbage or turnips today? I have a bit of bacon for them."

Devoy waved her away. "Whatever you think, Kate." He dug in his pocket for change. "But while you're out, pick me up some tobacco, won't you now?

"She doesn't like to know what we're doin'," Devoy said when she was gone. "I try to spare her as much as I can." It did not seem to Joseph that she had been spared much, except perhaps a decent place to live and the money to put meat on the table more than once a week.

"All right. I want to ask you about two other people, Mr. Devoy. You said you sometimes meet at the Ballyglass, and sometimes at St. Joseph's. Are Liam and Father O'Gara there for your meetings?"

The older man glared at Joseph over the rim of his glasses. "You can't be suggestin' that Father O'Gara is a murderer!"

"I have to consider every possibility, Mr. Devoy. I think we have to face the fact that you're not going to like it, no matter who it is. Father O'Gara is in a position to hear your men's confessions, among other things —"

Devoy's fist came down on the arm of his chair. "Our work does not require confessin'!"

"Your guns kill people, Mr. Devoy, and the last time I looked at a catechism, 'Thou shalt not kill' was still a commandment. But even if he's not hearing it in confession, could he be overhearing your meetings at the church?"

Devoy's intense look of consternation was answer enough. "But we don't always meet at the church. More often than not, we meet at the Ballyglass where we can have a dandy durin' the meetin'."

"And where is Liam?"

Devoy shrugged. "He goes to meetin's at the Hall, I think. Or maybe to see a friend. But he always leaves."

"You're sure?"

"He goes right out that back door of his, and one of us bolts it behind him. I can't be more sure than that."

"Then that leaves us with Dylan Moran."

"Dammit lad, I've already told you, Moran didn't know about the Glasgow operation, but the stag did! Have I not made myself clear on that point already?"

Joseph stood up and walked over to the window. Below, he could see Kate McBride making her slow progress down the street to the grocer. She looked older than her years and lonely. He wondered how she'd lost her husband.

"I have to draw him out," he said at length. "And it must be with information so important that he makes his contact in person."

Behind him, Devoy was silent. He turned around. Devoy was gazing into the distance, and Joseph knew he was coming to a decision. "I've been thinkin' of an operation for some time now. It's big. I hate to compromise it."

"But with a stag in your ranks, it's already compromised," Joseph said softly. "And besides that, it's the only way to bring him out."

CHAPTER
THIRTY-SIX

Rachel lay awake long after Joseph had left
her at her front door, and woke in the gray
pre-dawn light with the same questions on
her mind. He hadn't kissed her, not that
she had expected him to take such a liberty,
but she knew he had almost done so when
he helped her out of the carriage at the Astor, and, she conceded to herself, she had
wanted him to. But now she wasn't sure.

He was charming in his way, but often
autocratic. Still, he had integrity, and a gruff
sort of kindness. He had handled himself
admirably at the Yacht Club. But she was
doing it again — the very thing he loathed
in her. Yet how could she help but compare
his world to hers when they were so different? And now he was embarking on something dangerous, and she could not tell him
that she was afraid for him. It would not
matter. He was determined to find Cormac
Doyle's murderer whatever the cost. She

rose and dressed, her mind very much on the day before her and the plans that Joseph Hannegan refused to disclose to her. Time was growing short for Maggie. He would have to act quickly, and the knowledge that he would struck a deep chord of fear in her.

Her uncle, too, was worrying over Maggie at breakfast. "So far, I have nothing I can use to defend her," he said. "I've done everything I can to delay a court date — challenging jurisdiction, asking for more time to locate witnesses. I've even tried to find a forensic expert who might be able to tell us exactly when Doyle died. I don't have any more cards up my sleeve, Rachel. I need a professional investigator on this case. How am I to defend the girl when you and Hannegan are tying my hands behind my back? You wanted me to defend the girl and I agreed. Now you're making it impossible."

"If you'll give us just a few more days, Mr. Hannegan is on the brink of finding the murderer. Can't you contrive to get jury selection postponed?"

She reached over to scratch a dry spot of something off his suit jacket. Irene would never have let him leave the house with so much as a speck of dust on his clothing.

"I've done that. But they will not postpone indefinitely, and we're losing valuable hours here. Why is Hannegan so determined to keep an investigator out of it? Could he have something to do with the murder, Rachel?"

"No!"

"You don't know him all that well, after all. And he is Irish."

"Just what does that mean, Uncle Matt? Do you think Irene might be in on it too? After all, she's Irish." She regretted the words as soon as they were out of her mouth.

His shoulders slumped and he rubbed his face with an open palm. "Alma is complaining that she can't do Irene's job and hers, too. Mrs. Coffey is asking me for menus I don't have. She took great umbrage yesterday when I told her I didn't care whether she served tenderloin of pork or veal cutlet for dinner. And the dailies are wandering around as if they don't know what to do, and I don't know what to tell them, Rachel."

"I'll handle it," she said. "I'll leave a list for the dailies with Alma and discuss the menu with Mrs. Coffey. And tonight, I'll start interviewing for a new housekeeper. I'll contact an agency today."

"Yes. All right," he said. He stared down at his plate, where poached eggs and lamb chops were congealing from lack of interest.

"I miss her, Rachel. And I keep thinking about all the lost chances over the years."

"Then why lose another minute? Go to her, Uncle Matt, and ask her again. I know she loves you."

He dropped his napkin over his plate, as if he couldn't bear the sight of it. "And if you're right, if she were to say yes, then would it really be fair to her to subject her to the kind of scrutiny she would be under? I'm running on an anti-Tammany ticket, fighting corruption and vice. Wouldn't our adversaries have a heyday with her — my housekeeper? Can you imagine the innuendo about all our years together? Richard Croker will not think one second about making her out to be my mistress and the house where I raised you a den of iniquity if it suits his purposes. I've done enough to her, Rachel. I will not subject her to that."

Most people would have said that it was a fine fall day, although the wind was slightly brisk at the water's edge. The sharp blue of the sky was mirrored in the East River, disguising the seething filth beneath. Likewise, the ferry Rachel boarded could have been taking its few passengers to cozy homes in New Jersey or on a Coney Island excursion. Instead, it was taking them to one of the darkest places in New York. Rachel flashed her pass to the ferryman and boarded behind a priest carrying a bag like Father O'Gara's. He might be going to hear confessions. Perhaps even someone's last.

The Superintendent had given her leave to see Maggie on her way to work and deliver the news about Watchman Cain. It was a short crossing to Blackwell's Island — not a time to strike up conversation, nor did anyone on the ferry seem so inclined. Police patrol boats cruised the river, reminding those on board that theirs was a sobering excursion. On shore, guards seemed to be everywhere, stationed along the perimeter of the island, although it did not seem possible that anyone could escape the fortress, the penitentiary building with its thick, crenellated walls. Rachel trudged up the path beside the priest, who smiled bleakly at her. Inside, she waited while he was shown through a set of heavy iron doors before the desk sergeant took her through to a visitors' room. In a few minutes, they brought Maggie to her.

Something about the girl had changed. Her eyes were no longer vacant, but had taken on a sly, cunning light. She was losing weight — slight before, but now as thin and angular as a bundle of twigs. Her fingers reminded Rachel of chicken bones. Her face was slightly swollen and covered in greenish bruises.

"Maggie, what happened to you?"

Maggie's hand went to a particularly ugly bruise on her neck. "A bit of a donnybrook over breakfast," she said, as though it weren't important. She narrowed her gaze at the sight of Rachel, and crossed her arms tightly over her chest.

"Give me your worst, Miss Bonner," she said sharply.

"Sit down, Maggie." Rachel waited while the girl pulled out her chair and dropped into it. She folded her hands on the table. They were red and peeling, the cuticles ragged and the nails split. She was assigned to a janitorial detail that worked a far greater hardship on her hands than housemaid work in Ireland had ever done. She waited primly for Rachel to go on.

"The Superintendent has dismissed the watchman we believe raped you, Maggie. Right now dismissal is the best he can do, but he is hoping to gather more evidence against him. Is there anything you can tell me that would help us identify him specifically? Did you see anything — the color of his hair, the shape of his face?"

"Nothing. I told you, it was black as night.

But if you know who he is, what more do you need?"

"Evidence." Rachel explained that Cain had been dismissed not for rape, but for dereliction of duty.

"And yet, there's plenty of evidence against me for a crime I didn't do. A fine joke on me that is." Maggie snorted and shook her head.

Rachel leaned across the table. "Is there anything else I can do for you, Maggie? Anything I can bring you?"

"Some fine silk stockin's, perhaps," Maggie said. "And a box of chocolates to nibble on with me tea."

Rachel ignored the sarcasm. "Shouldn't we write to your family? The trial's coming up and they should know about it."

"Why, Miss Bonner? So they can sit under their leakin' roof and set aside their worries about how they're to feed the rest of the family this long winter, to brood instead about the daughter who was to send them money from America? The one who lied to them about havin' a good job to go to? Even now, they're lookin' for their first letter in the post, expectin' a little somethin' to help them get by, and I'm here, as close to hell as I can get on this earth. Better they think I drowned in the crossin' than to know

527

about my disgrace. No, we won't be writin' the family."

Rachel reached across the table to take Maggie's hands, but the girl withdrew them, tucking them back under her arms. Rachel tried to fill her voice with a confidence she did not feel. "You've got to hang on, Maggie. We're close to finding out who killed Cormac, but we have to prove it."

"Like you're provin' who raped me, Miss Bonner?"

"No! I swear to you Maggie, we'll find a way out of this somehow. Just a few more days. We'll get him. Mr. Hannegan —"

"I want to ask you somethin', Miss Bonner, and I want you to tell me the truth." Maggie's eyes bored into Rachel's. "The women here, they talk about somethin' called the electric chair."

A sick revulsion washed over Rachel. She fumbled in her bag for a handkerchief, aware of a sudden cold perspiration at the back of her neck.

"I want to know if it's true. Is there such a thing as that?"

"Maggie, please, you needn't worry —"

"Is there such a thing as a chair that burns you alive with electricity, Miss Bonner? They say it goes into your brain and sets your hair on fire. I want to know, is it true?"

Rachel turned away. There was nothing she could say.

The hot water felt good on Maggie's hands in a purging, punishing way. And punishment was just what she wanted. How could she have been such a fool as to love the likes of Cormac Doyle, and worse, to love him still? An able dealer, her father had called him, but she'd been too blind to see it. He had used her and gotten himself killed, leaving her to pay the price. And the price was high.

Even as she'd asked the question, she hadn't doubted that it was true. Jenny Moffat, who was a trollop and had stabbed a customer for beating her, first told her about the electric chair. Jenny was frightened, too. She had no reason to make up such a story. And Maria Savino nodded solemnly as she listened. She'd heard of it, she said in her broken English. It waited for her, too.

They strapped you into it, Jenny said. She'd heard about bodies catching on fire from it.

"Are they dead already?" Maggie whispered, her voice catching in her taut throat.

Jenny shrugged. "Does anyone really know? The electricity, it throws you around in the chair, so that's why they use the straps."

Even now, Maggie felt sick thinking about it. She set the pan she'd been washing onto the drying rack and leaned over the sink. She would not throw up. She would not stop thinking about it. She would think about it and think about it, and think about it some more, until she wasn't afraid any more. If only there were another way out. But there wasn't. She had no faith in what Miss Bonner had said — that they would find Cormac's killer. A man had raped her, and it had come to nothing for him.

Blackwell's Island had taught her the truth about justice in America. Jenny Moffat had no teeth, and her left arm had been broken by her customers so often, it hung lifeless at her side. The cop on the beat didn't care. Josie Teague killed her drunken father. Never mind that he'd raped and beaten her over and over again for three days. Maria Savino's husband had died in a sewer accident leaving her with a newborn and six other children to feed. She had no milk and in a fit of despair, had choked the child she could not nurse.

Maggie picked up another pot crusted black with the remains of the lunch stew. The warden and guards had eaten first, off the top, leaving the burned remains for the inmates. That was America — a stew, savory for those who ate off the top. But those at the bottom got only the dregs.

"You'll need a pot chain for that." The housekeeping matron peered over Maggie's shoulder, her expression pinched in distaste. "Get one out of the supply closet," she said, pointing across the kitchen with her billy club. "And another bar of soap while you're at it."

Maggie found it quickly and turned it over in her hand. The handle was iron, and the bulb of chain made of interlocking metal rings. It might make a weapon, if she thought hard enough about how to use it. That is what Cormac would do. Cormac would find a way to fight back. But even if she managed to disarm the housekeeping matron, how would she get out of the building, divided again and again as it was by iron doors and heavy bars? And then, she was on an island, and even if she could swim the distance, where would she go?

She turned back to the closet for the soap, hunting among bottles of carbolic acid and ammonia, Chinese laundry wax, and boxes of Roseine powder. And then the answer came to hand. She turned the small tin over in her palm before slipping it into the pocket of her skirt. She rearranged the bottles of carbolic acid, carefully covering the vacant spot on the shelf, her heart thumping heavily in her chest. But after all, who would miss a tin of rat poison?

Joseph picked up Billy Bell in Battery Park, just as he had expected. He hadn't exactly planned what he would do, but one way or another he must leave Bell behind. He would walk, that much he had decided, because the opportunities for losing Bell were far greater on foot than they would be in a car or on the el.

He stepped out at a rapid clip, forcing Bell to hurry to stay apace with him, across the park, past Bowling Green, the Produce Exchange, and Steamship Row and onto Broadway. Here, in the concentration of banks, brokers, and insurance companies, foot traffic was heavy as businessmen poured out of their offices for the trip home. The sidewalk ahead was a sea of bowlers and homburgs, pinstripes and herringbones, charcoal suits and cutaway frock coats. With luck, he might lose Bell naturally — a casualty of the congested sidewalks during the approaching dinner hour. He slowed at a corner just long enough to trade a coin with a newsie and grab a copy of the day's

Times, casually glancing behind him. Bell was a dogged shadow.

He continued up Broadway, weaving between other pedestrians, as elusive as he could be without attracting unwanted notice from others around him. Where was the cunning of his youth? There had been a time when he and Liam could evade three beat cops nipping at their heels after pinching a handful of cigars or a bucket of beer. But those days were gone, and Joseph was not sorry.

The Post Office was coming into view when he summarily decided to make a move. Ahead, the striped awnings of the Astor House jauntily beckoned the weary guest. Joseph took the steps two at a time, bursting into the lobby to lose himself among the out-of-town businessmen straggling in from the day's commerce. He snapped open the newspaper and pored over the inside page, one eye on the elevator. Billy Bell was scaling the hotel steps when Joseph stepped onto the car, just as the door was sliding closed on a tightly packed crowd.

"Five, please," he said to the operator.

The ride was morbidly slow. Joseph could scarcely contain his impatience, but leapt from the car on the third floor with apologies for misreading the number on his key. As he watched, the car continued its upward progress. He wondered if Billy Bell was watching it from the lobby, or had already taken the stairs. He could not afford to linger to find out.

Joseph had been in the hotel before and had an idea of the layout — a square, with a rotunda at its center. And where there were corners, there were also stairs. Bell would take the closest flight. Joseph plunged down the hall past the first exit, turning the corner and making for the rear doors. He had just reached the southwest corner of the building when he heard the door of the anterior stairwell slam back against its frame, footsteps into the hall, then retreating again into the hollow shaft of the stairs. He might go up another flight, maybe two. Either way, there wasn't much time. Joseph raced down the three flights to a rear hallway of the hotel and bolted through the exit to Barclay Street. As if he had personally ordered it, a hansom cab stood waiting to pull around the corner into a line in front of the Astor House. Joseph shortened the cabbie's wait.

"The Plaza Hotel," he said, and buried his head in the newspaper.

CHAPTER
THIRTY-SEVEN

Joseph took an unobtrusive seat in the Plaza lobby and unfolded his newspaper, surreptitiously glancing up toward the hotel desk to be sure he had not attracted attention. But the clerks were all busy registering guests and checking message boxes for men and women who were not accustomed to waiting. He hoped they would be this busy all night.

Ironic how much time he'd spent in the most unlikely places lately. First the Yacht Club, then the Astor Hotel and now this Italian Renaissance temple to affluence. He couldn't deny it was beautiful — all marble and gilt, crystal and mosaic. The leather chairs soft and deep as featherbeds. And all in the cause of a poor Irish croppy's daughter. But he was close now, he knew. He just needed a bit of that luck the Irish were always touting.

There were too many variables in this

plan. Captain Vine might be out for the evening, in which case all would be lost. Or he might merely receive a message. But Joseph had not been able to think of another way to draw out the informant, and he could not permanently neglect his duties at the station to follow Vine day and night until the stag showed himself.

He pulled out his watch and snapped it open. Within the next few minutes, Devoy would be meeting with his executive committee to announce a radical new operation — one which could turn the robust economy of Great Britain upside down. It was a daring idea, and what alarmed Joseph most deeply was that Devoy had planned it long before he knew he had a stag in his organization. But John Devoy had never been short on audacity. The *Catalpa* rescue was only one in his dossier of brazen moves against the Lion.

They had agreed that the meeting would be short, giving the stag plenty of time to contact and meet with Vine. Devoy would announce the first target of the operation, to be attacked tonight, and lay out a list of others that would follow. "But we are a democratic organization," he'd complained. "I've never made an independent decision of this magnitude."

536

"Then you will have to plead the case of luck. It was a unique opportunity which might not arise again. You had to make an immediate decision. Surely they will accept that."

Devoy had reluctantly agreed. The truth, Joseph suspected, was that Devoy did not want to disclose this plan at all, for he hoped to be able to undertake it when his organization was a bit larger. Joseph could only pray that it would never reach the stage of mature possibility. The aspect of destroying millions of dollars in British property, not to mention countless innocent lives, was too outrageous to contemplate.

"The important thing is that Moran must actually plant the dynamite, but his timing must be perfect, so that he does not have time to set it off before the police get there. And it is paramount that he escape. Under no circumstances is he to light that dynamite. Be sure he understands that, Mr. Devoy."

Devoy had glared at him with open contempt. "Are you tryin' to tell me how to run a subversive operation, lad?"

"I am trying to tell you that if he thinks he'll just take advantage of the opportunity to blow a hole in the Brits, I'll have him in jail before the sun is up." Joseph smiled to himself now. Perhaps he had been a bit impertinent, after all.

"Mr. Taggart? I do have that right, don't I?"

Joseph did not, at first, react to the name. But when he glanced up, Captain Arthur Vine was standing over him with a confidently extended hand. Joseph took it with all the aplomb he could muster.

"Captain Vine, isn't it?"

They exchanged the necessary cordialities before Vine cleared his throat with some embarrassment. "I find my dinner partner has been called out of town. I wonder, have you plans for the evening?"

Joseph scrambled for an answer. Here was a visit from his Irish luck, although he was not yet certain whether it was good or bad. But he was exposed now, and that left him little choice but to accept. "I had just planned to have dinner here in the hotel. I must be up early in the morning and would prefer to dine in," he said. "But I would be delighted if you'd join me."

It was the answer Vine had been looking for. He had heard the Plaza's cuisine was outstanding, he said as they made their way through the lobby to the Men's Café. "I am partial to prime ribs of beef, myself," he said.

Joseph agreed, although a good canvas-back duck made a very satisfying entree. He tried to draw upon Rachel's arts of fabrication. The evening would require some skill if he were not to reveal himself as an impostor. But he knew in his heart that he was no John Drew.

The Men's Café was a monument to masculinity, paneled in smooth mahogany with sturdy brass chandeliers and wall sconces. Joseph felt himself more at ease there, despite the company, than he had been in the lobby. "Have you been to Vancouver, Captain Vine?" he asked, as they were seated at their table.

"Regrettably not. Toronto, of course, and a brief visit to Montreal. I shall begin with a hot Irish whiskey," he said to the waiter, adding as an aside to Joseph, "Whatever you may say about the Irish, they do know whiskey."

Joseph felt his face flush. "Martini, please."

"But I do have an acquaintance in Vancouver," Vine said, studying his menu. "Sir Hubert McGee. Perhaps you know him?"

He felt a moment of panic. What would Rachel say now? He grinned affably. "I confess to being a bit of a recluse. Have you had the lobster mayonnaise? I'm told it is exceptionally good."

"Hmmph. Is it, I wonder? Fish for lobsters in your part of the world, don't they?"

Joseph had no idea. "Yes. Of course, salmon is our specialty," he said. "But I don't really keep up with the fishing industry."

Conversation ebbed as Vine became engrossed in his menu, but the dishes swam in Joseph's vision. He could discuss Vancouver only generally — how much had Vine learned from Sir Hiram? Hubert? Avoid the pulp and paper industry, British and Canadian politics, and sailing. And then Rachel's words came back to him, as clearly as if she were standing at his shoulder. *These people are only interested in themselves. Keep the conversation focused on them and you'll be fine.*

"I think the Rockaways, Consommé Britannia, and I'll be interested to see exactly what that is," Vine added parenthetically. "Then the caviar a la Russe, cucumber salad, and saddle of mutton, of course." He tapped his menu thoughtfully and glanced up at the waiter. "I haven't decided on my entree yet. Go ahead and take Mr. Taggart's order."

Joseph chose from the menu at random. "I'll begin with the Little Necks, consommé, no third or fourth course. Lamb chops, lobster mayonnaise, and Long Island duckling." Moira would faint when he told her what he'd eaten for dinner. He hoped he had enough money to pay for it. He placed his order of vegetables and abstained from dessert.

"Surely fruit and cheese, Mr. Taggart?" Joseph acquiesced.

"Did I understand that you are retired, Captain Vine," Joseph asked, when the waiter had gone away.

"Back injury in South Africa," he said. "Served as military attaché here in New York for several years, but I miss the climate of England." Vine chuckled. "I'm uncommonly fond of the dampness and fog, particularly after South Africa."

"And what will you do now?"

"Travel. Write my memoirs of the Boer War. Perhaps go to work in the Foreign Office. I have some expertise in the Irish Problem."

"Ah," Joseph said casually, despite his hammering pulse. "And it is a problem, isn't it? Will Home Rule pass?"

Vine sipped his whiskey and studied Joseph over the rim of his glass. "Not if I have anything to do with it."

The waiter set a plate of clams in front of

each of them. "Refresh this, please," Vine said, handing off his whiskey glass. "The Irish are incapable of compromise, Mr. Taggart. And Home Rule is nothing more than an embellished, glorified compromise. Mark my words, if it passes it will not succeed. The Irish will not be satisfied. They will push and push until we have to subdue them just as we've subdued the Boers."

A drumbeat pounded in Joseph's ears. By putting their women and children in concentration camps, by burning farms and poisoning wells? But Joseph Taggart, Protestant and loyal subject of the queen, would have no such sentiments. Vine seemed to sense them anyway.

"Believe me when I tell you, Mr. Taggart, that Kitchener's actions are entirely appropriate."

"And are the stories true? The typhoid, the starvation?"

Vine popped a clam in his mouth and shrugged. "One of the regrettable consequences of war, Mr. Taggart, but the guerrillas have brought it upon their families themselves, make no mistake."

Mother of God, no wonder Devoy and the others hated the British so much. For a moment, Joseph almost felt drawn to the Clan himself, but it was a passing sentiment.

Anyone who let a girl like Maggie sit on Blackwell's Island when they could have freed her any time was little better than Kitchener and his henchmen.

The clamshells were taken away and the consommé served as the conversation moved away from the dangerous subject of British colonialism. "Your Miss Bonner is quite an attractive young woman, Taggart. Do you mind my asking if you . . . well, have you an understanding, so to speak?"

Joseph smiled. "I'm afraid not. In fact, I don't know her all that well myself. I've had some dealings with her uncle, but he was not available for the reception last night. Miss Bonner kindly offered to accompany me."

"She's quite an enigma, I understand," Vine said. He exchanged his consommé for caviar canapés with scarcely a moment to take a breath. "My friends tell me that she is a matron at the local immigration center here in New York. Unusual for a young woman of her breeding."

Joseph set his cup aside and lit a cigarette, watching as Vine consumed his canapés as if they were a handful of nuts. "I'm afraid I know very little about that, Captain Vine. I confess I'd like to see more of Miss Bonner, but I'm not sure that time will permit it."

"Are you sure you won't have a canapé? The caviar is first rate." Vine watched Joseph shrewdly. "They had a shooting out there recently, perhaps you heard."

"A shooting? No, I'm afraid not. What was it about?"

"Oh, probably just one of those Irish brawls. Never seen a people so bad-tempered on the whole, but what else would one expect from an infer—"

"Captain Vine. Captain Arthur Vine."

Vine signaled to the bellman who was paging him through the dining room. "Right here."

The bellman handed him a folded piece of paper and received a dime in turn. Vine swabbed a glob of caviar off his lapel. "Excuse me," he said. "Probably something from my dinner companion."

Joseph profoundly hoped not. He drew on his cigarette and watched the smoke curl toward the ceiling, a study in nonchalance. Vine was taking his time, reading the message over several times. He glanced down at the saddle of mutton that the waiter had just set before him and returned once more to the message.

"I am afraid," he said, folding the note and sliding it into his watch pocket, "that I have been called away unexpectedly." He looked at the mutton and licked his lips.

"Nothing serious, I hope?"

Vine cut a piece of the meat and shoved it into his mouth before heaving himself out of his chair. "A friend in ill health. It appears to be more serious than we thought. I'm afraid I will have to leave you here, Mr. Taggart. My deepest regrets, but perhaps we can try again before you return to Vancouver."

"By all means."

Joseph rose as Vine signaled to the waiter. "I'm afraid I must leave. Put this on my bill, please. Room 324. And include Mr. Taggart's as well."

"That really isn't necessary —"

"Nonsense, Taggart. The least I can do."

Joseph waited until Vine had disappeared through the doorway before turning back to the waiter. "I'm afraid I'll have to miss the rest of this fine meal myself." He dropped some change on the table. "But by all means, charge the full amount of both to Captain Vine."

By the time Joseph reached the street, Vine had already crossed and was entering Central Park.

CHAPTER
THIRTY-EIGHT

Billy Bell had taught him a thing or two about not lapsing into obvious habits and the value of changing his appearance to fit a role. It would not do to continue the pose of Joseph Taggart, businessman. As soon as he was out of view of the hotel doorman, Joseph pulled his tweed cap out of the inside pocket of his jacket. He crossed Fifth Avenue to the Grand Army Plaza and stepped behind the monument to the *Maine* long enough to remove his tie, open his collar and take off his jacket. The latter he slung over his shoulder, covering the telltale straps of the holster that peeked out from under his vest. He pulled the bill of his cap down low on his forehead. It was not much of a disguise, but might work if Vine was not looking for him.

He started down the main thoroughfare, but soon realized that Vine was not in sight ahead of him. He must have taken one of the footpaths down toward the pond. Joseph turned back, choosing the first path he came to. He moved as quietly as he could without arousing suspicion, and employed the gait of his youth — the slouching ease of the Irish b'hoy — to aid his disguise. The park was all but deserted, throwing him into a conspicuous position. He was grateful for the darkness. Street lamps splashed light in puddles along the path, but wooded shadows camouflaged enough to provide him adequate cover. He bore on toward the pond, taking in turn each path that carried him closer, desperately hoping that his Irish luck would hold. It did.

Vine was on the path that immediately bordered the pond, moving northward, his erect back to Joseph. Joseph slipped back out of sight and quietly regained the outer path, moving along parallel to Vine. He could just see the other man between patches of trees and shrubbery — enough to follow him, but protected from exposure himself. Vine strode around the pond, coming to an abrupt stop when he reached the footbridge that crossed the basin's neck. The bridge, Joseph realized, was to be his point of rendezvous. It was well chosen. Joseph would have to get under it to hear what was being said. He waited until Vine had mounted it and stood gazing down the main body of the pond before circling around to come in behind him and fade into the darkness under the bridge. There he waited, afraid even to shift his weight for fear of making a noise that might alert the man above. By the time he heard another set of footsteps above him, his left foot had grown numb. He used the cover of the other man's arrival to shift position, leaning back against the brick, into the deepest cover of darkness.

"What in blazes were you thinking, sending that message to me?" Vine said. "We arranged a post office box for just that purpose. What could possibly be urgent enough to require meeting me face to face like this?"

"Dynamite in the British Consulate."

"What?" Vine's voice betrayed his horror. "When?"

"I'll get to that."

Joseph heard a scuffling movement above. "Tell me everything you know. Now!"

"Just a moment, chum. Information like this does not come free, if you recall."

"How much?"

"One thousand," the other voice said.

"Ridiculous."

"Well, if you think you're in a position to bargain —"

Vine apparently saw the futility of his bluff. He agreed to drop the money in their joint post office box the next day, but only if he had the information quickly enough to prevent disaster.

"They're arranging it for eleven o'clock, during the change of watch. But this is just the beginning, Vine, and we're going to have to renegotiate fees. Devoy has planned an extensive campaign against British businesses beginning with the White Star Line. Tea merchants, steel export — every important industry England has — and not just in the United States, but all over the world. He'll blow them to kingdom come."

Vine gasped. "Bloody shants and croppies."

"Present company excepted, of course."

Vine made no response to that. "Where? When?"

"They're meeting again tomorrow night to discuss the consulate bombing and begin planning other operations. I'll be there."

"You're going to have to get rid of Devoy."

There was a moment's hesitation. "No. Doyle was one thing. Kill Devoy and I'll have every scurvy rebel hunting me for the rest of my life. I'm not one of your bloody soldiers. This is business pure and simple, and I'll have none of killing Devoy."

"You have no choice," Vine said slowly, pronouncing each word distinctly, lest there be any confusion about his meaning. "If you don't eliminate John Devoy, I will turn you in for Cormac Doyle's murder."

"And betray yourself? Do you expect me to believe that? Besides, it would take you years to develop another informant close enough to the Clan to feed you information."

Vine laughed. "I have nothing to be ashamed of. The world will not judge us for preventing anarchy in our own empire, and if that requires hiring foreign agents then what of it? Every country does it. But I'll tell them that I did not authorize murder, and my conscience would not allow me to ignore it. Besides, I won't need another informant, don't you see? When the Clan discovers that one of their own murdered Doyle and betrayed their cause, it will destroy them. They'll never trust each other again."

Joseph heard it all. His plan had worked. At last he had drawn out the stag and confirmed that it was he who had shot and killed Cormac Doyle. But there was no triumph in it. Only a pain so great that even after the other two had left, Joseph sat huddled and shivering under the bridge in the dark.

Rachel was brushing her teeth when she heard the doorbell ring. She had interviewed potential housekeepers all evening with most unproductive results. None of them had the skills she required, and their deficiencies would only accentuate Irene's absence. Now one of them had forgotten something, or more likely had returned to plead more fervently for the job.

The bell rang again, this time with a more insistent twist of the key. Alma was surely in bed and her uncle had retired to his room with a bottle of scotch. Mrs. Coffey might get it, but the cook slept so soundly that her snoring sometimes reached the upper floors, and the groom slept in the carriage house. Rachel sighed, pulled her dressing gown closed and ran down the stairs.

Joseph Hannegan stood at the door. He was shaking, and his face was as pale and gray as moonlight.

"What is it?" she said, pulling him into the house. "What's happened? Are you sick?"

"I know it's late," he stammered. "I didn't have anywhere to go . . . anyone to —" He

551

left off, as if the exertion were too much for him.

She led him into the drawing room and left him slouched on a damask sofa, returning momentarily with the decanter of Cointreau and two snifters. "Here," she said, sloshing some of the liqueur into a glass. "Drink this."

He put the glass to his lips, but did not drink. It seemed to her that even the effort to swallow must be too painful for him. She touched his forehead, but it was cool. "Can you tell me?"

"The stag," he said. "It's Liam."

Rachel dropped onto the sofa next to him. "Oh Joseph, no. You're sure?"

The misery in his face confirmed it. He wove his fingers together, covered his face and hunched over his knees. "I can't tell her. I can't tell her," he said. "It will destroy her. She believes in him. Last night, he asked her to marry him. She accepted."

Rachel poured a glass of Cointreau for herself and drank deeply from it. It burned when she swallowed it, and she felt its progress into her veins. But it did not ease the problem or banish it away. Nothing would do that. She felt his agony, and a spasm tightened in her own throat.

"I suppose that part of me suspected him

all along. All his money and property. I knew he had no conscience and even if I'd doubted it, there was the tenement fire."

"Tenement fire?"

He told her then, about Liam setting the fire to display his own heroics. "Croker drove him out of Tammany — Croker!" He laughed and Rachel felt a chill travel over her. "Richard Croker booted Liam from his den of thieves, because he has no principles. Even the devil himself wouldn't have Liam O'Neill, but my sister is going to marry him."

Rachel laid her hand over his. "You'll have to tell her, Joseph. I know it's terrible for you, but you can't let her go on believing —"

"Tell her? I can't tell her that the man she loves is a murderer. She won't believe it. She knows I'm opposed to the marriage. She'll think I've made it up to frighten her away from him."

"She won't. She adores you; you've taken care of her all her life."

He put his glass to his lips, and this time swallowed the whole of it. His shivering had stopped, she saw, and color was beginning to come back into his face. He shook his head.

"I'll have to go on as I planned. They're

meeting tomorrow night. Liam knows it is important, and Vine will be waiting to hear from him. He'll be there." He snickered. "There's money to be made after all."

Rachel poured him another, smaller portion. "But how is he doing it? I thought you said that he leaves before the meeting, that they see him out and bar the door."

Joseph stood and walked over to the mantle, setting his glass down to stare into the empty grate. The drink seemed to have given him a better command of himself. "I don't know. He may be listening at the door outside. The only way to find out is to follow him."

"But it could be dangerous."

Joseph smiled at her, a strange, sad smile. "I think even Liam would find it difficult to kill his oldest friend."

Rachel's eyes grew wide at his revelation. Joseph nodded. "More than twenty years. We ran the streets of New York together as kids, a pair of b'hoys with big plans. Just see where they got us.

"Do you remember last night, when I told you about the men in the Clan who neglected their families for the cause? I was talking about Seamus O'Neill. He was no father to Liam or his brother and sister, and poor Cecilia, his mother, worked herself to death just to pay the rent. Liam got no encouragement to better himself at home. Seamus put him on the street to work when we were still in knee pants, and Liam learned to survive. Doreen and Kevin are another story, better left untold.

"It may be hard for you to understand, Rachel, but Liam is doing the only thing he knows how to do. He's fending for himself in a world that never wanted him to succeed. I'm not defending him, mind you, but I understand him. I wish to God I didn't. It would make this a great deal easier."

He returned to the sofa and took her hand. "I've come to ask a favor of you. It may seem the height of cowardice. It probably is. But I'd like you to be there when I tell her. She has no mother to turn to, and the women at the boarding house are not . . . well, I think they'll be little comfort to her. I have no one else to ask, and I think she'll need a woman with her."

"Of course," Rachel said immediately. "We were to go to the Susan B. Anthony rally tomorrow night, but —"

"Then you must go. I don't want her to know that anything is wrong until it's all over. When the time comes . . . by then my father will know the truth. Moira might not believe me, but she will believe him."

■ ■ ■ ■

Billy Bell slouched in the door of Rossi's store. Joseph had anticipated him, approaching from the west side where, if Bell were watching the house, he would not notice the man behind him.

"Well, well, if it's not my old friend Billy Bell." Bell swung around, backing into the doorway at the sight of Joseph's pistol.

"Who sent you, Bell?"

"Look, I ain't done nothin'. Don't know whatcher talkin' about. I'm just here —"

"Shut up and turn around."

"Watchin' my girl's house is all —"

"I said turn around."

Bell shrugged. "Sure, whatever you say."

Joseph patted him down, withdrawing a Derringer from Bell's jacket and a stiletto from an ankle sheath. "No sense putting these on the streets," he said, dropping them into his own pocket.

"Whaddaya mean puttin' them on the streets?" Bell said, a note of alarm creeping into his voice.

"You didn't answer my question. Who sent you?"

"I'm tellin' ya, nobody sent me. Ya know how it is. My girl's a dago. Her brother don't want her havin' nothin' to do with me. I watch the house. Soon as he leaves — you know these damn wops."

Joseph's patience snapped. "Enough of your blarney." He brought the butt of his pistol down on the base of Bell's skull. Bell dropped like a sandbag.

Joseph had picked up a pint of whiskey on his way home from Gramercy Park with vague plans of nursing it in the privacy of his bedroom. Instead, he cracked the seal, rolled Bell over and poured it down his neck and the front of his shirt. He stepped back out onto Sullivan Street and whistled for a cab that sat at the corner of Houston. Back in the doorway, he hauled Bell up, looping a lifeless arm over his shoulder, and dragged him out to the corner just as the cab came to a stop.

"My friend Mr. Bell, here," he said to the cabbie, "has had a wee bit more of the drink than is good for him, and the wife at home will be worryin' herself gray."

With the help of the cabbie, he shoved Bell up into the hansom. Billy slouched back in the seat, mouth agape. "Aye," Joseph said, "he'll be craw-sick in the mornin', and worse when Mrs. Bell gets hold of him. Better deliver him into her lovin' arms before she comes lookin' for him."

Joseph fished the fare out of his pocket and passed it to the cabbie, giving him the Tompkins Street address of his old cold water flat. The cabbie hesitated.

"The waterfront? Now I don't know as I wanna go down there."

Joseph added another bill to the fare. "Just leave him on the street. That fishwife of his'll find him." The cabbie reluctantly agreed. Joseph watched him off at a trot, the hollow clop of the horses' hooves reverberating on the street.

The crimps and muggers could keep their mickeys in their pockets. Billy Bell would be out for a while, and fair game for the water rats that ran the docks. Joseph seriously doubted he'd see Bell again.

When the cab was out of sight, Joseph turned toward home. The aromatic odor of pipe tobacco greeted him three doors down. Dennis sat on the steps alone, in the dark, drawing on his pipe and staring out into the darkness. "What were you up to down there at Rossi's, son?" he said quietly.

"Just pouring a drunk friend into a cab and now I'm off to bed." Joseph tried to climb past his father, but Dennis blocked the way with his crutch. "Sit down till I talk to you."

"Dad —"

"Sit down, Shosav! There are things to say between us."

Joseph hesitated. The last thing he needed was Dennis pressing him for information. "It won't do any good, Dad. I've nothing to tell you."

"I think you do, and anyway, I have somethin' to tell you."

Joseph fell wearily to the concrete step next to his father. "Go ahead, then."

Dennis knocked the ash out of his pipe and withdrew his tobacco pouch. "I heard somethin' tonight and I don't believe it myself." He scooped his pipe in the pouch and tamped down the tobacco, clamped the pipe in his teeth and struck a match on the concrete.

"Devoy called a special meeting tonight."

"Dad, you know how I feel about —

"You're not tellin' me you didn't already know about it?" Joseph waited. When he neither confirmed nor denied it, Dennis continued.

"He wanted to tell us about an operation, goin' on . . ." Dennis checked his watch and tucked it away. ". . . just about now, I'm guessin'. Said old Tom Gallagher was deliverin' a load of dynamite to the British Consulate — enough to blow them all to blazes."

Dennis turned to Joseph. "You're not surprised, are ya' lad?"

Joseph was grateful for the darkness. He poked a cigarette in his mouth and lit it. "I'm shocked, Dad. What could they be thinking?"

"I wouldn't know, Shosav," Dennis said thoughtfully. "But I can tell you this, Tom Gallagher made no such delivery."

"Dynamite takes an expert."

"It does, sure. Fact of the matter is, Tom's good with dynamite, but not good enough to keep him out of prison. The Brits had him in Kilmainham up to a year or two ago."

"Well, there you have it, Dad. He tried it again. Some people just won't learn their lesson."

Dennis took a jackknife out of his pocket and opened it to pare a broken thumbnail. "Tom Gallagher learned his lesson, Shosav. They sent him back to us a broken man. It wasn't Tom Gallagher deliverin' dynamite tonight. Tom's in a sanitarium in New Jersey." He folded the knife carefully and slipped it back in his pocket. "I know, because John and I took him there ourselves."

They sat together in silence, watching the traffic on the street. Directly across from them, Anna Ferrante washed her front steps with a scrub brush. Two doors down Mae Osterhaus was being courted on the front stoop by her young man. The occasional bicycle streaked across their view, and now and then a hansom or a delivery wagon rattled down the quiet street. The White Wings would be out with their brooms in another hour or two.

"You've found the stag, haven't you, son?"

"Dad —"

"John and I are the only ones who know about old Tom, although I think Clarke might have an idea, since he was in prison with Gallagher back in '98. You were plantin' information. You might've told me."

"I can't tell you anything, Dad. Not yet, anyway."

"Was there really dynamite?"

Joseph admitted that much. "Moran was to plant it. The information had to seem credible enough to draw the stag out again. Right now, Moran should be leading the cops a lively chase down State Street. It's risky, but he was willing to take the gamble. He's heard American prisons are elegant compared to Kilmainham. I hope he won't have to find out."

"He's a tough lad, and a smart one. He'll be all right no matter what. Then you have found him."

"I'm afraid so." Joseph stared out into the darkness.

"I'm sorry I got you into this, son. If I'd known it would come to this, that it would even touch you at all, I'd never have gone along with it."

Joseph's thoughts returned to Arthur Vine and his loathing for the Irish, to Kitchener's South African concentration camps riddled with typhoid and starvation. They brought it on themselves, he had said. But no child on earth deserved to die delirious with fever or so weak from hunger that his heart simply gave up beating. No child in South Africa today, and no child in Ireland fifty years ago.

"I'm sorry too. I know you believe in what you're doing, and even if I don't, I think I understand it better." He paused, struggling with what must come next.

"I want to tell you something, Dad. It's goin' to be hard on you, the truth. I want you to be prepared. It's worse than you might expect. I just want you to remember that there's an innocent girl on Blackwell's Island, and if we don't go through with this, no matter how bad it is, she's going to die in the electric chair."

"Who is the stag, Shosav?"

"I can't tell you that yet. You'll have to

trust that I've done the right thing."

Dennis struggled to his feet and grabbed his crutch, laying a hand on Joseph's shoulder. "I trust you, son," he said.

CHAPTER
THIRTY-NINE

The priests always said that hell was a raging inferno, but it didn't feel like it to Maggie. She pulled the thin blanket up under her chin, and clamped her jaws together to keep her teeth from chattering. The real hell could be no worse than its counterpart here on earth, and it would be a great deal warmer.

Miss Bonner had not returned since she asked her about the chair. She was as abandoned as any soul in hell. It hardly mattered that she hadn't killed Cormac. No one believed her — maybe even Miss Bonner had stopped believing her, and that's why she hadn't come back. Maggie couldn't think of another explanation for it.

Back home, her mother would be washing up the dishes from dinner, and Jerry would be reciting his catechism or spelling for school tomorrow. Da would be down in Drumcliffe — maybe at the pub, beating

Father Duffy and some of the boys at a friendly game of Twenty-five. But they'd all be waiting, wondering why her letter hadn't yet come from America.

"She's probably busy with that Mrs. Westcott," her mother would say.

"Aye, it takes a while to feel to home in a new place. Our Maggie'll be workin' hard and tired as Job when the day is done. She'll write when she gets her feet on the ground. Don't you worry."

Don't you worry. That, of course, was why Maggie refused to write to them. What could they do, there on the other side of the world, but worry helplessly, knowing that their oldest child was awaiting a chair that would blister the skin off her bones? And all for the love of a red-bearded man who cared more for a clod of Irish dirt than he did for one of Ireland's daughters. What a fool she'd been, but there was nothing for it now.

She felt in the pocket of her prison skirt and pulled out the tin from the kitchen. She wished she knew how it would be — slow and painful, or quick as the blink of an eye. Would it burn her throat or go down sweet as honey-root? She twisted the cap off the tin and felt of the powder with the tips of her fingers.

Would they bury her here, or send her

home? If they sent her home, Father Duffy might never know how she died, that her soul was not fit for a proper burial. He'd wear his black vestments, sprinkle her casket with holy water, and perfume it with incense. *Let perpetual light shine upon her,* he'd pray. Then they'd shoulder her casket and carry her to holy ground, with all of Drumcliffe to send her off. And no one would be the wiser that she was bound for hell, because the priests always said that suicide is the most grievous sin of all.

Joseph heard the bar on the door of the Ballyglass draw back and stepped into the shadows of the alley. He had taken the precaution to wear dark clothes, and pulled a black knit watch cap down on his forehead. His revolver was fitted snugly into the shoulder holster under his jacket. In his hand, he carried an electric candle from the station.

"Tell Brian I said to bring you a bottle of Monte Cristo on me," Liam called back into the light. "I'll be seein' you fellas."

The door closed behind him and the bar slid back into place. Liam stopped for a moment and glanced back. Joseph held his breath and waited. If Liam were listening from the alley, it would have to be somewhere other than through a steel door. But he lingered only a second before he strode down the alley and emerged onto Broadway. Joseph waited until he had exited the alley before following.

He'd half expected to see Liam turn back toward the front door of the Ballyglass on Murray Street, but Liam angled northward instead. He was moving quickly and without a backward glance. Joseph signaled to Moran, waiting on the corner of Murray Street, and set off in close pursuit of Liam.

The sidewalk was teeming with women. They seemed to part like the Red Sea for Liam. It had always been that way. The world, he thought, was more indulgent of the handsome and beautiful. Perhaps that was part of what was so wrong with Liam. Too much charm, too little conscience.

Across Broadway, a crowd of feathered, flowered, and fruited hats was collecting in City Hall Park to await the arrival of Susan B. Anthony. Somewhere in that crowd were Moira and Rachel. They were to meet at the fountain, she'd said.

Moira had been all aglow at dinner. On her left hand sparkled a diamond engagement ring of quite respectable proportions. Before the theater, Liam had been to see Dennis, to make his formal declaration for

Moira's hand. Dennis had, of course, embraced it. The actual proposal occurred on the Astor Roof Garden. Moira had spared no details in thrilling Miss Dove and Mrs. Shapiro with the story. Joseph had never seen her happier.

At Warren Street, Liam stopped to wait for a passing streetcar before crossing the intersection. Joseph kept an eye on him in a shop window ten paces back, while Moran bought a paper from a newsie. The car passed, and Liam moved, but not directly up Broadway, as Joseph had expected. Instead, he turned into another alley behind the row of buildings facing Warren Street Joseph hurried to the mouth of the alley. He could hear Liam's footsteps, but could scarcely make out his body in the darkness. Behind him, the streetlights of Broadway made too bright a backdrop. If Liam were to turn now, he'd surely see Joseph silhouetted against the light. Joseph slipped around the corner, pressing his back to the brick and hoping to melt into the darkness. Moran was right behind him.

Liam hadn't gone far, he realized. Joseph strained to hear over the beating pulse in his ears. He was close — twenty, maybe thirty feet away — standing still. He heard a scrape of metal against metal and the creak of a door. He could just make it out in the darkness as it opened and swung closed again. "Wait for me here," he whispered to Moran. The other man signed his assent.

Joseph crept forward, running his hand along the wall until it contacted a steel door slightly ajar. Inside, he heard a heavy thump. He pulled the door open a crack.

Light. The centralized glow of a lantern that soon dimmed and went dark. Joseph waited, thought. Was it extinguished or removed? Could Liam be in there, waiting for him in the darkness? There was only one way to know.

Joseph pulled the door wider, listening, watching for any indication of movement. An inch more, and then another. Ahead he saw a bleached spot in the darkness. He slid through the narrow opening and waited, but Liam did not show himself. At length, he left the door standing partially open and eased forward, laying heel and toe gently on the floor.

The spot was still visible ahead of him, and as he approached it resolved itself into a rectangle. A trap door in the floor, and a flight of stairs leading below. "Well, well, got yourself a bolting-hole, eh Liam, my friend?" he whispered to himself.

He took a tentative step onto the first

stair. It held fine, as sturdy as if the staircase had just been built. But the way below was too dark. He couldn't risk the noise he might make while feeling his way down. He turned away from the trap door and switched on the battery light, clamping his hand over the lens so that only the tiniest shaft of light protruded between two fingers. It was awkward and kept both hands engaged, but it provided enough light to go forward.

He had gone down five steps when he reached a makeshift landing, where the staircase intersected another at a right angle. He swung the light backward up the other stairs, but if his bearings were right, they led toward the street outside and had been walled up some time in the past. He turned on the landing and took the remaining steps down, ending in what appeared to be a long, narrow office of some kind.

He took his hand off the lens and let the full light play out over the room. On the far wall was a fresco of a cog-wheel and behind it, the remains of an immense paddlebox style blower. Several heavy oak desks sat at random angles, and a large wooden file cabinet hugged the wall to the right. What was this place?

He cast his light over the floor and the

clutter of tracks in the thick layer of dust. They led across the office and to the right through a long hall. He could see a faint glow at the end and stopped, extinguishing his light and moving forward in tense silence. At the end of the hall, he turned right again and descended three steps to a room flooded with light.

"Mother of God!"

He almost couldn't believe what he was seeing. In the center of the room a stately fountain waited only for the water to resume its flow. The walls were striped with pine and walnut molding and hung with paintings, mirrors, and brass gaslights every six feet. Maroon settees were carefully arranged in little groupings around the fountain and inside a railed area where a grand piano made up the centerpiece. A profuse pattern of deep red cabbage roses and bright green leaves covered the oilcloth flooring. Except for the gaslights, which Liam had thoughtfully lit, the fixtures were covered in dust and strung with cobwebs so thick as to create a filmy, diaphanous curtain. An airy room, haunted with ghosts of the past. He could almost hear the low murmur of their voices. The Beach subway line.

Joseph had been flippant with Miss Dove when she had told him the story over dinner. "Alfred Beach was a highly intelligent man, Mr. Hannegan," she'd said. "He designed the subway as a large pneumatic tube that would pull the cars from one stop to the next."

"Had a bit of the Jules Verne in him, did Mr. Beach?"

Two red spots of color had appeared on Miss Dove's cheeks. "In fact, he was the owner of *Scientific American* magazine. Anyway, Boss Tweed opposed it, so Mr. Beach built it in secret. The crew worked at night, right under Tweed's nose."

"And where was this rogue line, Miss Dove?"

"Beach built the reception room in the basement of Devlin's Clothing Store at 260 Broadway — that's on the corner of Broadway and Warren Street. The subway only ran a few blocks. It was a demonstration model, you understand, although his intention was to extend it all over the city as soon as he had the permits to do so. The terminus was on Murray Street."

"But Tweed put the kibosh on that idea."

"Yes," Miss Dove said, gazing down at her plate. "I'm afraid he did."

Alfred Beach always must have thought he'd be back some day to build the remainder of his remarkable underground tube.

Now Joseph felt the heavy sadness of the room, and was vaguely embarrassed to be witness to the death of another man's dream. Yet he was obscurely glad that it remained virtually untouched, even if known only to him and Liam, as a silent monument to one man's genius. He turned away reluctantly and took another short flight of steps down to the opening of the tube.

The exterior of the tunnel was of brick construction, and the entrance, perfectly round and about eight feet in diameter, with a row of gaslights encircling it. Liam had not lit these, depending, Joseph supposed, on his lantern for light in the tunnel. Joseph held his breath and listened, but he could not hear footsteps ahead of him. He cautiously switched on his battery light and peered down the length as far as he could see.

The tube was lined with iron plates and curved ribs, like the inside of a great serpent. Two tracks ran along its lower edges, with a brake rail in the center, but walking between them was perfectly feasible. Joseph set out, using minimal light, and followed the tunnel as it curved toward Broadway. After about fifty feet, the curve righted to a straightaway of all brick construction. It couldn't have been more than a block, but underground as it was, it seemed much longer.

Above, Joseph could hear the traffic on Broadway — the rumble of a streetcar passing overhead, the heavy clop of horses' hooves on the pavement — and suddenly felt that the steel plates were a very thin membrane between the street above and the tunnel below. If the plates were to suddenly give way, no one would know where he had disappeared to. "Get hold of yourself, man," he said, under his breath.

From the curve of the tunnel at Broadway, it spanned only another two hundred feet or perhaps a bit more. He mapped it in his mind sure, from what Miss Dove had said, that the curve turned the tunnel so that it ran directly beneath Broadway, ending at the corner of Murray Street. He reached the end of it, a plain wooden platform, sooner than he had expected. He switched off his light and stepped back into the darkness of the tunnel.

A flight of stairs, rising from the platform, led to a rectangular opening above. Another trap door spilled faint light onto the stairs. This was what he had come looking for. Up those stairs, he knew he would find Liam. The traitor was in his den.

CHAPTER FORTY

Joseph withdrew his revolver from its holster and stepped softly onto the first stair. Above, he could hear the murmur of voices, and behind it the muffled clamor of the front barroom. He crouched low as he ascended to the fourth step, slowly rising until he could just see into the room above, Liam's office, and the man himself standing, his back to the trap door and the rumpled Turkish carpet which normally covered it.

He had removed the picture of himself with Richard Croker from the office wall. Behind it, a square of plaster had been chipped away exposing the lath beneath. Liam wore a headset similar to a telephone exchange operator's, and held an attached black box close to the lath. Joseph ascended all but the last step and pointed his revolver at Liam.

"Learning anything valuable?" he said.

Liam turned with a start. "Joe! I was just —" He stopped as his dilemma became apparent. There was no innocent explanation for what he was doing. Joseph scaled the last step.

"You've caught me then," Liam said with a hollow laugh. He removed the headset and tossed it onto his desk. "Newest thing in hearing devices. Called an Akoulallion. Got the idea from the old man himself," he said, gesturing toward the office door and the room beyond it.

"The Brits pay good money for this nonsense. You know how these old duffers love to scheme. Same thing they've been doin' since we were ten. Why not make a little profit on their connivin'?"

"Arthur Vine pays well, does he?" Joseph took Liam's silence as assent. "And is Billy Bell on his payroll too, or are you paying him out of your own pocket?"

"Billy Bell?"

"He's not very discreet, Liam. I picked him up the first night he followed me."

A slow smile spread across Liam's face. "Someone's been followin' ya, Joe? Well, I didn't put him on it, so you must have an enemy out there." Joseph believed it was the truth, if only because Liam was enjoying it too much.

"Ya see?" Liam continued. "This is all a misunderstandin'. Sure, the Brits paid me a little for information from time to time, but between us, I got the better end of that bargain. Don't know why they're worried about a bunch of old men."

"And what about murder, Liam? How much did you make on Cormac Doyle?"

He didn't have the grace to blink. "Doyle? Don't know who you're talkin' about, Joe. Never heard of him."

"Explain that to John Devoy. They're waiting for you on the other side of that door. Unlock it."

"Joe, we can work this out, you and me. We understand each other, always have. You never wanted any part of that bunch, and we both know you don't care if I sell every secret they've got."

"I'm not in your class, Liam. I may not like what they do. I may even feel that it's a waste of time and energy, but I don't trade on their folly, and I don't commit murder. Now unlock the goddamn door."

O'Neill studied his old friend's face as if he were mystified by Joseph's reaction. At length, he shrugged. "Why not? Only thing I have to hide is a harmless prank. Oh, they'll be scalded all right, but they'll get over it. Probably kick me out of the Clan, but can't say I care much about that."

Joseph pushed him through the door. On the other side, six men were waiting for him. Liam greeted them with a broad smile. "Didja get that bottle of Monte Cristo, fellas?" He received no smiles in response.

"Here's your stag, gentlemen," Joseph said, and turned to Liam. "Mr. Devoy's been feeding you false information. The dynamite at the British Consulate was planted, my friend."

Liam faltered, the first missed beat in his song and dance. "Clever. So now you're going to shoot me, are you? Come on, Joe. You can't expect me to be afraid of my oldest friend. Or any of you. You've known me all my life. At least give me a chance to explain. You, of all people, Joe —" Liam took a step toward him.

"Don't move."

"What about Moira?" Liam took another step. "How do you think she'll feel when she learns that you've shot her sweetheart? You know I can't let you take me alive, dontcha now?"

Had Liam stabbed him with a stiletto, his pain could not have been sharper. And it was only a fraction of what Moira would experience once she knew the truth. Could he shoot Liam? He thought he could, but only because Liam's thoughtless, self-consumed scheming would deal Moira a mortal wound. "Don't tempt me," he said bitterly.

Liam saw that he had miscalculated Joseph's reaction. "Joe, listen to me." He spread his hands out, entreating his old friend. "I told you, I'm goin' to be legitimate as you. Even more."

He turned to Dennis. "You've given me your blessing —"

Dennis shook his head. "I'll kill you myself before I'll ever let Moira marry the likes of you. I should've listened to Shosav. He tried to tell me."

"But I've bought a house for us — a brownstone right there near Washington Square so she can see you every day. I have the deed right here." He reached into his jacket pocket.

It was coming, and Joseph knew it — Liam's last feint, his final deception — and the decision to fire was his. In the space of a breath, Joseph glimpsed their years together through a different lens. Liam, left on a dark street corner, following him with hungry eyes while Joseph went home for his supper. The gray misery of the O'Neill's flat, where five people slept, ate, but lived in stark isolation from one another. The bruises on Liam's neck and face the day after he'd lost at pitching pennies. His awkward laughter as he propped Seamus up against the door of a bucket shop long enough to empty his father's pockets. Images Joseph had buried in the deepest chambers of his memory now relentlessly fought their way to the surface, crowding out the dangers of the present. The revelation was bitter, the hesitation deadly. Liam lunged, grabbed at Joseph's gun hand with his left, and forced the barrel up. With his right hand, he pulled the Mauser out of his jacket and laid the muzzle against Joseph's temple.

"He who hesitates is lost, old friend. Give me the gun. Make no mistake. You might not be able to kill me, but if you force me, I'll do what I have to do. I've done it before."

"Doyle," Joseph said, as he passed the revolver to Liam. Liam flipped it open and emptied the bullets out before pocketing it.

"Of course, Doyle. I have a good thing here. I couldn't risk losing it. You," he said, gesturing at the other men, "do all the work, and I collect all the money. It is the perfect business arrangement."

Liam's glance traveled to the trap door. "There's no way out," Joseph said. "Moran's down there waiting for you. You'll never get out alive if he gets hold of you."

He saw the doubt in Liam's face. "Cormac Doyle was his best friend." Joseph laughed at the irony of it. "You know how it is with friends."

Susan B. Anthony held her hands up to quiet the applause of the crowd. Her advanced age had not slowed her. Her voice rang with authority and zeal. "One last thing," she cried. "You all know my position on the right of women to vote." The crowd cheered wildly until she silenced them again.

"I say to you now that not only *should* women vote, but that they *must* vote. We have entered the workforce and brought with us a new swell in men's moral development — in the pursuit of justice and service. And yet, in politics we remain excluded. It is only by the entrance of women in this arena that honor can and will be restored. Women will be kept silent no more!"

The women in City Hall Park took up the chant. "No more! No more!"

One of the women on Anthony's staff said something to her. "Ladies, I have a train to catch. I will carry your spirit with me to Buffalo. Let nothing stand in your way. Teach, learn, work, heal, organize yourselves. Women are moving forward in this country. We will never turn back!"

The women cheered as Miss Anthony was helped from the stage by her staff. Even after she had disappeared from view, they lingered, as if in hope of an encore. At length, the crowd began to disperse. Rachel took Moira's arm in hers.

"What did you think?"

"She was wonderful. Imagine her, eighty-one years old and still traveling and speaking. And here I am, more than fifty years younger. She makes me feel as though I'm not doing enough, but now . . . marrying Liam and all. We'll be starting a family right away, I imagine."

"But you can still work if you want to."

"And leave my children? No, I couldn't do that. My mother did it because she had to, but Liam says it won't be necessary."

Rachel heard all this, and responded to it as a woman going through the motions of intimacy but not participating in it. The effort of keeping up appearances was beginning to tell on her as she discussed the wedding that would not be celebrated and the children who would not be conceived.

"We should have tea," Rachel said abruptly.

"But I. . . ." Rachel saw that she had interrupted Moira. She hadn't been listening, had been making a conscious effort to close out Moira's voice.

"I'm sorry. What were you saying?"

Moira guided her forward, out of the park and onto Broadway. "That I want you to meet him. Tonight. Right away."

Rachel felt her knees sinking. "Oh no, Moira. Not tonight."

"Are you not feeling well? Perhaps you should go on home then. I can get a cab for you."

But she had promised Joseph that she would stay with Moira, no matter what. "I think a cup of tea —"

"Then tea it will be. Liam's bound to have a pot around the place somewhere."

"But a bar . . ."

"Don't worry. We'll go right through to the back, to his office. If you're worried about appearances, we can go out the back door when we leave. Here we are," she said, holding the door open for Rachel. "This is Liam's pub, the Ballyglass."

In the front room, the men from the Hall were celebrating a small chip in the glue of the Fusion ticket. Joseph could hear the clink of bottles and glasses, and the escalating voices of bravado. Too much confusion and disagreement between the candidates, they claimed. Too many differences on the issues. Croker was back, and all would be well, they said, boisterously rejoicing the return of the Boss. And meanwhile, they knew nothing of what was happening in the back room, and might not have cared had they known.

The men stood clustered in a rough semicircle. Joseph took in their faces one by one. Daniel Cohalan, attorney, and Patrick McCartain, physician. Both professional men who had never had to bloody their hands in the service of Clan na Gael. It was all theoretical to them, Joseph suspected, like a strategy or a treatment they had planned, but which was executed by others. How very easy it must be to send the guns when they didn't have to pull the triggers.

Tom Clarke, a delicate-looking man who had seen far more battle than most of the others and spent two years in Kilmainham Jail for it. His gaze darted around the room, as if he were looking for a weapon or any way to turn the advantage.

John Devoy. Suffused with rage, his hands opened and closed spasmodically, as if they would tear Liam O'Neill apart of their own will. His eyes bore into the stag with a hatred to sear the very soul.

And Dennis Hannegan. Here was the true face of betrayal. The white-haired boy was a stag and in Liam, Dennis would see the cancer that his politics had spread. Years of sacrifice and privation had brought the O'Neills to this and Dennis could not hide from it anymore. He hung his head and stared at the toes of his shoes.

Only Seamus O'Neill did not understand. "Liam, what's goin' on? John? What in blazes is this all about?"

"It's about your son, Seamus. He's been sellin' information to the Lion. Betrayed the guns — both operations — and killed one of our men. Bloody stag," he said. "You should be whipped and beaten and hung for the traitor you are."

Liam held up the Mauser. "Try it, old man."

"He wouldn't do that! Liam's a brother, John. Explain what happened, lad."

"Nothin' to explain, Da'. It's true."

Seamus stared at his son, unable to comprehend the truth even when Liam confirmed it. "But you took the oath! Have you no honor?"

Liam turned the Mauser on his father. "What would you know about honor? Was it honorable for Ma to kill herself to keep you and your cause alive? Did you ever once honor your vows to her?"

"She understood, Liam. The cause of

Ireland. It was what we both wanted."

"Shut yer gob! How do you think I felt, Da', Ma sendin' me out to comb the bars for you night after night? Bucket shop to bucket shop until there I'd find you, charmin' the b'hoys with your tales of glory. Oh, you always figured the hero then, martyr to the cause, banished from your homeland. You couldn't work like Dennis Hannegan and give your family a decent place to live. No, the cause of freedom might crumble without you. The plain truth of it, Da', is that you couldn't make it in America. Wouldn't hold onto a job because it was easier to be the hero of dreams than just a navvy on the docks. You're a scut, Da', and you always will be. So don't speak to me of honor. You don't even know the meanin' of the word. I did what I had to to get by. We all did. Doreen sold her body to every man jack who'd have her and God knows what Kevin had to do to get away. But did you go look for him? Not you. You had Ireland to save."

"I didn't see you knockin' yourself out to find him," Seamus said. "You're the very one — you said 'He'll come back when he's ready.' "

"He wasn't my son! It was all I could do to keep myself alive, can'tcha see? And here you were, such great friends with the likes of Dennis Hannegan and not a bit of him to rub off —"

The door from the bar opened. "His office is just back here. He's bound to have some tea. Or maybe a brandy would be better," Moira said, speaking over her shoulder to Rachel.

Liam backed up a pace and swung around, training the Mauser on the open door.

"Mother of God! Liam, what are ya doin'?"

"Come in, Moira *Aroun,*" he said. "And bring your friend with you."

"But —"

"Now shut the door. There's the girl."

Rachel sought out Joseph. "I tried to prevent it but —"

"It's all right," Joseph said. "Better she see for herself what he is."

Moira's gaze traveled from Liam to her brother and on to Rachel. Two bright, angry spots appeared on her cheeks. "See what for myself? Joseph, tell me what's goin' on."

"I'll tell you," Liam said. "Your brother and the rest of them — yeah, even your Da' — they have me for a traitor. Joe always told us they were mad over their harebrained causes. Now he's joined them, he's as daft as the rest."

"What are you talkin' about, Liam? Why do you have a gun?"

"He killed a man, Moira," Joseph said. "He's been eavesdropping on Clan meetings and informing to the Brits. That's where all his money's been coming from."

"No, Joseph, he's been workin' for Tammany. I'm not sayin' I like it, but I can live with it if I must."

Joseph heard himself shouting at her, but he couldn't seem to get through to her any other way. "He's not workin' for Tammany anymore. They threw him out for setting fire to that tenement he supposedly saved. Ask Croker, ask any one of the men in that bar out there, Moira, and they'll tell you. Even the crooks at the Hall didn't want him."

Joseph watched with sick helplessness while the truth revealed itself in Moira's changing expressions. She didn't want to believe it. She looked at Liam, but he turned away, shaking his head as though it were all a conspiracy against him.

"Liam?"

"Come away with me, Moira *Aroun.* We'll go away, where no one will ever find us. I have money enough for the rest of our lives now."

"Tell them they're wrong, Liam. Put the

gun away and tell them it isn't true," she pleaded.

He had no answer for her. In a fleeting, half-formed thought, Joseph realized that Liam O'Neill had no lies left, even to protect the only person who had ever really loved him. She waited, but no answer was forthcoming.

Behind her, Rachel stood waiting, as if to catch Moira lest she faint. But Moira was stronger than that, stronger than all of them. She put out her hand. "I'll stand by you, whatever you've done Liam O'Neill, but I won't let you kill anyone else. Give me the gun."

He shook his head. "There's still time, Moira. I won't hurt them, but you've got to come away with me now."

She took a step toward him. Rachel grabbed at her arm. "Moira, don't!"

But Moira shook her off, moving to Liam's side. "If I go away with you now, I'll never be able to live with what you've done."

She was next to him now, holding her hand out for the gun. He looked down at her outstretched palm and at the pistol in his own hand. "I've learned one thing in this life," he said. "The only way to get what I want is to take it."

He grabbed her arm and pulled her to

him, pushing the muzzle up under her neck. "Stay back," he shouted at the men.

"Liam," Joseph cried. "You don't want to do this. Not to Moira."

Liam smiled. "My old friend, you had my sister. Why shouldn't I have yours?"

Joseph saw clearly, then, what he had only glimpsed before. This was personal — a hatred deep and abiding that drove Liam in his relentless quest for more money, more power, more prominence. Anything to best his worst adversary, Joseph Hannegan.

"Liam, for the love of God, let her go!"

Liam secured his hold on Moira and turned the gun on his father. "I don't want to hear your voice, old man. Don't say another word or the first bullet will be yours. Ma loved you and how did you repay her? By workin' her till there was nothin' left in her but bitterness and heartache. She gave it all to you, for you, and all you gave her was three brats she didn't have the strength to love at the end of the day. Don't say another word to me about bein' your son. I'm bloody sick to death of you!"

Across the room, Joseph caught his father's eye. His grip had tightened on his crutch. He lifted it a fraction off the floor, looked at Liam, at the gun, and back at his son. Joseph nodded and turned toward Rachel. She had seen the silent exchange.

"You won't hurt me, Liam," Moira said. "I know that, and so do they."

"Even after all this, you still believe in him?" Joseph said.

Liam laughed and trained the pistol on Joseph. "She didn't learn that from you, did she, Joe lad? Oh, I was a great friend to find you whores and whiskey when you wanted them. But did you ever once look around you and see I was dyin'? I had nothin' and you had more than your share, but all you gave me was your pious disapproval. I had to take what I needed for myself." He stepped back, pulling Moira with him. "And I'm takin' her now, Joe."

Joseph stepped toward him. "I can't let you do that, Liam," he said quietly.

To Liam's right, Dennis moved a step forward too. "Liam, you've been a son to me —"

"Don't!" Liam cried. "I'm not your son, though God knows I wanted to be. I had to go home to the likes of him," he said, waving the gun at his father.

It was the opening they had hoped for. Dennis swung the crutch up, slamming it into Liam's hand. The gun discharged as it flew from his fingers. Joseph lunged for his sister, yanked her from Liam's grasp and passed her into Rachel's waiting arms. He dove for Liam, knocking him back against the wall with all the force he had in his body. Liam slammed backward, cracking his head against the plaster. He staggered, reeled, and righted himself, rushing Joseph with doubled fists.

But the gunshot dropped him at Joseph's feet. Joseph spun around, searching for the shooter. Seamus O'Neill stood with the Mauser still pointed at his son.

"There'll be no stags in the O'Neill family," he said, and pulled the trigger again.

CHAPTER
FORTY-ONE

They called it "the phantom limb." Joseph had heard his father speak of it, heard veterans of the Civil War complain of the missing limb that still caused them pain. He had never understood how it was possible for a part of oneself diseased, crushed, wasted, and pared away to ache *in absentia.* Never until now.

The afternoon sky was a glowering purple and the wind had picked up, blowing in gusts that whipped the trees first one way and then the other. Liam had been in the ground a week, and of those seven days, on three Joseph had returned to his grave. He couldn't have explained why, only that there were things unfinished between them.

No one would ever understand that Liam was his phantom limb — so much a part of him that despite the poison that had infected most of Liam's life, the loss of him still ached. He felt lopsided, as though his left hand had been severed at the joint. He did not need it to survive, but it gave him balance and symmetry. In some way, Liam had been like that.

Joseph had spent many hours gazing down the telescope of the years. But the memories he focused on were necessarily circumscribed by the borders of his own lens. He could not see beyond them, to what had happened to Liam outside of their experiences together. At the end, he thought he had finally understood what Liam wanted. Moira, whom he might have loved for herself, but he also coveted because she was so much a part of Joseph's life. Liam would have taken everything from him — his sister, his father, his good name — and yet Joseph never doubted that Liam had loved him as a brother. But Liam had been the prodigal, and there was no joyous homecoming awaiting him.

It almost seemed as if Liam had known how the end would come. Joseph took the note from his pocket, opened it and read it again. Not that he needed to, cemented into his memory as it was, but in every word, every syllable, he continued to search for what Liam had not said.

Joe,

I gave you a good race, didn't I?

In case you're tempted to forget me, I want Moira to have everything — the bar, the cash and the properties. The details are in the will, attached. I have named you as executor. As you will see, I have done very well for myself. There is enough money to take care of Moira for the rest of her life. I've also directed a substantial fee to be paid to you. The mortgage on the Ballyglass is almost paid off, and there is enough capital to pay it outright. Payment should be made to Richard Croker.

It was signed simply "Liam."

How like him! A last gesture of friendship or mortal enmity? His bequest would keep him a haunting presence in their lives. Worse, if they accepted it they would be tacitly accepting the way he had gotten it, complicit in graft, betrayal, and murder. Liam's final seduction.

"I want no part of it," Moira had said. "I don't need tainted money to remember that I loved him." Although Joseph agreed, they had gone to Matthew Bonner for advice and come away more bewildered.

"I can only tell you the way I see it, Miss

595

Hannegan. If you do not take it, it will go to the state of New York, and that means into the pockets of umpteen Tammany politicians, where it will do no one any good. My niece tells me that you want to go to nursing school. Why not use the money for good? Become a nurse and help some of the people out there who were hurt by the likes of Liam O'Neill."

"But the bar . . ."

"Will you put it back in the hands of Richard Croker? Let your father manage it and give some of the proceeds to charity. God knows, it's the only way they'll ever get a drop of Tammany money."

In the end, they had decided to take Matt Bonner's advice. Living with the money would be the penance that Joseph had to pay for failing his friend, for there was no denying that he had failed Liam O'Neill. He couldn't have said when the turning point had come, when he might have diverted Liam onto a better path, but he knew now that he had been the only stable influence in a life of chaos and rage, and when Liam had needed him most, Joseph had deserted him for a life of his own. If Liam had left Joseph nothing else, at least he had left him with a bitter knowledge of his own weaknesses. Liam had been his dark side, the man he might have been had he not been just a little bit luckier.

A few heavy raindrops began to fall, and the air was steeped with an earthen smell. Beneath his feet lay the body of his oldest friend. The only flowers on the grave had come from Joseph. The wind turned them over and beat their fragile heads to the ground. Joseph dug a hole in the dirt with his hands and set the vase down in it. It was the least he could do for Liam.

Joseph left for the station late the next morning, stopping at the public phone outside Rossi's grocery store. He asked Central to connect him to the station, and when the switchboard came on the line, affected a deep brogue to ask for Albert Lederman.

"Tell him it's his good friend Billy Bell waitin' to speak to him, there's the dear."

In a matter of seconds, Lederman was on the line. "Bell? What the hell are you doing, calling me here? I told you you'd get paid, but only what we agreed on. It's not my fault you got yourself rolled. Give me your address and I'll send it to you. Bell? Bell?"

Joseph returned the receiver to the cradle and walked to the corner. Traffic was unusually congested, but quiet, as though dampened by a great cloud of fog. A hushed crowd had gathered around a newsie with three piles of papers at his feet who passed them in silence to waiting hands. Joseph snatched up a black bordered *Times* and tossed a coin to the boy.

The President was dead. A week after he had been shot by the anarchist Leon Czolgosz, at 2:15 that morning, McKinley had taken his last breath. Joseph would read about it on the ferry, but now he picked up his pace. The station, like every other government office, would be in turmoil. By the time he reached it, McNabb had already called a meeting of all the division chiefs. Joseph slipped into the back of the room to listen.

"We will be receiving a shipment of black crepe before the day is over. Hannegan," McNabb said, over the heads of the others in the room, "you'll take charge of seeing it hung from the third floor balcony, and supervise the hanging of black wreaths on all the main doors.

"As to the rest of you, we will have to carry on with business as usual. There is to be no discussion with members of the press. If they pressure you for a reaction to the President's death, or more importantly, to Czolgosz, send them to me. Are we entirely clear on that point?" A general murmur indicated that they were.

"Fine. Let us all get back to work, then." McNabb dismissed all the division chiefs except Lederman, but caught Joseph at the door.

"You'll have to keep things under control here today, Hannegan. The Commissioner and I will probably be tied up with the press all day. The aliens are behaving like cattle in a thunderstorm out there," he said, pointing in the general direction of the Registry Room. "They've heard about the President, and they're worried they'll all be turned away now. God only knows how those people think. Take care of it," he said, and led Lederman away.

Joseph went immediately to the Registry Room. A palpable air of anxiety hung over the immigrants. Joseph could hardly blame them. For most, political change was a disquieting fact of life that could mean new pogroms, more economic hardship, political imprisonment, and even death. They could scarcely help but wonder what the President's assassination meant for them. Would they be allowed to enter? Would America still be the land of golden opportunity or had they come too late? There was little that Joseph, or anyone at the station, could do to ease their fears. Most did not care to try.

"Move along there!" A grouper shoved a man in a black coat, with long black curls dangling out from under his hat, into one of the holding pens. "This ain't some sight-seeing tour. Make room for him, the rest of you."

A mob of similarly dressed men pushed backward in the pen and stared forlornly at Joseph through the chain link fencing. The gateman slammed the iron door and turned his back on them. When he saw Joseph watching, he shrugged and glanced away.

Joseph withdrew a small pad and pencil from his pocket. "Take care there, Mr. . . ." He peered at the gateman's name badge. ". . . King," he said, carefully writing the name on his pad. He tucked the pad back in his pocket.

"Those men have done nothing to earn your contempt. Treat them with some respect, or you will be removed from your position."

King said nothing, but turned away to spit at a nearby cuspidor. Joseph pointed a warning finger and turned away. It would be like this all day. Polish immigrants cowered at the inspection desks, frightened that a fellow Pole had been the one to put McKinley in the grave. Joseph spent most of his day on the heels of the Polish interpreters, watching that no one was mistreated, ready to assure any incoming immigrant that no one held him to blame.

By four o'clock that afternoon, the crepe had been strung across the balcony overlooking the Registry Room — a dark and menacing cloud that hung over the immigrants' heads like their awaiting fates. Joseph thought that they could have well done without it, but it might be difficult to explain to the public why Ellis Island was above mourning their fallen chief. He returned to his office and the newspaper he had not had time to read.

McKinley's death had eclipsed the other news. Joseph paged through the *Times* until he found what he was looking for, mercifully hidden on page eighteen. *Immigrant Given Death Sentence,* the headline said. The *Times* reviewed the "bizarre case" in which Seamus O'Neill, of 67 9th Ave. had shot his son, Liam, during an argument in the latter's bar on September 8. More bizarre was the fact that O'Neill had also confessed to shooting another newly landed immigrant, Cormac Doyle of Drumcliffe, Ireland, a week previously. Witnesses to the shooting, including attorney and officer of the court Daniel Cohalan, could not shed any light on the cause of the altercation. The perpetrator had refused counsel and declined to state his motive for the killings. He was sentenced this morning to death in the electric chair.

Dennis Hannegan would not mark this article with a red pencil. It would not be clipped for his scrapbook. He was suffering mute grief for his lost friend, a conspirator once again in the silence of Clan na Gael. But that was the way Seamus O'Neill wanted it, and honoring his last wish was the only gift Dennis could give his old friend.

The other article was located on page twenty-two. *Immigration Service Investigation Suspended During Mourning for President.* So McNabb had found a way to delay the hearings indefinitely. That suited Joseph's purpose beautifully, giving him more time to gather evidence. The letter was just the beginning.

It was a gamble, he knew. After all, the case of Cormac Doyle's murder was closed and the threat of his own implication was behind him. The letter would just reopen the wound, and that might prove fatal for Joseph. But that was a risk he would have to take to put a stop to Boarding's negligence. An anarchist had just taken the

President's life. It was a very sobering message.

While he was willing to take the risk himself, he did not want to put Rachel's job in jeopardy. She'd been a source of help and support through the Flynn ordeal. Getting her fired was no way to repay her. He put in a call to the Head Matron, asking her to send Rachel to his office at the end of her shift. "And ask her to bring the envelope, please. She'll understand what I'm talking about."

Rachel turned the watch of the excluded women over to the night matron coming on duty and walked down the hall to the Superintendent's office. She had heard Joseph refer to the excluded wing as the first ring of hell and thought it an apt description. It was her least favorite work at the station. Thankfully, the appointment was only temporary until Maggie Flynn and Dylan Moran were safely on board a ship headed for Liverpool. They were leaving tomorrow.

Rachel had accompanied her uncle to Blackwell's Island the morning after Liam O'Neill was killed, and while Matt provided the necessary forms for her release, the matron had allowed Rachel to go to Maggie in her cell.

"It's over, Maggie," she said. "I'm here to get you released."

Maggie had slumped down on her cot, as if the news had been bad instead of good. "What am I to do now?" she said, after a protracted silence.

"Why, go home of course."

Maggie had looked up, her green eyes moist. "I haven't the passage," she said.

Rachel smiled. "Well, I have, but I don't think you're going to need it. Mr. Hannegan will be deporting you as an undesirable." Maggie had laughed until tears ran down her face.

"Come along. You change. I'll get your things. Let's not stay here another minute."

Rachel gave the girl the clothing she'd brought from the station and opened a Gladstone bag to receive the few possessions Maggie had been allowed to have. Toothbrush and tooth powder, a faded photograph of her father's cottage in Drumcliffe. A dog-eared volume of *The Lives of the Saints*. And a small tin.

"Maggie, my God, what are you doing with this?" Rachel stared at the container of rat poison lying in her open palm and up into Maggie's green eyes. The girl colored and turned away.

"Were you —"

"I couldn't do it, Miss Bonner," she said. "They would have buried me in unholy ground."

Rachel knocked on the Superintendent's door. He was sitting at his desk going through the day's mail. "It's tense out there," she said, taking a chair.

"Can you blame them?"

"No."

The Superintendent held up an envelope. "Another mystery solved. I received a letter from our embassy in London this morning. It seems that Captain Vine is returning to England by way of Canada. Apparently, he left for Quebec on September 9, and from there departed for home. Lucky coincidence for the Captain, eh?"

"What will happen now?"

"To Vine? Nothing. We could lodge a complaint with the British Foreign Office, but that would mean explaining Vine's association with Liam, and Seamus has muddied the water too much by claiming he killed Doyle. In all likelihood, Vine will be posted to Ireland next. I don't give him much of a chance once he gets there, though. John Devoy has very long arms. Did you bring the envelope I gave you?"

Rachel shook her head. "It isn't there. Someone took it from my locker. I assumed it was you, since you have a master key."

Joseph's expression hardened momentarily, then gradually softened until he was smiling broadly, even chuckling a bit under his breath. "Billy Bell," he said.

"Pardon me?"

"Billy Bell, the man who was following me. He saw us together and reported it to Lederman. Our friend Albert is anything but stupid, and McNabb has a master key, too."

Rachel caught her breath. "After all this, can they still hurt you?"

"On the contrary, Miss Bonner. By now they have destroyed the only evidence that could. It is regrettable that they have gotten away with it." He tapped the newspaper in front of him. "But we have a new President now, and Teddy, as we know, has little patience with corruption. I believe their days are numbered."

"Well," Rachel said, rising. "I'll say good-night, then." At the door, she stopped and turned back. "How is Moira?"

Joseph compressed his lips in a frown. "She doesn't say much. Doesn't talk about Liam at all. She's gone on with her chores as if none of it ever happened. But the light's gone out of her. She's quiet, and sad, and very much in need of a friend, Miss Bonner."

"I didn't want to inter— that is . . . I wasn't sure she'd want to see me. I'll call on her right away."

"Thank you. I'd be very grateful if you would."

There was so much to be said between them, and so little they could say. She would miss working with him so closely and more, being the one person in his trust. They would return to immigration station business as usual and their bond would dissolve over time. She hesitated for a moment at the door, but finding no words to suitably express her thoughts, turned the knob.

"Miss Bonner?"

When she turned back, he was standing. "I . . . I don't think I ever told you that I enjoyed dancing with you."

"No, you didn't. I enjoyed it too."

He cleared his throat and glanced away. "Perhaps some time we could do it again."

She felt her spirits lift. "Yes," she said. "I'd like that very much."

Matt Bonner sat in his study reading the newspaper accounts of McKinley's death. The world, he thought, had now changed.

With one flick of the finger, Leon Czolgosz had made the United States an infinitely more dangerous place to live simply by revealing, to a heretofore naive and trusting citizenry, the barbarous possibilities of assassination even in this civilized twentieth century. Political candidates would never feel entirely safe again. But Matt Bonner was not afraid of death. He had long known that working in the criminal world was perilous, no matter which side of the courtroom he sat on. He had come to terms with his own mortality long ago.

It was living, he now realized, that he was afraid of. Embracing life meant taking chances, being embarrassed and hurt. He knew, now, that he'd only ever had the shadow of Irene in his life. It had been enough until he'd lost her. But now, he wanted all of her. He wanted her across from him at the dinner table, not hovering outside the dining room doors. He wanted to say goodnight in the privacy of their own bedroom, not in his library or at the foot of the stairs. He wanted to feel her warm flesh not next to him, but in his arms. How could he have settled for so little for so long? He folded the newspaper neatly and set it aside.

"Alma," he called to the maid. "I'm going out. I don't know when I'll be back. Tell

Mrs. Coffey I won't be in for dinner."

He reached Seth Low's office shortly before five o'clock, marched past Low's secretary, and arrived in front of Low's desk just as he was hanging up the telephone.

"Bonner, I was just going to call you. Need you to speak at a rally in the sixteenth."

Matt held up his hand. "Won't keep you, Seth. Just wanted to tell you that I'm out of the race. I'll campaign for you and support you any way I can, but you'll have to find another D.A."

"But —"

"Think about Bill Jerome. He's a good man and he'll help the ticket. Let me know what you need from me and I'll be there." He was out the door before Low could call him back.

He went to three florists before he found what he wanted. "These are a hybrid," the clerk said. "They're very hardy, but the purer strains are more popular."

"A hybrid is exactly what I want," Matt said, choosing each stem individually.

"You're quite sure, sir?" the clerk asked. "They're not the most fashionable flowers for bouquets."

"Quite sure. Fashion does not interest the lady in question." Matt handed him a twenty-dollar bill and left without waiting for his change.

Matthew Bonner had not taken many chances in life. Vast wealth, he thought, was much like a coach and four, carrying him through the storms of life securely sheltered from their exigencies. But if he had never felt the sting of their sharp winds, he had likewise never experienced the exhilaration of enduring them. What he was about to do would plunge him naked into the eye of the storm. It was such a small gesture to most people. But to Matt Bonner, who had everything, but nothing, it was the biggest risk of his life.

He scaled the stairs on feet light for his considerable weight and pounded on the door with his fist. Irene opened it as if she knew it was he.

"I read somewhere," Matthew Bonner said, "that orchids grow wild in Ireland. I'd like to take you to see them."

She pulled back the door and took the flowers from his arms. "They're particularly lovely in County Clare. Come in, Matthew," she said. "I have a pot of tea waitin'."

ABOUT THE AUTHOR

Ann Stamos is the pen name for Takis and Judy Iakovou, authors of the Nick and Julia Lambros mystery series, an amateur sleuth series set in the fictitious city of Delphi, Georgia. *Bitter Tide* is the debut novel in their new Ellis Island mystery series. The couple lives in Athens, Georgia.

The employees of Thorndike Press hope you have enjoyed this Large Print book. All our Thorndike, Wheeler, and Kennebec Large Print titles are designed for easy reading, and all our books are made to last. Other Thorndike Press Large Print books are available at your library, through selected bookstores, or directly from us.

For information about titles, please call:
  (800) 223-1244

or visit our Web site at:
  http://gale.cengage.com/thorndike

To share your comments, please write:
  Publisher
  Thorndike Press
  295 Kennedy Memorial Drive
  Waterville, ME 04901